ILOBOLA

(The Marriage Fee)

TERRY FRANCIS

ISBN: 1-4392-4598-3
ISBN-13: 9781439245989

Visit www.booksurge.com to order additional copies.

To Lynette, you are sadly missed.

Acknowledgements

Thanks to my good friend Sue Roger for encouraging me to start writing. I'm deeply indebted to my friends Meredith Lambert, Ian and Liz Plane, Linda Taylor, and Alma Hooper, all of whom have read various versions of the manuscript and made invaluable suggestions and recommendations. I'm also grateful for the information obtained from Keith Middleman's book *Cabora Bassa Engineering and Politics in Southern Africa* as well as the historical details obtained from the F. A. Van Jaarsveld book *From Van Riebeeck to Voster*. Information relating to Mozambique, its people, as well as details relating the gold mining industry in South Africa was researched on the Internet and in the Sandton Library in Johannesburg. Last but not least, to my beloved late wife, Lynette, who always gave me encouragement and support to finish writing this book when I was discouraged and stopped for periods of time.

ILOBOLA

(The Marriage Fee)

Chapter 1

It was late in the afternoon and Mofola had just come out of the store, having purchased a bag of tobacco for his father and a few groceries for his mother. Victor Aguiar was waiting outside, sitting on the steps that led from the store's wide *veranda* to the dusty main road. It was hot in the direct sun and he wiped the perspiration from his greasy forehead with the back of his shirt sleeve. Victor was not a nice person; he had a bad attitude, especially when it came to the blacks. Like a lot of the Portuguese of that time he despised the black folk even though they were the ones that patronized his store.

He was waiting to confront Mofola, as he had spent more time than he thought was necessary in the store talking to Negome. He had been watching Mofola for months now and could see that he and Negome were developing a very friendly relationship and this was now starting to really annoy him. Victor stood up as Mofola started down the steps and grabbed Mofola by the arm, pulling him around to face him, causing Mofola to lose his grip on the brown paper bag he was carrying. It fell onto the last step scattering the contents onto the road.

"Look," said Victor, pointing his finger in Mofola's face, "Negome is going to be married to the eldest son of Mr. Costa, the owner of the cantina, as soon as he is twenty-one years old. I'm tired of you talking to her and wasting her time whenever you come into the store. She has better things to do than stand around talking to someone like you. When you come into this store, you can deal with me or one of the other girls. I don't ever want to see you talking to Negome again, do you hear me?

"You herder of cattle and goats," he went on, "will never be able to pay the *ilobola* for my Negome. So don't let me catch you talking to her again or I will get the commissioner to put you in jail, do you understand?" he said, waving his finger in Mofola's face. With that, Victor pushed Mofola off the last step and turned and went back up the stairs and into the store.

Mofola just stood there dumbfounded in the dusty road with the groceries he had just bought scattered around his bare feet. He looked up at the departing Victor going into the store. He did not understand. This was a terrible blow and it felt like his chest had just been crushed by the weight of a bull elephant. Mofola could not imagine that such a thing could ever happen to him and Negome. He had developed a crush on Negome when he was twelve years old, and he just naturally assumed that one day he would go to work on the mines like his father and brothers and earn enough money to pay Mr. Victor the *ilobola* for Negome. He had even told her so and Negome would often joke with him when he came into the store, saying, "Have you come to pay my father the *ilobola* today for this beautiful bride?" Then she would put her hands up under her shoulder-length hair, tilt her head to one side and smile at him.

He would then reply, "No, not today, but one day, one day," and they would laugh together.

Mofola picked up the groceries, dusted them off, and put them back in the brown paper bag. He took one last look up at the store to see if he could see Negome through the window, but she was not to be seen. He walked up the sand road, making his way back home, his feet making little puffs in the dust as he unconsciously put one foot in front of the other. His whole future that he had been planning in his mind during the years and months that he had spent up in the mountains with the cattle and goats, was now shattered like a glass bottle thrown against the face of a solid rock wall. He wished that it was already time again for him to take the herd up into the mountains to graze. Then he would not have to see the hurt in Negome's eyes when he came into the store and ignored her. But this was not to be, as he had only just come back and it would be several months before it was time to take the herd up into the mountains again. In any case, it was now time to teach his two young nephews, who were now seven and eight years old, the work of herding the animals, so that at the end of the dry season they could accompany him up into the mountains.

Mofola had looked forward to the day when he could start to teach his nephews the rudiments of herding. As soon as they were skilled enough to be able to look after the herds, he would be able to go to work on the mines in South Africa and earn big money so that he could one day afford to pay the *ilobola* for his bride, Negome. Things were now different and he wanted to get away so that he would not have to see Negome again.

Chapter 2

Negome Aguiar was born in a cool winter month in June 1944. She was the daughter of Victor Aguiar, an Afro-Portuguese storekeeper in the small town of Massangena in the province of Gaza in Mozambique. Massangena was situated on the banks of the Save River, seventy kilometres from the border of Rhodesia. Her mother, Margreta, was of Muslim descent. The Muslims had been trading on the southeast coast of Africa for centuries and had established settlements all along the north coast of Mozambique. Intermarriage between the Portuguese, Muslims, and the local black tribes was fairly common and dated back to the fourteenth century.

Negome had light coffee-coloured skin with the distinct high cheekbones and features of her Muslim descendants. Right from an early age it was clear that Negome was the Aguiars' brightest daughter and certainly the most attractive of the three, in fact she was quite striking. At the tender age of five she was already attending the Catholic mission school situated on the outskirts of town. She was a fast learner and even as a young child she would help in her father's store with the packing and cleaning, while her mother attended to her younger sisters in their house attached to the back of the store.

By the time Negome was twelve years old she could manage the store on her own. The Aguiars, like the rest of the townsfolk, were basic country people with a simple lifestyle. The Aguiar family, other than Victor Aguiar, had few luxuries. Not that they did not enjoy luxuries; it was just that they could never afford them, due mainly to Victor Aguiar's passion for gambling and red wine. Gambling had always been Victor's downfall in life and he had often ended up owing his gambling partners large sums of money which he somehow always eventually managed to repay. However, this passion would cost him dearly one day.

Although Massangena was not considered to be a big town, it was quite an important one, as it was situated on the cross roads that led to the north, south, east and west of the country. The road east followed the river Save to the eastern seaport of Nova Mambone, and south east to the port of Inhambane. North, the road led to the town of Espangabera on the border of Rhodesia. The road west was, at best, a track that went up over the mountains to where it stopped at the border of the Gonarezhou National Park of Rhodesia.

There was not much to Massangena other than a general dealer store owned by Victor Aguiar, a police station, petrol station, cantina-come-dingy hotel, Catholic mission school, clinic and a post office. A little way down the main street heading north was an open-air market where most things could be bought. There was not a lot going on in Massangena except for the transport trucks that passed through the town travelling to Rhodesia from Inhambane or Nova Mambone on the coast and back. Many of these truck drivers would overnight at Massangena. They parked their trucks in the open yard at the back of the cantina and would overnight in one of the cheap *rondavels*. They would inevitably end up sharing the room with one of the local "ladies of the night." Costa Xavair owned the cantina as well as the cheap rondavels situated at the back.

There were a number of small-time farmers in the district who farmed mainly with cattle and goats. They also grew *maize*, a few vegetables, and cashew nuts. They would sell these produce together with the goats at the open-air market. They would normally auction their cattle once a year just before the winter season, when buyers from the coastal region would come and bid for the best cattle in the district. The cattle would then be trucked down to Inhambane or Lourenco Marques where they would be resold to the abattoirs. The only other source of income that came into this region was from the migrant labourers working across the borders in South Africa and Rhodesia.

The South African and the Mozambican governments had agreements going back to 1897 on migrant labour for the South African mining industry. Over the years these agreements were amended and renegotiated several times by the various governments in power at that time. In 1940 Mozambique negotiated a special deal with the South African Chamber of Mines, whereby the deferred pay of the mineworkers coming from Mozambique would be paid in gold to the Mozambican government.

As the free world gold price increased, the Portuguese government then in power would make healthy profits on these deals. They would often hold back and purposely delay the payments to the migrant workers, capitalising as long as possible on the monies owed to them. This was a sore point and it eventually led to a breakdown of relationships and trust of the Portuguese government by the migrant workers, their families, and a large percentage of the poorer population living in and around the Gaza province.

As the gold price increased, so the demand for labour increased and, by 1940, there were more than one hundred thousand migrant labourers crisscrossing the borders of South Africa and Mozambique.

Much of Mozambique's Gaza province lies in the *lowveld* region with an altitude of less than five hundred meters above sea level. The climate here is hot and dry and often susceptible to drought. The land in this region is mainly made up of poor sandy soils that produce low crop yields, even during the good rainy seasons. In the previous centuries the area was teeming with game, but as the climatic conditions started to change and it became drier, the animals moved farther north in search of better grazing.

In the late nineteenth century there were only a few small herds of elephants remaining in the *lowveld* region of Mozambique. Most of the herds had moved north from this region, driven by intensified elephant hunting and drought. Before this period, the ivory trade had been an important part of this region's economy. With the elephant herds having moved north and those that remained having been incorporated into game reserves, an important part of this region's economy had dried up.

A large percentage of people in the Gaza region were destitute. They were considered easy pickings for the labour recruiters from the South African sugar estates and mining industries. If you signed up as a migrant worker, you would receive an official contract that could last for up to three years in one stretch or could be broken into single years. Your contract would also include a guaranteed free return passage to your homeland after your contract expired.

The people in the Gaza province commonly worked as migrant labourers in South Africa. Migrant workers could earn up to three times the amount of money that they could normally earn when working anywhere else in Mozambique as a labourer.

The terrible droughts of the early nineteenth century as well as the cattle raiding by the *Swazi* and *Zulu* tribes living south of the Mozambique borders had left the Gaza province's stocks of cattle very low. The young men could no longer afford the *ilobola* payment in cattle to the bride's parents for a wife. As a result, more and more migrant labourers were signing contracts to work on the South African mines.

At the end of their contracts they were able to afford the *ilobola* payment for a bride. The young men returning from their stint on the mines would pay in the region of thirty pounds sterling to the parents for a bride. In addition to the payment they would often have to shower the parents with gifts of clothes and other goods to persuade them to part with their daughters.

Chapter 3

Mofola Maraga was born on the eighth of December 1938; he was a year and six months older than Negome Aguiar and lived with his parents in a village *shamba* about five kilometres from Massangena. His father was from the *Shangane* tribe and a family descendent of the king of the Gaza province.

Mofola's two older brothers, Temba and Yussaf, had been working on the mines in South Africa for a number of years and they were now into their second three-year contract period. Their father had also worked on the mines; it was the only way in which he could support his family in the years of the terrible drought when the crops had failed time and time again and the cattle and goat herds had all but perished.

Occasionally the elders of the village would gather at the *shamba* of Mofola's father and they would sit around the fire drinking *Pombe*, the sour millet beer, telling stories until the early hours of the morning. At a young age Mofola would sit in the dark shadows out of sight of the men sitting around the fire. It was not customary for a child to listen to the talk of men. He would be enthralled by the stories they told of the great elephant herds that were trapped and slaughtered by the people of the villages so long ago.

"In the old days," Mofola recalled them saying, "long before the time when the rains no longer fell regularly in the Gaza, the elephants would come down to the southern lowlands from up north where they had been feeding for the winter months. Here they would feed on the new succulent leaves of the mapani trees that grew abundantly along the banks of the Save and the Sabie rivers."

They said that as soon as the rains started to fall in the lowlands and the new leaves appeared on the trees, the elephants would mysteriously appear like huge grey ghosts out of the dark of the night. They would travel in great herds, in small herds, and some, like the old bulls, would travel alone, carrying tusks so big and so heavy that they would drag along the ground. It was said that if the rains were late, then the elephants would be late coming down from the north; it was as if someone had sent them a message that it was still too early to travel south.

Each year they would journey along same paths that they had been travelling for decades. They would travel by day and by night, often covering distances of several hundred kilometres in a few days. Other game would follow the elephants in their *trek* south. Predators, both men and beasts, would lay in wait for them to pass, camouflaged in the long buffalo grass tanned golden brown by the winter sun. They would leap out catching any stragglers that may be too tired to keep up with the rest of the herd.

They said that during the winter months when the game had migrated back north, the people of the Gaza kingdom would gather from the neighbouring villages and dig huge pitfalls along the migrating game paths. These pitfalls could be as big as thirty paces long, ten paces wide, and as deep as the height of two standing men. Digging the pitfall was hard work and was not considered to be men's work but the work of the women. The work of men was hunting and warring with the neighbouring tribes. It was the work of women to till the ground, plant, and reap the crops. The men would not lower themselves to lift a hoe to dig in the ground; that was not men's work.

Back in those days they traded for iron implements such as hoes, axes, spearheads and knives from the tribes that originally emanated from the north. These were small nomadic tribes skilled in the mining and the founding of iron, gold, and silver. They would wander from one alluvial deposit to the next, working a site until the reef ran out, and then moving onto another prospected site. These people were not hunters or an aggressive warring tribe. Their only wealth lay in their ability to mine and found iron, tin, and gold, which they traded for animal skins, tusks, and food.

Once the site for an elephant pitfall was established by the elders of the neighbouring villages, the men would pace it out and the woman would start to dig. The choice of the site for the pitfall normally involved much argument and long debates by the elders of the villages and could last for many days or as long as the sour millet beer lasted. "Will the elephants cross the river at the bend this year or will they cross further upstream at the rapids?" they would debate.

"It all depends on the gods and whether they send much rain this season," one wise man would answer, and the discussions and arguments would continue from the day before into the early hours of the next morning. All the time the *calabash* of beer was being passed around the circle of wise men. Often the men would pass out drunk on the ground at the place they were sitting and awake in the morning to continue the discussion.

Once a unanimous decision had been reached, or more likely, when the beer came to an end, the wise men would stagger off to the chosen site and the debate would continue as to the size and positioning of the pit-fall. Normally this discussion would take place under a tree near the site and could last the better part of the day or until the men felt sober enough to pace the pitfall out without falling over in front of the village folk.

This, of course, was all considered to be men's work and Mofola was fascinated to hear the stories told over and over again. Each time he heard the story, there would be a little something different, depending on who was telling the story at the time. Mofola would hide in the shadows listening to the stories told by his elders, and his mother would often find him curled up asleep on the ground in the early hours of the morning, the men long gone back to their respective *shambas*.

Mofola would sit and listen to the elders describe how to summon the women to start to dig the pit. First the topsoil would be carefully removed and put aside close to where the pit was being dug. Only then would they begin to dig the pit. The soil would be dug out from the hole by one group of women while another group would be carrying the dug-out soil in baskets on their heads and scattering the soil over a wide area. In the rainy season the grass and the small bushes would grow up through the soil and camouflage any signs of an excavation having taken place in the area surrounding the pitfall.

It would take fifty women up to two months to dig the hole. Once the hole was completed to the elders' satisfaction, the men would start the delicate job of covering it. First bamboo sticks would be placed across the hole and then overlapping wild banana leaves laid on top of the sticks, forming a waterproof decking. Once this task was complete the women would then bring back the topsoil spreading it carefully over banana leaves. When the rains came and the grass grew the hole would be completely camouflaged.

The pitfall site would always be situated on ground sloping down toward the river. This was done for two reasons, one, so that once the trap was completed and the rains started to fall, the water would seep through the topsoil onto the overlapping banana leaves and run off down the slope, leaving the pitfall relatively dry. The second reason was that elephants are unsteady on their feet when going downhill, making it easier for them to fall into the trap.

The whole structure of the pitfall was designed so that any animal up to the size of a kudu bull could safely walk over it without it collapsing, but an elephant weighing several tons would fall right through the cladding, normally ending up breaking its front legs.

Up to seven elephants could be caught in such a trap at one time. This was not counting the others that would fall onto the ones already trapped in the hole, also breaking their legs or seriously injuring themselves trying to clamber out while others behind were pushing and trampling on each other in a mad frenzied stampede. It was a sight to see a whole herd of elephants stampeding down a slope, slipping and sliding, trying to stop from falling into the already full trap. They said the noise was deafening as the elephants trumpeted in fear, pain, and outrage at being tricked into the pitfall.

When the summer rains started to fall, new leaves appeared on the mapani trees along the river. The village people knew that it would not be long before the elephants started to migrate south to feed. The bush communication in those days was very effective. Once the people farther north saw the first signs of the migrating elephants, one would hear the sounds of drums in the distance, warning of the approaching herds. Information such as the size of the herd, its direction, and speed of travel would be communicated back and forth over long distances from one village drummer to the next.

As soon as the elders received the message that an elephant herd was approaching a village where a trap had been constructed, they would summon all the people of the village to congregate near the pitfall. Men, women, and children, young and old, would be assembled carrying metal containers or objects that could be beaten to create a loud clanging noise.

Often the group, consisting of several hundred, would form a V and fan out on either side of the game trail that had been trodden by a hundred thousand feet over many decades, with the pitfall being the bottom of the V. They would sit crouched, hidden in the long grass, out of sight and downwind from the approaching herd. The elephants would enter the top of the V formation and start to move down the game path toward the pitfall, browsing on the new leaves and young shoots of the trees they passed, unaware of the pending danger ahead.

Once the herd had passed some distance down the game trail, the group of people at the top of the formation would circle around crouched down, closing the top of the V. They would then jump up and start to bang and clang on the metal containers, this would be a sign for the rest of the group to rise up and follow suit. The elephants, now frightened, would start to stampede down the trail. The closer they got to the trap, the more the people closed in on them from the sides, shouting, banging their containers, and waving their arms in the air.

As the V formation got narrower, the elephants, realizing that they were boxed in would try to break to the left or right of the formation, only to be confronted by more waving and shouting people. The closer the herd got to the pitfall, the more dangerous it became for the people standing on the sides, especially if the herd was particularly large and the space to move became less and less. At this stage the elephants would be in an utter frenzy, mothers panicking, trumpeting for their young calves, and the matriarch trumpeting in rage and frustration having led the herd into danger.

Sometimes the herd was fortunate to be led by an old experienced matriarch; she would suddenly change direction and head straight for one of the sides of the V formation unperturbed by the shouting and waving people. Often in those instances many lives would be lost as the enraged elephants came stampeding toward the people with eyes glaring, ears flapping, their trunks aloft blaring and trumpeting as they crashed their way through the ranks of people, crushing them underfoot. Those that were not crushed to death would be badly maimed for life. This was the price that had to be paid for the spoils of the ivory trade in those days.

Long after the elders had left and gone back to their respective *shambas*, Mofola would lie on his back on the ground and look up at the stars so bright in the clear night sky. He thought about what it must have been like in the days when the elephants roamed in large herds through the land and men hunted the lion and elephant with only spears and axes in their hands. He wonder whether he would have been brave enough to stand and face a herd of charging elephants with only a spear and a metal pan in his hand. It was only the very brave young men from the village tribes that would be selected to form the bottom end of the V formation near the pitfall. It was considered to be a great privilege to have been selected to stand close to the pitfall. The young men would compete with one another to be able to take up the most dangerous position in the line.

Those that were the closest to the pitfall would be in the most danger of being killed or seriously injured. However, if they survived, then they would also be the first to claim an elephant that had fallen into the trap or had fallen on top of the ones already in the trap and now lay some distance from the trap seriously injured with a broken leg or some other injury, trumpeting and thrashing about, unable to get up.

Having claimed his elephant, the young man would stand guard over his prize waiting for the animal to succumb to its injuries. Sometimes, one of the less experienced young men would grow impatient with waiting and, thinking the animal had died, would venture near to the beast only to be crushed to the ground by a blow from a lashing elephant trunk. As the young man waited for the animal to die, family elders and other village members would gather around the fallen animal well out of reach of its lashing trunk.

The young maidens of the village would stand in the background giggling, laughing, and commenting about the braveness of the young man and they would speculate about the size of his penis and wonder if it might be as large as that of the elephant's trunk. The flirtation of the young maidens did not go unnoticed by the young man. He would already have singled out one or two of the giggling girls to choose as a future bride. The elephant tusks would make him a reasonably wealthy man and he would be able to afford to pay the *ilobola* to the bride's parents.

Once the elephant had died, the villagers would start the task of carving it up. It was customary for the young man to present the largest of the tusks to the chief *induna* of the village. This was payment for the privilege of being part of the village hunt and of having been selected to take up such a prominent position in the formation line. The second tusk he would sell to the ivory traders when they travelled up from the coast in the winter months to trade for tusks and animal skins from the various villages in the area.

When the tusks had been removed and the meat carved up, the meat would be distributed among the villagers with the delicacies, like the liver and testes going to the head of the young man's *shamba*. It was believed that the testis of the elephant would make a man as strong and as virile as the elephant and that his penis would stand up stout and erect as the trunk of an enraged elephant.

As Mofola lay there listening to the elders, he wished that there were still elephants to hunt so that he could somehow get a little piece of an elephant's testicle to eat. His brothers and sisters teased him about the small size of his penis. His mother had tied a thin leather thong to his penis and on the other end was a small stone the size of his fist; it was uncomfortable dangling between his legs but he persisted with it. His mother had told him that it would make it grow to the size of an ox's penis.

Mofola had to be at least twelve years old before he could attend the circumcision ceremony and he did not want the other boys there to see his small penis; he knew they would laugh and mock him. As he lay there on his back looking up at the stars, he thought to himself that it would have been much easier to have eaten a piece of the elephant's testicle, for that would have surely made it grow as big as an ox's.

As the story teller continued, Mofola listened to him describe how the elephants were hacked and chopped to pieces and how the pitfall became like a blood bath with hoards of people standing waist deep in blood and gore. People were like ants swarming over the elephant carcasses in the pit, hacking off great chunks of meat and passing it up to waiting hands above them who would carry it off in baskets on their heads to their respective *shambas*. The meat was carefully removed from around the tusks, and then the tusks were cut from the skull. Sometimes the tusks were so big that two men had to carry them but, as the years went by, they said the elephants with the big tusks slowly disappeared.

Those elephants that were still left with big tusks were seldom seen; these were the old bulls that had deserted the herd or had been kicked out by a younger bull and now moved around alone. With the elephants gone, the only way in which a man could afford the *ilobola* for a young bride was to go to work on the mines in South Africa. After working for three years on the mines, a man could afford to pay for a bride and still have money left to buy some cattle and goats.

Chapter 4

At fourteen Mofola was considered to be old enough to sit with the elders. He had already attended the circumcision ceremony just over a year ago and was now considered to be a man. He was now permitted to sit with the men around the fire and listen to the stories told by his father, his brothers and other men who had worked a contract period on the mines, but he was still not permitted to speak unless he was invited to do so by one of the elders.

The stories they told now were different from those told about the young brave elephant hunters. These stories were also about brave men. The difference being that these men were working deep underground where the heat was as hot as several suns, but where there was no sunlight, only the weak glow of a carbide lamp. Here, in this dark hole, the earth would tremble as the gods got angry and sent the rocks crashing down on men, crushing them to death just like the stampeding elephants would crush the hunters to death.

The migrant workers stayed in single quarter hostels on the mine property. Women were not permitted to be in the single quarters together with the men. Mining was considered to be men's work and far too dangerous for woman.

The hole going deep down into the bowels of the earth was as deep as the highest mountain was tall. The men would be lowered down into the hole in a big iron cage that could take fifty men at one time. An iron rope was fixed to the cage and then the rope went up high onto a wheel and then down again into a corrugated iron house where the big engine would wind the rope onto an even bigger wheel. The hole was called *eshafti* and the men would travel several hundred feet down the *eshafti* in the iron cage to tunnels that would lead to where the men would work all day, drilling and digging in the rock to find the *egoli*.

Digging a hole for the elephant trap was the work of women, but digging deep down in the *eshafti* to find the *egoli* was the work of men with strength and courage. Mofola longed for the day when he would be old enough to go to work in the mines in South Africa.

He would listen to the stories his brothers told, and his father would inform them that in the days when he worked on the mines things were much different. They would argue about when the work was the hardest, but one thing they never argued about was that it was still very dangerous to work in the mines. They spoke about how the singing rocks would warn them of an eminent rock burst. This was one of the miners' worst fears. Extreme pressure so deep underground caused the rocks to creak and groan as they moved and pushed against each other. Miners called this noise the "singing of the rocks," and when the rocks started to sing, it was time to get out of the mine as fast as possible.

The most dangerous job on in the mine was that of the rock driller. Because of the intense noise of the jackhammer drills and the hissing of compressed air, they could not hear the singing of the rocks. They would more than likely be the unfortunate ones trapped in a rock burst or crushed to death. Like the young hunters of the elephants who stood near the pitfall, their danger was much higher, and so too were their rewards. A good rock driller could earn up to three times the wages of a *lasher*, but he had to be strong and accept the dangers of the job. Mofola knew that when he went to the mines to work one day, he wanted to work as a rock driller and earn lots of money so that he could pay the *ilobola* for a beautiful wife.

To qualify to be a migrant worker on one of the mines, you had to be at least eighteen years old. You could then register with the Witwatersrand Native Labour Association (WNLA) who would check your date of birth and, if this proved to be in order, then you would have to undergo a medical examination. According to what Mofola's brothers had said, the doctor would hold a rubber pipe to your chest and listen to your breathing. Then he would hold your testicles in his hand and tell you to cough hard. If your chest did not sound like the distant thunder and your testicles jumped in his hand when you coughed, then you were considered to be fit to work on the mines.

The Portuguese government insisted that all migrant workers wishing to go and work in South Africa had to first register with the local labour recruiting office in their district before approaching the South African migrant-recruiting agent. This was so that the government could keep a strict control on the migrant workers leaving and returning to Mozambique. Once the migrant worker had signed up at the local recruiting office, he would be given an official stamped receipt bearing all his personal details. The worker could then present this document to the WNLA.

On returning to Mozambique after his contract had been completed, the migrant worker would present the Portuguese government with a similar receipt issued by the South African Chamber of Mines bearing the date of his first and last recorded shift. This receipt entitled the returning worker to collect his deferred wages that had been paid monthly to the Portuguese government by the South African Chamber of Mines for the duration of the worker's contract. This was the theory, but in practice it seldom had a positive outcome for the returning migrant worker. He would be confronted with a lot of paperwork and general bad administration, making it almost impossible for him to collect his deferred wages.

It paid the Portuguese government to make it as difficult as possible for the returning worker to collect his deferred wages, as the South African Chamber of Mines paid the deferred wages to the Portuguese in gold bullion. The Portuguese then traded the gold on the open market making handsome profits, which they used to bolster their sagging economy. The practice of holding on to the deferred wages for as long as possible was a great bone of contention among the migrant workers, and a deep resentment was building up against the government. The Portuguese government made handsome payouts to the Gaza monarchy to curry favour with them for the large number of migrant workers coming from that region, hoping that in this way they could appease the general populous.

Mofola despised the fact that at the age of sixteen, he was still expected by his family to herd the cattle and goats. Since his circumcision he was officially recognized as a man, but he still had to herd the animals, which was considered the work of boys and not the work of men. Over the last six years, Mofola had shot up; he was no longer a scrawny boy. The rock that had hung from his penis had long been removed and, as his mother had promised, he now sported a penis that any ox would have been proud of. The children no longer laughed at Mofola's small penis when they swam together in river swimming hole; the older boys stared at it instead in envy.

It was tradition that as soon as you were old enough, the duty of herding the animals would be handed down to one of your younger brothers, nephews, or cousins. Mofola had been herding the animals ever since he was eight years old and he was now sick and tired of this boy's work. The other young men in the village would mock and tease him. They would call him the little shepherd boy, despite the fact that age for age, he was much bigger than any of them. The other young men in the village had younger brothers, nephews, and cousins to hand the herding duty down to.

Mofola's brothers had married seven years ago when they first returned from the mines in South Africa, each having saved enough money to pay for a bride. Their sons were still too young to manage the herding of the animals by themselves. Mofola's eldest brother's first born was a girl, six years old. In any case, herding of the animals was not the work for girls. Their work was to collect wood and to fetch and carry water for the *shamba*. Mofola's sisters had also married but they had moved to their husbands' villages some distance away. So despite the fact that he was considered to be a man, Mofola was still stuck with the work of herding the animals until he could one day hand over this work to his nephews.

Cattle and goats were wealth; the more you owned the wealthier you were and the more respect you commanded with the community in the area. The low-lying area of the Gaza province was not really good cattle country, because it was too hot and humid in the summer months. The tsetse fly, foot and mouth disease, and severe drought could wipe out an entire herd in just one season. During the hot summer months the animals would be herded up into the mountains where it was much cooler and where the grazing was good.

For almost six months of the year Mofola would stay up in the mountains alone with the animals. He came home only occasionally to report back to his father on the condition of the herd and the number of calves that were born, and to refurbish his provisions. He would set up his camp in caves and under rock overhangs in the areas where the grazing was the best. During the day, while the cattle and goats were grazing, he would busy himself with the setting of snares and traps to catch small antelope, hares, and birds or he would fish in the clear mountain streams that flowed abundantly in the area.

The only weapons that Mofola had were a short stabbing *assegai*, a fighting stick, and a slingshot. The *assegai* was razor sharp, and he used it to cut the meat from the game he had caught into thin strips. He would then salt and hang the pieces on a rawhide thong strung between two trees, out of the reach of the wild animals. In the cool mountain breeze the salted meat would soon dry and then could be eaten at leisure. Salt was one of the few luxuries that Mofola had up in the mountains. His mother would pack him an ample supply of coarse salt in an old cloth tobacco bag that had been washed so many times, the picture of the boxer on the front of the bag had long faded away.

The only other possessions that he had were an old grey blanket, a small black cast-iron three-legged pot, and an empty Mills Special cigarette tin that he put his matches in to keep dry. When travelling from one grazing area to the next he would put the bag of salt into the pot and wrap it up in the old blanket, which he tied with a rawhide thong and slung this over his shoulder.

It was lonely up in the mountains, but Mofola did not mind because he was away from the mocking of the other young men from the neighbouring *shambas*. They occasionally would follow him a short way up into the hills, shouting names and throwing stones at him. This would enrage Mofola and he would come running down at them, waving his fighting stick like an *Impi* warrior. A stick fight would ensue, with the young Mofola normally getting the worst of the beating.

The years Mofola spent up in the mountains alone with the herd had made him hard and strong. He had also become an expert at stick fighting. He would practice for long periods, fighting against trees and imaginary foes while the cattle and goats grazed peacefully on the sweet mountain grasses. He would work out in his mind all the moves of his imaginary opponents and form counterattacking and defensive moves.

The young men of the other *shambas* that used to harass and tease Mofola, soon found out that it was no longer fun to follow him up into the mountains and provoke him into a stick fight, because whether there were three or four of them, Mofola always seemed to get the better of them.

So rather than take a beating from Mofola's fighting sticks, they reverted to standing some distance away and hurling stones at him and his herd. As a result, the herd would run off in different directions, giving Mofola a lot of work trying to round them all up again. However, this form of provocation had also come to a stop when a large stone flung with great accuracy from Mofola's slingshot hit one of the provokers. They now left him alone to tend his animals in peace.

Occasionally Mofola would see some of the other herd boys when they got careless and let their animals stray into Mofola's grazing area. They would then have to ask Mofola if they could please come into his territory to fetch their animals. They were all frightened of Mofola, not only because he was bigger than most of them, but because they all knew of his reputation with the fighting sticks and sling shot. Now, whenever their herds accidentally strayed into Mofola's territory they would send one of the smallest and youngest of the herd boys to go and fetch them. They knew, at worst, Mofola would give the young boy only a stiff lecture on being careless.

Over the years Mofola had marked out the best grazing area where the grass was sweet and there was an abundance of fresh water flowing from the mountain springs. As a result, the condition of his father's herd was recognized as being the best in the region. Because Mofola spent so much time with the herd up in the mountains, the animals grew accustomed to him and trusted him. He gave them all names, even the goats, and when he called them by their names they responded to him. He would often have to help a cow when it was having difficulty giving birth. He would stick his arm into the distressed cow's womb right up to his shoulder and pull the baby calf out. The animals were his only friends and he felt a certain bond with them and they with Mofola.

Chapter 5

In the late afternoon, Mofola would drive the herd back to his campsite, depending on which area they were in; it could be a cave or rock overhang. The herd would then be driven into an enclosure that Mofola had constructed with old dry thorn bushes piled on top of one another, forming a thick hedge the height of a man. Here the herd would overnight in the safety of the enclosure, out of reach of any prowling wild animals. Some nights Mofola would eat well, especially if he had been lucky that day and had managed to trap a guinea fowl or pheasant in one of the whip snares he had set.

A whip snare was one of the more common snares he used to trap birds and animals of various sizes. The bigger the bird or animal he wanted to trap, the bigger the construction of the snare would be, but the basic snare would always be the same. To construct a whip snare one would look for an ideal spot on a game path or in an area where the guinea fowl and pheasant normally feed.

As winter approached, the days grew shorter and nights grew colder up in the mountains. It would soon be time to drive the herd back down into the lowlands again. That morning when Mofola drove the herd out of the enclosure and into the *veld* to graze, he had noticed a large flock of crested guinea fowl feeding in an area where the grass seed was particularly abundant on the ground. The millet grass with its short bristlelike tufts containing the seed had started to turn golden brown and the cool westerly wind, blowing down from the high mountains, had scattered the seed over an open area where the grass had been grazed quite short.

The guinea fowl fed contentedly in the short open *veld*, moving about pecking up the fallen grass seeds. They could clearly see any approaching danger in the short open grass. Occasionally, one or two of the younger cocks would pick a fight with one of the mature cocks shattering the peace and tranquillity of the feeding flock for a short time. The rattling tick-tack-tirr-tirrr alarm call could be heard in the distance, as the mature cock, head down, wings spread out, charged at the challenging bird, scattering the rest of the flock as the young cock took off, not willing to stand up to the mature bird. These little tiffs never lasted very long and soon they would all be heads down feeding again.

Mofola knew that to catch a guinea fowl one had to be very skilful in setting up the snare and also very lucky, because the guinea fowl were very timid and also very suspicious, but when they were in a feeding frenzy one could get lucky.

Mofola decided to try his luck, and while the herd was grazing, he went about preparing the material he needed to make the whip snare. On that afternoon Mofola went back to his camp earlier than usual and put the herd into the thorn bush enclosure. He then went back to the place where he'd seen the guinea fowl feeding.

He chose a spot where the grass seed lay thick on the ground and set up the trap; all that remained was to set it and test it. He opened the slipknot in the long rawhide thong making a big loop, which he placed very carefully on the ground. He then used the back end of his *assegai* to touch the trigger stick, causing the bowed sapling to whip back, catching the end of the *assegai* in the now tightly closed slipknot.

Mofola reset the whip snare but this time he sprinkled ground over the looped slipknot covering it very lightly so that it could not be seen. He then pulled off a few handfuls of seed from the grass and scattered it on top of the ground, covering the loop. His snare now set and baited, he made his way back to camp as the sun dipped below the horizon.

The next day Mofola herded the cattle and goats out of their enclosure and down to the grazing area. As he approached the spot where he had set up the snare, he could see, even at that distance that there was something dangling from it. Catching a bird or small animal was one thing, but making sure you retrieved it before another predator did was not always possible.

Today the gods had looked favourably on him. Caught in the snare by its neck was a fat guinea fowl cock; it was still warm and must have been caught only a short while ago. Mofola was very pleased with himself, especially that no wild predator had found and taken a bite out of it. He untied the guinea fowl, dismantled the whip snare, and continued down to the grazing area near the stream.

While the animals were drinking, Mofola removed the entrails of the guinea fowl and then hung it up by its feet from the branch of a tree. The herd, having drunk their fill, started to move off to graze on the sweet grass still wet from the dew. Mofola, seeing that they were content, went off in search of dry kindling to start a fire.

Under a small rock outcrop he found a pile of dry leaves and twigs. He gathered them up and carried them back to the place where he had hung the bird. Mofola took the old empty Mills Special cigarette tin from his pocket, opened it and took out the box of matches. He had only four matches left, but that did not worry him particularly. He seldom needed to use matches, as the fire at the campsite rarely went out completely because the iron-hard wood he burned always left enough hot coals to kindle a fire again.

He soon had a roaring fire going in a shallow hole he had scooped in the ground. He kept the fire burning high until midday and then let it burn down to glowing coals. While the fire was burning down, Mofola took down the guinea fowl from the tree and packed it in clay which he had dug out from the bank of the stream. He scraped a hole out in the coals with a stick, placed the clay-covered guinea fowl in it and covered it with the red-hot coals.

Later that afternoon Mofola removed the guinea fowl from the coals and put it into a crude basket he had woven out of grass and slung it over his fighting stick on his shoulder. Mofola then kicked sand over the coals smothering them completely, rounded up the herd, and made his way back to camp.

After putting the cattle and goats in the thorn bush enclosure for the night, he settled himself down to enjoy the guinea fowl. Using a stone, he broke the hard baked clay covering the bird, pulling it away with the feathers. The meat was still warm and Mofola broke off chunks and ate with much relish, for it was not every day that one outsmarted the guinea fowl.

There was now a definite bite in the wind blowing down from the escarpment and Mofola decided it was time to pack up his few belongings and herd the animals back to his father's *shamba*. Early the next morning, long before the sun rose above the horizon, Mofola herded the animals out of the enclosure and set off back down to the lowlands. It was a long slow *trek* down the mountain and would take the better part of a whole day. At times the pathway was so narrow between the cliffs that only one animal could pass through at a time. As a result, they arrived at the *shamba* late in the afternoon.

There was always much rejoicing when Mofola arrived back at the *shamba* and there would be lots of discussion going on among his mother, his sisters-in-law and himself over the evening meal that night. He would want to know all about the news in the area and what news there was of his brothers in South Africa. His mother and sisters-in-law would want to know how he had coped up in the mountains this time and they would remark on how tall and strong he was looking and had he been fighting again with any of the other herd boys.

Only when everyone else had gone to bed, would Mofola and his father discuss the things that were important to men. Mofola would tell his father, going into great detail, about the new calves and kid goats that were born that season and the names he had given them all. They would sit and talk until the early hours of the morning. He would have to explain to his father about the grazing and was the rain sufficient to ensure good grazing next year and—the animals that got sick—did Mofola treat them with the right leaves and herbs and did he administer the *muti* the way his father had taught him. They discussed these things until the fire was just embers.

Chapter 6

With winter now finally on them Mofola was busy teaching his two nephews, Joseph and Emanuel, who were eight and six years old respectively, how to herd the animals out to the grazing and look after them during the day and then to herd them all safely back in the afternoon. Sometimes Mofola's mother would tell him to be back early, as she needed to send one of them to the store in Massangena to buy provisions and some tobacco for his father.

Mofola had always liked going to the store, as it gave him the opportunity to see the young girl who worked in the store behind the counter after school. Her name was Negome and she was the daughter of Victor Aguiar, the storekeeper. Normally Mofola was not comfortable around the young girls, as he was shy and they made him nervous, but Negome, she was somehow different. She had not tried to embarrass, or tease him in a nasty way, like the rest of the young girls did. She had always made an effort to come and serve him when he came into the store. She was also fond of Mofola because he was not like the other boys in the neighbourhood who were always forward and making rude suggestions to her. She had known Mofola for years, as he always came into the store to buy things for his mother, but mostly to buy a bag of Boxer tobacco and matches for his father. She also knew him from the short time he was at the mission school with her.

Her father had nicknamed him the Boxer Boy because he always bought Boxer tobacco for his father. The eight-ounce cotton bag carried a picture of a boxer printed on the outside. This brand of tobacco was imported from South Africa because of its popularity with the old mine labourers. Mofola's father had started to smoke a pipe with Boxer tobacco while in South Africa and ever since then that was the only tobacco that he would smoke. Despite the fact that Mofola's father was suffering from phthisis, a lung disease contracted on the gold mines, he continued to be a heavy smoker. Mofola or one of his nephews would have to go to the store at least once a week to get the old man's favourite tobacco.

Mofola had taken every opportunity to visit the store so that he could speak to Negome. Although it was a long walk from the *shamba* into town, Mofola did not mind the walk. He walked much longer distances with the herd; in any case, the way he felt about Negome he would walk for days if he had to, just to see her.

Mofola's attraction to Negome had not gone unnoticed by Victor Aguiar and he had told his daughter a number of times not to have anything to do with the Boxer Boy. Negome, being strong willed, chose to ignore her father's wishes and went out of her way to serve and speak to Mofola whenever he came into the store. This had annoyed Victor even more, for he had no intention of letting the cattle herding boy court his favourite daughter.

Chapter 7

Every day Mofola kept to himself watching his two nephews from a distance as they herded the animals in the winter grazing grounds. Mofola taught them all he knew about the cattle and goats, their sicknesses and how one prepared the cures from the herbs and roots that grew in the area. He taught them how to fish, hunt, snare, prepare, and cook what they had caught over an open fire.

The youngsters were keen and learned quickly. In the afternoon Mofola would send his nephews ahead with the herd and he would linger behind so that when his father asked his grandsons where Mofola was, they would inform the old man that Mofola was checking on the snares that they had set that day. If the old man needed someone to go to the store for tobacco, he would then have to send his two grandsons before it got too late, Mofola would thus avoid having to go to the store and face Negome whom he would now have to avoid and ignore. He remembered only too well that her father had forbidden him to ever talk to her again, or he would have him thrown in jail.

Many weeks had gone by and Negome was wondering why she had not seen Mofola for many weeks. She knew that it was not yet time for him to go up into the mountains again with the cattle and goats, so the next time she saw Mofola's nephews in the store, she asked them why she had not seen Mofola. "Is he ill, or did something happen to him?" she asked. When the two nephews returned home later that afternoon, they informed Mofola that Negome was asking where he was and why she had not seen him for such a along time.

Mofola was confused; surely Negome's father had told her that he had forbidden Mofola to speak to her, so why then would she want to see him? If her father had not informed Negome, then she would believe that it was Mofola that did not want to see her. He could not bear the thought that she would think this of him. He decided that he would have to go and see her immediately so that he could explain to her that it was her father that had forbidden him to speak to her.

None of the children were permitted to go into town without permission from one of the elders and even then they had to have a very good reason for wanting to go there. Mofola had no reason to want to go into town, except to go and see Negome and he did not want to tell his father about Mr. Victor forbidding him to see her. To try to explain the situation to his father was just too complicated and, in any case, the old man would side with Mr. Victor, as Mofola's father was a well-known figure in the area and he would not like to think that his son was making any trouble. Mofola asked his mother and his sisters-in-law whether they wanted anything from town.

They all replied that his young nephews had just come back from town and that there was no reason for him to have to go into town again that week.

Mofola tried to think of a good reason—other than to see Negome—why he needed to go into town, but he could think of no excuse that was good enough. He even told his nephews that if the old man sends them to town for tobacco, they must tell him so that he can accompany them.

When the old man had still not asked anyone to go into town after three days, Mofola decided to take matters into his own hands. He was becoming desperate; he wanted to clear up any misconceptions Negome may have about him as quickly as he could. Late that night when everybody in the *shamba* was asleep, he crept out of the hut he was sharing with his nephews and walked quickly across the yard to the hut where his father and mother slept.

Their *shamba* was situated on the top of a small hillock about five kilometres southeast of the town and was made up of five separate huts forming a half circle. A small stone and mud wall that came to waist height ran around the outside perimeter of the huts. There was small a wooden gate leading onto the cart track that led down to the dirt road going into town. The huts were all roughly the same size, measuring four by four paces with a grass thatched roof.

Mofola's brothers each had his own huts where wives and young children stayed; all the older children would stay in one hut together. One hut was bigger than the rest and was used as a common eating and meeting room. In the middle of the yard was the cooking area. This consisted of four upright gum poles the height of a tall man, forming a square, four by four paces with poles nailed across the top. Sheets of corrugated iron were laid on the top of the cross poles with large stones placed on top of the sheets to stop them from blowing away. Three sides of the enclosure were closed with tightly packed reeds. There was a small gap between the reed wall and the roof to allow the smoke from the cooking fire to escape, but still high enough to keep out the prevailing winds and rain.

As Mofola walked past the cooking shack, the dogs came running out to him whimpering and wagging their tails. During the day, the dogs, numbering between three and six, depending on who had puppies or who had picked up a stray, would lie around the base of the big acacia tree that grew in the yard. They might also go out with the boys herding the animals. At night all the dogs would curl up on the floor in the cooking shack.

The dogs belonged to nobody in particular. They were just there, and everyone fed them scraps when they felt like it, everyone patted them when they felt like it, and everyone kicked and swore at them when they felt like it. After all, they were just dogs. For as long as Mofola could remember there had always been dogs of some shape and size at the *shamba* to feed, kick, and shout at. He hushed them quiet, and with a short whispered command sent them all back to their sleeping place in the cooking shack, and then he proceeded over to his father's hut.

Mofola listened outside the closed door and could hear the loud snores of his father and the deep breathing of his sleeping mother. He knew his father was sleeping on his back with his hands behind his head. This was the only way that the old man could sleep and get enough air into his congested lungs. He slowly turned the latch of the door and opened it slightly, the snoring was louder now and through the gap in the door he could see the luminous hands and numbers of the old alarm clock that stood on the stool next to the old man's side of the bed.

Mofola knew that on the same stool there would be a box of matches, a pocket-knife, some loose change and a bag of Boxer tobacco. Slowly he pushed the door further open, hoping it would not make a noise, and stepped inside. Except for the luminous glow of the old alarm clock it was as black as the night sky without moon or stars. His plan was to take the bag of tobacco and hide it, making his father believe that he had misplaced it.

The old man would then instruct him or one of his nephews to go into town to buy a new bag of tobacco. At a later stage, he could then put the old bag he had taken where the old man could find it again. He crept toward the stool with his heart thumping so hard he was sure the noise was louder than his father's snoring and it would wake his parents. If his father woke up to find him standing there, he would think that it was a thief or that someone had come to do him harm. The old man would leap up out of bed, grab the short stabbing *assegai* that was next to his side of the bed, and stab him to death before he could even cry out.

As he moved toward the bedside stool he was careful not to fall over his father's shoes that he knew were put neatly at the side of the bed. He was just about to take another step forward, when one of the more curious of the younger dogs decided to see what was going on in the room and started to whine and scratch at the partially open door. The old man gave a loud snort and sat bolt upright in bed, at the same time grabbing the short stabbing *assegai*. At the first sound of the whimpering dog, Mofola jumped into the corner and sat crouched on his haunches with his head bent down between his knees and his arms covering it, expecting at any moment to feel the sharp point of the *assegai* penetrating his back.

"*Voertsek*," shouted his father, dropping the *assegai* and grabbing a shoe and throwing it in the direction of the now open door. The dog yelped as the shoe hit him square on the nose. It turned tail and ran off back to its sleeping place in the cooking shack. Mumbling to himself about his wife not having closed the door properly, Mofola's father got out of bed and slammed the door closed, turned around, and got back into bed again.

Mofola sat hunched up in the corner, not daring to move or breathe for fear that the old man would hear him. Mofola's mother said, "Go back to sleep, *Baba*, before you wake up the whole *shamba*." Within minutes the old man was snoring his head off again. Mofola sat dead still for another few minutes, then he got slowly to his feet and gingerly crept over to the stool and felt around for the bag of tobacco. He found the knife, the matches, and a few loose coins on the stool, but where was the bag of tobacco?

Chapter 8

Negome, not knowing that her father had forbidden Mofola to speak to her was concerned that Mofola no longer cared for her. It was three days since she had given the message to Mofola's nephew and she had heard nothing from Mofola or his nephews. She asked her mother and father if they had seen Mofola lately in the store when she was at school. They both said that they had not seen him for many weeks. Her father said he had heard that the Boxer Boy had gone up into the mountains again with his cattle and goats, but this was not what Mofola's nephew had told her. He said that Mofola was at the *shamba* and was helping them with the cattle and goats during the day.

Victor Aguiar loved to play poker and every Friday night he would go across the road to the cantina where he would play poker with Costa Xavier, the owner of the cantina, the commissioner of police, Carlos Chissano, and anyone in the cantina who was foolish enough to take on the trio. It was normally one of the new drivers or co-drivers—unfamiliar with the trio's tactics—that they could talk into playing with them.

Victor loved to play cards; that and a couple of bottles of red wine were his only once-a-week entertainment. He was not very good at poker, but because of an arrangement they had among the three of them, they would always take money off one of the drivers or co- drivers. This boosted Victor's ego as being a good card player. When no one else could be talked or enticed into playing with them, the three of them would play together. They would drink wine and play into the early hours of Saturday morning and large sums of money would cross the table.

Victor had lost a great deal of money at the gambling table and would often end up owing large gambling debts to his two friends, which, over the years he always managed somehow to pay back again. One day, Victor kept telling himself lady luck was going to smile down on him and he was going to win big and show his two friends up. It was this optimism that kept bringing him back to the card table, week after week.

Whenever a new victim could be found to take on the trio, it would create a bit of excitement in the cantina. The locals and the drivers that were staying overnight in the dingy rooms at the back of the cantina would gather around the poker table. They were all hoping to see if this new victim could take money off the trio. With all the people gathered around the card table it created quite an atmosphere; occasionally a drunken brawl would start but normally it was nothing that the commissioner himself could not handle. Anyway it all added to the Friday night excitement and entertainment.

For years the priest and nuns at the Catholic Mission had tried in vain to close down the gambling and prostitution at the cantina, but as long as the commissioner was party to the whole sordid affair there was very little that anyone could do about it.

Chapter 9

Unbeknownst to Mofola, the bag of tobacco that should have been standing on the stool next to the bed had been knocked off the stool and had fallen on the floor next to the bed when his father had grabbed for the stabbing *assegai*. Mofola quickly retreated from the room, his little mission unaccomplished. He now had to think of another way to visit Negome.

Mofola had heard that Mr. Victor would go over to the cantina every Friday night to play poker with Mr. Costa and the commissioner. If he could only find a way to see Negome at night when Mr. Victor was playing cards. He could then slip away from the *shamba* when everyone was asleep. Mofola tried hard to come up with a plan, but nothing would come to his mind. He therefore decided that even without a plan he would go to town on Friday night. Maybe when he was there, a plan would come to him. At least he would be doing something, which was far better than doing nothing, he thought to himself.

The village folk generally went to bed early, not only because they had to get up early, but also it cost money to burn candles and the *paraffin* lamps. That Friday night when everyone was asleep, Mofola slipped out of the *shamba*, closing the gate behind him so that the dogs would not follow him into town. The moon was full and already fairly high in the sky. Dark ominous clouds passed in front of it, casting weird shadows across the track that led down to the road that went into town. The shadows never bothered Mofola for he knew every rock and cranny on the track that led down to the road.

Mofola had never been into town at night before and when he arrived there he was amazed at how busy it was, especially around the cantina. He kept in the shadows, not wanting anyone to see or recognize him. He knew that if anyone recognized him it would surely get back to his father that he was seen in town that Friday night. As he passed the back of the cantina he could see three big trucks parked there. One was loaded with cement, covered partially by an old canvas that was tied down to the sides of the truck. The other two trucks were loaded with pipes and machinery that Mofola did not know.

He made his way across the road to the back of the store where the Aguiars' house stood. The house was not big and was built onto the back of the store with the same red sun-baked bricks that most of the other buildings in the town were built from. The once shiny corrugated iron roof now had rusty patches that could be clearly seen in the bright moonlight.

The back door led out onto a courtyard that was enclosed by an old rusty wire fence that was badly in need of repair. Near the one side of the house two peach trees grew. He knew they were peach trees, as he had often seen the trees full of peaches in the early summer. The house had five windows in all, one big window near the back door and two on each side of the house. He could see the glow of a *paraffin* lamp through the drawn curtains on the street side of the house as he walked past the house to the small gate leading into the courtyard.

He looked around to make sure that nobody was watching him before he pushed open the gate and walked into the courtyard. The house was built on sloping ground; as a result, the windows on the side of the house away from the street were much higher off the ground than those on the street side.

Mofola walked around the side of the house and he could see that the window nearest him had the curtains open. He stood on his toes, caught hold of the window ledge and pulled himself up so that he could see into the room. There was a light shining into the room from the room across the passage. He could just see the outline of a bed, but he could not see if there was anyone in it. By this time his fingers could no longer hold on to the window ledge and he dropped back onto the ground. He thought to himself that this room must be where Mr. Victor and his wife slept, as the bed was big enough for two grown people.

The window next to the one he had just looked in had the curtains closed. This window was even higher than the one he had first looked in. The light in the room was very bright, and he thought it had to be a Coleman pump lamp to be that bright. He could see that there were people moving about the room. When someone walked past the window and brushed against the curtains they would open for a short while, but he was too low down to recognize anyone. One of the peach trees was close to the window with the bright light. He clambered up the tree to a height where he could just see above the ledge of the window and waited.

From where he was sitting in the tree he could just see into the room through a small gap in the curtains. It looked as if there was someone sitting at a table, but he could not see who it was. He waited for someone to brush past the curtains again so that he could get a better look. Mofola's legs were starting to cramp, as he was perched in an awkward position with his one leg hooked around a branch to prevent him from falling out of the tree. Just as he was about to give up, someone brushed past the curtains again and they opened just long enough for him to get a quick glimpse of what he thought was Negome sitting at the table, but he could not be sure.

The person came back again brushing the curtains briefly open. This time he saw quite clearly that it definitely was Negome sitting at the table. He was so excited that he nearly shouted out her name, forgetting briefly that he was perched up a peach tree in the black of night.

Mofola quickly climbed down from the tree and broke off one of the long thin branches that so often grew out from the main trunk of old peach trees. He took the branch and went and stood under the window of the room where Negome was sitting. Holding the branch and stretching out he tapped on the window with it. He could not be sure if Negome was alone in the room. He decided that if someone other than Negome looked out the window he would quickly slip back into the shadows.

Negome was sitting at the dining room table doing her school homework. She heard a noise at the window that sounded like a branch of a tree rubbing against the glass pane. Thinking it was strange, as there were no trees that near to the house, she got up from the table and went over to the window to have a look at where the noise was coming from.

She pulled back the curtains and stared out into the blackness of the night not seeing anything. She stood there for a few seconds letting her eyes become accustomed to the dark, but she could still not see what had been making the noise on the window. She was just about to step back and close the curtain again, when she saw the thin end of a tree branch slapping against the window pane. Thinking this strange, she opened the window and looked down to the ground. She saw someone standing there with a long thin branch of a tree in his hand and a wide grin on his face.

"Negome" he whispered, "it is me, Mofola."

"Mofola what are you doing here?" she asked.

"Shhh! be quiet," he said. "I had to come to see you and explain why I have not seen you. It's because your father has forbidden me to ever speak to you again." Just then Negome's mother came into the room.

"What are you doing, child," she asked, "hanging out that window like that?"

"I was hot, Mother, so I opened the window to get some fresh air."

"Don't be so foolish, child," said her mother. "Do you want to let all the mosquitoes in the neighborhood into the house?" With that she walked over to the window, closed it again, and drew the curtains.

Negome now understood why she had not seen or heard from Mofola for such a long time and she decided to speak to her father the following morning. That night she slept well dreaming of being together with Mofola.

The next morning having slept on the problem she thought that maybe it was not such a good idea to confront her father about Mofola. At the best of times she knew her father was not a reasonable man, and confronting him might only make things worse for her and Mofola. She decided instead to send a message to Mofola with one of his nephews the next time she saw one of them in the store.

When Mrs.. Aguiar came to the window, Mofola thought that this was the end, but fortunately, Negome's quick-wittedness saved the situation. Mofola felt much happier as he made his way home again knowing that Negome now knew the reason why he had not been to see her for many weeks.

Negome did not have long to wait. By Wednesday the old man had just about smoked the last of his tobacco and had sent his two grandchildren to the store. It was just before closing time when Negome saw the two boys coming into the store and went over to serve them. She took down a bag of Boxer tobacco from the shelf and placed it on the counter. While she was counting out the change, she quickly told them about her plan to meet Mofola. He was to meet her in the old woodshed at the back of her father's house on Friday night at about ten o'clock.

When the two boys gave Mofola the message he swore them both to secrecy. He threatened that if they ever mentioned this to anyone, he would feed them to the lions up in the mountains.

Friday could not come fast enough for Mofola. It was eventually Friday night, but it seemed as if the whole *shamba* had decided to go to bed later than usual that night. At last it was quiet and everyone had gone off to bed. Mofola waited in the room where he slept with his two nephews until he thought it was time to go. He had no way of knowing what the actual time was. The only clock in the *shamba* was the one that stood next to his father's bed and he was not going to sneak into his parents' room again to check the time.

He slipped out of the *shamba*, closed the gate and ran all the way into town, convinced that he was late. He walked around to the back of the store, making sure he was not seen as he gingerly made his way over to the old woodshed. He looked around again before cautiously pushing the door open and whispering Negome's name. It was very dark inside the shed and he sensed rather than saw that there was no one there. He was now even more convinced that he was late and that Negome had grown tired of waiting for him.

It was quite a big woodshed, about three paces by three paces. Mofola felt his way around the inside, kicking his foot against a log on the floor and cursing under his breath. The wood was stacked along the back wall right up to the roof. The smell of chicken feed was quite strong in the enclosed shed. He felt his way around to where the smell was the strongest until he touched bags of feed stacked two high in the corner and sat down on the bags and waited. He decided to wait for a while just in case he was not late. Maybe Negome was late because she could not slip out, or maybe his nephews had gotten the message wrong and it was to be next Friday night. All these thoughts went through his mind as he sat there waiting.

He sat there waiting for what seemed to be an age and was just about to get up and go when he heard the distinct sound of a fly-screen door opening and closing. A short while later the door of the shed opened and Mofola could see the silhouette of Negome framed in the doorway by the light of the moon from outside.

The two of them had never been alone together before and for a brief moment, while she stood in the doorway, he wondered just what they would talk about. He need not have worried, because Negome had so much to talk about that he hardly got a chance to say anything. However, he did manage to tell her exactly what her father had said to him and how her father had threatened to have him thrown into jail if he continued to speak to her in the store.

He also told her that her father had plans for her to marry the eldest son of Mr. Costa as soon as he turned twenty-one. Negome was horrified that her father could even think like that. As far as she was concerned, Mr. Costa's son was an arrogant pig and she would never marry him even if he was the last man on the earth.

Negome sat on the sack of chicken feed next to Mofola. He could feel the warmth of her body pressing against his and he found this new sensation very exciting. The two of them sat in the darkness and spoke for a long time. Eventually Negome said that she had better go back inside in case her father came home earlier than usual and found that she was not in her bed. Her father always came into their room at night to say good night no matter how late it was. They decided that they would meet every Friday night in the woodshed at the same time and agreed that whoever was there first would wait for some time before leaving, just in case the other was held up for some reason or other. Mofola said that he would send a message with one of his nephews if he could not get there and Negome said she would do the same.

Every Friday night the two would meet in the old woodshed and discuss their future plans. Mofola would soon have to take the herd up into the mountains again, as the hot rainy season was nearing. This time he would be taking his two nephews to teach them how to herd and live up in the mountains. Because Negome's father would not consent to their marriage, they decided that the only alternative they had was to run away together, but first they had to have enough money to travel far away from Massangena. They would need to go where her father and the commissioner could not find them. The best thing would be for them to go to South Africa or Rhodesia.

"When I come back from the mountains, I will go to my brothers in South Africa where they are working on the mines. I will get work as a driller deep underground and I will earn big money. I will then come back and fetch you and we will both go back to South Africa where you can get work in a big store and I will go back and work on the mines again."

During the weeks that followed they would sit in the woodshed on Friday nights and discuss how much money they would need to travel to South Africa and how long it would take Mofola to earn that much money. "Maybe we could get a ride with one of the truck drivers," said Negome. "Surely one of the drivers would help us if we told them what our plans are." Negome knew that the truckers did not particularly like her father, as he was one of the three who was always taking their money at poker.

"If we could get a ride with a truck going to Rhodesia, we could then make our way from there to South Africa," said Mofola. "That would be a good plan, as we would then not have to spend so much money and we could save some and use it in South Africa to start our new life together."

Up until then they had met in the woodshed every Friday night without any problems, but Negome was now afraid that she would be missed by one of her sisters and could therefore not stay too long in the shed with Mofola. She explained to him that the last time when they met and she slipped back into the bedroom that she shared with her two sisters, her youngest sister Malaina was lying awake and asked where she had been. Negome explained to her sister that she was hot and could not sleep and that she had gone into the kitchen to drink some water.

Unbeknownst to Negome this was not the first time that her sister Malaina had seen her leaving and coming back into the bedroom. At first she thought nothing of it, but when she noticed that it was always on a Friday night she decided to ask her the next time she saw her do it. Negome insisted that she was hot and had gone into the kitchen for a drink of water. Malaina wondered why her sister took such a long time to have a drink of water. She decided next time she would follow her.

Mofola was now seventeen years old and he had only one year to go before he was old enough to enrol at the WNLA to register to go and work on the South African mines. Although he was big for his age and all the years up in the mountains had broadened his shoulders and toned the muscles of his arms and legs, he was still worried about being accepted by the WNLA.

Ever since hearing the stories from his brothers about the doctors at the WNLA who examined men for fitness, he had been testing himself every month to see if he would pass the test. He would hold his testicles in the cup of his hand and cough, but no matter how vigorously he coughed he could not get his testicles to jump in his hand. He even practiced twitching the muscles of his groin but he could still not get his testicles to even move let alone jump.

This was very worrying for him because if he did not pass the test then he would not be able to go to work in the mines and the plans that he and Negome had made would come to nothing. He wondered if it was maybe the stone that his mother had tied to his penis that had deprived his testicles of all the strength and growth. He wanted to ask his brothers, but they were in South Africa, and to ask his father was just out of the question, so he continued to check himself every month and hoped that one day they would just jump up in his hand.

Chapter 10

It was Friday night and the old grandmother clock in the dining room had just struck ten o' clock. The house was quiet, her father was playing poker at the cantina, and everyone else in the house was asleep, or so Negome thought. She slipped out of bed, put on her night robe, and went out of the bedroom, down the passage, and into the kitchen. She unlocked the back door, pulled it open, and looked out through the fly screen door to see if there was anyone around outside before pushing the screen door open and stepping out into the backyard, closing both doors softly behind her.

Malaina lay awake with her face to the wall, as soon as she heard Negome leaving the room she quietly got out of bed and tiptoed down the passage where she stood peeping from behind the passage door leading into the kitchen. She caught just a glimpse of Negome as she closed the back door. She quickly went into the kitchen, pulled back the curtain in the window that overlooked the backyard, and in the moonlight saw Negome walk across the yard to the woodshed. Why would Negome be going to the woodshed at this time of the night, she thought to herself. There was plenty of wood for the fire in the morning because she had brought in a load herself just after they had eaten dinner.

Malaina waited to see whether Negome was coming back and when, after a few minutes, she had not come out of the shed, Malaina decided to go and see what Negome found so interesting in the woodshed. She opened both doors very quietly, slipped out into the cool night and crept over to the shed on her bare feet, being extra careful not to kick her toe or stand on a stone. As she drew nearer to the shed she could hear muffled voices coming from inside.

She crept closer, making her way toward the back of the shed. If whoever was there came out, she could then hide behind it. She could now hear quite distinctly the voice of her sister, but who was she talking to? She stood there listening for several minutes until the other person spoke, but only a few words and then stopped, it was a man's voice that she recognized but she could not immediately put a face or name to it. Malaina waited while her sister continued to speak and then she stopped talking and the male voice said, "This will be my last trip up into the mountains." Then she suddenly realized that it was the voice of Mofola.

Malaina knew Mofola; all the girls in the area knew him or had heard about him. They had all heard how strong he was and how good he was at stick fighting; the other young men left him alone, as he would take two or three of them on at the same time and beat them. People also said that his penis was the size of a two-year-old baby's arm. Malaina liked Mofola. She would often serve him in the store when Negome was not there, but when she was in the store she would tell Malaina to go and serve another customer, Negome was always telling her what to do, as if she was the boss of the store.

Malaina knew that her father did not like Mofola, as she had often heard him tell Negome not to waste her time talking to the stupid herd boy. Malaina wondered why she had not seen Mofola coming into the store for such a long time, but then she did not think too much about it, as she knew that he was more than likely herding the cattle up in the mountains again.

Malaina stood listening to the two of them talking for a little while longer, and then she quickly went back into the house and got back into bed and pretended to be asleep. A short while later Negome came creeping back into the bedroom. She took off her night robe and got into bed and was asleep in a very short time. Malaina lay in her bed listening to the slow, steady breathing of her two sisters and tried to work out in her devious little mind how she could best use this information to get back at her bossy elder sister.

Malaina was deeply jealous of her father's affection for Negome. Her father could never see anything wrong with what Negome did or said, except he did not like it when Negome ignored his wishes that she should not waste her time talking to the Boxer Boy Mofola. Malaina decided that in the morning she would tell her father of Negome's little visits to the woodshed.

She was sure that this bit of information would bring her some good favour with her father who always seemed to shun her.

Victor Aguiar was not in a particularly good mood on Saturday morning. He had lost again at poker on Friday night and had also drunk too much wine, for which he was now paying with a bad headache.

Malaina knew that her father was in the habit of rising early, irrespective of how late he went to bed; he would stoke up the fire and put a pot of coffee on the stove to brew. He would then sit at the kitchen table quietly drinking a big mug of steaming coffee. Victor referred to this time as his thinking time and he did not look favourably on anyone who in any way disturbed his morning quiet time.

Malaina opened the passage door into the kitchen. She saw her father sitting at the kitchen table drinking his coffee. He looked up as the door opened. "Yes, child, what is it?" he asked irritably. "Can't you see that I'm busy?"

"Yes, Father, I can see that you are very busy," she said in her sweetest hushed voice. "I only wanted to tell you about Negome and that boy that Father calls the Boxer Boy, but if Father is too busy I can always tell you some other time."

Victor now a little more interested said, "Yes, yes, so tell me, child, what is it that is so interesting that you have to disturb your father's time of thinking?"

Malaina closed the door softly and went and sat opposite her father at the kitchen table. She then told her father that Negome was seeing Mofola in the old woodshed on Friday nights and that Negome had been seeing him there for the last six weeks every Friday night when everyone was asleep. "I heard them having sex," she added. She thought she would exaggerate a bit to make it sound better.

"So why is it that you only give me this very important information now after six weeks?" her father burst out.

"I'm so sorry, Father," she said, detecting the anger in his voice and thinking maybe she had over-exaggerated the situation. "I was not too sure until last night," she babbled with tears running down her cheeks, "when I followed Negome to the shed and I could hear them inside. They were talking and making love noises. The other times when Negome went out of the room I asked her where she was going and she told me to be quiet and go back to sleep. She said she was only going to the kitchen to drink some water."

"All right," said her father, "you did the right thing to tell me these things. Now be off with you and give your father time to think."

Victor was furious that Mofola had disobeyed his orders not to see or speak to Negome ever again and here now they were meeting at night and having sex together. If this information got to the ears of Costa he would never allow his son to marry Negome and all Victor's plans would come to nothing. But what would Costa's son think when he found out on his wedding night that Negome was not a virgin? Maybe he would not notice if Negome was clever enough. Anyway it would then be too late, as they would already be married and that would be Negome's problem not his.

Victor would not allow himself to even think that Negome might be pregnant. If the two of them had been having sex for the past six weeks, the possibility was very strong. "Jesus, I could kill the stupid little bitch," he said to himself. He would go and speak to his friend the commissioner and between the two of them he was sure they could come up with a plan, but first he must speak to Malaina again.

Victor went to find his daughter, who was in the bathroom washing the tear marks from her face. He went into the bathroom, closed the door and confronted Malaina again about what she had heard in the shed. "Are you sure that your sister and that Boxer Boy were having sex?" he asked, rather embarrassed, for the girls discussed sexual matters only with their mother and never with their father.

"I can't be positive, Father," she said. "I only heard what I thought was the noise people make when they have sex," she said, lying again, now realizing that she was getting herself into a big mess with all the exaggeration.

"So how is it that you know what noises people make when they have sex?" asked Victor.

Malaina, realizing that she was lying herself into a corner, started to sob again. "I only heard what the other children at school said it sounded like, I've never heard people having sex before." She sobbed. One of the things that Victor could not handle was a woman crying and especially when it was one of his own girls.

"Now, now," soothed Victor, patting Malaina on the back, "don't cry, child, I just wanted to be sure that I have all the facts," he said. "I want you to promise me that you will never repeat this to anyone, not even to your mother, do you understand? If I ever find out that you have told anyone about this little incident I will give you such a hiding that you will never forget it, is that clear?" he said.

Later that morning Victor went into the store and took a roll of bank notes out of the safe and walked up to the police station to speak to the commissioner. He was feeling a little better about the situation, having spoken again to Malaina. He was not convinced that Malaina knew that her sister and the Boxer Boy were having sex, and anyway there was very little he could do about it. If she was pregnant he would soon find out and then he could send her off to his brother and sister-in-law who lived in Inhambane. She could have the baby there and then come back after the birth. She could then explain that she had gone there to look after her sick aunt.

Victor explained the situation to the commissioner, leaving out the part about Negome and the Boxer Boy having sex. The commissioner was in a good mood having just received part of the outstanding debt owed to him by Victor. He took out a little black book from the inside pocket of his uniform jacket and made a few adjustments to the figures, smiled, and put it back in his pocket. The commissioner was very sympathetic and told him not to worry; he would take care of the situation.

With that the commissioner reached under the counter and pulled out a half bottle of wine and two glasses. He pulled the cork with his teeth, sloshed wine into the glasses, and pushed one glass over to Victor. Some wine spilled on the counter and he wiped it up with the sleeve of his jacket. By the time Victor left the police station he was feeling a lot happier. As he walked back home, he was congratulating himself on turning a negative situation into a rather positive one.

Victor was confident that the commissioner would find a way to sort out the Boxer Boy. The commissioner was feared by the people in the district for he was a hard man and did not take nonsense from anyone. Victor remembered hearing the commissioner once remark that one had to be hard on these black bastards, because if you showed them any kindness they would take it as a weakness. He said the Portuguese had learned this the hard way over the decades of conflict with the black people in their African colonies.

Chapter 11

The days between Fridays seemed to go so slowly for Mofola. This Friday would be the last Friday night that he would be able to visit with Negome, because his father had told him that it was time to take the cattle and goats as well as his two nephews up into the mountains to graze as the days grew hotter and the dreaded tsetse fly was starting to appear.

Mofola made his way into town that Friday night and sat in the woodshed waiting for Negome to arrive, she seemed to be late but he could not tell as he had no way of checking the time. He found it strange that the light in the kitchen was still burning, he could see the glow through the drawn curtains and every so often he saw the shadows of someone walk past the window.

Negome and her two sisters were just getting ready to go to bed, when there was a knock on the front door. Her mother was already in bed and her father was sitting at the kitchen table drinking wine. "Negome," he shouted from the kitchen, "see who's at the door."

She opened the door to find the commissioner standing there. "Good evening Negome," he greeted her, "is your father in?"

"Good evening, Commissioner," she said. "Yes, he is in the kitchen, please come in."

"Who is it?" shouted her father.

"It's the commissioner, Father," she answered. "Bring the commissioner into the kitchen," he shouted again.

She escorted the commissioner down the passage into the kitchen. "Good evening, Commissioner," greeted Victor. "Come, sit down and have a glass of wine." Negome left the kitchen and as she went through the door into the passage, her father called, "Close the door, my child. Negome turned and pulled the passage door closed and went off to bed.

Negome lay awake in bed listening to the muffled voices of her father and the commissioner talking in the kitchen. She knew that they had already finished one bottle of wine because she heard her father go into the store to fetch another bottle. The more they drank the louder they seemed to get. Although they were talking and laughing quite loudly she could still not quite make out what they were talking about, as the kitchen door into the passage was closed.

Negome was becoming quite agitated, because her father always went over to the cantina on Friday nights. She could remember only one other time he had not gone over to the cantina on a Friday night and that was when he was sick with malaria. Negome knew that tonight would possibly be the last time she would be able to see

Mofola for several months. He would soon be taking his father's herd up into the mountains. She lay in bed waiting; ten o' clock had come and gone. It was now half past ten, the old grandmother clock on the dining room wall had just struck the half hour and still the two men sat and talked and laughed in the kitchen.

Mofola could see the light in the kitchen through the gap in the partially closed shed door and realized that there must still be someone in the kitchen and that was why Negome could not slip out. Disappointed that he would not see her for some time he got up from the log that he had been sitting on next to the door and made his way out of the shed. He had just gone past the back of the shed when a strong pair of hands grabbed him from behind.

He tried to turn to see who had grabbed him when he was hit on the side of the head with something hard and his legs just buckled under him. As he hit the ground one of his attackers kicked him in the groin. He doubled up in pain. He lifted his hands and arms to protect his head from the boots that seemed to be raining down on him from all sides. As they kicked, one or another shouted over and over, "Thieving bastard, this will teach you to steal."

The noise and the disturbance outside brought the commissioner and Victor running out of the kitchen waving a *paraffin* lamp taken from the kitchen table. "What's going on here?" shouted the commissioner, as he ran over to the two men who were kicking the living daylights out of poor Mofola who lay semiconscious on the ground.

The commissioner lifted the light. "Ho! It's you," he said to his two black constables. "What is it we have here?"

"We were walking down the street, sir," said one of the constables, "when we saw this man sneak into Mr. Victor's backyard and take this trousers and this shirt," holding the shirt and pair of trousers up so that the commissioner could see them, "from the washing line there, sir," he said, pointing in the direction of the wash line. "So we hide here behind this shed and when he come past we shout to him to stop, but he try to run away so we grab him and then he try to cut me with this knife," holding up an old knife so the commissioner and Victor could see it.

Negome heard the back screen door slam as the commissioner and her father ran outside. She lay in bed wondering what was going on. Then she heard her mother at the kitchen door asking her father what all the noise was. "Don't worry, my dear," shouted Victor from the back of the shed. "Everything is fine, it is only a thief that the commissioner's constables have caught taking clothes off the washing line. You can go back to bed, the commissioner here will deal with the situation."

"There was no washing left on the line," Negome heard her mother say. "I brought it all in myself."

"You must have been mistaken," Victor said. "Go back to bed."

Negome lay in bed, wide awake. She could not go to sleep. She just hoped upon hope that it was not Mofola that they had caught but Mofola would have gone a long time ago if he saw that the light in the kitchen was still burning and he would not steal clothes from the washing line, she reasoned. Feeling more relieved with her self-explanation she eventually fell asleep. Mofola was dragged to his feet and marched off to the local jail in the old fort. Victor and the commissioner, pleased with their evening's little entertainment, went over to the cantina to see if there were still any takers for a few games of poker.

When the old man got up on Saturday morning and walked down to the cattle paddock he was surprised not to find Mofola there busy with the cattle. His grandsons were busy milking the two milk cows, but Mofola was nowhere to be seen. "Where is Mofola?" asked the old man.

"We don't know, Grandfather" said Joseph. "When we woke up this morning Mofola was already up. We thought that he was already down here with the cattle, but when we got here we could not find him and when we asked, no one had seen him this morning."

The old man thought that this was strange, as Mofola had never gone anywhere without first consulting him.

The sun was already high in the sky and still there was no sign of Mofola. The animals in the paddock were becoming restless. "Joseph," shouted the old man irritably above the noise of the animals, "take the herd out to graze. We can't wait all day for Mofola to decide to come home."

Late that afternoon when Joseph and his brother brought the herd home there was still no sign of Mofola. The old man was hoping that Mofola had joined his nephews with the herd sometime during the day, but when he did not arrive home with them he was annoyed but also worried, as it was not like Mofola to go off without telling him first.

That night after the evening meal when the *shamba* was quiet and the rest of the family had all gone to bed, the old man sat under the kitchen overhang near the fire. He sat there half asleep feeding the occasional log onto the fire, trying to think where Mofola could be. The more he pondered the more uneasy he became.

It was ironic that Mofola would spend weeks up in the mountains alone with the herd and the old man never worried about him, but now he had been away only one night and the old man had a bad feeling that something was not right.

It was Sunday morning, and the sun was still hiding below the horizon when the old man got up stiffly from the stool where he had spent the night next to the fire. He made his way over to the hut where Mofola and the grandchildren slept. He opened the door and looked inside to see if Mofola had perhaps slipped in during the night when he had nodded off to sleep next to the fire, but he was not there. The two boys were putting on their clothes. "Good morning, boys," greeted the old man.

"Good morning, Grandfather," the boys greeted in return.

"Joseph you know Mofola has not come home yet. Do you have any idea where he can be or where he might have gone?"

Joseph had a very good idea where Mofola had gone, but he dare not tell the old man, remembering too well Mofola's warning that he would feed him to the lions if he ever mentioned a word about him and Negome. "No, Grandfather, we have no idea where Mofola can be," he lied.

"Never mind," he said. "When you have finished milking the cows and have eaten, take the animals out to the grazing, I'm going into town to see if Mofola is perhaps there, so don't let the donkeys out to graze."

After breakfast the old man hitched up the donkey cart and went into town. He passed many of the townsfolk from out of town on their way to the mission church. Each time he passed people he knew, he would stop and ask them if they had seen Mofola in the last few days, but no one could remember seeing him recently.

The old man did not believe in the woman god of these Catholic people. He believed in many gods and the spirits of his ancestors. These were the gods that he called on to lead him to his youngest son. When he arrived in town he could hear the church bell ringing in the distance, he put his hand into his pocket and pulled out the old Zobo pocket watch attached to a silver chain and looked at the time—it was nine o'clock.

The old man hitched the donkeys to the hitching pole at the back of the cantina next to two freight trucks that were parked there for the night. There was very little activity in town that early on a Sunday morning. One of the truck drivers was washing some clothes in the concrete trough outside one of the *rondavel* rooms and had placed the clothes on the bonnet of the truck to dry. The old man walked around to the front of the cantina; it was still closed. It opened at eleven o'clock after the last service had finished at the mission church. This was an agreement the priest, Father Hogan, had with the commissioner.

A young man was polishing the red cement steps going up to the cantina with red wax polish. "Good morning, young man," greeted the old man.

"Good morning, *Baba*," said the younger one.

"The rains are late again this year," said the old man, "and the ground is so dry that if we do not have rains soon then we will have another bad season for the crops."

"Yes, *Baba*, the ground is dry and the dust so thick that when you spit, it makes holes in the dust like ant bear holes."

"Tell me, young man, do you know my youngest son Mofola?"

"Yes, *Baba*, we know him. He is called the Boxer Boy."

"That's right," said the old man. "Have you seen him lately?"

"No, *Baba*, we have not seen the Boxer Boy for a long time now. We used to see him when he would come to Mr. Victor's store to buy the tobacco. Now we don't see him anymore. We only see the young boys of the *Baba's* oldest son."

"Thank you, young man," said the old man. "My son he has been missing for two days now and no one seems to have seen him or knows where he might be."

With that the old man turned to walk away. "One thing," said the young man, "it may be a help to the *Baba*."

"Yes, what is it?" asked the old man turning around to face the young man now sitting on the step.

"On Friday night I was sweeping near the door. It was late and many people had already gone home, when the commissioner and Mr. Victor came into the cantina. They were laughing and talking and I'm sure I heard them talk about the Boxer Boy, maybe the *Baba* can go to the police station and ask there about his youngest son."

It had never occurred to the old man to inquire at the police station. Maybe it was because he knew his son would never get into any trouble, but maybe they had seen or heard where he might be found. He walked up the dusty street to the police station and went inside the building with the sign above the door saying "Charge Office." The constable on duty sat with his feet on the table, head resting on the back of the chair. The chair was precariously tilled back on its hind legs and he was half asleep. A well-thumbed greasy magazine lay open across his fat belly.

The old man walked up to the counter and cheerfully greeted the constable. "Good morning, Constable." The constable opened his one eye and looked at the old man, recognising him as Mofola's father; he closed his eye again, saying nothing. The old man stood at the counter waiting patiently for the constable to acknowledge his presence. The old man knew better than to speak again to the constable; it was far better to wait until the constable was ready to address you in his own good time. After what must have been at least five minutes the constable said with his eyes still closed, "So, old man, have you come to see your criminal son?"

"What do you mean criminal?" the old man burst out. "No son of mine is a criminal."

"That's what you think, old man," said the constable. "On Friday night your son was caught stealing clothes off the washing line at the back of Mr. Victor's house and when two of my colleagues tried to apprehend him, he resisted arrest and pulled out a knife and tried to stab one of my colleagues."

"These things you say cannot be true," stammered the old man. "My son would never do such a thing. He does not even possess a knife."

"Yes, yes," said the constable, dropping his legs to the floor and sitting up straight in the chair, "that's what all the parents of their troublesome children say; we see them all the time."

"Where is he, then?" anxiously asked the old man. "Can I see him?"

"Sorry, old man, he is in one of the cells at the back and the commissioner has given instructions that he is to have no visitors until the magistrate has heard his case."

Three times a year the magistrate from Inhambane would come up to hear cases in Massangena. If one happened to land in jail just after the magistrate left then one could be in jail for up to four months pending trial. The commissioner would normally allow the family to visit the accused every day and bring the accused food. This way the commissioner could save on feeding the prisoners and pocket the money budgeted for the prisoner's food.

"But how will I know that it's my son?" protested the old man.

"Look here, old man," said the constable. "I know you and your son, the Boxer Boy. I have often seen the two of you at the market in the donkey cart. Believe me, it is your son."

"Please, can I see him just for a minute?" pleaded the old man.

"All right then," said the constable, "but only for a minute and you are not to speak to him, do you hear?"

The constable slowly lifted his great weight out of the chair and lifted up the hatch in the counter and beckoned to the old man behind the counter. They went out the back door of the charge office into the bright sunlight and walked across the cobblestone courtyard to where the cells were situated against the back perimeter stone wall of the old fort.

There were ten cells in all, built up against the back wall. Three of the cells were occupied and the rest stood empty with their doors wide open. The fort was built back in the eighteenth century when the Portuguese were still fighting raging wars with the *Shangane* tribes in the Gaza province.

Each cell was originally designed for six prisoners but, during the years of conflict with the black tribes, up to fifteen prisoners were at times housed in one cell. Today it was very seldom that there were more than five prisoners in the fort at any one time. The roof of the cells was originally constructed with thick wooden beams clad on the outside with slate stone, but a fire had raged through the building many years ago and the wood and tile roof had been replaced with corrugated iron sheets. In the summer months, when the sun was overhead, it would beat down on the iron roof, making the heat in the cell almost unbearable.

Mofola had been placed in the far right-hand cell. Each cell was built with a single solid steel door and a small open barred window situated near the top of the wall looking out onto the courtyard. The old man stood on his toes and peered in through the bars of the cell window. He could see a naked figure sitting crouched in the corner but he could not recognize the person in the gloomy light.

"Mofola," he called, "is that you?"

Mofola turned his head and looked up at his father, their eyes briefly meeting. The old man hardly recognized him, as his face was so swollen from the beating he had taken.

"Hey! You, old man," shouted the constable. "I thought I told you no talking," he said as he pulled the old man away from the cell window. "Do you want to get me into trouble? Maybe I should put you in the next cell—then you can talk all day to your criminal son." With that he took the old man by the arm and led him back into the charge office. "Now you be off," he told the old man, "and don't let me see you here again until after the trial."

Chapter 12

There was no courthouse or town hall in Massangena, so three times a year; Costa Xavier would turn his cantina into a makeshift courtroom. The court proceedings never lasted longer than a day unless there were an abnormal number of cases to be heard. There was no official prosecutor and there was no defence lawyer, the whole procedure was very simple, efficient and effective.

The four hundred and fifty kilometres from Inhambane to Massangena took Antonio Nacapa the better part of a day. He would not drive at night because it was too dangerous with the big trucks on the roads. Most of the truck drivers were contract drivers who would drive through the night to earn extra money. They considered the roads their own private property and anyone, including magistrates, was considered fair game to be pushed off the road.

Antonio would normally leave Inhambane at first light and arrive in Massangena late in the afternoon. Sometimes he would have to leave later due to some important business, and then he would overnight at Chgubo, which was roughly two hundred kilometres from Massangena. He would then get up early and travel the remaining distance in approximately five hours—depending on the state of the road, which was normally very bad, especially when it rained—arriving some time in the late morning.

Communications were not that good, as the telephone line between Inhambane and Massangena was in a poor state of repair and constantly out of order. When the telephone lines were down, one had to rely on the integrity of the truck and bus drivers to get messages to the commissioner to inform him that he would arrive the next day. Often he would arrive there before the commissioner got the message and find that the court proceedings had been prepared for the day before and now nothing was prepared. It would take some time to get everyone reorganized and the cantina laid out again as a courtroom.

Depending on the number of cases, there would be two sessions, one that morning and one in the afternoon. The three-times-a-year court session was about the only entertainment that the townsfolk got, so the whole town was normally there to witness the proceedings.

Antonio hated the three-times-a-year trip up to Massangena, but because he was the junior magistrate he got all the unpleasant jobs. It wasn't that he did not like trying the cases in Massangena; on the contrary, he found the cases often amusing and very interesting. Antonio was basically a family man and he hated being away from his wife and two children. He hated even more the fact that he had to stay over at Costa Xavier's dingy hotel where the rooms constantly smelled of some whore who no doubt spent the previous night there with one of the truck drivers. The drive up to Massangena was long and dusty, but, except for the trucks trying to push one off the road, he enjoyed driving and being out in the country.

The magistrate sat at the back of the cantina near the big open window so he could feel the fresh breeze coming in from the river. He sat at a table placed on a small platform normally used for some entertainer who occasionally passed through the town. Another two tables and four chairs were placed just in front of the magistrate's table; they were for the commissioner, his chief constable, and the accused. Behind the commissioner's table were the rest of the cantina's chairs placed in neat rows with an aisle up the middle leading to the front door. The tables that were not being used were stacked on the side next to the counter.

As usual the cantina was full and people were standing outside on the *veranda* looking in through the door and the open windows. The prisoners would be walked down the road from the jail to the cantina in leg irons and handcuffed to a constable. They would be brought down just before their trial and would stand waiting on the *veranda* of the cantina where they would be chained to one of the poles supporting the roof.

There were only three cases today and Antonio was hoping to finish them before lunchtime. He could then leave immediately for Espangabera where he would spend the night; otherwise, if he finished only after lunch, it would mean he would have to spend another night in one of Costa's rooms and eat the greasy chicken curry that his wife always prepared for him.

Mofola's mother and father sat in the front row of seats directly behind the accused. These seats were reserved for the family members of the prisoner and witnesses, should there be any. It would seem that they were the only family there, as they were the only people sitting in the front row. Mofola's case would be the last one to be heard, they were told by the chief constable who came to see them at the *shamba* a week prior to the hearing.

The first case to be heard was for cattle theft. The accused was led into the cantina courthouse in leg irons and was marched down to the front, handcuffed to the constable. He was told to sit while the constable removed the handcuffs and then stood next to the prisoner.

"This court is now in session," declared the magistrate, banging with his gavel on the table. "Commissioner, let us hear the first case," requested the magistrate.

The commissioner got up from his chair and addressed the magistrate, "Your Honour, our first case is that of cattle theft. The accused here, Takane Nipodi," he said, pointing to the accused sitting in the front, "has been accused of stealing a young heifer from his neighbor, Ergo Mecca."

"Thank you, Commissioner. Will the accused rise?" The constable standing next to Nipodi nudged him in the ribs with his truncheon, indicating that he should stand. Nipodi stood up and faced the magistrate. "Takane Nipodi, how do you plead to this accusation? asked the magistrate." Guilty or not guilty?"

Nipodi turned to the constable next to him and asked him what the magistrate had said. The constable explained to the accused what the magistrate had said, as it was also part of his duty to act as an interpreter when necessary.

The accused turned to face the magistrate, shaking his head from side to side with a look of total indignation, and said, "Not guilty, sir,"

"Your Honour," corrected the chief constable, looking at the accused, "you address the magistrate as Your Honour,"

The accused first looked at the chief constable sitting on his right, nodded, then looked back at the magistrate and said in a loud voice that carried to the back of the room, "Not guilty, Your Honour, sir."

Antonio was used to the accused and witnesses addressing him as sir, your worship, magistrate, etc.; it did not bother him particularly. "So you say that you are not guilty? Then tell me," said the magistrate, "in your own words, why you think you are not guilty."

"As Your Honour, sir, knows, in the summer months when the cattle sickness is here in the lowlands we take the cattles up into the hills to graze where it is cool and there is no sickness."

"Yes," said the magistrate, "please continue."

"It was last year," Nipodi went on, "that I send my cattles to the hills with my two sons, my neighbor, he also send his cattles into the hills with his son like we do every year, Your Honour, sir.

"This year when she goes to the hills, one of my cattles *she* is big with calf, so when this cattle *she* is grazing in the hills, *she* born this young calf but my cattles *she* has got no milk after four days and this young calf *she* go to my neighbor's cattles, the one who *she* got milk.

I don't know why this cattles of mine *she* has a calf but *she* has no milk. Now when, after four months, the cattles they all come back from the hills and this calf of my cattles, *she* walk with the cattles of my neighbor. So when they come back I ask my eldest, where is the calf of the cattle that was big with calf when the cattles they go to the hills? My son, he tell me that this calf, *she* drink the milk from the teats of my neighbor's cattle and is now there by his *shamba*.

"The next day," said Nipodi, "I go with my eldest to my neighbor's *shamba* and my son, *she* show me that calf of my cattles, *she* standing there with the one cattles of my neighbor. So I tell my son to fetch that calf for my cattles and we take this calf to my *shamba*."

"Tell me, where was your neighbor when you took this calf back to your *shamba*?" asked the magistrate.

"That neighbor, *she* was by the beer party at the other neighbor *shamba*."

"Then what happened?" asked the magistrate.

"My neighbor, when *she* come back to his *shamba* and his son tell him we take that calf, he tell the police that I steal that calf from him and the police *she* come and *she* take that calf back to my neighbor's *shamba*."

"And where were you when the police came to take the calf back to your neighbor?"

"I was hiding," said Nipodi, "in the trees down by the river because I know the police, *she* put me in the jail if *she* find me."

"But the police did find you some months later, is that not so and put you in jail?"

"Yes," said Nipodi. "How long is it now that you have been in jail waiting to be tried?" asked the magistrate.

"It's now three months and two weeks, Your Honour, sir," replied Nipodi.

"Commissioner, is that the story as it was related to you?" asked the magistrate.

"Yes, Your Honour, that is the story as we have recorded it," replied the commissioner.

"Then let us hear what the neighbor has to say about this tale of woe, where is the neighbor?" asked the magistrate.

The chief constable stood up and called, "Ergo Mecca, come up to the front." A rather overweight man in his late forties got up from the middle row of seats and approached the magistrate. He stood on the other side of the constable.

"Are you Ergo Mecca, the neighbor of the accused Takane Nipodi?" asked the magistrate.

"Yes, Your Honour, I am Ergo Mecca."

"Mecca, have you heard the statement of the accused?" inquired the magistrate, "and would you say that this was a true reflection of what happened?"

"Yes, Your Honour, it is true what this man, he say," answered Mecca. "This heifer calf, *she* belong to me."

"Tell me," said the magistrate, "why is it that you believe that the heifer calf belongs to you when it is the calf of your neighbor's cow?"

"You see, Your Honour," said Mecca, "this calf, *she* is surely my calf, because this cattle for my neighbor *she* did not have milk to feed this young calf, so this calf, *she* come to my cattles to get the milk. No one bring this calf to my cattles, *she* come to my cattles by himself," explained Mecca. "If this cattles of mine *she* not give the milk to this calf, then this calf, *she* surely *she* die. The milk from my cattles make that this calf, *she* live, so this calf *she* now belong to me," went on Mecca.

"How old is this calf now?" asked the magistrate.

"*She* is over six months, Your Honour, and *she* is this big," said Mecca, extending his arm out, his fingers closed and hand facing upward, indicating that the calf was just over waist high.

"I see," said the magistrate, "the calf is now quite big. Is it still feeding on your cow?"

"Yes, Your Honour, *she* is big, this calf, because *she* drink the strong milk for my cattles that make this calf big and strong but now *she* no longer feeding by my cattles, *she* now eat the grass," explained Mecca.

The magistrate pondered on the case in silence for a few minutes and then said, "I think what we should do is we should kill the calf and each one of you will get a half, how does that sound to you?" said the magistrate looking at Mecca.

"This is a good plan, Your Honour," said Mecca.

"And what do you say, Nipodi, is this a good plan?" asked the magistrate.

"No, Your Honour, sir, this is not a good plan, better Your Honour, sir, *she* give this calf to my neighbor and let me go home to my *shamba* to be with my family."

"Mecca," said the magistrate, "if your wife has a child and *she* cannot feed the child because her milk has dried up and your neighbor's wife has milk and *she* feeds this child until this child can eat the normal food, who does this child belong to?"

"*She* is, of course, my child, Your Honour, for this child *she* come from the seed of my loins and *she* is born from the womb of my wife so *she* must be my child," answered Mecca.

"Why then is it different with the cattle?" asked the magistrate.

"The cattles *she* is different," Mecca went on. "They are not people, the cattles *she* is like the money, if the money from my neighbor pocket, *she* come to my pocket by himself, then this money *she* is mine."

"I see," said the magistrate, "you can go back to your seat," he told Mecca. "We will have a short break while I think about this case."

Nobody left the makeshift courthouse while the magistrate drank a glass of lemonade that Costa brought to him. As soon as the magistrate had finished drinking his lemonade he struck the table three times with his gavel and said, "This court is again in session, please take your seats and be quiet."

Quiet was not something the people understood very well and it took the commissioner's bellowing voice and several threats before there was at least a reasonable quiet. The commissioner stood up, faced the people and said, "The magistrate will now deliver his judgement, will the accused rise." The constable standing next to the accused gave him another nudge in the ribs, indicating to him to stand up.

"I find the accused, Takane Nipodi, not guilty of stealing what was rightfully his in the first place," said the magistrate. "Furthermore, I fine Ergo Mecca," the magistrate went on, "one hundred *escudos*, which is to be paid to the court for wasting the court's time, a further one hundred *escudos* you must pay to the court, which will in turn will be paid to Nipodi for being wrongly arrested and put in jail. If you do not have the two hundred *escudos*, you will be put in jail for six months or until your family is able to raise the money. Next case, please."

The next case was a simple case of being drunk, disorderly, and fighting in the cantina. After the normal formalities the magistrate asked the accused how he pleaded.

"Guilty, Your Honour," pleaded the accused.

"How long have you been in jail?" asked the magistrate.

"Six weeks now, Your Honour," replied the accused.

"I sentence you to a further six weeks in jail, and if you are arrested again for a similar offence, I will put you in jail for a long time, is that clear?"

"Yes, Your Honour, and thank you, Your Honour, for such a small sentence, I promise to not fight in the cantina again."

"Right," said the magistrate, "just make sure you keep your promise. Next case, please."

Negome, her mother, and two sisters sat in the middle of the cantina courtroom. Victor sat at the back with Costa, they were talking and laughing with one another while the magistrate drank some more lemonade and the constable brought Mofola to the front. The chains on the leg irons dragged along the wooden floor of the cantina, making a chinking sound as he shuffled along. He paused at the middle row and looked in the direction of Negome, and for a brief second their eyes met. The constable yanked his handcuffs, pulling him forward again.

The swelling and bruising on his face had now disappeared and he looked clean and neat in the new shirt and long pants that his mother had given the constable at the jail to give to him for the trial. He passed in front of the commissioner and the chief constable and went and sat in the chair for the accused. As he sat down he half turned his head to the right where his mother and father sat.

"I see you, my son," said his mother.

"No talking to the accused," said the commissioner, turning toward Mofola's mother.

When Negome found out the next day that the person that was arrested was Mofola she was deeply distressed. She did not know what to do, as when she tried to see him in jail, the constable had told her that Mofola was not allowed visitors until after the trial.

She had no idea what Mofola wanted her to do, so rather than do or say anything that might make things worse for him, she kept quiet, except she pleaded with her father to withdraw the charges against Mofola for stealing. Her father had explained that he had already spoken to the commissioner, but it was now a serious offence because Mofola had tried to stab the constable with a knife.

She could not believe that Mofola would steal, let alone try to stab someone with a knife; she just knew that there must be a simple explanation to this whole affair. As the weeks went by she went over in her mind what she was going to say if Mofola asked her to speak as a witness to his innocence. She had made up her mind that she would tell the magistrate that Mofola had been visiting her and that he would never steal her father's shirt or try to hurt anyone. It must be a bad mistake. Someone was trying to make trouble for him. Negome still had no idea that her sister was the cause of all this trouble.

The magistrate struck the table three times with his gavel, "Quiet please, court's in session, will the accused rise?"

The constable standing next to Mofola indicated that he should stand up and face the magistrate. The magistrate then asked Mofola the usual questions regarding his name, age, and place of abode, confirming that he was, in fact, the person mentioned on the charge sheet. "Commissioner, please read the charges against the accused," said the magistrate looking impatiently at his watch to see how much time he had, as he wanted to leave Massangena before noon to avoid Mrs. Xavier's curry chicken.

The commissioner rose, picked up a piece of paper and read, "The charges brought against the accused, Mofola Maraga, are as follows: There are two charges, Your Honour, against this man."

"Yes, I'm quite aware of that, Commissioner, I also have the charge sheet in front of me. Please continue," said the magistrate, irritated that the commissioner was wasting time.

The commissioner read on, "The first charge is that on the night of Friday the fourteenth of October of this year the accused stole a pair of trousers and a shirt," pointing to the shirt and pants that the chief constable was waving about above his head, "from the washing line at the back of Mr. Aguiar's house.

"The second charge is one of a more serious nature," said the commissioner. "It is that of resisting arrest by two of my constables. In the line of duty they tried to apprehend the accused on that same night as the accused sneaked out the gate of the backyard of Mr. Aguiar's house, carrying the shirt and trousers. The accused further tried to inflict serious bodily harm with a deadly weapon on one of the constables who was trying to apprehend the accused," he said, pointing again to the chief constable who was now dramatically waving an ugly looking knife in the air above his head.

"Is that it?"

"Yes, Your Honour," replied the commissioner.

"How do you plead to both of these serious charges, young man?" asked the magistrate. The courtroom went suddenly quiet. Mofola turned and looked at his father, he could see the terrible hurt in his eyes, he wanted so desperately to shout out, "Father, please believe me, I did not do these things they accuse me of," but he knew it would be all in vain; his father had already condemned him as guilty. Mofola turned around again to face the magistrate and said in a clear and loud voice, "Guilty, Your Honour."

"No! No!" shouted Negome, standing up. "He's innocent, and it's all a terrible mistake." The people sitting in the courtroom all turned around in unison to see who this desperate voice belonged to.

Her mother grabbed her by the arm and jerked her back into her seat, slapping her across the face, shouting, "Shut up, you stupid child, you know nothing of these things."

"Silence, silence," shouted the magistrate, but the crowd in the courtroom was now curious and started to shout, "Let her speak, Mama, let's us hear what she has to say."

"Order, order," shouted the magistrate, banging his gavel repeatedly on the table. "If we cannot have order in this court then I will clear you all out."

The crowd quieted down and the magistrate continued to address Mofola. "Young man, do you realize the seriousness of this crime?" Not waiting for a response, he continued, "It would seem that at this early stage of your life you have embarked on a career of crime and violence, and it is my duty to make sure that you are suitably punished and that you reform from this path. Do I make myself clear, young man?"

"Yes, Your Honour," replied Mofola.

At the back of the courtroom Victor leaned over and said something to Costa and they both started to laugh. The magistrate looked away from Mofola and stared at the two laughing and said, "Would the two of you like to share what you apparently find so amusing with the rest of the courtroom?" Victor and Costa immediately stopped laughing and sat there looking sheepish. "Well," said the magistrate, "I'm waiting."

"Sorry, Your Honour, it was a private matter," said Costa.

"Well then, I would greatly appreciate it if you could restrain yourselves until after the court session."

"Thank you, Your Honour, we will restrain ourselves."

The magistrate again addressed Mofola. "Young man, I have taken into consideration the fact that this is your first offence and that you are still a juvenile when passing sentence. However, one cannot overlook the fact that the crimes you have pleaded guilty to are all of a serious nature. For the first offence of stealing, I sentence you to six months in jail. For the second offence, and that is of resisting arrest and trying to inflict bodily harm with a knife, I sentence you to two years in jail. Both terms will be served consecutively in the Joao Belo Juvenile Centre in Inhambane. Seeing that you have already served some time in jail, and perhaps with good conduct, your two and a half years could be one and a half or two at the most. It all depends on your behaviour while in detention."

"Commissioner, are there any further cases to come before this court today?"

"No, Your Honour, there are no more cases today."

"There being no more business, I declare this court now closed," said the magistrate, hitting the table one more hefty blow with his gavel.

Victor could no longer restrain himself and jumped up shouting, "That will teach you, Boxer Boy, that will teach you not to listen to my warnings."

Mofola turned around and looked straight at Victor and said to himself, "Your day will come, Mr. Victor, as sure as the sun rises and sets in the sky."

The magistrate was pleased. Today's proceedings had taken less than two hours, it was now eleven o' clock and he could go to his room at the back of the cantina, pack his bag and then drive up to the police station to finish the last bit of business with the commissioner. With a bit of luck he could be on the road to Espangabera by noon, thus avoiding Mrs. Xavier's greasy chicken. Such was the administration of the law, quick, efficient, and extremely effective.

Chapter 13

Mofola had to spend another five weeks in the local jail where he had been kept pending the trial, before the prison transport came down from the north and took him to the juvenile prison in Inhambane. Although the local prison authorities were now more lenient, he was still only allowed family visitors.

His mother came to see him every day at noon; she brought him food and a small *calabash* containing sour milk. She never spoke one word to him. She would hand him the food through the bars of the cell, and then she would sit on the cobblestones outside his cell and wait until he had finished. She would then take the food containers and make her weary way back home along the dusty road.

For the first two weeks, Mofola pleaded with his mother not to come and visit him every day. Much as he loved to see her, he was worried about her well-being; it was such a long walk from the *shamba* to the jail and back for his frail mother. Despite all his pleading, she continued to come and after two weeks he stopped trying to persuade her not to come, as he knew it was futile.

His father came to see him only once. "You have shamed our family and the people of the royal family of Gaza," rebuked his father. "Did I not give you a trouser when you needed it, did I not give you a shirt when the one you wore was old and full of holes, did I not provide for you from the day you were born?"

"Yes," answered Mofola, "my father, he gave me all these things."

"Then why, I ask, do you need to steal these things when your father, he give them to you?" And the knife, did you steal this as well, or did you secretly sell one of our goats to buy the knife?"

"No, Father, it was not like that. I did none of these things they accused me of," answered Mofola.

"So, my son, am I now to believe you before I believe the commissioner, the constable, and Mr. Victor, who were all witness to these doings? You are not only a thief but a liar as well. You are a disgrace to the name of your father and I will have nothing more to do with you." With that the old man turned around and walked off across the prison courtyard before Mofola could utter any explanation.

Mofola was sad that his father had not given him the chance to explain his side of the story, but he also knew that his father was a very proud man and that he greatly respected the commissioner and what he stood for in the community. Nothing Mofola said or did would convince the old man differently.

The night after the trial, Victor Aguiar got blind, stupid drunk and was heard boasting about how he and his friend the commissioner had taught that stupid

Boxer Boy a lesson. Nobody could deceive Victor Aguiar, especially not that stupid Boxer Boy who was not even good enough to herd chickens, let alone cattle and goats. "What did this chicken herd boy think, hey?" he slurred, falling over the chair as he made his way to the bar counter. "Did he think that he was good enough to court my daughter? No not that chicken shit Boxer Boy, no, never. My friend the commissioner and me we fixed him real good, we fixed him."

Victor was making such a fool and nuisance of himself that eventually Costa sent for the commissioner who came down to the cantina and stood for awhile in the doorway and watched Victor staggering about and slurring to everyone he could hang on to.

Victor saw the commissioner standing in the door way and staggered toward him falling over several chairs shouting, "This is my friend the commissioner. Come in, Commissioner, and have a drink; tell these people how we fix that chicken shit Boxer Boy real good, hey."

The commissioner grabbed Victor as he staggered into his arms. "Shut your stupid mouth, you fool," whispered the commissioner in Victor's ear as he dragged him out of the cantina and across the street to the back of the Aguiars' house. He then helped him up the stairs into the kitchen where the rest of the Aguiar family were having their dinner.

"Good evening, Commissioner," said Mrs. Aguiar. "Thank you for helping Mr. Aguiar home, I'm sorry if he has caused you some inconvenience."

"Good evening, Mrs. Aguiar, young ladies, it's no problem," answered the commissioner, "no problem at all."

"Of course it's no problem, the commissioner and me, we are friends," slurred Victor as he fell into one of the kitchen chairs.

"Give my friend the commissioner a chair, child, can't you see he wants to sit down?"

Negome immediately jumped up and offered her chair to the commissioner.

"Thank you, Negome, but I can't stay, as I still have some work to do tonight."

"Come, Commissioner, we drink a salute to our accomplishment. Today we showed that stupid Boxer Boy not to meddle in the business of Victor Aguiar." "Child," he shouted. "Go fetch a bottle of the good wine from the store."

"Sorry, Victor, we drink a salute some other night." And with that the commissioner turned and went out the door calling over his shoulder, "Good night, Mrs. Aguiar, young ladies," as he went down the back stairs into the night.

As the screen door slammed closed, Victor's head hit the table, his arm knocking a plate from the table that smashed into several pieces as it hit the cement floor.

Mrs. Aguiar jumped up. "Come, girls," she said, "help me get your father to bed. He is not feeling well."

By Sunday there were rumours going around the town about Victor and the commissioner having set up Mofola, but nobody seemed to know for what reason. Negome also heard these rumours at church that morning. As she walked home from church with her mother and two sisters she thought about it and asked her mother what she thought.

Her mother stopped right there, shocked that her daughter should even think like this. "Don't be foolish, child," said her mother, "your father and the commissioner would never do such a thing. Never let your father hear you say such things; he will be extremely angry, do you all hear?"

"Yes, mother," answered the two younger daughters.

Negome did not answer; she started to walk on home ahead of the others. She was not at all convinced that her mother was, in fact, right in her judgement. Her mother was in many ways very naive.

At home Negome went and sat on the back steps of the house, she could just not get this thing out of her mind about Mofola being set up by her father and the commissioner. The more she thought about it the more it worried her. She cast her mind back to the night that Mofola was arrested. What was the commissioner doing at their house that night, she asked herself. They always played poker on Friday night in the cantina with Mr. Costa, no matter what happened.

Now it was slowly starting to make sense, they did set up Mofola that night, that's why they were sitting in the kitchen drinking. They were waiting for the constable to arrest Mofola as he left the woodshed. They then ran outside when they heard the constables shouting and witnessed the whole affair. Mofola never stole any clothes. Even her mother said there were no clothes on the wash line and her father never again mentioned his missing pants and shirt. The more she thought about it the more convinced she was that she was right. One thing still bothered her. How did her father find out that she was seeing Mofola in the woodshed on Friday nights? He was always at the cantina on Friday nights and the rest of the family were all asleep.

Then she remembered that one night when she got up to go and see Mofola, her youngest sister woke up just as she was leaving the room and asked Negome where she was going. She remembered getting such a fright when her sister spoke that she reacted immediately, telling her sister to keep quiet and go back to sleep, as she was hot and thirsty and was only going to get a drink of water.

Could it be that her sister did not go back to sleep again but secretly followed her and saw her going into the old woodshed? There was no one else that she could think of that could have known she was seeing Mofola in the shed. That's it, she thought, it had to be her little sister that had spied on her and had then gone and told their father.

As she sat on there on the steps and tried to reason the whole situation through in her mind, the more convinced she was that she was right. She got up and went to find her little sister and confront her with her deliberation. After all, what did she have to lose—Mofola was in jail for something he never did and she would probably never see him again.

Negome went back up the stairs into the kitchen. Her little sister was washing the breakfast dishes in the sink. When Negome saw her she became so angry, that she immediately began to shout at her little sister. "You little witch! So it was you that told father that I was seeing Mofola in the shed. You little shit, I'll kill you," she shouted as she made a lunge at her sister's long hair.

She ducked around the other side of the kitchen table, screaming, Father, Father, Negome wants to kill me."

Victor, Mrs. Aguiar, and their other daughter came running into the kitchen to see the two girls screaming at each other across the table. "Father," shouted the youngest girl, "Negome wants to kill me because I told you about her having sex with Mofola in the shed."

"You two-faced little shit," screamed Negome. "I never had sex with Mofola."

"Shut up, both of you," shouted her father. "Yes, you little slut, what do you think, I'm stupid? I know what you and Mofola were doing in the shed."

"We weren't doing anything, Father," protested Negome. "We were only talking."

"So who do you think is going to believe that stupid story?" shouted her father. "I'm telling you, child, you had better keep your mouth shut about this or the whole town will know what a slut you are and then no one will want you."

"I don't want anyone else but Mofola," she shouted back at her father.

Her father stretched across the table and slapped her hard across her face. "Don't you dare shout at me, you little whore. Now listen to me, all of you. I don't ever want to hear another word about this, do you understand?"

"The name of this family will be shamed forever, so it is in the interest of all of us not to speak to anyone about this matter," said her mother, now almost in tears.

"That's all you ever think of, Mother, your standing in the community. Not once did you ever think about my feelings, Negome said.

"I won't speak to you again," said her father. "Let me hear that any one of you has spoken about this I will knock your stupid heads off your shoulders. Is that now quite clear?" he said, looking at each one in turn. Both the younger girls nodded their heads, but Negome just looked at her father and walked out of the room.

Chapter 14

It was midday and five weeks exactly from the day of Mofola's trial when the prison truck finally arrived to pick him up. There were already nine other prisoners handcuffed to the steel railings of the open truck. Mofola was pushed up on to the back of the truck and hand-cuffed to the railings with the other prisoners.

Travelling on the back of the open truck was a lot more pleasant than being cooped up in the hot cell back in Massangena. However, after six hours of standing on the back of an open truck and not being able to sit because of the handcuffs, the pleasantness of the cool open air had long been forgotten. Mofola's legs were start-ing to ache and by the time the prison truck arrived at Chgubo where they would stay overnight before making the final trip to Inhambane, he and the other prisoners could hardly walk.

At Chgubo there was only one police officer and his house served as the police station. There was no jail building. The jail, as such, was situated under a big aca-cia tree next to the police officer's house. Around the trunk of the tree, which must have been over a metre in diameter, was a thick chain secured with a large padlock. Each prisoner in turn was allowed to relieve himself in the long drop toilet at the back of the house; he was then handcuffed to the chain around the tree.

Just after sunset an old lady came out from the back of the house with a big black cast iron pot containing a thick *maize* porridge. This was placed so that all the prisoners could reach it. She then brought them some clean drinking water in an old twenty-litre *paraffin* tin that had been made into a bucket. Inside the old *paraffin* tin bucket was a jam tin floating in the water, you could hear it knocking, "clink, clink," against the side as she carried it on her head from the house to the prisoners under the tree.

The next morning, just after dawn the prisoners were again allowed to relieve themselves before being hand-cuffed to the back of the truck where they would stand for another five to six gruelling hours before finally arriving in Inhambane.

The juvenile centre was situated twenty kilometres from Inhambane, close to the railway line going to Janniegama and ten kilometres from the coast. You could smell the sea when the wind was blowing from the east, which was most of the time. Mofola had never seen the sea before. He had only heard of this large expanse of water and for a while he forgot about his aching legs as he gazed in wonder at this great expanse of water.

All the other prisoners except Mofola and another youngster were dropped off just outside Inhambane at the prison called Maximax, which was short for maximum-security prison. To get to the main railway station the prison truck with its two prisoners had to cross over the Inhambane Bay by ferry. Mofola just hoped that the ferry would not tip over or sink, as he would sink to the bottom of the sea still handcuffed to the railings of the truck.

At the station they were handed over to two wardens who accompanied them on the short train journey to Joao Belo Juvenile Centre, or JBC, as it was more commonly referred to.

The Joao Belo Juvenile Centre was established in 1938, the year that Mofola was born and ten years after the premature and unexpected death of Joao Belo, the last republican minister of the Colonies of Mozambique. During his brief but successful tenure, he introduced far-reaching industrial and financial changes in the country, which successfully stimulated the sugar industry to abolish slave labour on the sugar plantations. Ten years before he died, in 1928, he promulgated a new and expansive labour relations act. This act proved to be a major revision from the previous code and was well received by the population at large.

(JBC) was established by Portugal in 1938 as a political showpiece to the rest of the world. Lisbon was coming under increasing criticism of its colonies in Africa and in particular by Great Britain and the United States of America. Lisbon decided to build the centre, as a bit of a showpiece where foreign dignitaries could be brought to see how well the Portuguese treated their juvenile criminals. The centre was therefore named after Joao Belo, a campaigner for human rights and the abolishment of slave labor.

Mofola quickly adapted to the routine at (JBC), school in the morning and work in the sugar cane fields and vegetable gardens in the afternoons. In fact, he found the life in the centre quite pleasant.

The magistrate who sentenced Mofola had been in the business for the last fifteen years and knew all the tricks in the book. He was not fooled by the slick story given by the commissioner and the constable. He had seen this sort of thing before and knew that there was something more sinister behind this so-called open-and-shut case. When Antonio first received the charges relating to Mofola's case, he went through them thoroughly. He decided, because this seemed such an open-and-shut case, to conduct his own discrete inquiry into Mofola and his family. The reports that he got back were not of a juvenile delinquent but of a well-disciplined young man coming from a family connected to the royalty of the Gaza province.

After hearing the case and witnessing the well-rehearsed procedures of the commissioner and his constables. He was now even more convinced that there was something more sinister about this case than what was portrayed at the trial. He therefore decided not to have Mofola imprisoned at Massangena where his life would have been hell, but to send him instead to JBC where he could keep an eye on him. He knew that a year or so in the centre would do him no harm; in fact it would give him a bit of education, which he would normally not get.

The rumours about Mofola's case being a put-up one soon died as more interesting gossip made the rounds.

Anyway, it was not good practice to speak badly of the commissioner, he was a powerful man in the district and one could get into a lot of trouble if it was established that you had spoken badly of him.

Mofola's parents had obviously also heard the rumours a number of times from different sources. His father immediately dismissed the rumours as being rumours spread by somebody trying to make trouble for the commissioner and Mr. Victor. His mother was a little more interested and when she was next in town she enquired at the regular stallholders at the market if they had heard anything. One old lady said that she should go and speak to the shoemaker, as it is believed that he was at the cantina the night after the trial and may have heard something.

She walked over to the old shoemaker's stall and greeted him, "Good morning *Baba* how is business your today?" 'today the business she is better than yesterday" he said, "but not better than the day before, but maybe tomorrow it will be good again, who knows, only the gods can tell." They exchanged small talk for a few minutes as she picked up some shoes, looked at them and put them down again.

It was considered bad manners to just ask a question out right. Slowly she got around to asking the old man if he had heard anything about her son Mofola and the trial. 'me" he said, "I no want no trouble, I'm an old man, I just do my work and I mind my own business but I see what I see and I hear what I hear."

"I am like you *Baba*, an old woman who just wants to know the truth about her son before one day she dies,

I too want no trouble. So what did you hear that night in the cantina?"

"Mr. Victor, he was very drunk that night, he even buy me some beer and tell me I make the best shoes."

"Yes" prompted Mofola's mother, "just what did he say?

"Mr. Victor he say, he and the commissioner, you know, Mr. Victor and the commissioner, they very good friends, they play cards every Friday night."

"Yes, yes," said Mofola's mother, now growing a little impatient with the ramblings of the old man, "just tell me what he said."

"Mr. Victor, he say that he and the commissioner, they trick the Boxer Boy real good."

"I see," she said, "but how did they trick the Boxer Boy?"

"You see I only hear what I hear."

"And what was it that you hear," she asked, with a little more irritation in her voice.

"The story is told by some," he went on, "that the commissioner, he get his constables to wait for the Boxer Boy when he come to see the daughter of Mr. Victor on that night when they catch him. The constables they beat him and kick him and then they take a trouser and a shirt from the wash line by Mr. Victor's house and they put by the hand of the Boxer Boy. They also take a knife and they put it with the trouser and the shirt."

"I see," said Mofola's mother, having at last got the information she wanted. "Thank you, *Baba*, and may the gods look kindly on your business to day, tomorrow, and the days thereafter."

With these greetings she left the shoemaker and went to find her husband to inform him of what she had learned.

At first the old man, as stubborn and proud as he was, would not believe the story. "Why do you not want to believe in your son, in all of his seventeen years did he ever let you down?" she asked.

"It is because he has disgraced the royal family of Gaza and I do not recognize him as my son anymore," he mumbled.

"It would seem that you are more concerned with this stupid notion of the royal family and your own reputation, than the truth about our son."

"What did the royal family ever do for our family all the years but take our money and our cattle? You never even gave our son a chance to explain his side of the story, you just condemn him like you condemn a poison snake in the grass." she rebuked.

"Yes, but there are so many stories being told. How do we know what to believe?" he mumbled, trying to defend his actions.

"Well, let us go and ask the daughter of Mr. Victor. Maybe she will tell us the truth."

Reluctantly he agreed.

They rode a short way up the road toward the school and waited under an acacia tree for the children to come out of school. The mission school was situated a short way out of town on the road to the Moraga's *shamba*. Mr. Victor's children would have to come past where they were sitting under the tree as they made their way back into town

Mofola's mother knew the Aguiar girls well, as she had been served by all of them at some time or other in the trading store. They did not have long to wait before the children came running out of the school gates. They saw the two youngest Aguiar girls first come running past with some other children laughing and chasing each other.

Negome came walking down the road by herself, ever since the confrontation with her sister and father about Mofola she had kept very much to herself. She had lost all interest in life and felt rejected by her whole family. She wanted to run away but she did not know where to go. As she walked down the road, she noticed Mofola's parents sitting in the donkey cart under the tree. As she was about to walk past them, they greeted her. She smiled and greeted them back.

"I wonder if I can have a word with you, my dear?" asked Mrs. Maraga.

"How is Mofola?" enquired Negome as she walked up to them. "We have not heard from him since they took him to Inhambane," she said. "We can only hope and pray that he is in good health. But maybe you can help us to clear up a matter about Mofola that has been burdening our heart and mind ever since he was arrested."

"Yes, of course," she said. "If I can be of any help, please, what is it you want to know?" she asked.

"There is a story that we hear in the town about you and our son Mofola," she said. "We just want to know if it's true."

Negome's heart nearly stopped. Had they heard the rumour that she and Mofola had sex together? Please, not that too, she thought. I'd just die if they asked me that.

"What is the story that you have heard?" she asked.

"All we want to know is did Mofola come to see you that night when the constables arrested him?" she asked.

"Yes, he did come to see me," she said.

"You see! I told you that he was guilty, said the old man.

"No, no, that is not true," protested Negome. "He did not steal the clothes from the wash line, and neither did he attack the constable with a knife. That was a terrible lie. The commissioner and my father, they planned all this when my youngest sister told my father that Mofola was visiting me on Friday nights in the old woodshed behind our house."

"But why would they do that?" asked the old man.

"Because my father did not want Mofola to speak to me. You see, he told Mofola that when he comes into the store he is forbidden to speak to me, because my father has promised that I shall marry the son of Mr. Costa, and I want nothing to do with the son of Mr. Costa," she stammered, now almost in tears.

"Well, I can understand why your father did the things he did. I would have done the same if someone disobeyed my wishes," said the old man.

"You be quiet," rebuked his wife. "Were you not once young, with feelings in your heart, or are you now too old to remember those things?"

Negome told them the whole story, leaving nothing out, "And now my father thinks that I'm a whore." She sobbed. "But I'm still a virgin, Mofola never touched me, I'm so sorry for what has happened, if only I had not liked your son, none of these things would have happened."

"You are not to be blamed, child, for your feelings. The feelings of the heart cannot be controlled," said Mrs. Maraga.

"But I feel so helpless—is there nothing I can do, or go to someone and explain what has happened?" She was whimpering.

"No, my child, there is nothing you can do that will make these things you have told us better. It is far better that we leave these things to the gods."

Mofola's mother had no intention of leaving any of this to the gods, despite how much her husband protested. The very next day she went to the mission school and asked one of the sisters there to help her write a letter to the magistrate in Inhambane.

It was another four weeks before she received a reply back from the magistrate. He explained that there was very little he could do, as Mofola had pleaded guilty to the charges; however, he assured her that he was well and that he was adapting quickly to the life in the centre. He further promised that he would look in on the centre from time to time to check on his progress and report back to her. This he did every two months. Mofola's mother would receive a short letter from the magistrate informing her of Mofola's progress.

When the first letter arrived from the magistrate, she told the old man to accompany her to the convent so he too could hear when the sister read the letter to her.

"This is your business," he said. "I want nothing to do with these things."

"You are a stupid, stubborn old fool," she rebuked and went off to the convent.

Mofola was one of the older boys in the centre He was certainly the biggest and as a result he had no trouble with any of the other one hundred and thirty boys in the centre. Mofola was by nature not an aggressive person and, as a result, he was well liked by the other boys and the wardens alike. Mofola worked hard in the fields in the afternoons as well as in the mornings at school. He would read and study well into the night; therefore, his reading, writing, and basic arithmetic improved greatly.

The time in the centre went by quickly; the months just seemed to fly past. He had received a few letters from his mother and was pleased to know that they now knew the truth and his father was no longer angry with him. As promised, the magistrate came to see him a few times, and at his last visit he told Mofola that the authorities at the centre were pleased with his behaviour and the way he had applied himself to his work and studies. He also informed Mofola that he should apply for parole, seeing that he had now completed fifteen months in the centre. The parole committee would shortly be looking at all the records of the boys who had spent a year or more in the centre. Provided he continued to behave himself the chances were good that he would be released early.

When Mofola was working in the fields he had a lot of time to think about Negome and how he could get Victor Aguiar to accept him. Then he could ask to marry her. But first he needed money, for money was power, and to get money he had to go to South Africa and work on the gold mines. He had just turned eighteen, but he knew that he would not be accepted by the WNLA as a migrant worker to go to South Africa with a prison record. He had even stopped testing himself to see if his testicles jumped when he coughed. He knew that the only way that he would get into South Africa was to slip through the border as an illegal immigrant. He would then go and find his two brothers and ask them to help him get work on the mines.

Two months later, Mofola's appeal was accepted and he was a free man again, except that he had to report to his parole officer once a week for the next six months. Antonio Nacapa, being a magistrate, had a lot of influence in the town and had therefore been able to arrange through the parole officer to get Mofola a job loading and off-loading goods at a transport company in Inhambane. This was one of the same companies that transported goods to the north via Massangena as well as down the coast to Lourenco Marques.

His parole officer had arranged accommodation at the single quarters situated in the transport company's yard. Mofola shared a room with seven co-workers. The room was very small and stuffy, with only one window that did not open. Because Mofola was the new recruit, he was allocated one of the top bunk beds that were so close to the corrugated tin roof that if you sat up too quickly you knocked your head. It was only possible to go to bed after ten at night when the tin roof had cooled down enough to make it bearable.

Mofola's basic wage was three *escudos* per day and with overtime he could earn up to twenty *escudos* per week. Because the room was virtually unbearable, Mofola worked as much overtime as he could get. He often worked late into the night and, as a result, he soon got to know many of the truck drivers and their co- drivers. He kept to himself, not because he wanted to, but because most of the other workers were from the northern Tete province. The Gaza people and the people from the Tete province had never gotten on together because of age-old tribal and territorial border conflicts.

After two months, Mofola got friendly with a particu-lar co-driver named Roberto. He was also from the Gaza province and frequently did the north trip via Massangena. When Mofola mentioned the incident he had with the storekeeper and the commissioner in Massangena. Roberto said that he remembered it well because he had been in the cantina the Monday after the trial. Everyone was still talk-ing about how he was set up.

Roberto invited Mofola to his house, which was situ-ated on the southern outskirts of Inhambane to meet his wife and two children. It would seem that Roberto's wife was having a problem with the eldest son's schoolwork. He had just turned twelve. Because Roberto was away from home the majority of the time, he was not there to discipline his children. Mofola and the two boys got on well and he helped the eldest with his schoolwork. Because the two boys had been brought up in the big town, they were fascinated with the stories Mofola told of the life in the country. They especially liked the many stories of the elephant hunts and the dangers he faced when herding the animals up in the mountains.

Because of Mofola's good relationship with his two boys, Roberto asked Mofola if he would like to stay at his house instead of the single quarters that were so cramped and hot. Mofola agreed on one condition and that was he be allowed to pay Roberto's wife for the accommodation. At first Roberto would not hear of it, but in the end they agreed on five *escudos* per week, the same amount he was paying at the single quarters.

The arrangement worked well, Mofola helped with the discipline and the school work of the two boys and Roberto was happy to have someone at home whom he could trust while he was away on his long trips.

Mofola saved all his wages except for the weekly amount he paid to Roberto's wife. The only problem now that he was staying with Roberto's family was he could not work the long overtime hours he had been working before. This meant that he would have to work longer to save enough to get him to South Africa.

After ten months working at the transport company, Mofola estimated that he had enough money to at least get him to South Africa. For the past six months he had been exchanging *escudos* for South African pounds at black market rates with the drivers who went across the border on a regular basis. Four months ago he was given a clearance by his probation officer and told to stay out of trouble. Now, having saved all the money, he was anxious to get going. Roberto was on a trip and would be back in a week's time. They had discussed Mofola's trip to South Africa many times. Roberto promised that when he got back from this trip, he would speak to one of the other drivers going down to Lourenco Marques to see if they would give him a ride. Two weeks later Mofola was on the back of a truck on its way to Lourenco Marques.

Chapter 15

Three hundred and twenty five kilometres from Inhambane, the main road goes through the small town of Xinavane where a small badly kept road leads westward for a hundred kilometres to Moaulanquene, high in the Lebombo Mountains. Here it is only ten kilometres from the South African border of the Kruger National Park Game Reserve and a hundred kilometres to the nearest South African town of Accornhoek. It might just as well have been a thousand kilometres, for one first had to penetrate the hostile Lebombo Mountains before crossing through fifty kilometres of lion- and other big-game-infested bush of the Kruger Park.

During the years 1840 to 1845 many wagon tracks crisscrossed the Lebombo Mountains to Delagoa Bay (Lourenco Marques) from the old Transvaal Republic, in South Africa. One of these tracks was known as the Trichardt Track, named after Louis Trichardt, one of the Great *Boer* Trekkers who lost his life trying to find an easier route to the coast. This track cut through the Lebombo Mountains along the steep treacherous gorge carved out by the Sweni River, which joins up with the Olifants River on its winding journey to the sea.

It was a similar route that Mofola had chosen, not because it was the shortest, but because it was one of the more difficult and dangerous of the various routes used by the illegal immigrants going to South Africa. He figured in his mind that the more dangerous and difficult the route was, the less chance there would be of being picked up by one of the border patrols. Mofola could not risk getting caught now that he had a prison record, the authorities would simply throw him back in jail again.

Mofola had discussed his plans with his friend Roberto many times. They had tried to get as much information about the route from anybody who professed to know something about it and what could be expected on the journey to the city of gold in South Africa. Many of the stories Mofola heard were, he suspected, not true, but told only to create an impression that the person telling the story had been there and had survived the dangerous journey.

Over the months, while he was working at the transport company, Mofola weighed all the information in his mind, sifted out all that he believed was not relevant and by the time he was ready to go, he believed that he had a fairly good picture of the route and what he could expect on the way.

Just outside Xinavane, the truck driver stopped at a roadside filling station to fill up with diesel and let Mofola get off before proceeding to Lourenco Marques. Mofola thanked the driver for the ride, put his suitcase with all his worldly possessions on his shoulder, and made his way into town. It was already past midday and he had not eaten since the night before. He made his way over to the local cantina and bought a bowl of curried prawn heads and thick *maize* porridge, the cheapest meal they served.

"So you are making your way to the Souse Africa?" inquired the fat little Portuguese man pleasantly while serving Mofola. He had seen many of the black people over the years that stopped at his cantina on their way to the border. He knew of the route only from what he had heard and knew that some made it and some didn't. "They tell me the river, she is in flood. Two people were killed there some days ago—you better be careful." Mofola thanked him for the information and took his meal and went and sat down at one of the empty tables outside on the *veranda*.

Mofola finished his meal and took his plate back to the counter and bought a few provisions for the trip. "Do you know if there is much traffic going up to Moaulanquene?" he asked.

"Sometime you can get lucky. They are building a dam at Lagone Nova. The construction trucks sometimes come this way on their way up from Lourenco Marques." Mofola thanked him again, picked up his suitcase, and went outside.

The next town on the road to Moaulanquene was Magude, about thirty kilometres from Xinavane, and Mofola decided that he would start to walk. He still had at least six hours of daylight left and he knew that even if he did not get a ride he could easily walk that distance in four to five hours. Just after sunset he arrived in

Magude, having walked the whole way. Not once did he see a vehicle coming or going on the road. On the out- skirts of the town he set up his primitive camp near the river, out of sight from the road, under a big acacia tree.

The next day, even before daybreak he woke up from the noise of the red-billed wood hoopoe birds cackling in the tree above him. He washed in the river and then stoked up the fire he had made the night before. He made a mug of sweet bush tea and ate a small piece of the dried fish and a chunk of bread broken from the loaf he had bought with the other provisions in Xinavane.

Before sunrise he was back on the road again carrying his suitcase on his shoulder. The sun was now hot on his back as he trudged along the dusty road and the sweat ran down the back of his head, soaking the bandanna around his neck. By midday, not only his bandanna, but his shirt too was soaked with sweat. He put his suitcase down next to the road and slid down the bank to a small stream to get a drink and wash the sweat from his face. He had just taken off his shirt when he heard the whine of a diesel truck as the driver geared down to negotiate the steep descent into the valley.

Mofola scrambled up the bank to the road, waving his shirt as the truck came into view, heavily laden with cement.

"Where are you going?" shouted the driver over the noise of the big engine as he pulled up in a cloud of dust on the side of the road next to where Mofola was standing.

"Up to Moaulanquene," shouted Mofola.

"We are going through Moaulanquene to the new dam site at Lagone Nova. If you can find a place on top of the cement, you are welcome to a ride."

Mofola needed no second invitation; he threw his suitcase up on top of the old faded green tarpaulin covering the cement bags and clambered up after it. The cool breeze created by the moving truck was a welcome relief from the heat of the burning sun on his back. Because of the heavy load, the truck's progress was slow as it made its way along the narrow winding road through the mountains. The driver was in second or first gear most of the time, either climbing up or descending down a difficult stretch of the mountain road.

It was the middle of the afternoon before they arrived on the outskirts of Moaulanquene. Mofola leaned over the back of the cab and shouted to the driver through the open side window to please drop him off about three kilometres on the other side of the town where the road crosses the Sweni River. Mofola then crawled under the tarpaulin with his suitcase and lay down flat in between the cement bags. He did not want to take any chances that someone of authority may see him. A stranger in a small town carrying a suitcase was bound to create some suspicion, especially knowing that this was where many of the illegal immigrants try to cross the border. They might stop him and ask him some awkward questions.

They dropped him on the north side of the old stone bridge that spanned the Sweni River gorge, before continuing their journey to the Lagone Nova dam site on the Olifants River some fifty kilometres further north.

Mofola stood and watched the truck as it disappeared in a cloud of dust, knowing that this would be the last time he would see a friendly face for some days, depending on how long took him to get to the border and through the Kruger National Park Game Reserve.

He picked up his suitcase and walked over to the middle of the bridge and looked down into the murky brown turbulent waters of the flooded Sweni River, seventy metres below. The sun had now disappeared behind the mountains and the gorge cast dark grey shadows across the water, making it look even more hostile. Somewhere down there was a path that had been cut out of the sides of the sheer granite rock face by the floodwaters of a thousand years.

For just on five kilometres the river wound its way through the gorge. In some places it was up to a hundred metres wide and in other places it narrowed down to less than four metres, here the water was deep and rushed through it with an arrogant force. It was too dangerous to try to find a way down to the water's edge in this light, so he decided instead to wait until the morning when the sun was shining from the east into the gorge.

The light was fading fast now and he needed to find a secure place for the night, away from the road and possible border patrols. He picked up his suitcase, walked back over the bridge, and started to climb up the mountain. The going was tough. It was extremely steep in places with very few footholds, and the fact that he was carrying a suitcase on his shoulder did not make the task any easier.

The Lebombo Mountains extended some three hundred and fifty kilometres from the Crocodile River in the south to the border of Rhodesia on the Limpopo River in the north. They formed an almost impregnable natural wall between South Africa and Mozambique. Millions of years ago when the earth was forming, this vast wall of granite was pushed up from the bowels of the earth, forming steep cliffs and high ridges of solid rock.

Over the years, the rain and wind had smoothed and rounded the ridges, depositing the dust in little nooks and crannies. Over time, small dwarfed trees and shrubs had taken root in these soil deposits, giving the appearance of a giant bonsai collection.

Finding shelter on this expanse of solid rock was an almost impossible task. By the time Mofola had found some form of shelter under a slight overhang behind a boulder, the sun had gone behind the mountains, leaving only a red glow in the early evening sky. Here he was out of the cool night breeze pushing up from the sea and out of sight of the town way down in the valley. If he stuck his head around the side of the boulder and looked down into the valley below he could see lights starting to come on in the town. It looked like little fireflies in the night.

For nearly six months of the year the Sweni River was dry or partially dry with small pools of water seeping up through the sand in the riverbed. In the early days before mankind interfered with nature by erecting boundary fences, thus restricting the natural movement of game to within the boundaries of the various game parks throughout sub-Saharan Africa. This had been a migration path of the herbivorous animals. Today this pathway carried only the footprints of illegal immigrants, poachers, and smugglers looking for better opportunities in the land of *egoli*.

The unexpected rains in April would give the vegetation an extra boost for the dry winter months that followed. The late rains had swollen many of the small side streams and creeks that feed the Sweni River, resulting in the accumulation of water through the narrow gorge. Although the unexpected rains were a bonus for the *veld* and animals, it could spell disaster for Mofola, as he would have to wait until the waters of the Sweni subsided before he could attempt to make his way through the narrow gorge. Every day he waited was another day his rations would have to last and another day he risked detection by the Mozambican border patrols.

Fortunately the Mozambican patrols were not that frequent or thorough. They were not even that concerned with people leaving Mozambique to look for work in South Africa, as these people inevitably sent money home, and any money was welcome in the impoverished economy of Mozambique. It was the South Africans who were the more concerned about illegal immigrants, poachers, and smugglers crossing their borders and, in agreement with the South African authorities, the Mozambicans patrolled their side of the mountain. Every now and again the Mozambicans put on a bit of a show by arresting someone just to show they were doing their job.

Although the wind was cold, the rock was still warm from the sun that had been beating down on it the whole day. Mofola wrapped himself in his blanket, and sat wedged upright in the corner between the rock overhang and the boulder with his suitcase propped up in front of him for some protection against the wind. It was too risky to make a fire, as the glow might be seen by someone in the town below—not that there was any wood to be had on this sparsely vegetated expanse of rock to even start a fire.

Mofola watched as the moon came up, bathing the mountain in eerie silver light. He hoped that his old rival, the mountain leopard that had so often prowled on his herds up in the Chimanimani Mountains when he was a herd boy, would not be hunting in the near vicinity tonight.

The only weapon he had was the blade of an old kitchen knife, the point of which he had honed sharp on a stone before he left Inhambane. He had hidden it in the bottom of his suitcase, in between the lining together with four thin wads of money, each tied with an elastic band and wedged into the corners. The last thing he wanted, was to get caught with a knife on him; he had enough bad experience with knives to last him a lifetime.

Now out here in the bush it was different. He removed the blade from its hiding place and wrapped his bandanna around the blunt end as a makeshift handle. Looking up at the familiar patterns of the stars in the clear night sky gave Mofola a sense that he was not alone.

Holding the knife in both hands in his lap, he nodded off to sleep.

As dawn broke the next morning, it found Mofola halfway down the mountain. He wanted to be down on the road again before the first rays of the sun splashed its light across the mountain's ridge, highlighting anything that might be moving. The sound of the water racing through the gorge carried up the mountain in the cool morning air and got louder with every step he took down toward the old stone bridge that spanned it.

By the time he got to the bridge, the sun was peeping over the horizon, casting long shadows across the road. He would have to wait until it got higher before he could attempt the steep descent down to the water's edge. Only then would he be able to assess if he would be able to push his way through the narrow parts of the gorge against the flood waters. He climbed under the bridge out of sight and sat down on a flat rock to wait. While he waited, he drank some water from the bottle he carried in his suitcase and ate some of the dried fish.

He made a harness from a piece of rope he had in his suitcase and tied it to the suitcase so that he could put it on his back like a school satchel, knowing that he would need both of his hands when he climbed down to the water's edge and made his way up the gorge against the flood waters of the swollen Sweni River.

The sun was now shining into the gorge and Mofola could see that there was a steep path on the other side of the bridge leading down to the water's edge. He climbed out from under the bridge and crossed over to the other side and started to climb down to the water. It was not a path as such, but a number of feet and hand holds and short narrow ledges going down at steep angles in the sheer rock face, the rocks had been worn smooth by many hands and feet over the years.

The rocks were still wet from the morning dew as he started his descent, climbing slowly down the seventy-metre drop making sure that he had a firm grip with the one hand before letting go with the other. As he got nearer to the water's edge he could see the water twirling around in little whirlpools as it rushed below him on its way to the sea. At this point, just below the bridge, the gorge was five metres wide at the water's edge. Mofola stood on a ledge with the water lapping at his bare feet. He looked farther up the gorge to the first bend about fifty metres away. It looked like the gorge widened out before disappearing around the bend.

The water level was high above its normal path in the gorge and far too dangerous to try to wade through, especially at this narrow point. He would have to wait until the water subsided. There was no way he could push his way up the gorge against that volume of water. He turned around again to the rock face to start the climb back out of the gorge. It was then that he noticed the ledge just above his head. Over the years the high flood water had washed out a reef of softer rock in the side of the cliff, leaving a shallow narrow ledge several metres above the riverbed. It extended up the gorge to where he lost sight of it as it followed the cliff around the bend. The ledge looked to be no more than forty to fifty centimetres in height and extended about the same into the side of the cliff.

Mofola thought that if he could get up to this ledge, he could pull himself along on his stomach, pushing his suitcase in front of him. The ledge was just too high for him to pull himself up onto it and there were no cracks or indents in the side of the cliff at this point for him to get a foothold.

He had an idea, if he removed his suitcase from his back and stood it up on its end against the side of the rock face he could then climb on it and pull himself up onto the ledge. He could then pull the suitcase up with the piece of rope he had used to tie it on his back.

The plan worked, but the progress was slow and many times, when the gap became too shallow to push his suitcase through, he had to dangle it over the side. Some times the gap was barely big enough to get his head through. By the time he got to where the gorge made a bend, his knees and elbows were bleeding from lifting himself up and pushing himself and his suitcase forward. The gorge was much wider here and the water was not that deep and as swift flowing as it was directly under the bridge. Leaving his suitcase wedged tight into the gap on the ledge, and still holding onto the rope tied to the case's handle, he lowered himself into the water.

As his feet touched the water they were swept out from under him, causing him to lose his balance and fall flat on his face in the water. Still clinging onto the rope, he managed to regain his balance and stand up. The water was just above his knees. Using every crack he could find in the rock face, he pulled himself forward against the current. He gave the rope tied to his suitcase a hard yank and it came flying off the ledge, landing just in front of him in the water. Fortunately his suitcase had landed the right way up and he quickly lifted it out of the water before it got any water inside. He tied the suitcase on his back again with the rope and continued to wade up the river.

Once he had gotten around the bend, the gorge widened up even more and here the water was only ankle deep. In some places the gorge was very wide, more like a canyon than a narrow gorge and he could walk in the soft river sand on the bank. He made good time walking on the bank of the river but farther up he could see that it started to narrow again. Soon he was back in the water, struggling to stay on his feet with the water at times up to his thighs. Holding onto whatever he could grab hold of on the rock face, he made his way slowly forward.

Progress was now very slow in water ranging from waist to knee deep. Mofola was now starting to feel the cold. Having been in the water for over two hours, the constant fight against the current had started to sap his strength, and a lesser man may have given up long ago. He looked up to see if he could see where the sun was, as he had become a little disorientated in the winding gorge, but all he could see far above him was a thin streak of pale blue light where the towering sidewalls of the gorge seemed to merge with the sky.

Looking down again he sensed rather than saw that something was different; the sound of the water had changed slightly. At first he could not see it because his eyes had as yet not adjusted from the bright sky to the gloominess of the gorge. Then he saw it, a huge tree that had been uprooted somewhere upstream was now bearing down on him at a fast rate, its branches extended out in front of it like huge extended hands sweeping everything in their path. He barely had time to turn before it crashed into him, his suitcase taking the full brunt of the impact, knocking him off his feet and forcing him under water.

He tried to turn over but his suitcase and right arm were firmly caught up in the branches of the tree, he tried desperately to slip his left arm out of the rope sling, but it was too tight; he needed his other hand to unhook it off his shoulder. By this time his lungs were bursting for air and his head was spinning from lack of oxygen. He thought of Negome and how he missed her and would she miss him, then he passed out.

Chapter 16

Having spoken to Mofola's parents, Negome felt as if a great weight had been lifted from her shoulders. She brightened up and became interested in what was going on around her again. She got more involved in the church and often stayed after school and helped the sisters with the administration work and any other chores they would let her do.

Her relationship with her parents, in particular her father, was cordial. She seldom worked in the store anymore; even over the weekends she would spend most of her time at the convent helping the sisters. Sister Veronica was her favourite sister. Negome had confided in her about what had transpired between her and Mofola. It was Sister Veronica who had helped her to come to terms with the situation, especially when she blamed herself for the trouble Mofola was in. She believed that it was because of her affection for him that he was in all this trouble.

Now she didn't care anymore if the people in the town thought that she was a slut. She hoped that Mr. Costa and his son had heard this rumour. That would make sure that he would not want to marry her if he thought that she was not a virgin. Ever since she had been spending more time at the mission her whole attitude had changed, even her sisters remarked on her sudden change of mood. She basically ignored them, especially the youngest that had betrayed her to their father.

She often saw Mofola's mother when she came to see the sisters at the mission, to help her with the reading and writing of letters to and from Mofola. This gave her the opportunity to enquire how Mofola was doing at the Joao Belo Juvenile Centre. The old lady had even tried to encourage her to write to Mofola but she said she would rather not, as she did not want to cause him any more pain.

"What nonsense, child, you must not think like that," reproached the old lady. "You write to him."

But she never did, she was still confused and at this stage she was not sure what she wanted to do with her life.

The more time she spent at the mission the more she felt the allure to its cause. Eighteen months had gone by since she last saw Mofola that day in the cantina when he was sentenced. It all seemed such a long time ago that they sat in the old woodshed and planned how they would one day go away together. Mofola's mother had told her that Mofola was soon to be released and that he was going to South Africa to find his brothers and try to get work on the gold mines. As time went by, the notion that one day Mofola would come back and take her away became less likely in her mind.

Sister Veronica had been encouraging her to come into the order and become a sister of the church. She explained that when she was young she had a bad experience with a man and it was as a result of that incident that she decided to join the church and take her vows and become a nun. But Negome was not sure at this point in her life whether she was prepared to make that commitment. At this stage she was happy to just help out at the mission whenever she could.

Chapter 17

Mofola was jolted to consciousness as the branches of the tree wedged into the bank in the shallow water where the gorge had widened out. His head was still under water but he managed to lift it up sufficiently to gasp a few mouthfuls of air before the strain on his neck was too much to bear and he had to put his head back under the water. He was now even more firmly trapped, pinned facedown between the branches of the tree and the riverbed. Every now and then he would lift his head briefly out of the water to breath some air. Was this to be his grave, trapped beneath the branches of a tree, half submerged in water?

He lay there for what seemed an age, his left arm trapped under his chest and the other firmly caught at an awkward angle behind his head in the branches. Try as he might, he could not get either arm free. His back and neck were aching from the constant lifting of his head to breath. He did not know how much longer he could hold out. Then he felt it, the tree moved, or was it just his imagination? No, there it was again, he definitely felt it move again.

The tree was moving, the current was pushing the trunk into the middle of the stream and, as a result, it was turning the tree around so that the trunk was now in the front. Slowly, bit by bit, the tree was being pulled back into the current and Mofola with it, into deeper water. He could now only get his nose out of the water to breath. Suddenly the tree jerked as the current caught it more squarely and it started to move faster. Mofola freed his arm that had been pinned under his chest and dug his hand into the sand trying to anchor onto anything he could grasp hold of to stop him from being dragged back into the deep water.

He could no longer breath, the water was too deep. Just as he thought it was all over again, his hand struck something solid in the sand, it felt like a branch of an old tree stump that had gotten buried. He closed his hand around it and held on. His lungs were bursting and it felt like his arm was going to be pulled out of its socket. Then there was a loud crack as the branch holding his right arm snapped and the tree pulled away from him. He tried to get up but he couldn't at first, as the suitcase had filled with water and it was weighing him down, but he managed to get to his knees and get his head out of the water.

Gasping for air, Mofola crawled to the bank, un-hooked the rope from his shoulder and fell flat on his back in the sand. He lay there sucking in great volumes of air, not believing that he was alive. By this time the sun was directly overhead, blazing down into the gorge. The sun was warm on his body as he just lay there sap-ping up its warmth and regaining his strength. It was the most beautiful warmth he could ever remember feeling. When he awoke, the sun was long gone and the light in the gorge was starting to fade. Mofola got up out of the sand. His legs were stiff and his shoulders and neck hurt badly.

He opened his suitcase, everything was wet, and without the sun it would take ages to dry. He needed to make a fire to keep himself warm from the cool night breeze and to help dry his clothes and blanket. He closed the suitcase and carried it up the bank and walked a short distance to the side of the cliff where a pile of driftwood had collected against the sidewall, washed down from previous storms.

Mofola had put a box of matches in the suitcase to keep them dry, but they too were wet, he would have to make a fire the hard way. The wood was tinder dry and it did not take him long to start a fire the old traditional way by rubbing a hard piece of drift wood on a softer piece. He built a nice big fire, and then made a wash line with the rope that he had used to tie his suitcase on his back.

The dry fish had also gotten wet and, as a result, all his clothes as well as the blanket smelled of fish, the fishy smell he did not particularly mind. He unwrapped the fish from the brown paper and hung it on the make-shift wash line with the other things to dry. The half loaf of soggy bread he threw away. He removed the wads of money from under the lining at the bottom of his suitcase, separated them into single notes, and placed them on rocks all around the fire with a small stone on the top of each note to prevent the wind from blowing them away.

He cut a few strips from the piece of fish hanging from the line and sat with his back to the sidewall of the cliff and chewed on them. He had not realized how hungry he was until he started to eat. The roaring fire soon dried his blanket which was hanging closest to the fire, the rest of his things including the suitcase he left to continue drying. He then added some large logs to the fire, scooped out a shallow hole in the sand near the fire, and wrapped himself in the blanket. He curled up in the hole and went to sleep with the sound of the gushing river nearby.

Mofola woke up from a deep sleep just before dawn; it was still dark in the gorge. All that remained of the roaring fire were red embers and two ends of a smouldering log. He got up and pushed the two ends into the embers and blew the hot coals to bright red, igniting the smouldering logs. There was a cool morning breeze being funnelled through the gorge, which sent a shiver down his back. Mofola added more driftwood to the fire and stood with his back to it facing the river. It was then that he realized that something was different.

The noise of the gushing water had stopped. It was still too dark to see the river from where he was standing next to the fire. He walked toward the river and stood on top of the bank that the floodwaters had cut out of the sand and looked down to where the water level was the day before. Slowly his eyes, which were still dilated from the light cast by the fire, became accustomed to the gloom of the first morning light. He could see that during the night the flooded river had subsided to a stream.

Mofola was delighted, this meant that he could now cover what remained of the gorge in good time, and if he was lucky, he might be able to get through the border fence before the patrols came out. He quickly packed his suitcase, slung it up on his shoulder and set off at a fast pace up the gorge. He had walked for about fifteen minutes in the riverbed, which was now only a trickling stream in the middle of a hundred-metre-wide canyon, and up ahead he could see there was a bend, perhaps the last one before the end of the canyon.

Around the bend the canyon opened up onto a vast plain that stretched for as far as the eye could see. Although the sun had already risen, it had as yet not cleared the Lebombo mountain ridge behind him. In the soft morning light, the haze caused by the smoke from the burning of winter fire breaks clung to the tops of the trees, creating an impression of a great expanse of water. Mofola stood and stared out at this splendour. As the first rays of the morning sun spilled over the ridge and came cascading down onto this vast plain, it shimmered like the sea and, for a moment, he thought that he was back on the shores of the Mozambique coast.

As the sun got higher he could see the border fence silhouetted against the black background of the fire-break and white smoke cloud. He was so pleased to see it that he had to consciously stop himself from wanting to run toward it. He was about half a kilometre from the fence when he heard the sound of an approaching aircraft. It must be flying very low, as he could not see it as yet. Mofola was out in the open, the nearest cover was at least a hundred meters away and very sparse at that.

He sprinted to the nearest bush that offered some meagre protection and dived under it just as the plane came into view, flying so low over him that he felt the wind of the propeller. He was sure that he must have been spotted as the plane climbed, turned, and came back, flying low over him again. Twice the plane turned and flew over him. Mofola was convinced he had been spotted and the pilot was trying to flush him out. It took all his nerve not to get up and run back to the safety of the canyon. After the third pass the plane continued its original flight path south.

Mofola lay under the bush for at least another ten minutes after the plane had gone, now even more sure that the plane had gone back to its base to get help. He crawled out from under the bush and started to run as fast as he could back to the canyon. By the time he got there he was completely out of breath. He collapsed in a heap under a thorn tree and lay there sucking in great mouthfuls of air with his heart in his throat. He was terrified that while he was running out in the open the plane would come back, sweeping out of the sky like a huge eagle and pluck him up like a chicken to take back to its nest.

Mofola knew that he was still in Mozambique, but he did not know whether the South African patrols would venture into Mozambique to follow him. Little did he know that he was already in South Africa and had been for quite some time—he had crossed the actual border about two kilometres back in the gorge. The imaginary borderline ran through the middle of the Lebombo

Mountains. The fence was only the game fence of the Kruger National Park.

He decided that he would have to find a place to hide and wait and see if a patrol came to look for him. It was a chance he would have to take. He climbed a little way up the side of the canyon and hid himself behind some large rocks. From here he could see all the way to the fence and beyond. He opened his suitcase and took out the bottle of water and had a long drink, put it back, and sat with his back against the rock and waited.

The sun was already high in the sky when he heard the sound of vehicles in the distance. It was not long before two trucks appeared out of the bush. One was loaded with equipment and the other with men. The one with the men on board stopped at the fence on the bank of the river. The other drove down into the riverbed out of sight. The men on the first truck all got out carrying what appeared to be rifles over their shoulders. They too disappeared down the bank into the riverbed.

From where he was sitting he could not see down into the riverbed where the fence crossed the river. Mofola reasoned that the riverbed would be the easiest place to get through the fence and in a short while he would see them coming out of the riverbed on his side of the fence to search for him. He could not understand why they were taking so long, maybe they weren't in any hurry, as they knew he could only go back into the canyon and back to Mozambique. Maybe they had already informed the Mozambican border patrol to be on the lookout for him when he came out of the gorge on their side.

Mofola sat in the burning hot sun waiting and watching, his eyes playing tricks on him in the hot midday sun. Mirages of soldiers and trucks, all heavily armed, sprang up out of the plains before him; he closed his eyes and opened them again only to see there was nothing there. A number of times he nodded off to sleep, only to wake up with a start as his chin flopped onto his chest. He could not work out in his mind what the patrol was up to.

The sun was a bright orange ball on the western horizon when he saw the first of the men appear back on the bank of the river. One by one they climbed back onto the truck. The other truck came up out of the riverbed and took off into the bush, the first truck waited until all the men were on board and it too followed the other truck into the bush. Mofola, now even more confused, stood up and stretched his aching limbs. He climbed down from his hiding place in the rocks and went and sat back under the thorn tree, trying to work out what the patrol was doing.

The only logical explanation he could come to was that the patrol had simply sat in the riverbed under a tree, waiting to see that he did not try to come back. They would expect that he had been picked up by the Mozambican patrol as he came out of the gorge near the bridge that crossed the Sweni River.

Mofola reasoned that it was well past midnight. The first star of the night had dipped below the horizon and the moon was high in the evening sky, casting ghostly shadows all around him. There was a chill in the air he wrapped the blanket tighter around his upper body, hefted his suitcase onto his shoulder and made his way in the moonlight toward where the fence crossed over the riverbed.

This time he walked along the bank of the winding river. He was afraid to walk up the riverbed just in case they had left a few soldiers behind to make sure he did not come back at night. Following the riverbank was not the shortest distance to the fence, but in the dark it was the safest, the last thing he wanted was to get lost in the dark. By the light of the moon he was able to see the riverbank and was able to weave his way through the trees and bush growing above the river. Every time he startled an animal and it went crashing off through the bush, his heart would leap up into his throat. Other than the odd scratch he received from a thorn bush, he arrived at the fence without any problem.

The game fence was made up of two metres of heavy wire mesh with a further half a metre section of barbed wire angled out toward the outside. The fence went down the side of the riverbank, through the riverbed and up the other side. Mofola could smell the fresh smell of creosote paint as he got closer and it suddenly occurred to him that it was not a patrol that had been waiting in the riverbed for him to come back, but a work team repairing the fence that had been damaged by the floodwaters. The pilot of the plane had not seen him, he was merely checking the fence for possible damage caused by the storm and that was why he flew over the site several times to see the extent of the damage. Mofola wondered why he had not thought of that before. It would have saved him a lot of anguish.

Mofola didn't know whether to laugh or cry as he slid down the side of the riverbank to the riverbed. Sure enough they had replaced a whole new section from the one side of the river to the other. He found a place where the fence went over some soft sand and dug a hole under it, pushed his suitcase through and crawled through after it. On the other side, he jumped up and down shouting, "I'm in South Africa, I'm in South Africa," over and over again as he danced around on the sand.

He soon came to his senses, thanking the gods that there was no one about to hear him shouting. He quickly covered the hole and started to walk along the almost dry riverbed. Now he needed to find a tree that he could climb, before one of the carnivorous animals found him. Finding a tree was easy, both sides of the river were full of them, but finding one in the dark that he could climb and a lion couldn't was not that easy. He eventually settled on a fever tree with its straight trunk going up over two metres before the first branches started to appear. He climbed up into the upper branches and tied himself around the waist to the trunk.

Sleeping in a tree was not very comfortable, but at least he was out of reach of the lions he heard roaring and humphing all night somewhere in the distance. He slept restlessly, waking up every time he heard the sound of game moving about below the tree. Every now and then he would have to move to stop his legs from cramping and readjust his blanket around his shoulders. By the time the first signs of the dawn arrived he was more than ready to abandon his perch in the tree.

The first thing he did when he got down from the tree was to fashion a spear. Using the kitchen knife blade, he cut a straight stout sapling of about a metre in length. He then cut two slits in the thin end of the sapling and inserted the blunt end of the blade in one of the slits. Unravelling a piece of the rope he tightly bound the blade securely to the sapling. He now at least had some means of defence.

He took a tin of pilchards from his suitcase and opened it with his new spear. Using a stick for a fork, he quickly ate the fish and then took some water from his drinking bottle, swirled it around in the tin, and drank it. He folded his blanket and put it in his suitcase, hefted it up onto his shoulder, and climbed down the bank into the riverbed. He had been told that it would take two or three days to cross through the Kruger National Game Park, depending on whether or not he would have to hide and skirt around any patrols he came upon.

His plan was to follow the Sweni River to where it crossed the main road going north and south through the middle of the park; this should take him the better part of the day. Once he had crossed the main road he would have to leave the river and head southwest until he reached the Ngwenyeni River. He could then follow the river right to the western fence. Once he was out of the game park he would be able to continue with the river to where the road to Accornhoek crossed it.

By midday of the third day he had reached the western fence without any problem. He saw no one during the two and a half days, only animals in the distance. They would see him long before he saw them and, as a result, they would stay out of his way. There was a small bush camp on the banks of the river near the fence that was used by the game rangers as a base to patrol from. Mofola had been warned about it and when he saw the smoke from their campfire he took a wide detour around it, before digging a hole under the western border fence and making his way back to the Ngwenyeni River again, more than a kilometre from where it crossed into the park.

By late afternoon he had reached the point where the road to Accornhoek crossed the river. There was no point going any further, as it would soon be dark, so he decided to set up camp in the dry riverbed under the bridge. Someone had made a fire there before, close to where the wall of the bridge dug into the side of the riverbank. There were stones packed in a circle with the remains of half-burned wood and ashes.

He gathered more wood and kindling and then went about making a fire. The matches were now dry so he did not have to make a fire the hard way again. By the time the sun had set, he had a small fire going. He opened the last tin of pilchards and put the tin on a stone next to the fire to get hot. After he had eaten he dragged a dry driftwood log onto the fire that he had collected earlier, wrapped himself in his blanket, and sat next to the fire with his back leaning against the bridge wall and his makeshift spear next to him.

Chapter 18

He woke up just as dawn was breaking with the sound of a heavy truck crossing the bridge. He packed up his things and backtracked along the dry riverbed to a large water hole that he had passed the day before. He stripped off the tattered shirt and pants and washed, standing knee deep in the water. He left his suitcase and old clothes and spear on the grass bank, walked around to the other side of the water hole, and climbed up on top of the three-metre-high rock overhang to catch the first rays of the rising sun.

The sun was warm on his back and he felt clean having washed three days of sweat and dirt from his body, he was also pleased with himself and he sat there daydreaming, thinking what Negome would have said if she knew that he had gotten this far. He was now in South Africa the land of *egoli*. He was soon shaken out of his daydreaming by the sound of voices coming down toward the river. Before he could react, three young girls carrying large tin cans on their heads came down the path to collect water.

He quickly lay down flat on the rock, trying to make himself as inconspicuous as possible, hoping that they would not see him. He judged the three girls to be between fourteen and eighteen. They approached the pool just where Mofola had stood and washed himself a short while ago. The water where he had been standing was still murky. "Be careful," said the one girl to the other, "there could be a crocodile in the water. Look how muddy it is."

They stopped a few metres from the edge of the water and looked around them. It was then that they saw Mofola's suitcase and his old shirt and pants lying in the grass on the bank of the river. "Look there," said the one, "a suitcase and someone's old dirty pants and shirt. Maybe the crocodile has eaten him and spat out these old dirty clothes."

They put down their water tins and walked over to the suitcase; they were now directly opposite the rock overhang. All that separated Mofola from them was about ten metres of water. Mofola could now see the side profile of the eldest of the three girls and even at that distance he could see the outline of her firm breasts pushing against the light fabric of her dress as she stooped to pick up his spear.

She hooked up Mofola's pants on the end of the spear. "Look at the holes in these, she said. "The man who wore these pants might as well have worn no pants because they will hide nothing," she said, holding the pants on the spear up to the sun.

It was then that they saw Mofola lying flat on the top of the rock overhang across the water from where they stood. "Hey you," shouted the eldest of the three, waving the spear at him with his pants still hanging from the end, "why are you lying up there like a lizard, flat on the rock? Do these dirty old clothes belong to you?"

"Yes, they are mine," shouted Mofola. "I have just washed and now I am trying to get dry in the sun."

"But lizards do not like water," teased the eldest girl and the other two laughed and shouted, "Lizard, lizard, lying on the rock."

"I'm not a lizard," shouted Mofola. "I'm a man, can't you see?"

"Stand up," they shouted, "so we can see if you are a man. We think you are a lizard."

"You see, lizards don't have penises," shouted the eldest. "These are lizard's pants, see," she said and held up the pants again on the spear. "These pants could never hide a penis." They all laughed. "Come on, Mr. Lizard, stand up so we can see if you are a man or a lizard."

"I'm getting dry in the sun. That is why I am lying up here. Can't you understand?" shouted Mofola irritably.

"We still think you are a lizard and lizards don't need these clothes, or this suitcase so we will just take these things back to our father's *shamba*." And with that the girls picked up his suitcase and old clothes and started to walk back down to where they had left the water tins.

"Hey you," shouted Mofola, jumping up, "you can't take those things. They belong to me."

The three girls turned around and looked up at the rock where Mofola was now standing in all his glory, shouting down at them. "Look," shouted the eldest of the girls. "It is a man and quite a handsome man too. What's your name, Lizard man?"

"My name is Mofola. Can I now have my suitcase so I can be on my way?"

"So where are you going, Mr. Lizard?" asked the smallest of the three girls.

"That is my business and not yours," he said irately. "Just leave my clothes and my suitcase and I will not hurt you."

"We are very frightened, Mr. Mofola, see how we tremble," the eldest girl said, and the three of them started to shake their arms and legs in a mock act of trembling. "How do you think you are going to hurt us?" the eldest girl asked. "You are up there and we are down here, by the time you climb down from the rock we will have disappeared into the bush with your suitcase and dirty old clothes, so Mr. Mofola, lizard man, where are you going?"

Mofola was not used to dealing with girls. They made him feel awkward and stupid. He sat down again on the rock and looked down at the three young girls who were teasing him. "What is it you want from me?" he asked, "I have done you no harm or disturbed you in any way."

"Yes you have" said the eldest girl. "You have muddied the water and you are trespassing on our father's land. I think you had better come back to our father's *shamba* and explain to him what you are doing here."

Mofola knew that to argue with the three girls was only a waste of time because he was not going to get anywhere with them unless he did what they wanted of him. He had to trick them somehow. "Yes I will come back to your father's *shamba*," he said, "but first I need some clothes to wear. I cannot disgrace your father's *shamba* with my naked body."

"You are too clever," said the eldest girl. "What do you think—we were born only the day before? As soon as we give you some clothes you will run off."

"No, that is not so," protested Mofola, knowing full well that was exactly what he was going to do.

"I'll tell you what we will do," said the eldest girl. "We will leave you your old clothes, and my little sister here will take your suitcase and spear to the *shamba,* and you can carry her tin of water.

"But carrying water is not a man's work," protested Mofola again.

"You, Mr. Mofola, lizard man, have no choice," with that she gave the suitcase and spear to the youngest and she ran off up the path and disappeared from sight.

Mofola climbed slowly down from the rock and walked around the water hole to where the two girls stood watching him approach, snickering behind their hands about the size of his penis. Mofola picked up his old shirt and pants and put them on. He then went and filled one of the tins with water and stood in silence while the girls filled the other two tins. The girls balanced the tins of water on buns of woven grass on their heads and started to walk back up along the path they had come down. Mofola hefted the tin of water onto his shoulder and followed the two girls back to their father's *shamba*.

The youngest of the three girls sat on his suitcase outside the waist-high wall around the *shamba* waiting for them to arrive. As they approached, she got up and went in through the gate, followed by the other two and Mofola. The three girls walked over to the cooking area where an old lady stood stooped over a big black cast-iron pot.

"Mama," said the eldest girl as she lifted the tin of water from her head and placed it on the ground under the overhang of the cooking area, "we have brought a visitor. We found him down at the river and he looked so thin and hungry that we invited him to come and have some food with us."

"Yes," said the youngest smiling, "he even insisted on carrying my tin of water, so I carried his suitcase for him. His name is Mofola." Mofola just stood there with the tin of water on his shoulder and looked from one smiling girl to the other in amazement.

The old lady looked up from the pot she was stirring and said, "Well, young man, do you just want to stand there with the water on your shoulder all day, or do you want to stay for something to eat?" The girls laughed and took the tin of water from him and put it on the ground next to the other two.

"By the state of your shirt and pants," said the old lady, "it looks like you have come a long way and I would say that even the gods would have difficulty in mending them."

"I was busy washing when your daughters came down to fetch water," said Mofola, "and I did not have time to put on clean clothes, these old pants and shirt I was going to throw away."

"Maybe you would like to change into your other clothes before we sit down here to eat," said the old lady. "Yes, thank you, I will quickly go and change," he said, and with that he picked up his suitcase and went behind one of the thatched huts and changed into the only other set of clothes he had, they consisted of long grey pants, a light blue shirt, black socks and white *takkies*.

The clothes not only smelled strongly of fish, they were also badly creased from when he had rung the water out of them after he so nearly drowned in the river. Mofola threw the old shirt and pants over the wall of the *shamba* into the *veld*, picked up his suitcase and walked back to the cooking area.

"Look, Mama," said the youngest of the three girls, "how handsome our young man is in his new clothes."

"Yes I see," said the old lady, "and I can also smell that the young man comes from Mozambique. Those clothes will have to be washed before you can travel any further. Smelling like a fish market, the authorities will soon find you out and put you in jail until they can send you back to where you have come from. But first we eat and then we will see what we can do with those smelly clothes."

Mofola was surprised at the old lady's wisdom and her ability to smell the fish from at least three paces. He did not think the smell was that bad, but maybe he had gotten used to the smell. Even though the dry fish was finished, every time he opened his suitcase he still got a whiff of it. They sat on the ground and ate thick *maize* porridge with sour goat's milk. Mofola did not realize how hungry he was until he had started to eat; he had three helpings before his hunger was satisfied.

"It is just as well that my daughters do not bring hungry fish-smelling men home every day to eat, or we would soon be without food, said the old lady. This one eats like three men. Next time you bring visitors home, make sure first that they are not hungry."

The girls laughed. Mofola felt awkward again, and offered to pay for the food.

"No," said the old lady, "you keep your money. There will be enough cheats and dishonest people to take it from you on your journey."

As they ate, the old lady quizzed Mofola on where he had come from, how long he had been travelling, which way had he come and where he was heading. The girls wanted to know how many wives he already had and when he told them that as yet he had none, they were very surprised that such a handsome man did not have at least one wife to look after him. Mofola in turn asked where their father was.

"My husband," said the old lady, "and my son, who is the eldest of my four children, are working on the mines in Pilgrim's Rest. They sometimes come home at the end of the month, when they can get a bus to Bushbuck-ridge and then to Accornhoek which is not too far from here. But now, young man, we need to make a plan to wash those clothes of yours. What else have you to wear while we get those smelly clothes clean and pressed with a hot iron?"

Mofola opened his case and took out his blanket, "I can put this around me," he said.

"Ooh, that blanket smells worse than the clothes you are wearing," said the youngest girl sitting next to him.

"Well, we will just have to wash that too," said the old lady. "Dumbe, she said, referring to the youngest child, go and fetch a pair of your brother's old pants for Mr. Mofola to put on while your sister Tindela washes his things. Do you have anything else in that suitcase of yours that smells of fish and needs to be washed?"

"No, that's all that I have," lied Mofola, for he was certainly not going to let them wash his money that was stuffed in between the lining at the bottom of his suitcase.

Tindela fetched a tin basin and a bar of blue soap, picked up his clothes and blanket, and started to walk back down to the river from where they had come a short while ago. As she got to the gate she turned and called to Mofola, "So are you coming to wash your fish-smelling body or are you going to put clean clothes on a smelly body?"

"Yes, you had better go and wash that smell from your body," said the old lady.

"Shall we go and help Tindela with washing Mofola's clothes?" asked one of the other girls.

"What do you think, that your sister can't wash a few things? You both have other chores to do, now be off and get them done."

Mofola followed Tindela down to the water hole, remaining a few paces behind her, not wanting to engage her in conversation for fear that she may make a fool of him again.

A few paces from the water's edge there was a large flat rock that Tindela used for washing clothes. Tindela dropped the washing on the rock, filled the basin with water, and started to wash Mofola's things, first soaping them and then beating them on the rock.

Mofola sat opposite her on the grass and watched her kneeling on the rock with her dress tucked up in her panties, pounding his clothes and blanket on the rock to clean them. Every time she stooped forward to pound the washing, he could see straight down the front of her dress to her breasts that bounced up and down in time with the pounding. He felt himself getting hard and put his hands in front of his pants to hide his erection, embarrassed that she might see it.

Tindela must have sensed it. She looked up at him and said, "Are you just going to sit there, or are you going to wash?"

"I was waiting for the soap," stammered Mofola."

"I have finished with the soap," she said, and with that she picked it up and threw it to him. Mofola caught the soap, revealing the huge bulge in his pants.

"It would seem that my swaying breasts have aroused a tree trunk in your pants," she teased.

Even more embarrassed, Mofola quickly stood up walked down to the water's edge, dropped his pants, and walked waist deep into the cool water.

Tindela shook out the blanket and clothes and laid them on the grass bank to dry in the sun. She also went down to the water's edge, pulled her dress up over her head, dropped it on the sand, and walked into the water to where Mofola stood with his back to her soaping himself. She came and stood directly behind him, pressing her firm breasts against his back and put her arms around the front of him. Give me the soap," she said, "you have missed a spot on your back."

Mofola dropped the soap into her cupped hands. His erection was now so hard he thought his penis was going to burst. Tindela soaped his back down to his waist, and then let her right hand slip down below the water to his buttocks and then around to his bulging penis. "This tree trunk is now just right for planting," she said and moved around to the front of him still grasping his penis in her hand. With her left hand she pulled her pants down and threw them onto the sand near to where she had dropped her dress.

She guided him into her. Mofola put his arms around her and slowly pushed his throbbing penis inside her. Tindela grasped him with both hands locked behind his neck and crossed her legs around his waist. They both moved in rhythm, water splashing all around as their rhythm became faster and faster until they were both spent.

They remained locked together for a few minutes, both panting and out of breath. Slowly she dropped her legs from around his waist and moved away from him, feeling more satisfied than she had ever felt before with any of the other young men she had been with. Mofola ducked his head under the water for a few seconds to cool off and then shot up, jumping up out of the water, shaking the water from his head. They both walked out of the water and went and sat on the washing rock in the sun, neither speaking. It was not necessary.

Tindela pressed his pants and shirt with a hot iron and a lot of supervision from the other two girls. Then Mofola dressed in his freshly ironed clothes. They felt good on his body and his body felt more relaxed than he could ever remember. It was way past midday and time that he was on his way. He thanked the old lady and the girls for their hospitality and made his way to the gate.

"Wait for me," shouted Tindela as he got to the gate. "I will show you a short way to the road," she said "and you forgot your spear." She came running up to the gate, handed him the spear and walked with him along a path that led to the road going to Accornhoek.

When they reached the road she advised him to get rid of the spear, as no one would give him a ride if they saw him with a spear. He removed the blade from the stick and hid it again in the lining of his suitcase.

"Mr. Lizard man, go well."

"Yes," said Mofola. "You stay well and may the gods bring us together again one day."

With that he turned from her and made his way along the road, not looking back to see if she had gone back to the *shamba*.

Chapter 19

Mofola trudged along the dirt road in the early afternoon. A few cars and trucks had passed him going in
both directions, leaving him standing in their dust.
White people drove most of them. He was not used to
walking in long pants and shoes; the shoes hurt his feet
and after a while he took them off, tucked his socks into
them, tied the laces together, and hung them around
his neck.

Every so often he would pass a white stone on the
side of the road with a number; the last one said nine.
A short distance from where he had gotten onto the road
there was a stone marked twelve. He could not understand it. The distances between the stones here seemed
to be much longer than the distances between the stones
in Mozambique. What he did not know, was that in
South Africa, the white stones on the road were marked
in miles and not in kilometres.

Not long after he had passed the last milestone, an
old man came past in a small cart pulled by two donkeys.
The old man stopped about five paces further on, looked
back, and said, "Do you want a third class ride or do you

prefer a first class walk?" Mofola thought of his father in his old donkey cart, which was not unlike the one this old man had.

"I see you are going to the city of gold," said the old man, after they had travelled some distance in silence.

"How did you know that I was going to the city of *egoli*?"

"I see many people who come along this road, some going and some returning from the *egoli* mines. Many like you are full of hope and have great expectations, many who return, are full of bitterness and disappointment. Be careful, young man the *egoli* never brought happiness to anyone. It is like a huge python that slowly devours you and then, after a period of time, it spits out that what is no longer of use and what you have left is the mere skeleton of a once good man."

The old man dropped Mofola off at the bus depot and told him to ask for the bus that goes to Nelspruit. "From there you can get the train that goes to the *egoli* mines near the big city of Johannesburg."

Mofola thanked the old man for the ride and the words of wisdom, and made his way over to the bus depot. It was now late afternoon on Sunday and he was informed that the bus would leave shortly. He bought a ticket and went and stood in the long line.

Mofola could not believe that all these people with their boxes and luggage could possibly fit into one bus. There must be at least two buses, he thought to himself. A big green bus arrived and the people started to get on, passing their boxes and other luggage up to the two men on the roof of the bus that were packing and tying it down on the roof rack. By the time it was Mofola's turn to get on the bus, it was, by his understanding, now full.

"Pass me your suitcase," shouted one of the men on top of the bus. Mofola was very reluctant to part with his suitcase; he wanted to take it with him on the bus. "Hey you," shouted the man on top of the bus, "do you want to get on this bus or don't you?"

"I will wait for the next bus, this one's full," said Mofola.

"OK, you can wait till tomorrow. Next," shouted the man on the roof. Mofola reluctantly passed his suitcase up to the man on the roof and pushed his way onto the already full bus.

Even with all the windows open it was unbearably hot. The people were packed into the bus like sardines in a tin. It was a slow trip, the bus stopping at every bus stop to let people off and let new people on. Every time, the two men on the roof would untie and then retie the luggage back on the roof. Every time the bus stopped, Mofola would try to see from where he was standing in the middle of the bus, if his suitcase had not been taken by someone, not that he could do anything about it if they had.

It was dark by the time they arrived in Nelspruit and, by the number of electric lights that were burning, he could see that it was a big town. The bus stopped at the bus depot, which was a short distance from the station. Parked under a street light was a black police van with four policemen standing next to it; two were white and two were black. As the people got out of the bus, they would stop some of the passengers and ask them for their reference books.

In 1950, the controversial Group Areas Act, commonly known as apartheid, came into being in South Africa. It basically legislated that there were to be different domain areas for different population groups, and in 1952 the old pass law was abolished to make way for the personal reference book. This book contained details of the person's place of abode, place of work, tribe, tax details, thumb print, and picture. Anyone caught without this document was immediately arrested and put in jail.

The Group Areas Act was promulgated to basically control the influx of blacks into the white towns and cities. If your reference book did not reflect that you stayed or worked in a certain area, then, without special written clearance from the Native Affairs commissioner, you could not travel to another area of your choice.

Mofola had heard his father and brothers discussing this subject but it made very little sense to him at that time. Now it was 1962 and Dr. H. F. Verwoerd, the former minister of Native Affairs, was now prime minister of South Africa He was the architect of apartheid and was enforcing strict controls on the movement of blacks in the country. At the time, Mofola did not know this.

"Why are the police stopping those people?" asked Mofola, speaking to the old man standing squashed next to him, waiting to get off.

"They are looking at their reference books," said the old man.

"What is a reference book?"

"You mean you don't have a reference book?"

"No, I don't have one," admitted Mofola.

"Young man, where do you think you are going then without a reference book?"

"I'm going to Johannesburg to meet my two brothers who work there on the mines."

"Young man, you can't even buy a train ticket without a reference book. Without a reference book, they will put you in jail and if you are a foreigner, they will beat you up badly before sending you back to your country, to make sure you don't try to come back again," he said.

Look," he said as he started to move forward to get off, 'try to avoid them and if you are successful, meet me down the road there by that cafe," he said, pointing to a cafe on the corner, "I might be able to help you." With that the old man got off the bus.

Mofola stood in the aisle, blocking the way for the people behind him. "Move," shouted the people behind.

One person said, "If you don't want to get off, then move out of the way so we can get off."

Mofola moved into one of the now empty seats in front of him and watched the people getting off, collecting their belongings that were being systematically off- loaded from the roof and placed next to the bus. As the people got off the bus they picked up their goods and either went into the railway station or went in some other direction. He noticed that the police were mainly concentrating on those people who were going to the railway station.

He waited until he saw his suitcase being off-loaded and the police had stopped a large group of people heading for the station. He then quickly got off the bus, picked up his suitcase, and made off down the road toward the cafe on the corner.

When he got to the cafe he looked for the old man, but he was nowhere to be seen. Then he spotted him in the cafe store standing, waiting at the counter to be served. Mofola walked into the nearest entrance, but before he had taken two steps the white storekeeper shouted at him in the *Afrikaans* language that he could not understand, "Hey! Where the fuck do you think you are going, *kaffir*, this is the white's side, when will you fucking blacks learn to fucking read?"

The old man heard the storekeeper shouting and saw Mofola standing dumbstruck in the middle of the store. He called over to Mofola from where he was standing in the black section of the store, and told Mofola to wait outside for him. Mofola, still confused, turned around and made his way back out of the store and stood waiting for the old man to finish buying bread and milk.

"Young man, you had better start learning the ways in this country very fast or you will find yourself in jail before very long. Come with me, you can sleep at my place tonight. I have a room at the back of my master's house, I'm the gardener, I do his garden twice a week and clean his car. For that he lets me stay in the room at the back of his garage. We must walk fast, as it is still a long way to go and we must be inside before nine o' clock when the siren sounds."

"But why must we be inside before nine?" Mofola wanted to know.

"Because that is the law, there is a curfew, no blacks are allowed out on the streets after nine at night, so don't forget it."

They ate some of the bread that the old man had bought and drank some tea that he had made on a Primus *paraffin* stove. They spoke about many things, but mainly about the many strange customs that were law in this country. The old man explained that he had been home for the weekend to go and see his family in Bushbuckridge. "It was lucky that you spoke to me, said the old man; otherwise, you would be sleeping on the floor of a different small room tonight," he joked.

It so happened that the old man also worked in the garden of another white man who was involved with recruiting and transporting black labour up to the Witwatersrand. He said that he would speak to him on Monday when he went to work there and see if he could arrange something for Mofola.

Jan Smit was involved with the recruiting of black labour for the mines and the sugar plantations around Nelspruit and Komatiepoort, but with the new legislation, the recruiting business was becoming more and more difficult, and he often had to break the law to meet the ever-increasing labour demands of the mining magnates and sugar cane plantation owners. However, a bottle of whisky or a bottle of brandy, put in the right person's hand, was normally all that was needed to get a few extra names and numbers on the recruiting documentation.

The next morning, as promised, the old man spoke to his other employer, Mr. Jan Smit about Mofola. "You tell your little illegal immigrant friend it's going to cost him ten pounds if he wants to go to Jo'burg and tell him I want the money first."

"Yes, boss, I tell to him tonight."

Smit had promised East Vaal Mining Enterprise (EVME) that he would recruit fifty new labourers for them at fifty pounds sterling each. He had managed to get only forty-five legally, another three illegally, plus the new one tonight gave him forty nine, still one short. He was already two weeks late and EVME were threatening to cancel the contract. "What the fuck," he said to himself. "I've taken ten pounds sterling off each of the illegals, so I will only lose out on ten pounds. But if I don't get this bunch of kaffirs up to Jo'burg this week they will be sure to cancel the contract and that's goodbye to two thousand five hundred pounds sterling."

The next day was Wednesday and the old man quickly went along to Mr. Smit's house with the ten pounds. He had told Mofola that it would cost him fifteen pounds to get to Johannesburg, the five pounds he put in his own pocket.

Smit took the money and told him, "Make sure that you tell your little illegal immigrant to get his fucking ass over to WLNA's recruiting offices at five o' clock on Friday morning. If he's not there, I'll have your ass on the end of my boot, do you understand, *madala*?"

"Yes, boss, I understand, he be there in time on Friday."

"What's your friend's name?" asked Smit."

"Mofola Maraga, boss. See, here I write it on this piece of paper." With that the old man gave the piece of paper to Smit who took it and put it in the top pocket of his shirt.

Five o' clock on Friday morning saw Mofola standing outside the WNLA's offices with a whole lot of other blacks. At about seven o' clock a black man came out of the offices and started to call out names and told them which truck to get onto. Mofola had to hold his excitement and relief when he heard his name being called. He climbed up into the truck with the other labourers all clutching bags and suitcases as if it were the last thing they had in the world and maybe it was. Mofola knew that for him it was, for three days ago he had handed over nearly all of what remained of his hard-earned money to the old man to pay for his trip to the city of *egoli*.

Little did Mofola know, he was not destined for Johannesburg, but for the town of Boksburg, where the EVME was situated. This he only found out after they had been underway for a few hours and everybody started to relax a bit and talk to each other. Some of the chaps were going on their second contract period and it was from one of them that he learned that they were all destined for EVME in Boksburg and not, as he thought, Johannesburg. He also noted that Roodepoort Frontier Mining where his two brothers worked was about twenty miles from Boksburg.

Chapter 20

At midday they stopped just outside the town of Witbank to relieve themselves in the Wattle plantation alongside the road. In the town they stopped for diesel, and some of the chaps bought cool drinks. Mofola drank some water from the tap at the filling station, filled his water bottle, and bought a half a loaf of bread. The few shillings he still had left he wanted to save to buy a bus ticket to Johannesburg from Boksburg.

They arrived at the EVME late in the afternoon and stopped outside the main gates to the mine property. Smit got out and told his black driver to tell everyone to stay on the truck until he had got the necessary paper work completed at the mine offices. The driver was quite used to the routine. He had been driving for boss Smit for years and every few months they would make this trip up to Johannesburg to deliver labourers to one of the mines.

Mofola waited for his chance to jump off the truck and when the driver was engaged in small talk with one of the security guards at the gate, Mofola quickly climbed over the side of the truck and disappeared into the crowd milling around the gate. He had no idea where he was going so he just followed the people who were going away from the mine property.

After walking for half an hour he ended up in the northern part of Boksburg and made his way over to where a group of black people were waiting at a bus stop. He wanted to get as far away as possible from EVME in case they came looking for him. He asked one of the men he followed from the mine if he knew what bus he should get to go to Roodepoort Frontier Mining. The man explained to him that he would first have to get a bus to Johannesburg central and then get another bus to Roodepoort and get off at Roodepoort Frontier Mining.

Jan Smit walked into the personnel office at EVME and greeted the woman behind the counter. "Hello, Marietjie, how are you?"

"Hello, Mr. Smit, we haven't seen you for some time."

"Ya, it's been awhile. Is Mr. Young in?"

"Yes, let me see if he will see you." And with that she got up from her desk and walked over to the adjoining office, knocked on the closed door, waited a moment, and then went in, closing it after her.

After a few minutes she came out and informed him that Mr. Young would see him now. Smit walked over to Mr. Young's office and went in. "Hello, Dave, how's things, man? Sorry I'm a bit late getting your boys, but it's getting more and more difficult to get boys with the government's new policies."

"A bit late, Christ you're fucking three weeks late. I've had to contract another bloke to get me boys.

He brought them the day before yesterday. Smitty, I've told you a hundred fucking times that when we give you a contract with dates, you agree to those dates and we expect you to adhere to them. I can understand a few days late but not three bloody weeks."

"Jees, Dave, I said I'm sorry, man, what do you want me to do? They don't just grow on fucking trees you know, this is 1962 not 1952. It's not like the old days. Verwoerd has tightened up on all the migrant workers coming into the country and the local blacks don't want to work on the mines."

"Smitty, that's your problem, the other blokes seem to be able to get their quota and get them here on time."

"Ya but not at fifty quid each, hey!"

"So it costs a few pounds extra but at least we get them on time. I've told you that when their contracts are up they want to go home and they won't work an extra day over their contract date."

"Come on, Dave, man, do me a favour. I can't take them back again; there'll be a fucking riot."

"OK , I'll tell you what! Ill give you thirty pounds each for them."

"Jees, Dave that's what I paid for them, give us a break, man."

"Look, I had to pay sixty quid for the ones that came in the other day, so take it or leave it."

"OK, OK, I'll take it."

"Good. Then I'll make out the clearance papers so you can go and off-load them at the compound, but it's too late to organize the payment, the accounts office closes at four, so you will have to come back tomorrow for your money." "No that's fine, I was going to stay with my sister in Benoni anyway so I'll come back tomorrow for the cheque."

"When you get to the compound tell the compound manager to give me a ring."

Smit and the driver offloaded the new labourers at the gate to the compound, gave the paperwork to the manager, and gave him Dave's message. They then drove through to Benoni to his sister's place. "Jees, he thought to himself, that Dave is some kind of shit. Thirty fucking pounds. Anyway I still make a small profit, seeing I only paid twenty-five each for the fuckers, it was better than nothing."

Mofola got off the bus at Johannesburg central and stood around waiting for the bus to Roodepoort, it was getting late and he wanted to be with his brothers before it got dark. There were several people waiting for buses to various places, some white folk and some black standing apart. Mofola was tired and went and sat down on one of the empty benches near where all the white people were standing. Mofola plunked himself down next to a white man on the bench where there was a space.

"What the fuck do you think you are doing, *kaffir*," said the man next to him in a language that he did not understand. "Can't you fucking read? This is for whites only, so get your fucking black ass off this bench and go and sit with the other kaffirs over there," he said, pointing to where the black people were sitting on occupied benches, "before I give you a good fucking *klap*.

Mofola did not understand a word the man was saying and wasn't sure whether he was speaking to him anyway, so he just sat there looking straight in front of him.

The white, now furious that Mofola dared ignore him, jumped up and grabbed Mofola by the front of his shirt, yanked him to his feet, and slapped him hard on the side of the face, knocking him off his feet. Mofola, not knowing what was going on and now incensed that this man had just assaulted him for no reason at all, got up and promptly hit the white with his fist square on the jaw, knocking him to the ground.

By this time they had attracted the interest of the other whites that now started to shout encouragement to the white on the ground that was trying to stand, obviously dazed and shaken that a black could even dare hit him back.

"*Bliksem* him," another white man shouted, fuck him up good."

Mofola sensed that this was not the time to stand and fight; this was different from a good old stick fight with the other herd boys. He grabbed his suitcase and took off down the street with the sound of whistles in his ears. Looking back over his shoulder he could see two police constables hard on his heels.

Johannesburg was a jungle to Mofola. There were buildings higher than the highest trees and equally as many as the trees in the forest, one place looked the same as the part he had just run from and yet different. He had long since outrun the two police constables, but every now and then he could hear the shrill sounds of whistles in the distance. He had no idea where he was, only that he was somewhere in the back streets of Johannesburg.

He needed to find a safe place to hide. It was dark by this time and soon it would be curfew and he would be in even more trouble out on the streets. He found a little alley that went into a dead-end with a whole lot of old cardboard boxes piled up at the end. He crawled under the boxes, pulling more boxes on top of him and sat there to await the coming of what he hoped would be a better day.

Mofola did not sleep very well under the pile of boxes, right through the night he heard police blowing their whistles and some times they seemed to be close. He was terrified that they would come down the alley and find him under the pile of cardboard boxes. When morning finally broke, he was relieved but quite exhausted. Being Saturday, he thought that it would be best to remain where he was until there were more people on the streets before he ventured out from his hiding place.

He lay there for a long time, he could already hear the traffic in the street and he thought that it would now be all right to leave his hiding place. He was just about to crawl out from under the boxes when he heard people coming down the alleyway. They were banging tins and shouting to one another. They started to pull the boxes away from where he was hiding, and he thought that this was now the end. There was nowhere to run and this was a dead end with a solid three-metre wall behind him.

"Hey you, up you get, the time for sleeping is over, the sun is in the sky and some of us have work to do, even if some like you don't, so move or we will throw you in the truck with the rest of the rubbish."

Mofola had no idea what they were saying but he soon got the message that they weren't the police looking for him. He quickly got up and made his way to the front of the alley where three other black chaps were breaking up the boxes and throwing the pieces onto the back of a big truck.

Mofola asked one of the three if he could direct him to where the bus for Roodepoort stopped. One of the three, having worked on the mines for sometime, could understand and speak a little *Shangane*. He directed Mofola to the central bus station. That was the last place that Mofola wanted to be at this moment, so he asked him if there were any other place he could get the bus from, other than the central bus station.

"Oh yes, but it is much further away," he said. "The next nearest is at Jeppe station. We are going past there so if you follow us, I'll show you when we get there."

Mofola followed the rubbish truck down the hill from Hillbrow to Jeppe station, which took the better part of an hour. Mofola was amazed at the speed that the rubbish men went about their work, they ran from one point to the next collecting rubbish and dumping it in the big open truck, he felt awkward and wanted to help them but was told that this was their work and that he should not get involved.

Being Saturday the buses were not that frequent; he had to wait until ten o' clock before a bus came that was going to Roodepoort. The bus ride cost him one and six pence and, had it not been for the driver, he would have gotten off the bus several times at the wrong place. When the bus got to the Roodepoort Frontier Mining bus stop the driver indicated to him that he should get off and pointed to the large gate a little way down the road with the name of the mine on it.

Mofola stood outside the mine property and looked up at the huge double gates with the arch spanning across the top with the wording, Roodepoort Frontier Mining, and said to himself, "Now I have arrived in the land of *egoli.*" Outside the gates there were two mine security police controlling the people and various vehicles coming and going from the mine property. They would stop all the vehicles and check the paperwork and the load before letting it proceed onto the mine property. People walked in and out of the gate and the security guard on the gate took very little notice of them, as they waved some form of identification as they passed through the gates.

Mofola had heard his brothers talking about the identification tags that the black mine workers wore around their necks and how important it was to make sure that you did not lose it, as without the tag you did not get your wages. Mofola did not want to take the chance and approach the guards at the gate to ask them if he could go and find his brothers—even if they did look friendly—he'd had enough of the authorities for quite some time.

He went back across the road and sat down on the grass and leaned against one of the many big eucalyptus trees growing along the side of the road, to contemplate how he was going to contact his brothers. It was cool under the trees out of the midday sun and Mofola was weary after all the excitement of the past days and the lack of sleep. He sat there watching the people coming and going from the mine property, some were white folk, but many were black folk dressed in yellow waterproofs and wearing tin hats. He wondered how best he could go about finding his brothers.

He must have dosed off for a few minutes, for he got such a fright when the mine hooter sounded at midday. He jumped up looking around to establish where the loud sound was coming from; it continued for at least twenty seconds. Within minutes of the hooter blowing, people and all kinds of vehicles came streaming out of the mine property. On Saturdays the mine worked officially only until midday, but many of the maintenance divisions worked a full day on Saturday and sometimes on Sunday as well, servicing the many machines and equipment needed to run a big mining operation.

He stood and watched, amazed at the vast number of people coming out of the mine property. Two men walked across the road toward him and, as they approached, he could hear that they were speaking *Shangane*, his home language. As they were about to pass, Mofola greeted them, "I see you, my brother,"

"Yes, we see you too," they greeted back, only stopping their conversation long enough to greet Mofola as they continued on their way down the road. Mofola hesitated a few seconds, picked up his suitcase and ran after them.

"Sorry, my brothers, but can you please help me?"

The two men stopped and turned around as they heard Mofola calling after them. "Yes, young man, what is it you want?"

"I'm trying to contact my blood brothers who work here in the mine and the police at the gate will not let me into the mine property to go and find them," he lied.

"That is true," said the one man. "You cannot go into the mine without a permit. What are the names of your blood brothers that you seek?"

"Temba and Yussaf, we are the sons Maraga from the Gaza province in Mozambique."

"There are many hundred people working here in this mine from the Gaza province, even ourselves, we are from the Gaza province. Where is it in the mine that your brothers work?"

"Yussaf, he works with the people who work with the electric, and Temba, he is a driller," replied Mofola.

"That is strange," said the one man, "I work in the fitting and turning workshop, which is right next to the electric workshop, and I don't know anyone in the electric workshop who is named Yussaf, maybe they work at another mine."

"No, no," protested Mofola, "they work here at this mine, Roodepoort Frontier Mining."

"I'm sorry, my young friend, we cannot help you," and they turned to go.

"Wait," shouted Mofola, remembering that his brother had said that they call him Joe in the mine, which is short for Yussaf. "Do you maybe know a Joe with the people who work with the electric?"

The one man stopped again and said, "Joe, yes, of course I know Joe in the electric workshop. Everyone knows Joe, he's the one who always makes the jokes. I'll tell you what, we are going to the trading store down there," he said, pointing to a corrugated tin building a short way down the road. "When we come back we will go past the workshop and see if he is there and we will tell him his young brother is here to see him."

Some time later they came back and as they passed Mofola sitting on the grass one of them said, "Don't worry, my young friend we will find your brother Joe and tell him you are here. Who shall we say you are if he should ask?"

Mofola thought for a second then said, "Tell him his brother Boxer Boy is here."

"OK, Boxer, we will tell him you are here, so don't go away." Mofola lay on the grass and waited anxiously for his brother Joe to come out through the big mine gates across the road.

The sun had long gone down and in the distance there was thunder and lightning, typical of the summer season up on the *highveld*. Soon Mofola would have to find a place to hide for the night. The big double gates to the mine property had been closed and the security guards on the gate had changed shifts; the new guards were checking the identity of everyone that passed through the gates. Every time a black man came out, Mofola would jump up and strain his eyes in the now fast-fading light to see across the road if it was Joe coming out.

The floodlights around the mine property's surrounding walls had come on some time ago, bathing the area in an eerie orange glow. Everywhere else it was pitch dark except for the occasional flash of lightning that would streak across the sky, lighting it up for a brief moment. At nine o' clock the mine hooter sounded again, signalling the start of the curfew.

While he was waiting for Joe to come out, Mofola had been looking around for a place to spend the night, and a little way down the road toward the trading post the road crossed over a ditch. He had decided to spend the rest of the night in the ditch in a concrete storm water pipe under the road. There was a cool breeze blowing through the concrete pipe, so he wrapped his blanket around himself and curled up in the pipe with his head on his suitcase and was soon sound asleep.

As promised, the two men went over to the workshop on their way back to the compound, but it was already locked up and everyone had gone home. They did not know in which of the four compounds Joe stayed so they decided to wait until the next day, Sunday. Maybe Joe was working overtime like them and then they could tell him about his brother.

During the early hours of the morning the storm had moved over to the Roodepoort area and the rain came down in buckets, pouring off the sides of the hills and roads and into the drains and ditches. The thunder and lightning had woken Mofola a few times, but he was used to storms, having experienced many while he was herding up in the mountains. He simply pulled the blanket tighter over his head and went back to sleep.

One minute he was sleeping and the next he was being tumbled head over heels down the pipe by a huge force of water. He came shooting out the end of the pipe and continued to be swept down the ditch by the water. It was only after he had been carried along some distance that he was able to find his feet and get up, clutching a sopping wet blanket. His suitcase had been swept away into the darkness of the night to who knows where.

He pulled himself up out of the ditch and walked back along the top of it, crossing over the road and into the eucalyptus plantation that grew next to it. He was soaked to the skin, cold, and miserable, "It would seem," he thought to himself, "that I must surely be destined to one day die in water."

Joe and his boss stood waiting for the cage to take them underground. It was seven o' clock Sunday morning, the ground was still wet from the rainstorm early that morning, but now the sky was clear and it looked like it was going to be another fine day. However, he would not see much of it, as he and his white boss, the electrician, had to go underground to repair an electric cable that had been damaged in a rock fall.

They were waiting for the Mary-Anne hoist to come up from underground. The main hoist was hauling rock, so they all had to go down in the small Mary-Anne hoist. Had they all been going down on shift on a normal working day, they would have gone down in the main man-hoist, with all the blacks packed tightly into the bottom half of the double decker cage and all the white bosses with plenty of room in the top half, but today they would all ride together in the Mary-Anne hoist.

The steel grid door of the Mary-Anne cage closed, and the onsetter man rang the bell twice, signalling the winding-engine driver to lower the cage into the shaft.

Just as the cage started to drop slowly away from the bank, the man that worked in the fitters workshop came running up to the cage and shouted to Joe through the grid door, "Hey Joe, do you have a younger brother? He says he is from our home country."

"Yes, how do you know?" shouted Joe as the cage started to drop below the surface on its journey into the bowels of the earth. The last Joe heard was "I saw him"—and the rest was lost in the rattling noise of the cage gathering speed.

The clouds had all blown away, the rain had stopped, and the dawn was breaking in the eastern sky. Mofola walked into the plantation well out of sight from the road and the mine gate and took off all his clothes and rung them out. He did the same with his blanket. He wrapped the damp blanket around himself, shook his clothes out and hung them on the branches of the eucalyptus trees where they could catch the early morning sun.

Mofola could not afford to stand around and feel sorry for himself. He had to get back to the grass bank opposite the mine gate just in case his brother Yussaf came looking for him. He pulled on his damp pants and shirt and carried his shoes and socks to the grass bank opposite the gate and sat down to wait for his brother to come out and find him.

Mofola watched the people coming in and out of the mine property, they were mostly black people and they were all dressed in their Sunday best. A few cars and small trucks driven by white folk also moved through the gates. Other than that, it was very quiet.

The sun was already high in the sky and had long since dried his clothes and his blanket that he had spread out on the grass. He was hungry and thirsty, the last time he had anything to eat was when they stopped to put diesel in the truck in Witbank and the last of the water he had drunk last night before his suitcase had been swept away by the storm water. All he had left now was what he had on, his blanket, and a few shillings and pence in his pocket. There was not much in the suitcase that he needed but somehow he felt lost without it, the suitcase had been like a companion to him.

Mofola was tempted to go down the road to the trading store and buy some bread with the money he still had left in his pocket, but he was afraid that if he went to the store he might just miss his brothers. Little did he know that in South Africa the stores all closed on Sunday, so it would not have helped him anyway.

All day while he was working underground Joe wondered about what his colleague who worked in the fitters workshop said; did he hear him correctly? He was not sure, the noise of the cage blotted out what the man was trying to say. They had finished repairing the damaged cable and were now waiting at twelfth-level station for the cage to come and lift them to the surface.

By the time Joe had surfaced from underground, cleaned the tools, cleaned the boss's boots and fetched the boss a mug of tea, it was already four o' clock in the afternoon. Not that it made much difference, as the chaps from the fitters workshop were still not up from underground where they had been installing a new scraper winch at fourteenth level, so he still did not know what the full message was about his younger brother.

Joe decided to go and have a shower at the change rooms and then he could come back to the workshops and see if the fitters had surfaced yet. He went and said good-bye to his boss, Vissie, who was sitting on his steel tool trunk talking to some of the other electricians who had also been working overtime.

"I go now, boss, everything, she is clean, OK?"

"*Ja*, OK, Joe, I'll see you tomorrow. Hey, before you go, get me some more tea, and tell that *madala* prick that I want two spoons of condensed milk and three spoons of sugar in my tea. You would think that the old fart would remember after three years," he said to the rest of the chaps sitting around drinking their tea. "I swear he does it just to annoy me."

"Vissie you see that's what you get when you fuck the old tea man around like you do."

"Fuck him, he is just another *kaffir*, he must pull himself toward himself or he will get a good *klap* from me."

Joe fetched another cup of tea from the old man and gave it to his boss. He then made his way to the change rooms, which were on the other side of the shaft. Just as he got to the shaft, the fitters were surfacing from fourteenth level.

"Hey, Joe," shouted the fitter man as he stepped out of the cage onto the bank, "did you find your brother?"

"No, where is he?" asked Joe as he walked over to the shaft bank. "He is outside the main gate on the other side of the road."

"Are you sure it's my brother?" asked Joe, rather sceptical. "Well he sounded very convincing; he said you would know him as Boxer Boy."

"Oh yes! That can only be Mofola, my youngest brother. Where did you say he was waiting?"

"On the other side of the road opposite the main gate. I saw him there yesterday; maybe he is still waiting there now."

Chapter 21

Joe ran down to the main gate still dressed in his yellow waterproofs and mine boots, typical of those worn by all the workers going underground. He went through the gate and looked across the road to the grass bank on the other side. He could see someone there, but it was four years since he had seen Mofola and he could not be sure if it was actually him or not.

Mofola saw this person walking across the road toward him dressed in yellow waterproofs and wearing a tin miner's hat. He looked like hundreds of other mineworkers who had been passing in and out of the gate all yesterday and today. He was wondering just what to do now. Maybe the man he spoke to yesterday could not find Yussaf and that is why he had not come to find him. Up until now he was always confident that he would find his brothers and get a job on the mine and make big money so that he could go back home and take Negome for his wife. It was this that had kept him going all the time, through all that had happened to him over the past few years. Now that he was so close, he suddenly felt his confidence waning and wondered if he had done the right thing after all.

As Joe got closer, he saw it was Mofola, he looked tired and his clothes looked like they had never seen a hot iron. "Hey, little brother, what brings you to the big *egoli* city?" he shouted across the road, taking his tin hat off so that Mofola could recognize him.

Mofola jumped up and ran to meet his brother. They embraced each other right there on the side of the road. Tears of joy and relief flowed down Mofola's cheeks. The pent-up frustration and bitterness of the past years seemed to just flow out from him as he collapsed on the grass bank with his head between his knees.

"Why did you take so long to come and find me? I have been waiting here now for two days, do you have any idea what I have been through over the past few years?" stammered Mofola, trying to hold back the tears.

Yussaf sat down next to his younger brother and put his arm around him and let him ramble on about his various ordeals. There was no point at that moment to explain to him why he hadn't come sooner to find him. Yussaf knew that was not the problem, it was everything else and it was best to let it all come out now, then it would be over. So he just sat there next to him and listened.

After a while Mofola calmed down and looked at his brother and said "I'm sorry, my brother, I know it was not your doing what has happened to me over the past years, I'm just so thankful that I have at last gotten here."

"Don't be sorry, my little brother, a lesser man than you would not have survived this ordeal. It is surely the gods that are putting your strength to the test. Come, we must get you inside to the compound before it gets too late."

"How are we going to get in through the gate?" Mofola wanted to know.

"Come, we'll go into the eucalyptus plantation and change clothes."

The two brothers walked casually into the plantation, out of sight of the main entrance, and they changed clothes there. Mofola put the yellow waterproofs that Yussaf had on over his crumpled up shirt and pants. Yussaf's gumboots were a little too small for Mofola's feet, but he managed to force them on. Fortunately Yussaf had his normal working clothes on under the waterproofs and, with Mofola's *takkies* on his feet, the two of them emerged from the trees as if nothing had changed.

"Put on the hard hat and just walk next to me. I will show my identity tag, but you just walk and continue to talk to me as we go through the gate." Yussaf, carrying Mofola's old blanket rolled up under his arm flashed the ID tag hanging from his neck at the guards as the brothers passed through the gate. The security guards never even looked at them and they continued on through the mine property to the compound where Yussaf was staying.

The compound was situated on the far perimeter of the mine property. There were eight double-story hostels, each accommodating one hundred people. The hostels were arranged in a semicircle with the mess and kitchen closing the circle.

The long-term workers were situated in the new wing of the hostel where there were only eight to a room.

In the other rooms there were twelve to a room and the rooms were much smaller. Yussaf and Temba shared a room with six other men, all of them from Mozambique. When they got to the hostel, Temba was sitting on the steps leading up to their room, talking to one of the roommates. He did not see them approaching and when they were a few metres away Yussaf called out, "Temba, see who has come to visit us."

Temba did not recognize Mofola dressed in Yussaf's yellow waterproofs and his mine tin hat. Mofola removed the tin hat and said, "My big brother, don't you want to greet your youngest brother?" Only then did Temba recognize Mofola.

Temba jumped up and gave Mofola a big bear hug, and said, "My little brother, how did you get here? The last we heard you were working in Inhambane." Temba put his hands on Mofola's shoulders and took a step back, "Just look at our little brother—he is bigger than me."

The three brothers sat on the steps talking, the mine hooter had sounded at six o'clock signalling that it was time for dinner, but they carried on talking, it was only when the outside lights came on that they realized that they had not yet eaten; the mess would close at half past seven. "Come, little brother," said Yussaf, "we must get you into some other clothes and go and get some food. I'm sure you must be very hungry."

Between the two brothers they managed to find some clothes that fit him, as well as a spare tin mug, plate, and spoon. They then all walked over to the mess and stood in the queue waiting to be served.

With all the excitement of meeting his brothers, Mofola had forgotten how hungry he was and when he got the first smell of food his empty stomach started to rumble, reminding him that he had not eaten for two days.

As they got to the serving area, Yussaf said something to the serving cook, and when Mofola put out his plate to be served he got a double helping of *maize-samp*, beans and meat. Mofola's plate was so full he had to hold it with two hands. Most of the workers had already eaten, so the three of them managed to find a table where they could sit alone. As soon as he sat down, Mofola started to eat. He could not remember having tasted food so good. He finished what he had on his own plate and then ate what Yussaf and Temba had left on their plates.

Temba took the three mugs and went and filled them up with hot coffee from one of the urns near the serving area. "No wonder our young brother is so big, he eats like a hungry lion," said Yussaf as Temba put down the tin mugs of hot coffee on the table.

They sat around the table in the mess discussing how they could get Mofola a job on the mine until the cleaners told them that they were going to lock up the mess for the night.

They decided that Yussaf would speak to his boss Vissie in the morning, as he had a good relationship with him. Yussaf knew the whole family, as he would go over to boss Vissie's house on the Sundays that they did not have to work on the mine. He would do garden work and any other odd job that Vissie wanted him to do.

They walked back to the compound and sat outside on the steps with some of the other men who shared the room with the two brothers, Yussaf introduced Mofola to their roommates. They all wanted to know what was going on back home as most of them had not been home for two to three years. They continued to talk, sitting on the steps until the first hooter sounded, signalling that it was ten minutes to nine o' clock and that in ten minutes the lights in the rooms would be switched off.

They all lent Mofola their extra blankets and when he protested that he was quite used to sleeping on the hard ground, one of them said, "Here we are all family—one day you can help one of us."

Mofola folded the blankets in half and laid them on the floor between the beds of his two brothers. He could not remember when he had last slept on such a soft bed.

Chapter 22

The next morning the hooter sounded at five o' clock, signalling that it was time to get up and get ready for work. The two brothers told Mofola to stay near their room. He could sleep on one of their beds if he liked and no one would take any notice of him, as there were lots of men who were sleeping during the day because they worked the night shift.

On Mondays, Vissie and Joe did maintenance on the surface. They were busy in the compressor house checking the switchgear and motors. They were alone, so Joe spoke to Vissie about Mofola. At twelve o'clock they went back to the workshop to eat their lunch sandwiches and have a mug of tea. They agreed that Joe would go back to the compound and bring Mofola down to the workshop to meet Vissie. If he liked Mofola, then he would give him a job at home doing the garden and other odd jobs.

Joe went back to the compound to fetch Mofola. Mofola was sleeping on Joe's bed. "Hey, little brother, wake up, my boss wants to see you, and if he likes you he will give you a job at his home."

"But what do I say, I can't speak *Afrikaans.*"

"Look, all you have to say is *ja* to my boss when I nod my head like this and *nee* to my boss when I shake my head like this," he said, nodding and shaking his head to demonstrate. "Come, we must go quickly before the lunch break is over."

They hurried back to the workshop. "You stand here outside and wait. I'll go and tell boss Vissie you are here. If someone speaks to you just say 'boss Vissie,' OK?"

Mofola stood and waited outside the workshop, very nervous, not daring to look at anyone who went into or left the workshop. He had been standing there just outside the door where Joe had left him for about five minutes when the electrical workshop foreman came walking up to the door.

"Who you waiting for?" asked the foreman.

"Boss Vissie," replied Mofola.

"OK, " said the foreman as he stepped into the workshop, then took a step back and asked, "does he know you are waiting for him?"

"Boss Vissie," replied Mofola again.

"Yes, I know it's boss Vissie you are waiting for, you stupid *houtkop,* but does he know you are here?"

Just then Vissie and Joe came out of the workshop. "Hello, Vissie," said the foreman. "This *houtkop* here says he's waiting for you."

"Thank you, sir," said Vissie, and the foreman went on inside.

"So you are Joe's youngest brother?" asked Vissie.

Joe, standing just behind his boss, smiled and nodded his head.

Mofola smiled and said, "*Ja*, boss."

"Can you work in the garden?"

Joe smiled again and nodded.

Mofola smiled and said "*Ja*, boss."

"Joe tells me you got no permit to work in South Africa?"

Joe looked sad and shook his head.

Mofola looked sad and said, "*Nee*, boss."

"OK, Joe, tell your brother to meet us at my car when we knock off," As he turned to go back into the workshop, he looked again at Mofola and asked, "So what's your name?"

Mofola looked at Joe and Joe pulled a face and shrugged his shoulders.

Mofola looked at Vissie and shrugged his shoulders.

Vissie looked again at Joe and asked, "He does have a name, doesn't he?" and looked questioningly again at Mofola.

Joe quickly made his hands into a fist and brought them up to his face.

Mofola smiled and said, "Boxer."

"Your name's Boxer?" asked Vissie.

Joe smiled and nodded his head.

Mofola smiled and said "*Ja,* boss."

"OK, Boxer, you come with your brother to my house this afternoon and we will see how you work in the garden.

That afternoon Joe and Mofola worked in the garden. Joe showed him how to push the lawnmower, pick up the grass, cut the edges with the clippers, and dig out the weeds. By six o'clock they had finished the whole garden. Vissie and his wife, Riana, came outside to inspect what they had done. Riana walked around the garden with her two boys, Gerrie, six, and Danie, three; their baby daughter of four months was asleep in the house. Riana was impressed with what she saw. Riana was very house proud, she kept it spotlessly clean and tidy without a housemaid. She insisted that if she could keep the house clean and tidy then Vissie could keep the garden the same way.

Vissie and his wife went back inside the house, Joe and Mofola sat outside on the steps of the back porch with the two boys who were jabbering away to them in *Afrikaans*. Mofola could not understand a word they were saying, so Joe translated some of the things they said and they would all laugh. The little ones did not know what the men were laughing at, but because Joe and Mofola were laughing, they laughed as well.

Vissie came out onto the back porch and spoke to Joe, as he had now realized that Mofola could not understand a thing. "My wife and I have discussed it and we have decided that Boxer can stay here in the *kaffir* room at the back of the garage. We can't pay him much but we will give him food. There is an old bed in the room that the *kaffir* girl used that was here before we came to this house two years ago. He must just clean out the room, as it is full of junk."

Vissie was pleased that Riana had agreed to let Boxer help around the house, as cleaning, gardening, and that sort of thing was not on the list of things he liked to do most. What Vissie liked most was to tinker in his garage, work on his car, and drink beer. With the new baby, Riana was finding it difficult to cope with the two boys and do all the housework; as a result, when Vissie came home from work he would have to do a lot of the chores around the house and he hated that. Boxer would be a big help and this would take a lot of the pressure off him.

Joe and Boxer immediately started to clean out the old maid's room at the back of the garage. Riana gave Mofola an old blanket and cushion, there was a small iron bed that was tied together with wire with an old coyer-hair mattress that was full of holes but it was better than sleeping on the floor.

It was starting to get dark and Joe said he had better be going back to the compound, as blacks walking in the streets at night got arrested even if it was before the nine o' clock curfew. Mofola continued to sort out his new accommodation and by eight o' clock the room was liveable.

Mofola, or Boxer as he was now known, soon fit into the Vissers' way of life. Riana would have to take the baby to the mine hospital once a week and lug the boys along with her. It was quite a business pushing the pram and trying to control the two boys and stop them from running in the road.

The mine hospital was situated outside the main mine property about a mile from the Visser house and Riana would end up having to carry the youngest boy most of the time. After two weeks, Riana decided to leave the two boys in Boxer's care.

"You look after my two boys," she said to Boxer, explaining to him in broken *Afrikaans* and sign language that she was taking the baby to the hospital and he must look after the boys until she came back. She also made it quite clear to him that if anything happened to them she would cut his throat, drawing her flat hand across her throat. "You understand, Boxer, what I say?"

By this time, with the two boys following him around all day jabbering away to him in their language, he soon got to understand a bit of *Afrikaans* and knew what Riana meant, and said, "Yes, Missus, Boxer look for the boys, Missus go hospital, boys OK, no cut Boxer throat." He said it in broken *Afrikaans* and they all laughed. The boys were only too glad to stay with Boxer and not have to walk all the way to the hospital with their mother.

Boxer got on well with the two boys; they reminded him of his two nephews back home. Using pieces of thin rubber strips cut from an old motor car inner tube that Boxer had found when he cleared out his room and a Y-shaped stick cut from an old peach tree branch, they made a catapult. They put up tin cans on the fence that bordered the open *veld* and shot at them with stones collected in the garden.

By the end of the second month Boxer could make himself understood in *Afrikaans* and the boys could speak quite a few words in *Shangane*. Riana would send him to the store with a list of things to buy. He was now used to the money and already knew the prices of the more common commodities.

On Saturday afternoon Joe would come to visit him at the Visser's house and he and Joe would clean and polish Vissie's car. That's when the Vissers didn't go out with the car. If they did, then Joe and Mofola would wander around Roodepoort and window-shop, as all the stores closed at one o'clock on Saturday afternoon and only opened again on Monday morning at eight. Some of the cafes remained open until six o'clock and there was one particular cafe that sold fish and chips that Mofola frequented. He would buy a packet of fish and chips for six pence and a soft drink for three pence; that was the only luxury he would afford himself.

The Vissers paid him six pence a day, which came to one pound two and six pence a month. Most of this he saved in an old coffee tin that he hid in the roof rafters of his room.

Boxer still had his sights firmly fixed on working underground on the mine but without a work permit he could not get a job on the mine. Vissie had a friend who worked in the Native Affairs commissioner's office on Jeppe Street in Johannesburg who was trying to arrange a reference book and a work permit for him. It was going to cost him five pounds, which was nearly five months' wages, but he did not mind, as he would be able to earn big money on the mine once he had the work permit.

The Saturday before Christmas of 1962, Vissie had a barbecue party at home in the backyard. Both Joe and Boxer were there to help with the making of the fires and the cooking of the meat. Riana had made them both long white aprons so that they looked the part. One thing you could not teach Boxer was how to cook meat on an open fire—he was an expert, having spent a good part of his youth up in the mountains cooking for himself on an open fire.

Vissie had learned some time ago, that Boxer was an expert when it came to a barbecue, so he left the cooking to Boxer and Joe. This gave Vissie more time to stand around the fire with his friends and get drunk. The womenfolk sat in the living room and kitchen discussing their respective husbands and gossiping about each other. The children ran around screaming and shouting and being raucous as only children can be, and occasionally one of the mothers would come out and tell her respective children to shut up and stop screaming, but other than that they all seemed to be having a good time.

The more the men drank the more generous they became offering Joe and Boxer beer and a tot or two of brandy and water. Boxer did not like the taste of alcohol, but Joe was quick to accept the occasional beer or tot; he said it was Christmas and one should be happy. Boxer knew of much better things to make him happy.

By eight o' clock most of the guests, with the exception of the immediate family, had all gone home. Joe was very unsteady on his feet so Boxer told him to sleep with him in his room for the night; if he walked back to the compound in that state he would surely get arrested and be put in jail.

Boxer went into the kitchen and asked Riana if he could help with the washing of the dishes and other things before he went to bed.

"No, Boxer, you can go to bed and in the morning you can clean up outside."

When he got to his room Joe was lying on his back on Boxer's bed fast asleep and snoring. Boxer took one of the blankets and curled up on the cold cement floor and went to sleep.

On Sunday morning Boxer was up early cleaning up outside, picking up all the empty beer bottles and putting them into wooden crates ready to take back to the liquor store. By the time Joe got up, Boxer had finished cleaning up outside. Joe decided to go back to the compound, as he was not feeling very well.

At half past nine Vissie came out on the back porch half dressed for church with his black shoes in his hand. "Boxer," he shouted, "where are you?"

Boxer came running out from his room and said, "Morning, my boss, how the boss feeling today?"

"Don't you even ask, we are already late for bloody church and my shoes are dirty, here," he said, passing the shoes to Boxer's outstretched hand. "Get the polish from the kitchen and clean them quick, quick." He then went back into the house to finish dressing. Boxer quickly cleaned them and put them inside the kitchen door.

Ten minutes later the whole family came running out of the house. "Boxer, open the gate," shouted Vissie as he pulled the car out of the garage. Boxer stood at the gate waiting for them to drive out so he could close it again. As the car drew alongside him, Vissie wound down the widow and handed Boxer a brown envelope.

"What's this, boss?" asked Boxer.

"Well, open it, you dumbhead" Boxer quickly opened the envelope and took out the official looking letter.

"So what's it say?" asked Vissie, knowing full well that Boxer could not read *Afrikaans*. "Here, give it to me," he said, taking the letter back from him.

"Come on now, Vissie, we are already late for church. You know how all the people stare at you when you come in late," protested Riana.

"So let them look, what's the difference if we are five minutes or ten minutes late? They are still going to look; it gives them something to talk about after the service."

"It's from the commissioner of Native Affairs, it's your work permit for three years," said Vissie, giving it back to him. Boss Lombard gave it to me last night at the party, I did not give it to you then, because I thought you might have gotten drunk and burned the meat."

"Thank you, thank you, my boss," shouted Boxer clapping his hands and making little bows as Vissie pulled the car out onto the road.

"Next week you must go and get your reference book," shouted Vissie through the open window as he pulled away up the road.

When the Vissers got back from church, Boxer was waiting at the gate for them. He opened the gate and Vissie pulled up outside the garage. Vissie got out of the car with the rest of the family, then waited for Boxer to close the gate and come up the driveway while the others went inside the house. "So are you going to work for me for five months or are you going to pay me the five pounds I paid to boss Lombard?" asked Vissie.

"If the boss want me to work, then Boxer work for the boss for five months. If the boss want, I pay the boss the money, it is also good, just like the boss and the missus want Boxer can do."

"Look, the missus and me, we have talked about this when we came from the church. The missus wants you to stay and work because you help her so much with the boys and you keep the garden nice and clean, but she also knows how much you want to go and work on the mine, so we think we will let you go to the mine as soon as you get a job there.

"Thank you, my boss. The boss and the missus is too good."

"Yes, but there is one condition, you must come every Sunday and clean the garden and help the missus with cleaning the windows and that sort of thing for the whole of next year, then you don't have to pay me back the five pounds, so what you think?"

"The boss is too good. Boxer will work for the boss and the missus every Sunday, no problem."

"OK, Boxer, that's a deal. Now, you know boss Jannie Grobler, that big man who comes here sometimes to visit. He was here last night at the party, and he tells me that his piccaninny is going back to Mozambique in January and he is looking for a new assistant boy. If you want, I will speak to him on Monday."

Chapter 23

On the morning of January, 3, 1963, Boxer stood on the bank of number two shaft at Roodepoort Frontier Mining waiting with fifty-odd other mine workers for the man-hoist to take them underground. True to his word, Vissie had spoken to Jannie and he had organized Boxer a job through the mine personnel department as Jannie's *piccanin*.

Boxer spent the first three weeks at the mine training school, learning the various aspects of the job as well as the language spoken on the mines called *Fanagalo*. *Piccanin* was the name given to a miner's assistant. He would carry the miner's bag, which contained his breakfast, lunch, and thermos flask of tea or coffee and anything else he needed. He would also carry the charging stick, which was similar in size to a broomstick handle and used to push the sticks of dynamite into the holes in the rock drilled by the drilling team.

At first Boxer wanted to be a driller, or machine boy, as they were referred to on the mine but when Vissie told him that he could earn just as much and more if he proved himself a *good piccanin* and assisted the miner in all aspects of the job, he could earn good bonus money. Boxer thought that this *piccanin* job could also be good.

At the mine school they tested his IQ and found it to be of a higher percentage than the average laborer, they also suggested that Boxer learn the job of a *piccanin* as it carried more responsibility and was more intellectually demanding than the other jobs.

Then as now, mining was a dangerous job and miners had to always keep a cool head. The miner, his *piccanin*, and the machine boys formed a team. The better the team worked together, the less chance that accidents would happen.

Once the man-hoist off-loaded the miners and their teams at the various levels, the men made their way on foot along the winding tunnels to their respective working sites. They would then inspect the previous day's blasts to see how clean the cut was and, most important, check to see if there were any misfires.

When the miner was satisfied that the working face was safe, he would pry off any loose rock from the roof, or hanging wall, as it was referred to in mining terms, with a large crowbar and start to hose down the working face. As soon as he accomplished this, the timber men would move in to shore up the hanging wall. The ventilation team would be busy connecting more ventilation ducting to the existing ducting and replacing any ducting that may have gotten damaged during the blast. As soon as this was all done to the miner's satisfaction, the lashers would move in and start clearing the rock from the blast. The loose rock would be shovelled into cocopans and trammed back to the ore pass bins, where it would later be loaded into the skip and hoisted to the surface. The miner would then start to mark the face with crosses, indicating where the drilling team should drill. Once the shot holes were marked, the drilling team would move in and start drilling. When the machine boys were finished with the drilling operation, the miner would then charge the holes with explosives ready for the next blast. This was basically the daily exercise carried out by the miner and his team.

The miner's wage or salary was determined by the cubic capacity of rock or ore he mined from his *stope*. This was referred to as fathomage and was measured by the surveyors once a month.

Boxer was still very nervous about going into this deep hole; it was as if they were going into the very bowels of the earth. He had been down underground a number of times with the training school, but they never went very deep, just a hundred feet or so down an incline shaft that they walked down and up. He had heard stories from the old hands about the steel rope breaking and the cage with all the men plunging to the bottom of the shaft, killing all the occupants. He remembered his father speaking about it when he worked on the mines back in the thirties.

The miners would sometimes play pranks on the new recruits and arrange with the hoist driver to uncouple the winder from the clutch and let the cage full of workers free-fall for three or four seconds before applying the brakes.

This was the most frightening experience, as you assume in those few seconds that the rope has broken and you are falling to your death at the bottom of the shaft. Suddenly the brakes come on and the cage jerks to a stop and then shoots up the shaft again as if it were tied to a piece of elastic. It would continue to yo-yo for some time before the hoist driver would lower it to its first destination.

Many grown men have been known to mess in their pants under such circumstances. Of course such pranks were strictly forbidden and the culprits, if found out, would be immediately dismissed, but this did not seem to deter the men from having what they regarded as just a bit of fun.

The double-decker man-hoist would arrive at the bank and the onsetter would signal to the hoist driver by ringing a bell that people would be entering the cage. The hoist driver gave the same signal back, acknowledging that the message was understood. Only then would the banksman open the cage door and let the men enter. All the black workers would travel in the lower part of the double-decker cage and all the white workers would travel in the upper part. The theory being, that if the rope broke, then the black people in the lower part of the cage would somehow cushion the impact of hitting the bottom.

Boxer got into the cage with about forty other workers. He kept quiet, not wanting to show the others that he was a "newy." He hoped that they did not notice how his legs were trembling. In any case, the brand-new overall he was wearing was a sure give away that he was a new recruit. The workers had their own way of initiation, as the hoist dropped below the surface into the complete darkness. The "oldies" would all switch off their battery-operated cap lamps and then someone behind the new recruit would bang him on his tin hardhat. As he turned to see who it was, someone on the opposite side or in front of him would do the same. This would continue until the cage came to rest at the station where they all got out. Once they got onto the station the "oldies" would all stand together, remove their tin hats, and bang them against their battery packs as a salute to the "newy."

Joe had warned Boxer that this may happen so when the lamps went out he braced himself for the volley of blows that followed. When he alighted from the cage they all gave him the traditional salute. "Go well, my brother, and may the sunlight forever hit your eyes," they all shouted as they moved off to their respective working areas. The daylight hitting your eyes was the first thing that one noticed as you broke surface coming up from underground.

Boxer stood and looked around at the station of number twelve level, waiting for his boss Jannie to get out of the upper deck of the cage that had to be lowered to the station floor once all the blacks had got out from the lower deck. He was surprised at how big the chamber was that was blasted out from the side of the shaft and how brightly it was lit up with electric lights. There were wire mesh enclosures with locked gates with signs saying "Store" and "First Aid" with a big red cross on the side. The signs were in English, *Afrikaans*, and *Fanagalo*. further down there were other mesh enclosures but he could not see the signs.

On the one side of the station another chamber had been blasted out to make a big room. Boxer could not see inside from where he was standing, but at the entrance it said "Number 5 Pump Station."

"Hey! Boxer, we have work to do, or are you going to stand there all day dreaming?" Jannie took off at a fast pace down the haulage, walking next to the tramming line. Boxer had not heard his boss come up behind him because of all the noise in the station, he picked up the brown cloth bag that contained Jannie's breakfast and thermos flask of tea, slung it over his shoulder, and ran down the haulage to catch up with Jannie.

"Hey, you watch what you are doing with that bag, dom kop. If you break my thermos I'll break your fucking head."

"Sorry, my boss," panted Boxer, having caught up with Jannie. He was finding it a bit difficult to run in the rubber boots that had been issued to him; they seemed a bit big for his feet.

"Hey! you keep the light from your cap lamp on your head out of my eyes when you talk to me and you had better learn this fast if you want to stay working for me," said Jannie, getting irritated with his new *piccanin*, "The next time I'll knock the fucking thing right off your head, do you hear me?"

"Yes, my boss, sorry, boss, I not do it again."

"You had better not. Come on, we have still a long walk to the working *stope* and time is money, just you remember that."

"Yes, boss," replied Boxer as they walked the rest of the fifteen minutes in silence at a fast pace down the dark haulages to Jannie's box.

Boxer thought to himself as they walked along that he was not getting off on a good foot with his new boss. He knew that boss Jannie was a difficult man and that he did not take nonsense from anyone, especially the kaffirs. He should have remembered what they taught him in the training school—never to shine your light in the face of a person, but with all the excitement of his first day he had forgotten and he cursed himself under his breath for this.

The miner's box was just that, a wooden box the size of a two-seater table nailed together from bits of scrap wood, with two stools made from sawn off logs with a piece of plank nailed to it as the seat. It was situated in a convenient little alcove in the haulage, about three or four hundred yards from the working face. As the working face moved with each blast, after a week or so the box would be moved to a new site so as not to be too far from the working face.

Boxer took the tin of sandwiches and thermos flask out of the bag and put them both in the box. Jannie took two thick yellow crayons from inside the box and gave them to Boxer together with a hundred-foot cloth tape measure. Boxer put the things into a canvas bag. "Come, we need to go and inspect the last blast." Boxer slung the bag over his shoulder and followed Jannie to the *stope* face.

When they got to the working face, having slid along the floor of the *stope* on their backsides—the *stope,* being only about three feet high—the drilling team were already there connecting up their machines to the compressed air and getting ready to start drilling. The timber men had already pried off all the loose hanging rock and were shoring up the roof with timbers. The ventilation crew were connecting up more piping to the existing ventilation pipe.

Jannie passed the beam of his lamp over the working face to see if there were any misfires. Satisfied that there weren't any, he then checked to see that the "reef" was still running in the right direction. The thin two-inch-wide carbon leader referred to as the reef was what contained the gold deposit. He proceeded to mark the places where he wanted the machine boys to drill, explaining to Boxer all the time as he went along what he was doing and why he was marking the face in that specific way. He was very thorough and took time to explain in detail to Boxer when he thought he did not understand.

Jannie took out his notebook and recorded the number of holes to be drilled and also took note of the rock formation. They then moved onto the next *stope*, but this time Jannie told Boxer "Now it's your turn, let's see if you took note of what I was doing."

Boxer unclipped the lamp from his tin hat and cast the beam over the working face paying special attention to what he had learned at the mine school and what Jannie had said. Satisfied that there were no misfires, he took the thick yellow crayon out of the bag and proceeded to mark the face. Just before he made the cross on the rock face with the crayon he would hold it on the spot and look at Jannie who would give his approval or would shake his head. He would then move in closer and explain why here and not there and so they marked the whole face with Jannie correcting Boxer every time he made a mistake; in this aspect Jannie was very patient.

Back at the box, Jannie took out his notebook and worked out how many sticks of dynamite, detonators, and rolls of fuse wire he needed. While he was busy working this all out, he ate one of his sandwiches for breakfast or "*samies,*" as they were known on the mines, and drank a mug of tea poured from his thermos flask.

"Come, Boxer, I'll show you where the explosives are stored, put that *golavan* onto the track he said pointing to a small flatbed tramcar lying on its side next to the tramway. Boxer turned it over and hefted it onto the track, first the front wheels and then the back two.

They moved down the haulage in the direction they had come from the shaft, with Jannie leading the way and Boxer pushing the *golavan* behind him. After walking for ten minutes they took a branch tunnel which led to a cavern. Electric lights were suspended from a steel wire rope running down the centre of the cavern's roof. There was a store area fenced off like the other ones Boxer had seen near the station. On the gate was the wording "Explosive Magazine" with big yellow and red "Danger" signs tied all over the fence.

"Morning, *madala,*" said Jannie, greeting the old man sitting behind the gate of the magazine. "How is the explosive this week, old or fresh?" Not waiting for him to reply, he said, "This is my new *piccanin*, Boxer," and handed him the list of explosives they required. The old man looked at the list, unlocked the gate and started to pass out boxes of explosives, detonators, and fuse wire to Boxer who loaded them onto the *golavan*.

Jannie picked up one of the rolls of fuse wire and examined it. "Why do they keep buying this shit?" he said to the old man holding up the fuse wire.

"I don't know, boss," said the old man. "I just issue it, I don't buy it."

"*Ja, ja*," said Jannie, "that's what you always say. One day we are going to have an accident and then those 'know it all cheapskate managers' will listen to us and not buy this crap." He threw the roll back onto the tramcar. He signed the book, making a squiggle next to his name where the old man had written in the amount of explosives he had handed out.

Boxer pushed the tramcar back to the box and they immediately started to prepare the explosive they needed for each working site. Jannie showed Boxer how to measure the length of fuse wire and how to connect it to the detonator and insert it into the stick of dynamite using a thick piece of copper wire with one end sharpened to a point, much like a thick knitting needle. The stick of dynamite would be pierced on the side at the top end of the stick with the sharp end of the piece of copper wire to a depth to accommodate the length of the detonator.

By the time they had finished fusing the explosives the drilling team had finished drilling in the first *stope* and had moved on to the second *stope*. "Come, let us take this lot here," he said, pointing to one pile of explosives stacked on one side with their individual fuse wires neatly coiled up, "and go and charge up G *stope*."

Boxer loaded the pile of explosives onto the *golavan* and pushed it along the haulage to where the track ended. Jannie took a bundle of explosives under his one arm with his arm through the coils of fuse wire and made his way into the slope, half crawling and half sliding on his backside. Boxer followed him with another bundle of explosives and the charging stick. It was very hot and humid in the *stope* and there was still a lot of moisture hanging in the air that had been created by the machine boys' drilling operation. The ventilation system would still take some time to clear the air in the *stope*.

By the time they had reached the face they were both wet from perspiration and breathing heavily. Jannie used the charging sick to tamp the explosive into the holes drilled by the drilling team, pushing the sticks of dynamite as far as they would go to the end of the holes.

Boxer watched carefully what Jannie was doing, passing him the explosives as he finished charging a hole. When all the holes were filled, Jannie uncoiled the fuse wires from each charge, carefully laying them out and cutting them all to the right length so that when he lit the fuses the explosives would all explode in the sequence he wanted.

Jannie could manage up to three stopes a shift with his old *piccanin*. This would push up his fathomage and bonus considerably. It would still be some time before he could let Boxer charge up a *stope* on his own, although this was highly illegal; the mine management turned a blind eye to it, as it gave them a bigger production.

They made their way back to the box with Boxer pushing the empty *golavan* behind Jannie. "Now we wait for the machine boys to finish drilling F *stope*," said Jannie, reaching inside the box for his tin of *samies* and thermos flask. "We can then go and charge up that section." He was hungry and could already taste the bacon and egg *samie* he had left over from breakfast.

As he picked up the samie tin he knew without looking inside that it was empty. "Who the fuck has been eating my *samies* again, was it you?" he asked, shining his light into the empty box and showing it to Boxer sitting on the other side of the box. Jannie knew full well that it was not Boxer, but he was so mad he had to pick on someone.

"No, never, my boss, I never eat the boss's food. I was with the boss all the time," protested Boxer. "*Ja, ja*, I know," said Jannie. "It's got to be that thieving bastard again up to his bloody tricks. One day I'm going to catch the bastard and I'll cut his balls out."

"But who take the food from the boss?" inquired Boxer.

"I don't know. It started last year. Every now and then some bastard would steal my *samies*. I swear if I catch the son of a bitch I'll kill him."

They waited at the box, sitting in silence until the boss-boy of the drilling team came and told them they were finished at F *stope*.

"Come load the explosives. Let's go and charge up F slope," said Jannie as he stormed off down the tunnel leading to the *stope*, not waiting for Boxer to finish loading the *golavan*. Boxer took off after him at a trot pushing the *golavan* in front of him.

When Boxer arrived at the end of the tramline a few minutes later out of breath, Jannie was waiting for him. "What took you so bloody long?" he shouted. "Do you want to carry all the explosives into the *stope* by yourself?" asked Jannie now in a foul mood. He'd had his *samies* stolen and Boxer was the nearest one to take his anger out on.

They quickly charged up F *stope* and went back to the box to wait until ten past two, which was the time that Jannie started to walk down to G *stope*. Boxer could already hear the rumblings of blasting further away from them. They had to wait until the other miners came past his section before he could light up his sections.

One of the *piccanins* of the other miners came to them as they stood waiting at the entrance to the *stope* and told them it was OK, they could light up their sections, as the miners in front of them were now all making their way back to the shaft station.

"Give me a *cheesa-stick*," said Jannie, holding out his hand for Boxer to hand him an igniter stick. Jannie took out his pocket-knife and cut the tip off the *cheesa-stick* and lit the cut-off end with a match. It burned with an orange glow much like a sparkler on Guy Fawkes night. Using the *cheesa-stick* he proceeded to light the fuses in sequence. When there was only a short piece of the igniter left in his hand he said to Boxer, "Quickly get another one ready."

"Sorry, boss, I don't have a knife."

"If you don't have a knife then bite the fucking top off and hurry up. This one is about to die." The *cheesa-stick* is about ten inches long, as thick as a man's finger, and looks much like a long thin cigar.

Boxer pulled out another stick from the bag, bit the top off and handed it to Jannie who took the small burning piece and lit the new stick and threw the small piece still burning on the ground where it rolled into a pool of water and lay there burning and spluttering until it had burned itself out. Jannie finished lighting the rest of the fuses, took out his knife again and cut the top off the stick that was burning.

Boxer knew that cutting the burning end off was the only way to stop it burning all the way through to the end. He had learned that in the mine school. He was very relieved that Jannie was not that angry to make him bite the end off the burning *cheesa-stick*.

They finished lighting up F *stope*, went back to the box to pick up the flask and empty samie tin, and made their way to the shaft station. Boxer's mouth was burning from the cordite in the igniter-sticks he had bitten off and no matter how much he spat, it did not seem to help; his tongue was blistered and felt thick in his mouth.

As they walked back down the tunnel to the shaft station Boxer could hear explosions all around and feel the shock waves as the first of their sections went off. His first instinct was to run, but he restrained himself and continued to follow in the footsteps of Jannie down the haulage.

At the station they had some time to wait before the next cage arrived at their level. They sat waiting on a pile of timbers. "Hand me my tea flask," said Jannie. Boxer took the thermos flask out of the bag and passed it to Jannie. "Where's your mug?" asked Jannie.

"It's in the bag, my boss," replied Boxer.

"Well it's no fucking good in the bag, is it? Give it here." Boxer handed his mug to Jannie who poured the rest of the tea in the flask into Boxer's mug. "Rinse your mouth with the tea and don't ever forget your knife again," he said, handing the mug of tea to Boxer.

Back on surface Jannie showed Boxer where to wash all his things in the outside sinks right next to the white men's change rooms. "When you have finished, put the flask and the mug back in the bag and hang it up on this peg here," he said, pointing to where there were rows of pegs on the *veranda* of the change room. Each miner had a peg with his name stamped on a brass tag directly above each peg. After you have washed my overalls and socks, you hang them up on this hanger and hang them on the same peg. I will collect them when I have finished showering and put the clothes in the change room to dry overnight before I go home."

"Now, this is what I want you to do every day unless I tell you otherwise, do you understand?"

Boxer nodded his head and said, "Yes, my boss, every day I make like this."

"Good, as long as you understand, we will get on OK," said Jannie as he walked into the change room.

As soon as Boxer got the job on the mine, he moved from Vissie's old servant's quarters into the mine compound. He was now staying in the old section of the mine compound with twelve other new recruits in a dormitory. As soon as he had finished cleaning Jannie's things and had hung them all up, he went and showered in the blacks' change rooms and changed into other clothes. He then went in search of his brother Joe, whom he found sitting on the steps polishing his shoes.

"So, my little brother," inquired Joe, as Boxer approached him, "how was your first day underground?"

Boxer sat down on the steps next to Joe and told him step by step how his day had gone. When he got to the part where he bit the end off the *cheesa-stick* Joe could not stop himself from laughing. Boxer did not think it was so funny and stuck out his tongue to show Joe. "Look," he said, pointing to his tongue and trying to talk with it still sticking out. Well, Joe nearly fell off the steps, he was laughing so much at Boxer, now trying to talk with his tongue sticking out.

"Hey, little brother, one learns fast here on the mine, so where is your knife?"

"I didn't get a chance to go to the trading store to buy one yet," protested Boxer, rather annoyed that his brother should laugh at his misfortune.

"Come my brother, let me help you," said Joe as he got up and went into his room. Boxer followed him inside. Joe opened his steel locker and from under some clothes he took out a piece of hacksaw blade about six inches long. The teeth had been ground away and it had been sharpened like the blade of a knife, half of the blade was wrapped in insulation tape to form a handle. "Here," he said, "you can use this until you get a chance to go and buy a pocket-knife."

The rest of the month went by without further incident, except Jannie's *samies* were being stolen every so often, which put him in a bad mood again. Boxer was getting to know his boss and managed to keep out of his way and not make mistakes. The piece of cut-off hacksaw blade worked well, so there was no immediate rush to go out and buy a pocket-knife.

On Friday afternoon after payday, Boxer walked down to the trading store where one could buy almost anything, from a box of matches to a bicycle. He walked into the store and went over to the glass display counter where all the different knives were laid out. There were big ones, small ones, and ones with brightly coloured handles and even some with pictures on the handles. All the knives had blades that were less than four inches long, because by law blacks were not allowed to carry a knife with a blade longer than four inches.

The trading store was run by an Indian family. One of them came over to him when he saw that Boxer was looking at the pocket-knives. "So you want to buy a knife?" Boxer nodded his head. The store assistant took out a key, unlocked the showcase, took out five knives, and placed them on the top of the counter. "Which one you like?" he asked. "What about this one here," he suggested, pointing to one of the brightly coloured ones, "or this one with the picture of the Zebra is very nice, and for you I make very special price."

Boxer picked up one or two of the knives, examined them, and put them back on the counter. He shook his head, looked at the store assistant, and pointed to a folding knife with a plain black handle lying by itself on one side. "You want to see this one?" he said as he put his hand inside the showcase and came out with the knife that Boxer had pointed at and put it on the counter in front of him. "This one is too expensive for you," he said and picked it up again and was about to put it back inside of the showcase.

In a flash Boxer's left hand shot out and closed like a vice on the wrist of the storekeeper. Boxer looked the assistant in the eyes and squeezed his wrist until he opened his hand. Boxer picked up the knife with his right hand and then let go of the assistant's wrist. "OK," said the assistant, rubbing his wrist, "you want that knife, and it will cost you seven shillings."

Boxer opened the blade of the knife, turned it over and read the name Joseph Rodger stamped on the back end of the blade. He closed it again and put it on the counter and made to walk away. "What, it's too much?" asked the assistant, "I tell you what, I make for you a special price, just because you my friend. What you say, we make it only six shillings, that a very good price."

Boxer picked up the knife again, opened it and ran his finger over the blade, a small trickle of blood appeared on his finger where he had tested the sharpness of the blade. Boxer had asked Jannie about his knife and he said it was a Joseph Rodger and that it was the best knife to have, but it was also expensive, today maybe four and six pence or even five *bob*.

Boxer closed the knife again and put it back on top of the counter. He put his hand in his pocket and pulled out some coins, he counted five shillings out on the counter and put the rest back in his pocket, picked up the Joseph

Rodger, and pointed it at the assistant and said, "Coolie, don't try to cheat me. You see this blood?" and he turned his finger over revealing the bleeding cut. "This could be your blood next time," he said, and walked out of the store with the knife.

That same Friday afternoon Jannie, Vissie, and two other miners were having a few drinks and playing snooker in the mine recreation club. The subject of eating came up and Kobus, one of the miners, said "You know, guys, I'm getting so fat my clothes don't fit me anymore, my wife feeds me like she's fattening me up for next year's Christmas dinner."

"You know, Kobus, why your wife is making you fat? It's because she caught you with that girl who worked in the assay's office and now she wants you to be a fat slob so the women don't fancy you anymore."

"Ag no, man, do you really think so?"

"Yes, man," teased Vissie. "That's the way the women think today. If they feed you enough then you get too fat and lazy to worry about a bit on the side."

"Ag, man, don't joke, you guys. You must see how much breakfast and lunch she packs me for work, I end up giving most of it to my *piccanin*."

"So why don't you just tell her to give you less to eat?" said Jannie.

"No shit, I can't tell her that, she'll think I don't like her food then she'll give me bugger-all."

The guys laughed and continued to play and chaff each other.

"You know, guys, it reminds me," said Jannie, "have any of you guys had your *samies* pinched underground?"

"Well, not lately," said Kobus, "but some time ago I thought my *piccanin* was helping himself to my grub. Then the one day I found out it wasn't him, because, when they went missing we were together all the time, so I knew it wasn't him."

"So did you find out who it was?" asked Jannie.

"No, not really, because of all the food the wife gave me I didn't worry too much."

"That's funny you should say that," said Arthur, the other miner. "My *samies* also used to go missing every now and then and I also blamed my *piccanin* for stealing them. I nearly fired the little bastard, but then it stopped."

"You know what, chaps? I don't think it's the kaffirs that's stealing our grub. I think it's that fat gut, Sampie Pretorious."

"What makes you say that?" asked Jannie, potting another red ball into the corner pocket.

"Man, it was last year sometime, we all got out of the cage on surface and I was standing on the bank with my samie tin in my hand. I was waiting for my *piccanin* to get out of the bottom deck so I could give him the *samies* that were left over. Sampie, who was also in the cage with me came over to me and said, 'Hey! Are you going to give those leftover *samies* to your *kaffir* boy?' 'Yes,' I said. 'Why do you ask?' 'Ag no, man, don't give those good *samies* to the kaffirs, rather give them to me,' he said."

"So what did you do?" asked Jannie.

"Hell, man, I was a bit embarrassed, so I said, '*Ja*, here, you can have them.' There were two *samies* left in the tin, so I took them out and gave them to him. I tell you, man, before we got to the change room he had stuffed them both in his mouth."

"That fat gut had no shame and whenever we came up from underground at the same time he would ask me if I had any *samies* or fruit left over. Eventually I got sick of him asking me, so I used to just say no. I think he got the message because he stopped pestering me after that. What I want to know is how did he know my wife gave me fruit every now and then?"

Maybe he just guessed," said one of the other guys.

"No, I don't think so," said Kobus, because shortly after that he took over a section near your section, Jannie, and ever since my *samies* have not been touched."

That's it then," said André, "it must have been Sampie who was stealing my grub as well, because about a year ago he was in a section near me and if I remember right it was about that time that my *samies* would go missing and I was blaming the *piccanin*."

"That man's a fat pig," said Jannie, "and he needs to be taught a bloody lesson."

The more the guys drank, the more convinced they got that they had to teach Sampie a lesson. By the end of the night they had worked out a plan to catch Mr. "Fat Gut" Sampie Pretorious. They called their plan the "XYZ Plan" and Jannie said this would be the code he would use for the others to play along.

They did not have long to wait. By Wednesday the following week Janine's *samies* had disappeared again. On the way up from underground that afternoon Jannie got into the cage and moved over next to Kobus. As the cage moved up the shaft to surface, Jannie put his mouth to Kobus's ear and said, "Plan XYZ."

When they got to the change room, Arthur was already in the change room, sitting on the bench next to his locker, taking off his boots. He had come up in the cage before them. As Jannie walked past him on the way to his own locker, he bent over and whispered, "Plan XYZ," and carried on to his locker. Jannie sat down on the bench and started to untie his boots and looked over at Kobus and winked.

The tea boy brought them all tea and they sat around chatting, waiting for their colleagues to finish in the showers. Sampie Pretorious had just finished showering and was standing outside the shower on a wooden duckboard drying himself with his towel.

Vissie walked in and went past Arthur to his own locker. As he passed him, Arthur said, "Hey! Vissie, it's 'XYZ' today."

"OK, I got you," said Vissie and went on and sat down on the bench next to his locker. Kobus looked over at Jannie and said, "Hey, Jannie, why so quiet today, man, did your mother in-law die or something?" The whole change room laughed, as they all knew Jannie didn't get on with his mother in-law, whom he normally referred to as the old bag.

"Hey, guys, don't joke. I did a bloody stupid thing today, man."

"How come?" asked Kobus.

"Well, remember I told you guys that some *kaffir* was always stealing my *samies* and if I ever caught the bastard I would kill him?"

"*Ja*, man, I remember that," said Kobus laughing and playing along.

"So don't tell me you caught someone and dumped him down the mine shaft," said Arthur, joining in on the "XYZ Plan."

Hey, guys, this is serious, man, don't joke, I'm worried sick that I may have killed someone. Now the whole change room went quiet and Jannie had everyone's attention.

"Jees, man, what the hell did you do?" asked Kobus with concern in his voice.

"On Friday my *samies* went missing again," said Jannie and I was so mad that over the weekend I bought some rat poison and the last three days I have made two of the *samies* with rat poison in them. The ones with rat poison had a blob of red jam on the outside, so I would know which ones not to eat. Today I ate the two good ones for breakfast and left the ones with the poison in the tin and then went off to mark up my section. When I got back at about twelve the *samies* were gone."

"Jees! Jannie are you mad?" said Vissie, that stuff can kill you, man. My wife was talking to one of the sisters down at the hospital not so long ago when she used to go down there for her check-ups and the sister was telling her about a young *litie*. Apparently he put some rat poison on his porridge thinking it was sugar. She said the kid was brought in about four hours after he had eaten the stuff. You know it's got quite a delayed action. The poor kid was in a bad way. He had terrible stomach pains and was vomiting all over the place."

"Did he die?" asked Kobus.

"No, lucky not, the hospital made him drink gallons of salty water and they gave him a whole lot of enemas, but at one stage I believe it was touch and go."

"I tell you, man, that *kaffir* who ate those *samies* of yours is soon going to know all about it."

"But what if he dies?" asked one of the other miners in the change room.

"You know, Jannie, you'll be up for culpable homicide," said another.

"No way," you'll be up for murder, Jannie," said one of the others, "because it was premeditated."

Everyone in the change room except Sampie was now discussing the whole affair.

Sampie Pretorious got paler and paler as the discussion went on around the room with everyone now speculating.

"I say if it was one of the kaffirs then he deserves what's coming to him."

"And if he dies?" said another.

"Ag, so what, there's plenty more where he came from."

"*Ja*, but it still will be murder," said another.

"Who's to know? Kaffirs are dying every day, nobody cares. They will think he drank some bad *skokkejaan*, or something."

The talk went on everyone now convinced that it was a black worker. Having decided that it was a black and not a white person, the discussion lost its flavour and soon came to an end.

Sampie could not get his clothes on fast enough, he didn't even bother to tie his shoelaces or button his shirt. He grabbed his things and shot out of the change room nearly knocking the poor old tea boy over as he brought in tea for some of the latecomers.

"What's the rush, Sampie?" shouted Kobus trying to hold back his laughter as Sampie stormed out the door muttering something about having forgotten to pick up his wife.

The next day Sampie's wife phoned the shift boss and told him Sampie was not well and would not be coming in to work, as the doctor had booked him off until Monday. When the shift boss asked what was wrong with him, she said Sampie came home and was complaining of terrible cramps in his stomach and insisted that she should take him to hospital, as he was sure he had eaten rat poison.

"Rat poison?" asked the shift boss. "Where did he eat the rat poison?"

"He wouldn't say," she replied, "but he said he was very sure that it was rat poison."

"And what did the doctor say?"

"He said that if it was rat poison he would have been dead long ago and in any case all the tests that the hospital did on him came up negative."

"So is he all right now?" asked the shift boss.

"Well, not really," she said. The doctor gave him some tablets for the cramps and sent him home, but the thing is when he came home he started to drink glass after glass of salt water which made him so sick that I had to take him back to the hospital, as he became totally dehydrated. They are now keeping him there for a few days under observation."

As it is in most small communities the word soon got around about Sampie Pretorious and the "XYZ Plan." He became the laughing stock of the mine. As result, Sampie could not take the teasing and resigned and went to work on EVME mine in Boksburg.

Chapter 24

Three months later Jannie was back to working three sections, he was so impressed with Boxer's progress that he was even considering opening up a fourth section, as they still had some spare time on their hands.

Jannie and Boxer would each mark up one section and the third one they would do together. Not once did Boxer have a misfire or a bad blast. Jannie's fathomage was up and so was his and Boxer's bonus.

After they had finished charging up their sections they would sit and play cards at the box, using washers as money. Jannie had taught Boxer how to play poker, and Boxer enjoyed the game; it was just another challenge to him to show the boss that he was not stupid. He picked up the game very quickly, and found it very easy to remember the different cards. It was like remembering all the names he had given the cattle and goats. The kings were the bulls, spades were black bulls, clubs the black speckled ones, hearts were the brown bulls and diamonds were the brown and white ones. The queens were the cows and the young calves were the jacks and so on.

For a black man with very little formal schooling, Boxer had a very sharp and analytical mind; he could work out the various card sequences and picture them in his mind. Shuffling the pack was like all the cattle and the goats milling around in one big herd and then breaking up into smaller ones and going off to graze in different areas. He could remember which ones were in which group and when one or two moved into another group he would remember which ones they were.

Playing cards was the same. The black bull cards went into that grazing pile while the brown cow went into another grazing pile and so he remembered the movements of the cards. After three weeks Jannie got tired of playing cards with Boxer as he seldom won a hand. He was convinced that Boxer was cheating but he could never find out how.

Jannie suggested that they increase the numbers on their drilling team and see whether they could manage another section. Early the next morning while they were all waiting for the cage to take them underground, they spoke to the drilling team and asked them how many extra machine boys they would need to drill a fourth section. The drilling team said that they would discuss it and come back tomorrow with an answer. They knew that the more faces they drilled the bigger their pay packet was at the end of the month.

The next day, while waiting for the cage again, the boss boy of the drilling team came over to talk to Jannie and Boxer. "We have spoken to each other and we will try to see if we can manage to drill four stopes on one shift."

"OK," said Jannie, "how many more machine boys will you need?"

"We think only four, but you must let us pick the new ones we need, the guys that can work hard."

"Do you know of any good guys?" asked Jannie.

"Yes we know the good guys, but they work for the other bosses and if we take them then boss Jannie can have the trouble with that other boss."

"Fuck the other bosses," he said. "They must get their asses into gear and do some work for a change. If they can't get organized then we will take their boys. If any of the other bosses gives you trouble, you talk to me and I will sort the buggers out very quickly."

Jannie was known on the mine as a hard worker and, as a result, Jannie always had a nice new car and his pretty wife always had new expensive clothes. There was a lot of jealousy among the other miners but they kept their feelings to themselves, as they knew Jannie had a bad temper and a reputation for sorting out anyone who upset him. Some had already been on the receiving end of Jannie's huge fists.

Two weeks later, they were working five sections, but only blasting four. The way they had organized it was, as soon as they had each charged up two sections, they would quickly go and mark up the fifth section. The drilling team, now with four extra men, would make sure that they were among the first of the workers to go underground at six o' clock in the morning. By the time Jannie and Boxer got to their box, the drilling team had already started drilling the section marked the day before.

By the end of the month they were averaging four blasts for twenty days in a working month. Jannie's team was now cashing in large bonuses. Boxer saved most of his wages in a post office savings account that he had opened. He would write to his mother once a month and post the letter when he went to deposit his wages into his saving account. He would always ask about Negome in his letters to her, but when his mother occasionally wrote back she never ever mentioned Negome.

Although Negome was so far away she was constantly in his mind, and his only goal was to make enough money to be able to go back home and throw it all in front of Victor Aguiar and say to him, "Here is the *ilobola* for Negome." Boxer reasoned that Victor, being a greedy man, would say, "Yes, you can take her, you have anyway destroyed her name so you might as well have her."

He could see Victor's greedy little eyes as he scooped up the money off the counter in his arms, but he would need more money; one hundred pounds sterling would not be enough. Two hundred would be better, especially if he changed it into *escudos*. It would be 12,000 *escudos*, and Victor would surely not be able to resist so much money.

Boxer had worked out that with the money he had already saved and if he continued to save just about all of his wages, by the end of his two-year contract he would have over two hundred pounds sterling. He could even have some extra money to buy some more cattle and goats to add to those his father had given him.

Chapter 25

Vissie was a nonactive member of the OB (Ossewa Brandwag), an extreme right-wing Afrikaner organisation that was founded in 1938 as a cultural organisation based on the old commando system, and which advocated a non-party-political authoritarian state in South Africa. They were a small group who were vehemently against the British and actively protested against the South African Union taking any part in the Second World War. They had a sort of romantic longing to perform heroic deeds in the so-called interest of Afrikanerdom and, as a result, sided with Nazi Germany in the Second World War. Their subversive activities included blowing up railway lines, bridges, roads, and anything that could hinder the Allies.

When the Nationalist Party came into power in 1948, having defeated the former United Party run then by General Smuts, who was pro-British, their activities had curtailed, as their goal to have a government in place that was independent of Great Britain had been partially fulfilled. In their minds, however, there were still too many so-called liberal Afrikaners in the new National

Party and in government. Dr. Malan, the then prime minister, issued warnings against unconstitutional activities, stating that these flirtations and romantic National-Socialistic ideologies were dangerous, unacceptable and had no place in present day society. As a result, a heated dispute developed between the leaders of the National Party and the OB.

After the war, having had their wings somewhat clipped, by a lack of popular support in the party, they took on many other causes that they deemed needed their support, to satisfy their ever-growing egoistic and heroic needs. There were people in high office in government who secretly supported the OB and controlled their subversive activities to a degree. However, in any organisation there are the small groups who always want to be heroes and think that they can go beyond their leader's advice, purely for their own self-interest and satisfaction. The little OB group that Vissie belonged to was just such a rebel group.

The group would often meet at Vissie's house on Saturday afternoons and Boxer would be given the task of making a fire and cooking for them while they drank beer and brandy mixed with Coca-Cola. Over the months, Boxer got to remember their faces. Most of them did not take very well to him at first. They would order him about saying things like, "Hey, you *kaffir*, do this" or, "*Kaffir*, this meat is cooked too much or too little." Boxer just laughed and was always polite to them. As time went by they got used to Boxer being around.

One such Saturday afternoon, after they all had had a good few brandies and Coke, one of them said to Vissie in front of Boxer, "You know, Vissie, there aren't very many good *kaffirs* around, but this one here," he said, pointing to Boxer, "is a *kaffir* who knows his place. He doesn't drink or fuck around, that's what I like."

Thereafter, whenever they came to Vissie's house and Boxer was there, they would joke with him and ask him if he could box and generally make small talk with him while he was cooking.

One Saturday afternoon Vissie came strolling over to Boxer while he was cleaning the car and stood there talking to him with a beer in his hand. "How would you like to make some extra money?" asked Vissie. Vissie knew that Boxer was saving all his money to go back to Mozambique and get married and that he needed a lot of money to pay for his would-be wife.

"The money is always good when you can get it," said Boxer.

"This is good money" said Vissie, rubbing a little mark on the car with the sleeve of his shirt. "If you can help my friend—you see, he has a farm and he is building a dam. But there are a lot of big rocks that he needs to break up, and he needs some explosive, do you think you can get some for my friend?"

Boxer stopped cleaning and leaned back against the car and said, "To take the explosive from the mine, she is not a good thing, because if they catch me they will first put me in the jail and then they will beat me to tell them why I take the dynamite. So I'm thinking maybe this is not so good to do this thing."

"No, well that's fine, no problem. I thought maybe you could help this friend of mine and make some good money, but I will tell him he must try somewhere else," said Vissie, as he walked casually back to the house.

Boxer finished cleaning the car and put all the gardening tools back in the garage and then took the bucket and cleaning cloth back to the kitchen. "I go now, boss," called Boxer from the kitchen.

Vissie came out of the sitting room where he had been listening to the radio and where Sannie was making a dress on her new Singer sewing machine. "OK, Boxer, I'll see you next week," said Vissie.

"This other boss," said Boxer, "how much this good money?"

"One pound," said Vissie."

"I see," said Boxer. "This one pound how many dynamite?"

"One stick and one detonator is one pound," said Vissie.

"I see she is good money but how many sticks this friend for the boss want?"

"Maybe ten will be enough to break all the rock," said Vissie. "You think about it and let me know."

Walking back to the hostel that afternoon, all Boxer could think about was the ten pounds he could make, if he got Vissie the explosive. Ten pounds was more than he could earn in one month even with a bonus. The whole of the following week Boxer looked at means and ways he could get the explosive to Vissie and by the end of the week he had a plan worked out.

The following Saturday in Vissie's garage they discussed Boxer's plan, Vissie making a few suggestions, but overall he thought it was a good plan. Boxer said that it would take at least two weeks to get the ten sticks.

"No, that's fine," said Vissie. "When you give me the last one I will give you the money, is that OK? "If the boss, she think this plan is OK, then we start on Monday."

On Monday, Boxer booked out an extra stick of dynamite and a detonator and when he and Jannie were fusing up the explosives he hid one stick complete with detonator in the back of the box when Jannie was not looking.

As soon as Boxer had lit up his two sections he ran back to the box to make sure he got there before Jannie. He quickly emptied the little tea that was left in Jannie's thermos flask and carefully put the stick of dynamite in the empty flask, screwed the top back on and put it in the bag with Jannie's empty samie tin. By the time Jannie got back to the box, Boxer was all packed up and ready to go, which was not unusual, as he often finished before Jannie.

Once they got to surface Boxer walked straight over to the change rooms where all the *piccanins* were washing their boss's things in the sinks outside. Joe was also there washing Vissie's things. He would normally have washed Vissie's things long before the miners came up from underground, but today Vissie had deliberately kept him busy until he saw the miners walking back to the change rooms past the electrical workshop.

Joe was in a hurry, he had already cleaned Vissie's things and was just putting Vissie's flask and mug in the bag when Boxer arrived at the sink. Joe greeted him and beckoned him over, "Here, you can use this sink. I'm finished I need to go quickly, as I am meeting someone at the gate at three o' clock."

"One of your many girlfriends again, I suppose," teased Boxer. "Leave boss Vissie's bag, I will hang it up when I take boss Jannie's things to hang up." "Thank you, my brother, take care," and Joe was off to meet his someone at the main mine gates.

Boxer took Vissie's thermos flask out of the bag and put it in the bottom of the empty stainless steel sink together with Jannie's flask and mug. He quickly opened both flasks and gently tipped the one into the other making sure the dynamite stick slid into Vissie's flask without breaking the glass inside. He then screwed the top back on and put the flask back in the bag. He then washed all Jannie's things and took the two bags up to the whites' change rooms and hung the bags up on the pegs where they would be picked up by the individuals on their way home.

By the following Wednesday, Vissie had already taken eight sticks of explosives with detonators home and had them safely locked in his steel cabinet in the garage. Boxer had to change his tactics at the washing up sinks to avoid Joe getting suspicious. The one day when Joe had already taken Vissie's bag and hung it up, Boxer was busy doing a transfer from the one flask to the other outside the whites' change room when one of the men came walking out. "Hey what the fuck do you think you are doing? That's not the bag of your boss, that bag is for boss Vissie."

As luck would have it, Vissie was also just about to leave the change rooms when he heard the commotion outside and came running out. "No, it's OK, Gert. I asked him to bring me my flask, as my *houtkop* left it at the wash-up. Thanks anyway for checking."

"No, it's OK, Vissie, anytime, see you around."

On Friday Boxer had the last of the ten explosives in Jannie's flask. He was glad that it was the last one, as he was becoming very nervous and Jannie had noticed and asked him what was wrong with him as it was affecting his work.

The whole of Friday was just one of those days when everything seemed to go wrong. They were running late and, as a result, Jannie never even got to finish his lunch. They had to run to catch the last cage leaving from twelfth level and by the time they got to the station they were both out of breath. Fortunately the cage was also late and they sat on a pile of timbers to catch their breath.

"Pour me some of that tea in my flask," said Jannie. "I'm so damn thirsty having had to run to catch the bloody last cage and now it's late and I promised the missus I would be home early and not go to the club today." Boxer went cold when Jannie asked him for some tea, normally there was seldom any tea left in the flask, but today because they were late Jannie had not had time to finish the tea and Boxer had poured out what was left so that he could put the last stick of dynamite in it.

"I'm sorry, my boss, the tea, she is all finished," said Boxer, hoping Jannie would not remember that he had not finished it all. "Are you sure? I can't remember drinking two mugs today. Give me the flask—let me see." Boxer opened the bag and removed the flask. Instead of putting it in Jannie's outstretched hand he quickly turned off the top and put his finger on the lip of the flask and slowly tipped it up, the stick of dynamite slid down to the opening and stuck on his finger. "You see, my boss, the tea, she is all finished."

Just then the cage arrived, so Jannie had no time to question where the rest of his tea had gone.

As luck would have it, Vissie was still underground repairing an electric feeder cable that had been damaged in a small rock fall the night before. When Boxer went to put Jannie's bag on the peg he could not find Vissie's bag, and didn't know that Vissie was still underground. He quickly turned around and went back to the wash-up sinks to wait for Joe to come. He did not know what else to do, so he took the things out of the bag and made as if he was still washing them.

Then he heard Jannie shouting for him as he came walking down to the wash-up. "What the fuck's taking you so long today, you know I'm in a fucking hurry, haven't you bloody finished yet?" he asked when he saw Boxer with his hands in the sink.

"I sorry, my boss, I still wash the socks for the boss," protested Boxer.

"I haven't time to wait for you to finish, why didn't you first wash the flask and mug? Lately I don't know what's with you, are you trying to fuck with me or something? Give me the flask. The missus can wash it out at home."

Boxer had already unscrewed the top while Jannie was blasting him, and when Jannie asked for the flask he just turned it upside down and let the dynamite stick slide out into the dirty water in the sink. He then quickly put the top on and put it in the bag and gave it to Jannie who grabbed it and stormed off to the car park.

Boxer now had a stick of dynamite with detonator sticking in it lying in the bottom of the sink, he could not risk standing there any longer waiting for Vissie to arrive, he might not even come today, so he took one of Jannie's wet socks and stuffed the dynamite stick into it and put it in the pocket of his yellow waterproof jacket.

Boxer walked down to the blacks' change room, took off his waterproofs, hung them in his wire locker, and went and showered. In the shower he was thinking what to do now, he could not leave the dynamite stick wrapped in the sock, and he had to get the socks back to the whites' change room; otherwise, Jannie would have no socks to wear tomorrow.

Boxer thought he had a plan. He finished showering, got dressed, and took his yellow waterproof and rolled it up with the dynamite stick and Jannie's other sock. He casually walked out of the change room and all the way back to his room in the compound.

Lucky there was no one in the room so he quickly removed the wet dynamite stick and wrapped it in an old newspaper and stuck it under some of his clothes in his locker. Boxer didn't like the idea of having a wet stick of dynamite in his locker. Dynamite becomes unstable, especially when it starts to sweat. He remembered they had taught him that at the mine school, but he had no other place to hide it. He then took Jannie's socks and walked back to the whites' change room and hung the two socks on Jannie's peg and then went back to the compound.

Vissie came up an hour later, he was hoping that Boxer had not brought the last stick of dynamite up from underground today, but there was no way he could tell. For all he knew, Boxer might already be sitting in jail. He asked Joe to go and see Boxer that night and tell him that he would meet him at his car as usual tomorrow after work. "But Boxer knows he must come to you tomorrow after work. He comes every Saturday," said Joe.

"Yes I know, but last Saturday I told him not to come, as we were going away, but we have decided not to go now," lied Vissie.

"OK, my boss, I go tell him."

That night, just before lights out, Joe came over to Boxer's room and gave him the message from Vissie. Boxer asked Joe where he was today as he had not seen him at the change rooms. Joe told him that they were fixing a damaged cable on eighth level and then went back to his own room. Boxer thought at first it was strange that Vissie should send Joe to tell him to be at the car park, but then he realized that Vissie was trying to tell him to bring the dynamite with him the following afternoon when he came to the car.

Saturday afternoon, Boxer stood waiting next to Vissie's car in the car park with a rolled up newspaper under his arm. Vissie was much relieved the next morning when Joe told him that he had given Boxer the message to meet him as usual in the car park. When he saw Boxer standing next to the car with the rolled up newspaper under his arm he knew immediately what was in the newspaper.

"I see you are reading the newspaper now, Boxer," said Vissie when he got within hearing range.

"Yes, my boss, and this newspaper, she is very expensive," said Boxer with a smile on his face. In the car Boxer told Vissie what had happened to him the previous day and they both laughed when he told Vissie how angry boss Jannie was.

"Well, thank god, that's now the lot," said Vissie, as he packed the last stick of dynamite complete with detonator in the steel cabinet with the other sticks. The new stick had started to sweat having been immersed in water. Vissie not being a miner didn't know the difference between stable and unstable dynamite. "Boxer, here is your ten pounds," said Vissie. "I will get it back from my friend when he comes to collect the explosives on Sunday."

Boxer took the ten pound note and kissed it. "This ten pounds nearly make me an old man," he said and they both laughed. Boxer picked up the gardening tools in the garage and went outside to go and start the gardening.

Vissie called after him, "Make sure there is some wood for the fire, I want to *braai* at lunchtime tomorrow."

"OK, my boss. I can chop some wood for the boss—does the boss want me to help him tomorrow with the *braai*?"

"No it's OK, Boxer, it will just be me the missus and the children. You go and have a rest. You deserve one," he said.

Late that afternoon, Boxer went to inform Vissie that he was going back to the mine hostel and that he had cut a pile of wood and stacked it next to the *braai*. "When the boss, he get a chance, he must please sharpen the axe, she is too blunt, and that hard wood, she make the axe blunt too quickly."

"Just leave it on the work bench in the garage and I will sharpen it tomorrow if I get a chance," said Vissie. "See you again next week."

After church on Sunday, Vissie went over to one of the OB members who attended the same church and pulled him aside. "I've got a parcel for you at home," said Vissie. "If you come around eight tonight it will be OK. And don't forget your wallet. It's an expensive parcel."

"How expensive?" inquired the man.

"As we agreed, two for one complete with cap," said Vissie. "And we have ten in the parcel."

"OK, that makes it twenty for the lot. I will collect the package tonight. Well done." And they both joined their families again.

"What was that all about?" asked Riana.

"Old Sarel wants to borrow some tools to fix his car, so I told him OK but he must come after eight," lied Vissie.

"Why so late, man? You know I like to go to bed early on Sunday night and listen to the service on the radio."

"*Ja*, I know, that's why I told him to come late; otherwise, we would have to invite him for dinner and, remember, we were going to have a quiet *braai*, with just the family."

"Yes, that's right, now I remember. You can then tell him I'm already in bed, so I won't have to speak to him, as he gives me the creeps," said Riana.

When Vissie got home after church he changed into a pair of shorts and an old shirt. He sat outside on the back *veranda* with a cold beer and read the Sunday newspaper. Having read all there was to read in the paper, he looked over to where they normally have the *braai* and saw the pile of wood stacked next to it. He then remembered that Boxer had asked him to sharpen the axe.

He stepped off the *veranda* and realized how hot it was. The sun was really baking hot today and he thought to himself that he should move the car into the garage out of the sun. Vissie fetched the keys from inside the house and moved the car three-quarters of the way into garage. He needed some space in front of it where he had his workbench against the back wall.

"It's hot as hell in here," he said to himself as he switched on the light over the workbench, unlocked the tool cabinet, and took out a pair of goggles. The ten sticks of dynamite lay neatly packed one on top of the other in the bottom of the cabinet with a sheet of newspaper over the top of them. One of the top sticks had small beads of sweat clinging to it that had already soaked through the newspaper.

Vissie put on the goggles, switched on the electric grinding wheel, and started to sharpen the blade of the axe. He had hardly started when he felt someone tugging on his pants. He stopped grinding, pulled up the goggles onto his forehead, and looked down at his eldest son.

"Pa, Mamma said I must call you for lunch, she said you must come now before the food gets cold."

"Tell Mamma I'm coming. I just want to finish sharpening this axe, and I will only be a few minutes."

"Can I watch you, Pappie?"

"No, my son, the sparks from the grinding will get in your eyes and burn you. Go inside. I'm coming soon, soon."

Vissie watched as his son ran out of the garage, pulled the grinding goggles down over his eyes and continued to sharpen the axe. That was the last thing that Vissie ever did. Suddenly there was a terrific explosion, followed immediately by a second, as the petrol tank of the car exploded. The garage, its contents, and the car disintegrated in a ball of fire. Pieces of brick, corrugated tin from what was the garage roof, with bits of metal from the car were scattered all over the neighbourhood with every window in the immediate vicinity being shattered. How nobody else got killed or even hurt was a miracle.

The fire truck came from the mine and tried to douse the fire that was raging due to the pile of old tires and paint that Vissie had stored in Boxer's old room behind the garage. The *veld* behind the house had also caught fire and the neighbours were trying to beat it out with wet sacks. The fire brigade from Roodepoort came and sprayed foam on the pile of burning tires, on the car wreckage, and the tires that were lying burning in the *veld* and in the garden.

Black smoke from the burning tires hung like a huge black cloud over the area in the windless afternoon. The fires had all been put out and the fire department was performing the gruesome task of picking up the pieces of Vissie that had not been totally burned or disintegrated and were putting them into plastic bags. People stood around in little groups talking softly, still in shock, not knowing what to do or say. The whole area around the Vissers' house was a mess, the water and foam from the fire department were all over the place and the smell of burned meat and burned tires was still strong in the air.

One of the neighbours had managed to make some strong sweet tea and was trying to get Riana to drink some of it. She was sitting on the bench on the front *veranda* with her youngest on her lap and the other boys clinging to her dress. They were surrounded by broken glass and other debris. The fire chief from the Roodepoort fire station came over to her and offered her his sympathy and asked her what she thought had happened. She said she didn't know. All she could tell the chief was that she had sent her eldest son to go and call his father in the garage, and as the youngster came running into the dining room, having told his father lunch was ready, there was this terrible explosion that threw them all off their feet. Glass came falling in all around them. They were lucky they weren't cut by the falling glass.

"You were all lucky," said the fire chief making a note in his little black book. "If any of you had been in the kitchen when it happened then someone would have been seriously injured, as the whole back side of the house closest to the garage was badly damaged."

"Do you mind if I ask your little boy some questions?" asked the fire chief.

"No, you can ask him," said Riana, "but I don't think he knows much about what happened."

"Hey, big boy," said the fire chief kneeling down in front of him so that they were on the same level, "how are you, OK? Can this uncle ask you some questions? Is that all right, hey?" The youngster continued to look at his feet and nodded his head. "OK, big boy," said the fire chief, "the uncle won't be long, just tell the uncle, when you went into the garage to call your pappie, what was he doing, can you remember?"

"Pappie was making the axe sharp on the machine, he said I mustn't look because the sparks would come in my eyes and burn me."

"So then you ran inside?" said the fire chief.

"Yes, then I ran inside and the big bang make me fall on the floor, when's Pappie coming for lunch, Mama?" he asked as he looked up at her.

"Mrs. Visser, do you know if your husband kept any petrol or old paint and thinners in the garage?"

"Yes he always had a spare tin of petrol for the car and there were also tins of paint and stuff at the back of the garage, I was always telling him he must throw the rubbish away, it smelt like a paint store in there sometimes."

The fire chief went around the back of the house where most of his men were scratching in the rubble. "Well," he said, "have you found anything of interest?"

"No," replied the second in charge, "nothing significant. I think we have gathered up most of the remains of the guy—the rest of him has been blown to little pieces and we will never find them."

"OK," said the fire chief, "let's call it a day. I think I have enough information to make out a report."

"So what's the verdict?" asked the second in charge.

"The bloke was grinding an axe and he had all sorts of flammable stuff in the garage that caught fire from the sparks from the grinding wheel. Then it must have ignited the tin of petrol and then the car's petrol tank exploded."

The funeral for the remains of Vissie took place on Wednesday at the Nederduitse Hervormde Church in Roodepoort, which was the church the Vissers normally attended every Sunday. The service was attended by a large contingency of the mine personnel. Boxer and Joe went to the cemetery and stood with some other blacks on the side, away from the rest of the white people.

A few days later a general notice came around from the mine management banning all forms of flammable liquid from being stored in garages of homes belonging to the mine. Old tires were to be thrown on the dump and not stored on the property. Riana and the boys went and stayed with Vissie's parents in Roodepoort. Six weeks later she received a fat cheque from the mine's benefit and insurance company and with all the other benefits, Vissie's wages, overtime, and leave pay, she was quite a wealthy widow.

Chapter 26

On January 14, 1965, just over a year after the Vissie incident, Boxer stood outside the mine's main gate with about thirty other contract workers. They were all dressed in their best clothes and standing next to new suitcases, tin trunks, and duffel bags, all waiting for the arranged transport to take them to Johannesburg main station and then by train on to Lourenco Marques in Mozambique.

Boxer had been given an excellent reference by the mine personnel department and they told him that he could come back any time and they would have a job for him. They had also provided him with a travel document issued by the Native Affairs Commission office. The issuing of work permits and travel documents to clandestine workers was quite a common practice. Although the official figures for the number of migrant workers, recruited through the WNLA was in the order of three hundred thousand a year, it was estimated that there were close to six hundred thousand migrant workers employed on the South African mines alone at the end of 1959. By far, more clandestine workers than those recruited by the

WNLA, so the authorities were quite familiar with the coming and going of these people.

Boxer stood on the platform of Johannesburg main station with hundreds of other black workers who were returning home to Mozambique. The last time he had travelled on a train was when he was being transported to JBC centre outside Inhambane in Mozambique. This time it was quite different, as everyone was excited and in high spirits, talking and laughing at the top of their voices—the noise was unbelievable, it was like a carnival with everyone in brightly coloured shirts and fancy new hats. The railway personnel had a tough time trying to control the rowdy crowd.

"Stand clear, stand clear on platform three," shouted the voice over the PA system. With much huffing and puffing, the train eased into the station with smoke billowing out of the smoke stack and steam hissing out from under the garratt and locomotive. The smoke from the train hung in the station like a huge grey cloud, unable to quickly escape into the blue sky above, because of the low roof covering the platform.

As soon as the train pulled into the station there was a surge of bodies moving toward the slow moving train. "Stand back, stand back," shouted the voice over the PA system, but it was like telling a whole bunch of children there was free ice cream and they should all stand in a line. Before the train had even stopped, doors were being opened and people were clambering in, opening windows, and taking luggage from those on the platform. It was total chaos, how someone never got pushed under the moving wheels of the train was a miracle in itself.

Boxer was swept along with the rest and eventually found a seat. The luggage racks above the seats were jam-packed with suitcases, boxes, tin trunks, and what could not fit on the rack was packed in the aisles and between the seats. There was little room to move. There was no way the train conductor could walk down the aisles of the carriages, so they walked up and down the platform, leaning into windows, checking the travel documents, and clipping tickets as well as possible.

Satisfied that they had at least checked the major-ity of the passengers, the conductor signalled the driver and, with two toots from the train's whistle, the train slowly pulled out of the station, with three or four heads and waving arms hanging out of every window, shout-ing farewells to friends, colleagues from the mines, and pregnant girlfriends.

The train travelled first to Pretoria and then on to Nelspruit, crossing the border at Komatiepoort and ar-riving in Lourenco Marques some fourteen hours later. The trains carrying migrant workers to and from the neighbouring countries got special clearance and stopped only to take on water and coal at small sidings along the way. The train was never allowed to stop in any major city or town, as the authorities were afraid that once the workers got off the train in a town or city they would never get them all back on board again.

At the sidings where they stopped, there were no facilities to buy anything or toilets so whatever you wanted to eat and drink you took along with you on the train. No alcohol of any kind was allowed on the train, but to control it was an exercise in futility. When the train infrequently stopped, passengers would madly scramble out through doors and windows to any nearby tree or bush to go and relieve themselves.

At first the trip was exciting, but as the time went by and it got hotter, tempers became shorter. Sporadic fights broke out among those who had been drinking alcohol smuggled onto the train and were now wanting to settle old arguments about money borrowed or a girlfriend that was taken from them. The South African Railway Police had a torrid time trying to control the fighting on the crowded train.

There was normally a long delay at the border post as customs checked documents and checked bags and suitcases. They could never search everyone's luggage, but when they did find something illegal, the person would be imprisoned and given a thorough beating. The punishment handed out by the Portuguese was severe and this was common knowledge to all returning workers. Only the really stupid and desperate would risk losing everything they had worked for over their contract period, but every now and then one would get caught and he would be made an example of, to discourage others in the future.

Once they arrived in Lourenco Marques they would be bussed to a recruiting centre outside the city, where they would overnight in a compound. The following day they would register to collect their deferred wages that had been paid to the Portuguese authorities by the Chamber of Mines. The problem was, that unless you could prove that you had legally gone to work in South Africa and had registered with the WNLA prior to leaving

Mozambique you had no chance of getting your money out of the government. The clandestine workers like Boxer were fully aware of this practice and did not even bother to try, as they knew it was a futile exercise.

By the time the train pulled into Lourenco Marques it was just before 10:00 p.m. The PA system was announcing that all returning migrant workers from South Africa should proceed to the buses standing in the front of the main station entrance. Boxer, as well as many others, carried their luggage out the side entrance of the station; they had no intention of getting on any bus that was going to the recruiting centre.

Boxer put his suitcase on his shoulder and walked the nine blocks up Avendia Fernandes to where it crosses with Avendia Emilia. The city was still very much alive. There were cars on the roads, people walking, others were sitting at little sidewalk cafes eating and drinking. He had forgotten what it was like to be back in Mozambique. In South Africa at this time of the night the streets were almost deserted because of the nine o' clock curfew. He crossed the street and went through the open double gates into the truck yard of the depot of the old transport company he had worked for before he went to South Africa.

The transport company was open twenty four hours a day. There were four trucks parked in the yard, two were loaded and had their loads covered with green canvas tied to the sides with ropes. There was some very basic sleeping accommodation at the back of the office building. Boxer hoped that there might be someone there he might recognize. More often than not, if the drivers did not have a trip the next morning, they would all be down at their favourite cantina having a good time.

Boxer walked around the back to where the accommodation was situated. As luck would have it there were four men sitting outside the dormitory playing cards. Boxer immediately recognized the one driver, he was from Inhambane. Boxer walked over to where they were seated on old *paraffin* boxes around a wooden crate turned upside down as a makeshift table. He greeted them in his home language.

They looked up and the one who Boxer recognized said, "Hey! I know you. You used to work with us in Inhambane, what's your name again?"

"Yes, you remember, I'm Boxer, I mean Mofola," he corrected himself. "I used to load the trucks up in Inhambane."

They spoke awhile about the old days and what Mofola had been doing the past two years. Mofola explained that he was looking for a ride to Inhambane and then up to his hometown Massangena. The driver said that he was leaving for Inhambane the next morning at five o' clock and would speak to the manager to see if it was alright to give him a ride.

The next morning just before sunrise Mofola was perched up on top of the fertilizer bags on the back of the truck going to Inhambane. The driver had invited him to sit inside. Mofola thanked the driver and explained that he was tired and would prefer to lie and sleep on top of the bags. That was one reason, the other reason was that three in the front cab was crowded and hot and he had had enough of crowded seating on the train.

It was quite cool on the back of the truck as it made its way out of the city on to the north road that followed the coastline for 450 kilometres all the way up to Inhambane. Mofola made himself comfortable on the bags, used his suitcase as a headrest and slept for the better part of the journey.

They arrived in Inhambane late that afternoon. Mofola thanked the driver and went into the office to see if the old dispatch clerk was still there. "Hello, *Baba*," said Mofola, recognizing the old man behind the despatch counter.

"Hello, yourself," said the old dispatch clerk, also recognizing Mofola, "I'm far too good looking to be your *Baba*," he gibed Mofola. "Where have you been these last months?" he asked, knowing full well that it must be years since he last saw Mofola.

"Months—you mean years," said Mofola, removing his hat and walking around to the back of the counter. The old man got up from his desk and grasped Mofola's hand in his and shook it in the traditional African way.

"So where have you been these past years?" enquired the old man.

Mofola told him briefly where he had been and what he had been doing, and then asked, "So, old man, what has been going on here at the company?"

They exchanged some more pleasantries and spoke about some of the staff that had come and gone. "Tell me, *Baba*, does Roberto Gumane still work here as a co-driver?"

"Roberto," said the old man. "No, he no longer works here as a co-driver," he said, not volunteering any more information.

"Do you perhaps know then where he is working?" asked Mofola.

"Yes, he is still working here," said the old man.

"But you just said he wasn't working here any-more."

"No, I said he did not work here anymore as a co-driver. He is now a full driver."

Mofola play punched the old man and said, "*Baba*, one day I'm really going to smack you," and they both had a good laugh. "Yes, he is on a trip and will be back on Friday afternoon." "Do you know if he is still staying at the same address? Mofola enquired.

"Yes, I think so," said the old man. "Let me have a quick look in the records. "Yes," he said, "he has been at the same address for the past seven years."

Mofola made his way to Roberto's house. Roberto's wife was preparing dinner for herself and the two boys. She was very surprised to see Mofola. The boys had grown much taller since he had seen them last, they were now eight and ten years old. Roberto's wife invited Mofola to stay with them. "Roberto will be very angry if I tell him you were here and I did not invite you to stay," she said.

Mofola thanked her and said he would like to stay and see Roberto.

Late on Friday afternoon Mofola went and sat outside the house on an upturned crate with his legs stretched out in front of him and his hat pulled down over his eyes. Looking from under his hat he could see a long way down the street and he recognized Roberto from his peculiar walk as he loped along at a fair pace. As he got closer, Roberto could see a figure sitting next to the house and as he drew alongside, he said, "Can I help you?" with irritation in his voice, not recognizing Mofola with his hat still pulled down over his eyes.

"Maybe you can and maybe you can't," said Mofola in a disguised voice not attempting to look or get up.

"So what do you want?" said Roberto, now even more annoyed that this person was just sitting there outside his house.

"I want a ride to Massangena," shouted Mofola jumping up.

"Mofola, you devil, what are you doing here?" shouted Roberto, gripping Mofola's outstretched hand in both of his and shaking it vigorously. The two boys and Roberto's wife came out of the house laughing, having watched the whole incident from behind the curtains.

Roberto told Mofola that he was off until next week Thursday and that he was leaving early that morning to take a load up north. He was sure that they could get permission from the transport manager to give him a ride up as far as Massangena. That night the two men went into town and they got just a little drunk.

On Wednesday morning Mofola went into town and went to the bank and changed two hundred pounds sterling into *escudos*, which came to thirteen thousand and fifty *escudos*. He wrapped the money in a long piece of cloth and tied it around his waist under his shirt.

The next morning, Thursday, they left the house early before light, Mofola having said good-bye to the two boys and thanking Roberto's wife for her hospitality the night before. They arrived at the transport company before 6:00 a.m. Roberto went and spoke to the transport manager on duty to get permission to give Mofola a ride up to Massangena.

The road north was not in very good condition as usual and although it was only four hundred and fifty kilometres to Massangena it would take them just short of two days to get there with the heavily loaded truck.

On Thursday night they stopped over at Chuguto, which was roughly halfway to Massangena. Roberto and the co-driver slept in the cab, saving the money they had been paid for their overnight accommodation. Mofola slept on top of the bags of *maize* meal on the back of the truck under the tarpaulin that was covering the cargo. He lay on his back looking up at the stars. They looked much brighter and there seemed to be so many more compared to the stars he saw in the city. It reminded him of the nights up in the mountains where the nights were crisp and clear.

He lay there trying to count them, if only he had as much money as the stars in the sky then he could buy Victor Aguiar's store. Then he and Negome would run the store together—that would be a good plan—unfortunately, he did not have that much money, only enough to pay the *ilobola* for Negome. Tomorrow afternoon they would arrive in Massangena and he planned to go straight to Victor Aguiar's store and claim his bride with all the money he had wrapped in the cloth tied around his waist.

He could not wait to see the look on Victor Aguiar's face when he threw all the money on the counter. Victor Aguiar, being such a greedy man, would surely be very impressed when he saw so much money and would gladly let him take Negome for his wife. With those happy thoughts Mofola drifted off to sleep, dreaming that he was with Negome up in the mountains and they were swimming naked in one of the cool mountain streams. They then walked in among the cattle and goats and he pointed out his cattle to her. He woke up with Roberto pulling his foot. "Come on, dreamer, it is nearly time to go."

Mofola climbed down from the back of the truck and went across the road to the garage and washed his face with cold water under the tap. The dawn was just breaking when the big diesel truck pulled slowly out of Chuguto. Mofola sat up front with the others. As they got farther away from the coast it became drier and drier and the road got even dustier, Mofola mentioned it to Roberto. "Yes, it is very dry," Roberto said. "These last years, there has been very little rain, but for us it has been good business taking food up north."

The sun was just going down behind the mountains when they arrived in Massangena. Roberto pulled the truck into the yard at the back of Costa Xavier's cantina. Mofola got his suitcase down from the back of the truck. It was covered in white powder dust from the road. He went over to the outdoor ablution to wash and change his clothes; he wanted to make sure he made a good first impression when he saw Negome and her father.

Mofola went to find Roberto and thank him for everything and promised to keep in touch. "Before you go to your father's house tonight come back to the cantina and tell us what the storekeeper's face looked like when you put all the money on the counter," said Roberto. Mofola agreed he would come and tell them what had happened. He picked up his suitcase and walked over to the store.

Chapter 27

Mofola took out his Zobo pocket watch and looked at the time, it was just after six, and there was still plenty of time, as the store wouldn't close until seven o'clock. He walked up the three steps onto the wide *veranda* that went all the way around the front of the store. He put his suitcase down and cupped his hands to the big window and looked in. The window was dusty from the wind blowing dust up from the road, so he wiped a patch with the cuff of his shirt sleeve so that he could see better. There were a few people in the store and Negome was attending to one of them. His heart skipped a beat, she had grown into a woman, and her long black hair that once hung way below her shoulders was now cut to shoulder length. He could not see Mr. Victor—he must be at the back or in the house, but decided to go inside anyway.

Negome did not see him when he came into the store; she was still busy with a customer. Mofola walked over to the counter dressed in long brown pants, brown leather shoes, and a light blue shirt with a dirty mark on the sleeve where he had wiped the window clean. On his head he wore a dark brown trilby hat. He had removed the money from around his waist and had bundled it up in the cloth and put it in his suitcase, which he placed next to him on the wooden floor, and waited, looking around to see if he could see Mr. Victor.

The customer that Negome had been serving walked out of the store. She put some money in the till and then looked up and saw Mofola standing at the other end of the counter—she did not recognize him. She walked down to that end of the counter and said, "Good afternoon, sir, can I help you?"

Mofola removed his hat and said, "Hello, Negome, you are now even more beautiful than before," was all he could think of to say.

"Mofola," she gasped, "is it really you?" she asked, putting her hands up to her mouth. "I can't believe it is you. What are you doing here? My father told us that he heard you were killed trying to cross the border into South Africa over two years ago and now you appear here in front of my eyes."

"Did my mother not tell you about me and give you my messages?" he asked.

"Your father and mother have not come into this store since the day they took you away. Your parents buy whatever they can on the market and whatever else they need they would send one of your nephews to buy at the store and they would never say anything about you.

Mofola's parents had decided that they would not tell anyone about Mofola. They said it was better that way; rather, let the daughter of Mr. Victor marry the son of Mr. Costa, then things would be better again. At first Mofola's mother felt sympathy for Negome, but as the months went by and she thought of her innocent son in jail so far away, her heart hardened and she became resentful and bitter and blamed Negome for what had happened to Mofola. If it were not for her then Mofola would not have gone to prison, she reasoned to herself.

"I have come to take you away," he said as he opened up the suitcase and took out the bundle of money. He opened it up on the counter. "See, here is the *ilobola* to pay your father.

"Oh! Mofola," she said, "it is too late. My father has already agreed with Mr. Costa that I will marry his oldest son next year."

"But surely your father will change his mind when he sees all this money I have brought for the *ilobola*. Remember, I told you that I would be back one day."

"I know," she said, "and I prayed to the Madonna at the church that you would come and take me away from this place, but when I heard that you were dead, a piece of me inside died too."

Just then Victor Aguiar came into the store from the house and saw Negome talking to a stranger and there was a heap of money in a cloth lying on the counter. "Good evening," he said smiling, thinking that the stranger was about to make a big purchase.

"Hello, Mr. Victor," said Mofola, "I have come with all this money for the *ilobola* for Negome, your eldest daughter," he said, pointing to the pile of money lying in the cloth on the counter.

"Well, well, well, it's the Boxer Boy, I did not recognize you," said Victor. "But I knew that one day you would come back to make more trouble for me."

"But, Father, you said he was dead, protested Negome."

"Of course I told you he was dead," said Victor. "You were walking around like a sick cow. Did you think I did not hear you praying at night to the Madonna to bring him back, you stupid little slut. Now we have the herd boy back again," he said, pointing to Mofola, "and he's come to pay me *ilobola* with these few crumbs. I told you once before, she goes to Costa's son and next month they will be married. Now take your crumbs and get out of my store before I call the commissioner to come and arrest you again." With that he took hold of the cloth and shook it, the money went flying in the air floating down all over the store. "You could not buy a hair on her head," said Victor, "with those crumbs," and he walked out the back of the store into the house.

Several customers heard and saw what had transpired and helped Mofola gather up his money. He tied it up in the cloth and put it back in his suitcase.

Negome was sobbing. "Again my father has lied to me. All he cares about is himself. He has never asked me what I want for my life—he does not even care, as long as he gets what he wants. Please, Mofola, take me away with you," she pleaded, sobbing with big tears rolling down her cheeks. "I can't stand it any more."

Mofola looked at her and the hatred he once felt for Victor Aguiar when he was in jail came flashing back. The man did not deserve to have children, but to run away with Negome was not the thing to do; they would always be looking over their shoulders. "No, Negome, that is not the way. I will think of another plan—just trust in me." He picked up his suitcase and walked out of the store.

Mofola walked over to the cantina where Robert and his co-driver were each drinking a cold beer. They saw him come in and called out cheerfully for him to come and join them at the table, at the same time calling for another beer. Mofola sat down next to the co-driver. "So, my lovesick friend, when is the big wedding day going to be?" asked Roberto.

Mofola took a long drink from the bottle of beer that the waiter had put down in front of him and then told them exactly what had happened a few minutes ago in the store. "Hey, man, that Victor Aguiar is one greedy son of a bitch, if I were you," said Roberto, "I would forget all this and go home, leave the greedy pig and his daughter. They are only going to be bad trouble for you."

The two friends continued to give Mofola advice on what he should do and should not do. Mofola sat quietly sipping his beer, listening only with half an ear. His mind was racing ahead, trying to work out a way to get even with Victor Aguiar and have Negome as his bride. It was now dark outside. They had finished their beer so Mofola called one of the waiters over to the table and ordered three more beers.

Costa had seen Mofola come in earlier and sit down with the two truck drivers and wondered what had brought him back to Massangena, so he decided to take the beers to the table himself. "Well, if it's not the jail-bird himself come to pay us a visit. I see they eventually let you out," he said with a laugh. "Well, I must say you don't look too bad for a jail bird. Now I don't know why you have come back and I don't care. The thing between you the commissioner and Aguiar is none of my business. All I have to say is I don't want any trouble here, is that clear?" He put the three beers down on the table and walked back behind the bar counter.

The commissioner came in and went and sat down at his regular table, Costa saw him come in and immediately opened a bottle of red wine and took it over to the table. They spoke for a few minutes and then Costa pointed in the direction of the table where Mofola was sitting. The commissioner got up and Costa went into the kitchen.

The commissioner walked casually over to the table where Mofola and his friends were sitting. "I see you have come back," said the commissioner. "Did you have a nice holiday down by the sea? So what is it that brings the jailbird back here again?"

"Is this not a country where a man can come and go as he would like?" asked Mofola sarcastically.

"Yes, you are right, a man can come and go as he pleases, but this is my town and I don't like jailbirds, so stay out of trouble." He turned to walk away.

"Does that mean you would frame me again?" said Mofola rather louder than was necessary.

The commissioner turned and smiled at him, leaned over the table and said softly, "Yes, if that's what it takes, then so be it." He then turned and went and sat down at his table and poured a glass of wine from the bottle Costa had put there.

"You know, Mofola, if I were you," said Roberto, "I would take my things and get out of this town. There are too many people here who don't particularly like you and you will always be unwelcome in this town as long as this commissioner and his friends are here.

A little later Victor Aguiar came into the cantina and went and sat down at the table with the commissioner. Costa joined them with two glasses in his hand. He poured some wine into both of them and topped up the commissioner's glass. The three were immediately in deep discussion, occasionally glancing over to the table where Mofola was sitting. They then laughed out loudly, lifted their glasses over to where Mofola was sitting, and mockingly saluted him.

Costa went back behind the bar and returned with two packs of playing cards, which he brought back to their table. He opened them and gave a pack to the commissioner, who proceeded to shuffle them. The commissioner said something to Costa and they all laughed again. Costa got up from the table and walked over to the table where Mofola and his two friends were sitting. "Would any of you three gentlemen like to join us in a game of cards? No, I guess not," he said sarcastically as he proceeded on over to the bar where there were a number of drivers with some "ladies of the night" standing there drinking.

Mofola swallowed the rest of his beer and got up from the table. "Well, my friends, I believe it's time I went home. Thank you once again for all your help and advice. Maybe I will see you some time again when you pass through here—that is, of course, if I'm not locked up in jail again," he said with a laugh.

"Hey, man, don't make jokes," said Roberto, shaking Mofola's outstretched hand. "These guys are serious trouble, don't mess around with them. Remember what I said, forget this woman and get out of here, she is not worth all this trouble."

Mofola said he would think about it, and then walked out of the cantina. As he got to the door he turned and lifted his hand as a last farewell to his friends. Roberto returned the gesture and shouted, "You think about it," but Mofola had already disappeared into the night.

With his suitcase on his shoulder, Mofola trekked up the dusty road past the mission school, church, and clinic. There was a cool breeze coming down off the mountains. It was most welcome after the hot summer day and it made walking a pleasure. The moon was bright in the clear sky, lighting the way before him, not that he needed any light, as he could walk the road with a blindfold. As he walked along, a plan on how to get back at Victor was slowly forming in his mind.

As he approached the gate of the *shamba* the dogs came running up, barking. He called out the names of some of the dogs that he thought might still be alive. They came whimpering up to him crablike with their tails between their legs. Mofola crouched down, patting them as he spoke to them with the words and phrases he used up in the mountains when he was a herd boy. The older dogs, recognizing his voice, were now all over him with excitement and almost pushed him over. The younger ones stayed at a distance not quite sure what to do.

"At least the dogs were pleased to see me," he said to himself. "Well, most of them anyway." What the rest of the family's reaction would be when they saw him would have to wait until tomorrow as the *shamba* was in darkness. Like most rural communities, everyone went to bed early and got up early. Mofola made his way down to the cooking area where the dogs had been sleeping. He put his suitcase down and sat on one of the old wooden stools under the corrugated overhang. The coals in the fireplace were still hot so he took a few dry twigs from the wood box that stood in the corner and soon had flames splashing orange light around the cooking enclosure. He pushed the three smouldering logs back into the fire again. They had been pulled to one side earlier when the cooking was done.

The clay drinking pot wrapped in sacking hung from the same beam in the far corner. It still had the same old enamel plate acting as the lid with the tin mug turned bottom up on top of it. Mofola lifted up the enamel plate and dipped the mug into the water. The water was cool and sweet to the taste and it brought back fond memories of his mother and sister carrying water from the spring.

In his mind he could see his mother with a large clay pot on her head and following close behind was his little sister with a smaller pot on her head. They would scoop up water from the pool with a little blue enamel bowl and pour it into the clay pots. The water dripped from the rock overhang and collected in a shallow pool at the base of the rock outcrop, it was not a strong spring but Mofola could not remember it ever having dried up.

Once the pots were full they would put a small woven ring of grass on their heads and then place the pot of water on top of the grass ring. The two of them would slowly walk back down the pathway to the *shamba*. He could see clearly in his mind how the little blue scooping bowl that was floating on top of the water in the pot bobbed up and down as his mother took each step, he could even hear the clink, clink sound as it knocked against the sides of the pot.

The flickering firelight cast shadows against the reed sides of the enclosure. Mofola looked around in the dying light of the fire—nothing had really changed, and everything was as he remembered it. The dogs had all settled down again, curled up as close to the fire as possible. He often wondered to himself how it was that they didn't burn themselves. He counted them, there were six, they looked quite thin and he thought that was strange, as there were always enough scraps left over to feed all the dogs. He was pleased that the barking dogs had not stirred the family. He did not feel like talking tonight. Tomorrow, in the light, things would seem better. Mofola put his feet up on one of the other stools, leaned his back against an upright pole, and dosed off with his chin on his chest.

In the early part of the morning the dogs started to stir and one by one they got up stretched and went outside to do their business. Mofola had a restless night, it seemed that whenever he managed to dose off he dreamed of killing Victor Aguiar. They were strange dreams and left him feeling uneasy. In the early hours of the morning it had gotten cold so he kicked the logs into the fire and removed one of his blankets from his suitcase. He wrapped it around himself and sat there staring at the fire, not wanting to fall asleep for fear of dreaming the strange dreams again. He was pleased when the first signs of light appeared on the eastern horizon.

Mofola got up and stretched, his muscles were stiff from sitting the whole night on the stool. He went outside and got some more logs from the pile next to the cooking enclosure and got the fire burning again. The big black cast-iron kettle was in its usual place, it was still half full of water. He scraped some hot coals from the middle of the fire to one side and put the iron triangle with legs over the coals and the kettle on top of it.

Outside the enclosure Mofola dipped his hand into one of the clay pots containing water and splashed some on his face. He had almost forgotten what life was like back here. On the mines, everything was taken care of, from food to ablution. The life in the city seemed much easier than it was out here in the rural area.

Here there was no running water, no electricity, no water-flushing toilets, no tarred roads, and very sporadic public transport. These were basic things that you took for granted when you lived long enough in the city; you soon forgot about the hardships of the people back home.

He stood outside the cooking area with his back to the *shamba* enjoying the warmth from the first rays of the sun as it peeped over the horizon. Mofola's sister-in-law was the first to appear from their hut. She saw Mofola standing there with his back to her and did not recognize him at first. She was about to call out when

Mofola, sensing that someone was watching him, turned around to see her. She then immediately recognized him and shouted, "Mofola, it is you," and came running to greet him.

She was full of questions. "What are you doing back home, when did you leave South Africa, how were Temba and Yussaf, when did you see them last?"

"Slow down, slow down, one question at a time," said Mofola. With all the excited jabbering from his sister-in-law the rest of the *shamba* started to come to life.

His mother hugged him and said, "My youngest went away a boy and has returned a grown man, look at him—he is as tall as a giraffe."

"Yes, and so handsome," said his sister-in-law jokingly, "and I'm sure as strong as a lion," she said, taking Mofola's arm and bending it to show the muscle.

His father greeted him with a hug and said with a tear in his eye, "Welcome home, my son, we have sorely missed you."

They all went and sat in the cooking enclosure and Mofola's mother and sister-in-law prepared some thick *maize* porridge, which they ate with sour milk while they talked. Mofola's two nephews had grown from little children into grown-up boys. They sat quietly on one stool listening to every word Mofola said, as he was their mentor.

"Why are the two of you not up in the mountains with the cattle and goats?" inquired Mofola. The two looked into the fire and said nothing. It was as if the jovial atmosphere that had prevailed a few seconds ago had been switched off like an electric light bulb.

Mofola looked questioningly at his father. The old man looked up from where he had been staring into the fire. "The past two years have not been easy, my son, the rain has been so scarce that last year the spring at the top of the hill dried up for the first time in my memory. We had to go into town with the donkey cart and fetch water from the dry riverbed. The townspeople had dug a deep hole where the water came up from deep down. Sometimes we would have to wait the whole day to get enough water to last for a week. There was sometimes only enough for us so the animals had to go without water for days. Many of them have perished these last two years."

"This year the rain has been a little better and the spring is giving us enough water to live on again, but the earth has been scorched by devastating fires and, as a result, there is little if any grazing for the animals down here on the flatlands. The animals that have survived are too weak to *trek* up into the mountains. Come and see for yourself." The old man got up and shuffled his way to the cattle paddock at the back of the *shamba*. Mofola was shocked at how the health of his father had deteriorated over past years.

When Mofola saw what was left of the great herd they once had he was devastated. He counted nine skinny cows, two bulls, and six goats. Two of the cows were already so weak that they could no longer stand. "But, Father, when I left here some five years ago, we had one of the biggest and strongest herds in the district. Is this all that is left?"

"Yes, my son, I'm afraid these here are all that is left of our great herd of cattle and goats."

"We have been more fortunate than many others who have lost everything, including some of their family members. Others have moved north where the rainfall has been much better, but there too they have found more trouble. The people in the Tete province have chased them off the good lands into the swamplands where many have perished from the black water sickness."

"But, Father," protested Mofola, "surely there is something we can do to save these animals, can we not buy fodder from another district?"

"I'm afraid, my son, it is the gods that are punishing us for not thanking them enough for the good times," went on the old man philosophically. "There is no fodder to be bought in the area, it is no use. We cannot fight the gods. However, we must not complain, we are more fortunate than many others; we can still manage to survive on the money we have saved."

Mofola could see that the old man had all but given up; he was not well, and the phthisis sickness from the mines was slowly eating his lungs away. He could hardly complete a sentence without having a coughing spasm. Although he had stopped smoking some three years ago, according to Mofola's mother, it was far too late to make any significant difference to the old man's health.

The old man had gone to lie down; the excitement of the morning was too much and it had tired him out. Mofola went and spoke to his mother. "Why did you not write to us that there was this terrible drought?" asked Mofola.

"My son, at first, we thought that it would soon end and that it would not be so bad, but then when the rains did not arrive, it was already too late. Your father, as you know, is a proud and often very stubborn man. He said we should not burden our children with this punishment from the gods."

"But how could he say that? This affects all of us. He had no right to take this on himself. He should have called us to come and help."

"So now that you know, are you going to call your brothers?" asked his mother.

"No, I will deal with it."

"So who then has given you the right to take these things on by yourself?"

"This is different. I'm here and my brothers are in South Africa."

"Yes, my son, if you say it's different then so be it," his mother said, and then went into their hut to care for the old man.

Mofola called his nephew Joseph and together they hitched up the donkey cart to the two scrawny donkeys and made their way slowly into town. They first went to the marketplace on the other side of town to see if there was anything there they could buy to feed the cattle. It was only then that Mofola grasped the full impact of the drought. What was once a thriving marketplace with thirty or more stalls selling fruit, vegetables, tinned food, clothes, pots and pans, and many other items was now literally empty.

As much as he hated it, they would have to go into town and see what they could buy from Victor Aguiar's store. Mofola sent young Joseph into the store to see if they had any chicken feed. He knew that the cattle would eat it, as he could remember feeding it to the young calves. Joseph came out of the store and told him what the price was of a fifty-kilogram bag of chicken meal. Mofola could remember five years ago his father having paid three time less for chicken feed at the market.

They bought two bags, which was all that Mofola thought the donkeys could carry in their weak condition. At home they mixed the meal with a little water and fed it to the animals. They had to force-feed by hand the two cows that were lying down. It was Mofola's plan to try to get their strength up so that he could *trek* them up into the mountains where he was sure there must be at least some grazing and water.

When the old man saw what they were doing, he said that they were wasting money and that they could not fight the will of the gods. Mofola told him that it was his money and if he chose to spend it to fight the gods then it was his doing and not that of his father. Five years ago Mofola would never have dared talk to his father in that manner, but the years away had given him confidence, wisdom, and determination.

By the end of the first week there was a big difference in the condition of the animals. The two cows that were lying down were now standing and eating by themselves. Mofola had already bought another four bags of chicken feed and he thought that in another week or so the stronger of the animals would be able to *trek* up into the mountains.

Mofola decided that he would take young Joseph and go up into the mountains to see where they could find grazing before taking the cattle all that way up there and not finding any suitable grazing. The two of them left early the next morning, leaving instructions for the younger nephew to continue feeding the animals until they returned. It would take them a minimum of two days and maybe three to do a proper search in the area.

Mofola had a place in mind where he thought the fire would not have caused so much devastation. It was a small valley that was completely encircled by high cliffs. He had come upon it one day completely by accident while looking for stray cattle that had found their way into a winding passage between high cliffs that led into a small valley. Normally one would walk past the entrance, as it was overgrown with thick bush, but he had heard the cattle calling and had thought that they were trapped somewhere. It was then that he found the concealed entrance to the valley. Two cows had gone into the passage and had gotten stuck there where rocks and boulders had blocked the way.

Mofola and Joseph each bundled up some bread and a bottle of water in his blanket and tied the bundle to his back like Mofola used to do when he was the herd boy. They jogged and walked, jogged and walked along the pathways that led up into the mountains. The only thing that was different was there was hardly any vegetation and Mofola's fitness was not what it used to be. By the time the sun was high in the sky they had to stop to rest, five years ago he could have walked and jogged the whole day without a rest. They ate some bread and drank some water and rested for about half an hour and then started off again.

By the middle of the afternoon they had reached the foothills of the Chimanimani Mountains. They could no longer run, as the going was too steep, Mofola found the walking bad enough, he could not believe that he was so unfit, but he set a fairly fast pace to keep his image with Joseph. He also wanted to find the valley before it got dark.

It was late in the afternoon when they came to the cliff face where he thought the entrance to the valley should be. Somehow it looked different with all the burned vegetation. The land marks were gone and all Mofola could go on was what he remembered of the shape of the cliff. The problem was that one cliff looked very similar to ten others.

They walked along the foot of the cliff, first going east and then going west but they could not find the entrance to the valley. Mofola was starting to doubt that they were in the right place. It was now getting dark and they decided to spend the night under a rock overhang and continue the search the next morning. They ate some more bread and drank some water from the bottles they had brought along. There was no wood to make a fire, so they wrapped themselves in their blankets and curled up back to back on the floor of the cliff overhang. Mofola was so tired that he fell asleep instantly.

They were awake before dawn and sat huddled together in their blankets, waiting for the dawn to break. Mofola was stiff from the unusual exercise; every muscle in his body was sore, but he said nothing to young Joseph.

Mofola sat there trying to picture in his mind where the entrance could be. "Maybe it was on the higher plateau," he said to himself, "that must be it. I must have been on the higher plains that day when the cattle wandered into the passage leading to the hidden valley." As soon as it was light enough to see, they ate some more bread and drank a little water before packing up their few things and setting out again.

Mofola told Joseph what he thought, so they made their way back to the main footpath that would take them up the narrow valley that cut its way up onto the higher plains. The sun was hot on their backs by the time they reached the higher plateau. Mofola was already sweating. The stiffness in his legs had all but gone but the rest of his body still ached. There were now little pools of water here and there in the dry stream that followed the valley down to the lower plains. Even this high up, the *veld* had not escaped the ravaging fire. Close to the dry stream, young green grass shoots popped out in the burned *veld*.

Mofola stood and looked out over the burned plateau, remembering the lush tall grasses that grew so abundantly here in the summer months and how the gentle mountain breeze created waves in the sea of grass that ran to where it stopped at the foot of the high cliffs that went straight up, creating a new horizon. Somehow this looked more promising; they followed the dry stream heading toward the cliffs.

At the foot of the cliffs they walked eastward along the base of the towering cliffs. High above, a solitary black eagle soared in the updraft created by the warm air from the plains hitting the cliffs and rising up to where the eagle circled, looking for some sign of prey on the burned plains below.

As Mofola watched the flight of the majestic eagle, it folded its wings and dived toward the ground some five hundred meters in front of them along the base of the cliff and then swooped up again with what looked like a grey hare in its talons. Mofola and Joseph watched as it carried its prey westward until it was a small speck on the horizon.

Curious as to why the hare should venture out of its hole in the broad daylight when there was so little ground cover, they made their way toward the spot where the eagle had caught it. On arrival there was nothing there to indicate why the hare should be so stupid as to leave its hole in the broad daylight. The steep cliffs towered above them, continuing uninterrupted, circumventing the burnt plain they had just crossed. Mofola cast his eyes along the cliffs, but could see no other obvious cutting, other than the one they had come up through earlier that morning some kilometres to the southeast of where they were now standing.

Mofola was again beginning to doubt that they were in the right area and was just about to suggest that they turn back and try the west side, when he noticed that black dust from the burned grass was being blown back from where the cliff jutted out about twenty meters in front of where they were standing.

Mofola walked along the base to where the cliff jutted out and then continued on its journey. He climbed over some rocks that must have peeled off the sides of the cliff some centuries ago and peered around the outcrop. The unexpected breeze that hit him in the face startled him and he pulled his face back for a few seconds. He climbed around the outcrop to find a gap about a metre wide in the cliff face. This was it. This was what they had been looking for.

It must have been this gap in the cliff that the hare had been making for when the eagle caught it. Mofola and Joseph made their way along the narrow winding cutting in the cliff, climbing over rocks and small boulders littering the floor of the passage. The cutting continued for about five hundred meters to where it opened up into a beautiful lush valley. The contrast was so different from the burned vegetation from which they had just come, that they just stood in silence and looked down on it. The valley was surrounded on all sides by steep cliffs; it looked like a huge extinct volcano, several kilometres in circumference.

It was close to midday when Mofola and Joseph finished clearing the passage of fallen rocks that would hinder access to the cattle. There was no space in the narrow passage to pile the rubble so they had to carry and roll the big boulders to either of the entrances, whichever was the closest.

Once they had finished, they went down into the valley to see if there was enough water and built an enclosure out of thorn trees to keep the cattle safe from predators at night. Mofola had no doubt that there was water there, as there were plenty of signs of wildlife; their spoor and droppings were to be seen all over, but he wanted to know where the wildlife was and how abundant it was. He knew that when they got the cattle there, they would be exhausted and weak, and he would need to direct them straight to the water.

They followed the game path that wound its way down to the floor of the valley. Every now and then they would startle some wild animal and it would go crashing off through the thick bush. The floor of the valley was covered in lush grass that stood at least a metre high and, in the far distance, game could be seen grazing. A small but strong stream flowed from a fountain spring forming drinking holes everywhere as it made its way to the other side of the valley where it again disappeared as mysteriously as it had appeared, back into the ground.

They chose a spot under a big umbrella thorn tree that would form the centre of the enclosure for the cattle. They then collected dead thorn branches and piled them up on top of each other forming a twenty-metre circle, the height of a grown man, around the tree. By the time they had finished, the sun had disappeared behind the cliffs.

They made a small fire and heated up a tin of corned beef and ate the remainder of the now stale bread with the beef. Although there was plenty of game around for them to trap for food, there was no time for those sorts of luxuries this time; they needed to get back and bring the cattle back here. So this would be their last meal until they got back home.

As soon as it was light they filled their bottles with water and made their way back up the game path to the passage between the cliffs. Once on the other side they started to run at a slow comfortable pace that would slowly but surely eat up the kilometres, now taking the shortest route across the burned *veld*. They ran in silence one behind the other, only talking when Mofola pointed out a landmark to remember for the return trip. They stopped every so often to rest and drink a little water. By late afternoon they arrived back at the *shamba*. Mofola told his father that they had found good grazing but it was at least a day and a half or maybe two days' *trek* with the weak cattle.

The next day they planned and prepared what they needed for the trip back to the hidden valley and the following morning they left the *shamba* as soon as it was light enough to see their way. Emanuel would stay behind to continue to feed the two weak cows and go into town to buy provisions when needed for the family. Mofola led the two donkeys that were loaded with provisions for the two-day *trek*, Joseph and two of the dogs followed behind the cattle and the few goats. The going was very slow and they had to stop frequently for the animals to rest and drink a little water that they had brought along in two old twenty- five-litre *paraffin* tins strapped to the backs of the donkeys.

Just before sunset they reached the valley that cut its way up onto the upper plateau and decided to camp there for the night in the dry riverbed. They mixed some feed with the rest of the water and fed the animals. Some of them were so tired that they had to hand-feed them.

Mofola hoped that the animals would be able to make it to the first water hole on the upper plateau about a three-hour *trek* from where they were now.

The next morning they started off again just before sunrise. The cattle were weak and tired and they struggled to get some of them to stand up. One very weak cow just refused to get up, they tried to pull her up by her horns but she was like a dead weight. Mofola decided to leave her there, as the longer they stayed the hotter it would get and he needed to get to the water hole on the upper plateau before the other animals started to falter. Once they got to the hidden valley he would come back with some water and try to coax her to get up.

It took longer than what they had expected to reach the first water hole, they practically had to drive the cattle along and by the time they had reached the water another cow had lain down and refused to get up again. Mofola allowed the animals a two-hour rest at the water hole, they drank deeply, pushing and shoving each other to get to the small pool of water. Once they had drunk their fill from the water hole, they moved off and munched the short green grass shoots that had started to appear here and there between the burned *veld*.

While the animals were resting, Mofola took some water back to the cow that had stopped and would not get up. When he reached her she was standing again. He poured some water into a tin drinking pan and put it down in front of her. After she had drunk all the water, Mofola prodded her into a walk and slowly drove her back to the water hole and the rest of the animals.

They left the riverbed and cut across the burned *veld*, taking the shortest route to the entrance to the hidden valley. Once the animals were through the cutting it was difficult to keep them together and stop them from grazing. With much poking and prodding they managed to get them all into the thorn bush enclosure just before the light faded.

The next morning they were woken up just as dawn was breaking by the restlessness of the animals; they wanted to get out there and munch on the long dew-covered grass. Mofola and Joseph pulled a section of the thick thorn bush away making a gate for the animals to go out. There was a sudden rush to get out, some getting pushed into the thorn bush in their eagerness to get out. Within twenty seconds the enclosure was empty. Mofola and Joseph stood and looked as they grazed right in front of them. They looked at each other and smiled, pleased that their plan had worked out well.

They sat around the fire and ate some *maize* porridge that Joseph had cooked in a little black cast-iron pot. Mofola told Joseph that he was going to go back and fetch the other cow and while he was gone Joseph should start cutting saplings, as they would need to build a shelter for themselves. Mofola took the empty *paraffin* tin and the tin drinking pan and set off up the hill to rescue the abandoned cow.

Mofola stopped at the water hole and half filled the *paraffin* tin with water. He carried on down the valley, following the dry riverbed to the plains below. Long before he could see the place where they had left the tired cow he knew it was too late to rescue the poor animal, high in the sky above the area where they left the cow he could see tiny specks circling. Without even being able to identify the birds at that distance he knew that they were vultures.

There was a battle going on between the vultures and the jackals. At least twenty vultures hopped around on the ground grabbing pieces of the dead cow and hopping out of reach of the snapping jackals that were fighting a losing battle trying to defend their prey from the vultures. Above, still circling, were at least another twenty waiting their opportunity to feed. Mofola stood back about a hundred paces and watched for a few minutes. He suspected that the jackals had come in the night and attacked the poor defenceless cow on the ground. He hoped she died quickly but he knew that was unlikely.

Mofola planned to stay a week with Joseph to make sure everything was in order before he returned home; he still had some other unfinished business to attend to back in Massangena. The past weeks he had not thought a lot about Negome; there were just so many other things that had occupied his mind. But now he had time and his thoughts were seldom very far from her.

The days were sunny and fine. They had built a shelter, caught an Impala in a snare, cut up the meat, salted it, and hung it in a cool place to dry. All they had to do now was to watch that the animals did not stray too far from them.

Chapter 28

Mofola had brought the pack of cards with him that his nephews had bought for him when they went to buy the chicken feed, so he taught Joseph how to play poker, his favourite game. They used pebbles collected from the stream as money. Mofola showed him all the tricks he had learned and how to remember the cards by giving them the names of animals. By the end of the week Joseph had become quite good. Mofola let him win a few games every now and then just to encourage him. But it was now time Mofola got back home to attend to his other business. The animals had made a remarkable recovery; the grasses in the hidden valley were sweet and succulent and, as a result, the animals had already put on weight.

Mofola said good-bye to his nephew and, leading the donkeys with his few things strapped to their backs, he made his way back up the hill to the cutting in the cliff that would take him back to a different world from which he had just left. It was like leaving paradise. Even the donkeys were reluctant to leave.

In the afternoon of the day after he had left the hidden valley, he walked into the yard of his father's *shamba* leading the two donkeys. Everyone came to greet him. It was as if he had been away for years again. Even his father wanted to know how it went. Mofola told them what had happened and how one of the cows did not make it. Mofola's father said it was a sacrifice to the gods for letting the other animals get there safely, one cow was a small sacrifice to pay.

The following day was Thursday. It was exactly a month since he arrived back in Massangena. Mofola stayed at the *shamba* and spoke to his mother and sister-in-law and helped with the general chores around the house. The next day was Friday. He wandered around the *shamba* like a bear with a sore head until the late afternoon. He then had a wash, put on clean clothes, and told his folks he was going into town. Gone were the days when he had to ask permission to go into town. By the time he walked into town it was already getting dark.

Mofola stuck his head into the door of the cantina to see if Roberto was perhaps there, but he could not see him or his co-driver so he walked around the back to see if the big diesel truck was parked there. There were quite a few other trucks, but it was not there, so he went back to the cantina and ordered a beer, Costa must have been in the back because he could not see him either. For a Friday night there were only a few people in the cantina, Mofola thought this was a bit strange and then he remembered the drought and what his father had said about all the people moving to other provinces. One of the locals in the cantina recognized Mofola and came over to greet him. They made small talk about the bad drought and how it had affected everyone, and then went on to discuss what it was like in South Africa in the gold mines.

It was just after eight o'clock, Mofola was sucking on his second beer when the commissioner and Victor came in and went and sat at their usual table. One of the workers must have gone and called Costa, because it was not long after that he came over and placed an open bottle of red wine on the table together with three glasses. By this time the cantina had filled up a bit more. Mofola suspected that it must be that the truck drivers, having cleaned up, were now coming in for a beer and something to eat.

The trio played a few hands among themselves and then Costa came over to the bar and asked if anyone was interested in joining them for a game. He saw Mofola standing there but did not acknowledge him. Two drivers that had previously lost money to the trio were keen to get even and decided to play. The two drivers sat down at the table and were greeted by Victor and the commissioner. The commissioner recognized the two from a few weeks ago and asked them sarcastically whether they liked to give their money away. Victor laughed a bit more than was necessary, only to butter up the commissioner. After all, the joke was not that funny.

"I only give money to beggars in the street," said one of the drivers.

"I hope your mind is as sharp as your tongue," said the commissioner, "or you could find yourself out begging in the street."

The scene was set for real grudge game; this is what the locals liked, a bit of excitement in their lives. They gathered around the table where the five were playing poker, hoping to see the outsiders take money off the trio.

Mofola picked up his beer, strolled over to the table, and watched the game progress. After an hour or so the one driver who had made the beggar remark was losing badly and one could see the sarcastic remarks being made by the trio were getting at him, but this was all part of their game plan, to upset the opponent and make him reckless in his betting.

It soon became quite clear to Mofola why the trio always won, or won so often. The cards were marked. When the trio played among themselves they would obviously use a clean pack. Mofola walked around the table to make sure his theory was correct, yes the cards had thin finger nail marks in the centre of the card, and unless you were looking for them you would not notice them. One nail mark indicated the card was an ace, two for a king, and three for a queen.

It was not much later when the same driver, having lost again, pushed his chair back and stood up. "You three are cheating us drivers out of our hard-earned money."

"You are just a bad loser—did any of you here see any cheating going on?" asked Victor, looking around the table at the observers, seeking confirmation.

The crowd did not particularly like what they suspected was going on but they had no proof that the trio were cheating so they just shook their heads as Victor caught their eyes as he looked around the table. Victor always became a lot braver once he had a few glasses of wine in his fat belly and especially when the commissioner was at his side. His eyes eventually came to rest on Mofola, who just looked him straight in the eye, not moving his head.

"So, Boxer Boy, what about you did you, see us cheating, hey?"

Mofola kept quiet and just continued to look Victor in the eye. A deadly silence fell over the crowd of observers as everyone waited for this so-called Boxer Boy to reply. He certainly was no boy; he was a big strapping man. The tension was mounting and Costa could see a nasty situation boiling over into something more serious.

"Hey, I see we have a strong and silent one here. Maybe you would like to take the place of our driver friend?" Costa said as he kicked the chair further away from the table and indicated to Mofola that he should sit.

Mofola continued to look Victor in the eye and then slowly made his way around the table to the empty chair, sat down, and pulled the chair up to the table. The tension was broken. It was like someone had flicked a switch, on and off. The crowd began to buzz.

"So, Boxer," said Costa, careful not to include the word boy in his address, "do you think you can fare better than our driver friend? But let's see your money first before we deal you in."

Mofola had taken two thousand *escudos* from a hiding place and stuffed the notes in his pocket before he left home.

He reached into his pocket and placed a wad of notes on the table in front of him. The commissioner looked at the pile of money and said, "That should be enough to get you started."

"That seems a nice lot of money for a herder of cattle and goats," said Victor. "I suppose back in South Africa they don't know of your criminal record."

"Shut your mouth, Victor. The man's money is as good as any," said the commissioner, as the tension started to mount again. "The man has done his time, let the past be the past. Do you want to play cards or sit here and make unfounded remarks?"

The commissioner placed the pack of cards in front of Victor and said, "Deal." Victor was not happy that the commissioner had rebuked him in front of everyone. He had now lost face, but he did as he was told and thought to himself that one day lady luck would turn and he would take all the money back from them that they had taken off of him over the years.

Victor picked up the cards, shuffled them and placed the pack in front of the driver sitting next to him to cut. Victor dealt five cards to each player. Mofola kept three and discarded two, he had two kings and a jack. He did not fan the cards out in his hand but kept them closed so that no one could see the nail marks on the back of his cards. Mofola sat opposite Victor who had the driver on his right and the commissioner on his left, Costa sat on the commissioner's left next to Mofola. Mofola could see the backs of all the players' cards with the exception of Costa's.

Everyone was playing, so each put one hundred in the middle. Victor dealt new cards to those who had discarded; Mofola put his hand on the cards as they were dealt to him, slid them toward him and then picked them up and placed them behind the ones he was holding. He had been dealt a jack and a nine of spades. By the marks on the back of the cards Mofola could see that the driver had two aces, the commissioner had three queens, and Victor had no high cards that he could see and Costa's cards he could not see, as he was too close to him on the right.

It was the driver's call. "I go one" he said and put a hundred in the middle. Mofola also went one. Costa and the commissioner went two and Victor went three. It was the driver's turn again. "I will see you," he said, referring to Victor, and added another two hundred into the middle. Mofola suspected that the driver had a full house and the commissioner was also likely to have a full house, he had no idea what Costa had and Victor was either bluffing or he had a good hand, but by the look on his face he thought that he was not bluffing.

Mofola thought that he would play along just to ease the tension and see what Victor was up to, he knew his hand was not a good one. "I'll see you too," he said and put in two hundred more. Costa and the commissioner also decided to see Victor and each put two hundred in the middle.

"OK," said the commissioner, "let's see what you have."

Victor could hardly contain himself as he spread his cards out on the table in front of him. He had four fives and a ten of clubs.

"Four of a kind beats my full house," said the commissioner, throwing his three kings and two sevens on the table.

"And my straight," said Costa, putting his cards down on the table.

"Yes, beats my full house as well," said the driver.

"Beats me too," said Mofola and he laid his cards face down on the table in front of him.

"It's nice doing business with you," said Victor. He then stretched across the table to pick up Mofola's cards. "Let's see what the Boxer Boy had." But before he could even lift the cards off of the table a big hand shot out, grasping his wrist in a vicelike grip.

"If you want to see my cards then first let me see your money," said Mofola, looking Victor straight in the eyes.

"I see we have a sensitive player," said Victor, trying to save face as he let go of the cards."

"You should know better," said the commissioner. "Take your money so we can continue the game." Victor scooped up the money in the centre of the table and placed it on the pile of notes in front of him.

"Well, it will have to be without me," said the driver, as he got up from the table. "It would seem it's just not my night tonight." He walked over to join his friend who was standing at the bar.

Because the driver had pulled out, it was Mofola's turn to deal. He gathered up the cards and shuffled them like a professional, first shuffling them from one hand to the other in quick succession and then splitting the pack into two, with a half a pack in each hand he quickly thumbed each pack simultaneously blending one pack neatly into the other. Mofola's skill in shuffling had brought a buzz to the crowd of onlookers. He quickly dealt the cards, making sure that his cards were placed one on top of the other.

By midnight, Mofola had taken more than five thousand from the trio, at least three thousand of which had come from Victor's pile that was now dwindling fast. The more Victor drank, the more reckless he became, determined to beat Mofola at all costs. It was Mofola's turn to deal again. "I will play one more game and then I will be on my way home," said Mofola.

"Not so fast, boy," said Victor. "I want a chance to win back my money before you go anywhere."

"I'll stay for one more game or I can leave now—it's up to you," said Mofola.

"One more," said the commissioner.

"One more is also fine with me," said Costa.

But Victor was more determined to settle the odds with Mofola. "All right," he said, "one more game, but we make the minimum bet five hundred." Costa looked at the commissioner and they both shook their heads.

"Count me out," said Costa.

"And me too," said the commissioner.

"Well then, it's just you and me, Boxer Boy."

Mofola counted out five hundred *escudos* and placed them in the middle of the table, picked up the cards, shuffled, and dealt five cards to Victor and five to himself. The onlookers were quiet as the two players picked up their cards. Mofola picked up his one by one, not fanning them out, remembering each card as he picked it up, and placed one behind the other. "Not a great hand," said Mofola to himself remembering the cards he had dealt himself.

He looked across at Victor's hand and could see that he held two aces and one king, he could not be sure of one of the cards because Victor's fingers covered the place where the nail marks usually were. Victor discarded two cards and Mofola one.

Mofola dealt Victor two cards and gave himself one. He looked at his card and put it face down on top of his other cards lying on the table. Mofola could see that Victor had picked up another king and some other unmarked card, he knew that at best Victor held two pairs.

Victor was agitated that Mofola had not picked up his cards. "Well, are you playing or aren't you playing?"

"It's your call," said Mofola.

"Well then pick up your fucking cards so we can see if you are playing or not playing."

Mofola obliged, picked up his cards, and fanned them out. But he held them close to his chest to make sure no one behind could see his hand. He had no high cards, so it was not necessary to hide the backside of his hand to Victor.

Victor was visibly irritated. He could see the backs of all Mofola's cards but he still had no idea what Mofola held so he decided to bluff. "I'll go two thousand," he said and pushed the money into the middle of the table.

Mofola looked at his cards for a while, then closed them and made as if he was going to fold and put his cards down on the table. Victor's face lit up like a light bulb, and he was about to scoop up the money when Mofola said, "OK, Mr. Victor, your two thousand and another two."

"You can't frighten me, boy, you got nothing. Commissioner, lend me two thousand so I can call this boy's bluff."

The commissioner took out a roll of notes, counted out two thousand *escudos*, and handed the notes to Victor. He then took out a little black notebook and made an entry. Victor took the money and threw it down on top of the pile in the centre of the table. "Let's see what a pile of shit you have."

Mofola spread his cards out on the table in front of him. There was a four of hearts, six of spades, three of diamonds, seven of clubs and five of clubs. "Just as I thought, nothing," Victor said, paying little attention to Mofola's cards on the table. "There," he said, "two pairs beats that load of shit," and he tossed his cards on the table revealing the two kings, the two aces and a nine of hearts.

Victor started to pick up the money. "Wait a minute, Mr. Victor, where I learned to play poker, a straight beats two pairs or do you play a different set of rules here?" asked Mofola, looking questioningly at Costa and the commissioner.

"Straight," said Victor, "where's the fucking straight?"

"Look carefully, Mr. Victor," said Mofola as he rearranged his cards on the table, three of diamonds, four of hearts, five of clubs, six of spades and seven of clubs. "That looks like a straight to me."

"You cheating bastard," shouted Victor, jumping up from the table and knocking it over onto Mofola who fell over backward in his chair with the cards and money all over him and over the floor. "I'll fucking kill you, you cheating bastard," shouted Victor as he tried to get around the table to Mofola.

The commissioner stepped in his way and said, "There will be no killing here tonight, so sit down and shut your big mouth before I shut it for you."

One of the spectators picked up the table and helped Mofola to his feet, some of the others helped him pick up the cards and money and put it back on the table. Mofola thanked them and asked, "Did anyone here see me cheat? As he looked at each man, he shook his head as Mofola's eyes went from person to person around the table. Mofola gathered up his winnings and walked over to the bar where the two drivers that had played with them were sitting, watching from afar.

"How much did you lose?" he asked.

"Seven hundred," said the one.

"Nine hundred," said the other.

Mofola counted out seven hundred and then nine hundred onto the counter in front of them. "Just remember one thing."

"What's that?" one of them asked, looking at the money in front of them.

"You can't win against those three; the cards are always stacked against you. So take the money, I had a good night," said Mofola turning to go.

"No, wait, we can't take your money, you won it fairly and we lost it fairly."

"Maybe you did and maybe you didn't," said Mofola as he made his way to the door.

"What are you saying?" the other man asked, "Were they cheating?"

"I'm not saying a thing," said Mofola over his shoulder and continued to walk to the door.

Victor saw Mofola making his way to the door and got up from where he was sitting quietly with Costa and the commissioner. He was desperately trying to drown his sorrows in red wine. "Hey, you," he shouted above the noise in the cantina.

Suddenly the place went all quiet. Mofola turned around just as he got to the door and said, "You talking to me?"

"Yes, I'm talking to you, herd boy, you fucking owe me."

"I owe you nothing," said Mofola, turning to go out the door.

"Yes you do, you bastard, you took over ten thousand from me tonight and I want a chance to get it back."Mofola stopped again and looked over at Victor. "Firstly, Mr. Victor, I took nothing from you. I won it playing poker against you and your friends, or have you forgotten? And secondly, I'm not a bastard, I have a legitimate mother and father, so if you don't mind, I would like to go home. I still have a long walk ahead of me."

By this time Victor was making his way to the door where Mofola was standing. "So what are you saying?" he slurred, trying to get the words around his thick tongue. "You are afraid to give me the chance to win back my money?"

"No, Mr. Victor, I'm not afraid to give you a chance to win back your money, but I'm tired and I want to go home and, you see, playing against a drunk is not much of a challenge."

"Challenge, challenge, let me tell you, boy," by this time Victor was standing almost on top of Mofola, "I was playing poker long before you were even born and I'm more than a match for you and you know it." He grabbed Mofola's arm stopping him from going out the door.

"Mr. Victor," said Mofola very quietly so only he could hear, "let go of my arm before I break your neck like I would a chicken." The way Mofola said it and the look in his eyes made Victor immediately let go of Mofola's arm. "If you want another chance, then be here tomorrow night at eight," Mofola said and he walked out the door.

By this time Victor had regained his composure and shouted after him, "You had better be here tomorrow night at eight or I'll come and drag your black ass down here."

Mofola ignored him and laughed to himself as he made his way home. It had been a good night. His plan was coming together very nicely. It was almost as good as boss Jannie's "XYZ Plan." He laughed out loud when he thought about it. Those days now seemed so far in the past and yet they were not so long ago. He slept well that night and for once had no bad dreams about Mr. Victor.

Since the incident with Mofola and her father in the store almost a month ago, Negome had not heard from or seen Mofola. She had seen his nephews in the store a few times but Mofola had told them that if Negome asked where he was, to just say that he was busy attending to family matters.

It was Saturday and, being Victor's custom, he got up late, around eleven o'clock. He was in a foul mood and nursing a sore head from all the wine he had drunk the night before. His family were attending the store by themselves. Victor seldom went into the store on a Saturday. He would get up late, pour himself a mug of coffee from the pot on the stove and sit in the kitchen drinking it. After he had washed and shaved, he would walk down to the cantina to get something to eat and drink.

"Do you have to make so much noise when you close that damn door? Can't you close it softly? No wonder the hinges are always falling off."

"I'm sorry, Father, I did not mean to startle you. We thought that you were down at the cantina."

"Because I'm not here is no excuse to go around banging doors."

"I'm sorry, Father," protested the youngest. "I will be more careful in the future."

Victor got up from the rocking chair and went inside. "So, woman, what's for supper? I'm hungry. I have not eaten all day."

"We thought you were at the cantina," said his wife, surprised to find him still at home. "We had not planned on cooking a big supper."

"Why is it that everyone in this house assumes so much? Just get on with it and make me something to eat, as I'm going out at eight o'clock."

Just before eight, Victor walked down to the cantina. The place was full. It would seem that the whole town was there to see the contest between Victor and Mofola. Victor went over to his normal table where the commissioner was sitting.

"Good evening, Commissioner," said Victor.

"Yes," said the commissioner, "and how is your head today? We missed you at lunch. I hope for your sake it is clearer than it was last night or you could be losing your shirt tonight. That Boxer is no fool, you know!"

"Yes, I'm aware of that, Commissioner. That is why I thought I would have a sleep this afternoon so that my mind would be fresh for the game tonight. But don't you worry, Commissioner, that Boxer Boy is no match for me. Tonight I will take every *escudo* from him and send him back to where he belongs, herding goats."

"That's fighting talk," said the commissioner. "I like your spirit. Do you mind if Costa and I play a few hands with you? After all, the Boxer took money off us as well."

Victor's chest filled out when the commissioner mentioned that he had spirit. Tonight he would show them. Yes, let them all play. After all, they had taken a lot of money from him over the years. Tonight was his big chance to get even with them as well as take the shirt off Mofola's back. "Yes, of course you are welcome to play," said Victor. "We will all show that Boxer Boy who the best poker players are in Massangena."

It was already quarter past eight and there was still no sign of Mofola. Victor had still not had a drink, but he was slowly becoming irritable. He sloshed some wine into a glass and drank it in one gulp. By five to nine he was already on his third glass and was making all sorts of idle threats about what he was going to do to that no good son of a bitch herd boy when he saw him again.

At nine o' clock on the button, Mofola casually walked into the full cantina. He had deliberately come late because he knew it would really get Victor worked up. Mofola pushed his way to the bar counter and ordered a beer.

Costa served him. "This one's on me. You seem to have attracted a large gathering tonight—we thought that you were not coming."

"Well, I'm here," he said and made his way over to the table just as Victor was getting up to come and confront him.

"Where the fuck have you been?" asked Victor. "Don't you have a fucking clock in your house?"

Mofola put his hand into his pocket and pulled out his Zobo watch that hung from a thin silver chain. He casually flicked open the lid and looked at the time. It had just gone five past nine. "I'm sorry I'm five minutes late. Please forgive me; I know it's bad manners to be late for an appointment."

"Five fucking minutes, you're one hour and five fucking minutes late. Can't you even tell the time?" shouted Victor, right in Mofola's face.

"Wasn't our appointment for nine o' clock?" asked Mofola with a serious look on his face. "I'm sure I said nine, but then again I could be wrong."

"Wrong, of course you're fucking wrong and you know it, so don't give me any of that shit. Sit your ass down and let's play poker or have you changed your mind?"

By this time there was a crowd around the table and they loved every minute of this. This is what they had come to see, a good tense contest. Mofola obliged and sat down opposite Victor.

The commissioner asked Mofola whether he minded if he and Costa sat in for a few games. "After all, we would like the opportunity to win our money back again," said the commissioner.

Mofola said he had no problem with that, providing Mr. Victor agreed.

Costa came and joined them, bringing another bottle of wine and a pack of cards. Victor picked up the pack of cards that Costa had brought and said, "Seeing this is such an important game, I thought we should use a nice new pack of cards that I took from the store this afternoon."

Mofola was pleased with that decision, as he was going to make the same suggestion and had also brought along new a pack of cards.

The commissioner and Costa looked questioningly at each other, but said they had no problem, and Mofola said he had no problem either. The commissioner thought it a bit strange that Victor wanted to use a new pack of cards; they always played with the specially marked cards when playing against someone other than themselves. That was the only way that Victor could win. Although Victor thought of himself as a good poker player, the commissioner knew he was not and wondered just what Victor was up to.

The commissioner picked up the new pack of cards that Victor had brought and casually turned it over in his hand before tearing off the cellophane wrapping. He then split the seal on the box with his thumbnail and removed the cards from their box. He took the two jokers off of the top and put them back in the box. Every thing looked quite normal. He then handed the pack to Mofola and said, "Seeing you shuffle so well you can have the first honour."

One could almost feel Victor tense up when the commissioner took the cards and then sense the relief when he handed the cards to Mofola to shuffle and deal. By the time they had played a few hands Victor had regained his composure and was feeling quite confident, he had won two out of the three hands played. His little modification to the cards was working well and no one suspected anything.

By eleven o'clock Mofola had lost five thousand, at first he thought that they were all playing against him, but the commissioner and Costa had also lost quite heavily. He was now not sure what their game plan was. Victor seemed to win all the big hands and his cocky attitude and apparent good luck were beginning to irritate the commissioner. Mofola suspected the cards had somehow been doctored but he could detect nothing.

When eleven thirty came and the commissioner, not having won another hand, said, "Well that's me for the night. This is obviously your lucky night, Victor." He took out his little book and totalled up what he had lost. "I'm at least nine thousand down and I suspect that a good portion of that is now sitting with you. If you carry on this way, you will be able to pay me back what you owe me in cash."

Costa was not faring any better, having lost the last hand to Victor. He threw his cards into the middle and said, "That's me out as well. You just can't play against someone when the luck is running their way."

"This has got nothing to do with luck, it is just skilful playing," said Victor arrogantly, pouring the rest of the wine from the bottle into his glass. The commissioner scoffed at Victor's remark and went out the back to the toilet.

"Well, it looks like it's just you and me again," said Victor with more than a bit of sarcasm in his voice. "The cards are stacked against you tonight, boy, I'm going to take the shirt from your back still tonight." And he slapped the pack of cards down on the table in front of Mofola, "Or are you also going to pack it in? You still owe me, boy, from last night."

Mofola had already lost six thousand five hundred *escudos*. He was still a few hundred up from the previous night, but the way things were going it would not last very long, this was not what he had planed, his "XYZ Plan" was not going well at all. He would have to do something soon or he would be broke.

"I'll tell you what," said Victor, "let's make it a minimum bet of five hundred again." And with that he threw five hundred into the middle. "Or are you not the poker player you make out to be with all that fancy shuffling stuff you do?"

The spectators were all urging Mofola to continue, so he took five hundred and tossed it on top of Victor's five, picked up the cards shuffled, them and started to deal.

Mofola discarded three cards and kept a queen of hearts and a jack of hearts. Victor also discarded three cards. Mofola dealt Victor three cards, stretching across the table, and as he dealt the last card he knocked Victor's glass of wine over that was standing in front of him, Mofola in his haste to try to stop it falling dropped the pack of cards in the wine.

"Mother of Jesus Christ, you fucking idiot, look what you have done!" shouted Victor, jumping up from the table with wine dripping from his pants and running off the table onto the floor.

Costa quickly ran into the kitchen and got some cloths. He gave one to Victor to wipe himself and with the others he wiped the table and tried to dry the cards that were soaked in red wine. "Jesus Christ," swore Victor. "Not only have you fucked up my pants but you have fucked up a brand new pack of cards."

"I'm very sorry," protested Mofola, "I will pay for your pants to be cleaned."

"Cleaned!" shouted Victor. "Don't you know that red wine stains?"

"I'm sorry," said Mofola. "Then I will buy you a new pair of pants."

"You're fucking right you will—and look at these cards," said Victor, picking one up from the pile that Costa was still trying to wipe. "We can't play with these again," he said and threw the card back on the pile of cards.

"I said I was sorry," said Mofola. "It was an accident but we can still play." And he took a new pack of cards from his pocket and put them on the table. "You can have this pack" said Mofola. "This pack was bought from your store just the other day by my young nephew, and see, it is brand new, it still has the cellophane wrapping on it."

Victor picked up the pack and examined it, turning it over in his hand looking to see if the cellophane was still intact. "No, I don't feel like playing anymore," he said and put the pack back on the table.

"So who's backing down now?" said Mofola. "Just awhile ago, I thought you said you wanted to take the shirt from my back. Now it seems it's you that wants to back down."

The commissioner had come back from the toilet and was standing next to the table watching all the fuss. "Come now, Victor, he said, "show Boxer you're not afraid to play him."

"Yes, yes," chanted the crowd, urging Victor to play. After all, that's what they had come to see. The commissioner picked up the new pack of cards, opened them, and put them in front of Victor. He then gathered up the wet cards and the empty bottle, "I will even buy you another bottle of wine. Come, Costa let's go and find our friend Victor a nice bottle of your best wine." And with that he took Costa by the elbow and steered him to the bar.

At the bar the commissioner took the cards, put them on the counter, and started to spread some of them out. Costa got a bottle of wine from behind the counter, opened it, and put it on the counter in front of the commissioner, who said, "Look here. Our little fat friend has been cheating us; the greedy little bastard has doctored these cards. He has scraped some of the patterns off on the backs of the high cards. Here," he said, pointing to where the varnish had been scraped away. "The wine has soaked in and stained the cards. If it weren't for the Boxer knocking over the wine we would never have known. After all we have done for him—the ungrateful little bastard cheats his best and only friends. Come, let's make sure our greedy little friend plays some more."

Victor was trapped. He had no option but to play on. He could not lose face in front of the commissioner and the crowd of onlookers. After all, he was a better card player than this Boxer Boy, he reasoned to himself. How much of the money he had already won could he lose anyway? Even if he lost a few hands it could not be that bad, so he picked up the cards and started to shuffle them. "OK," he said, "but only three hands because I'm getting tired now."

"Fine" said Mofola, "but then let's make it a little more challenging and play minimum bet one thousand."

"Yes, yes," chanted the crowd, "one thousand, one thousand, come on, Mr. Victor, tell him you play for one thousand, you're not afraid."

By this time the commissioner and Costa had returned to the table and sat down.

"Come on Victor," said the commissioner, "deal the damn cards—this is, after all, your lucky night." He sloshed some wine into Victor's glass,

Mofola won the first hand, taking four thousand off Victor. It was Mofola's turn to deal. He shuffled the pack and put it in front of Victor to cut. Victor carefully cut the pack. There were beads of sweat now forming on his forehead as he placed one half next to the other. Mofola completed the cut by placing one half on top of the other and dealt five cards to each of them.

Victor looked at his cards, quickly discarded one card, and gulped down the glass of wine, which the commissioner promptly refilled. Mofola discarded two cards. Victor had been dealt two jacks and two tens; he needed another ten or a jack for a full house. Mofola dealt one card to Victor and two cards to himself. Victor grabbed his glass and gulped down the wine. He then slowly lifted the corner of the card on the table in front of him as if there were a snake under it. He then quickly picked it up and put it on top of his other cards and then picked the lot up and fanned them out in his hand. With the ten he had been dealt he now had a full house.

Victor was now feeling a lot more confident. "OK, Boxer Boy, let's see what you can do with this," he said and put five thousand in the middle of the table. There was a deadly silence around the table.

"Your five and ten more," said Mofola, not even looking at the cards he had dealt himself.

"Ten thousand, ten thousand," they whispered around the table.

"You can't frighten me with the oldest trick in the book," said Victor, counting out ten thousand into the middle of the table. He gulped a mouthful of wine and said, "Your ten and eight more." He would have liked to have gone another ten but that was all the money he had with him.

"OK," said Mofola and he undid the buttons of his shirt and then untied the bandana he had around his waist. He unwrapped the cloth and took out the rest of his money. "Your eight and ten more."

Small beads of sweat had again appeared on Victor's forehead. "You think you are so fucking clever. I told you, you can't frighten me. Commissioner, please lend me twenty thousand so I can really teach this fucking herd boy a lesson in poker he will never forget."

"Don't you remember?" said the commissioner. "You took all my money from me at the table tonight; I don't have that sort of money on me."

"Just give me an IOU like you always do, you know I will pay you back. As you said, Commissioner, tonight is my lucky night."

"No," said the commissioner, "no more IOUs, you are on your own. If you can't pay then you shouldn't play."

"Costa, you lend me the money," said Victor, now almost pleading. "I'm going to kick this boy's ass. This money is as good as all mine," he said pointing to the pile of money on the table and downing the glass of wine.

"Sorry, Victor, I can't help you tonight."

"Come on, somebody here, please lend me ten thousand." Victor was now getting desperate as he looked around the table. "Come on, I will give you back fifteen as soon as I finish this game, your money is safe." Nobody was prepared to lend Victor a cent. "What's the matter? Don't any of you trust me? What about you, Boxer Boy? Let me see you, you know I'm good for ten thousand. If I lose then I will give you fifteen from the store in the morning."

"I'll tell you what, Mr. Victor, I'll make you a deal," said Mofola. "Seeing you are so sure that you are going to win then you will get all this," he said, picking up a handful of notes from the table centre and letting them float back down again onto the pile. "If you lose then I take your daughter Negome's hand in marriage."

"You think I'm fucking mad? I'll never give my daughter to some fucking herder of goats. Over my dead body will that happen," he said and pushed his chair from the table and got up.

"Come on, Mr. Victor, you play, you win this time, no problem," shouted the crowd of onlookers trying to encourage him to play on.

The commissioner pushed his way around the table and came and stood next to Victor. While the crowd was still cheering him to play on, the commissioner pulled Victor closer to him and whispered in his ear, "You had better play on, you little piece of shit. You have been cheating us. Those cards you brought were doctored, the red wine stained the places where you scraped away the varnish—that's how you won. You are a greedy piece of shit. To think of all the times we helped you and you go and cheat on your only friends. I think you had better sit down and play, because if you don't then I will have to tell these people how you have been cheating them all these years."

The commissioner went and stood back where he came from and gestured to Victor with his outstretched hand that he should sit. Victor was obviously very shaken by what the commissioner had said. His whole future now lay in a game of cards. He wiped the sweat from his forehead with the sleeve of his shirt, looked at the commissioner and then at Costa who nodded his head in agreement. He then looked down at his cards lying face down on the table and then at Mofola's cards, still laying face down where they had been dealt. "You're fucking bluffing. You haven't even looked at your last two cards," he said and slowly sat down. The crowd cheered and clapped their hands. Victor picked up his cards and stared at them for some time. There was no other way out, and he had to call Mofola's bluff. "OK, you fucker, I'll call your bluff. My daughter's hand is at stake. Let's see what you have."

The crowd suddenly went quiet as Mofola took the top card from the pile of three that was lying on the table in front of him and turned it over to reveal a seven of clubs. The next card was a king of hearts and the last card was a seven of spades.

"Nothing, fucking nothing, that's what you got," shouted Victor across the table.

Mofola looked Victor straight in the face and without dropping his eyes he turned the top card over from the last two cards he had dealt himself. The first card was a seven of hearts. He put his hand on the last card, you could feel the tension and people were holding their breath, as he slowly turned it over to reveal the seven of diamonds.

The crowd around the table went wild slapping Mofola on the back and congratulating him as if he were a prize-fighter who had just won a world title bout. Little did they know that shuffling was only one of the card skills that he had learned, arranging the pack in a certain sequence as he shuffled and dealing from the bottom of the pack were other skills he had taught himself over the years.

The commissioner came around to where Victor was still sitting staring at the last two cards Mofola had turned over. "It seems that it was not quite your lucky night after all. You see what happens when you double-cross your friends? I'll be around on Monday to collect what you took from me and Costa tonight, make sure you have the cash or you could find yourself not only without one of your daughters but also without a business."

Mofola gathered up all the money on the table and tied it up in the bandana. It was funny—he felt no sense of victory as he got up from the table and said to Victor, who continued to stare at the cards on the table as if he were in a trance, "I'll be around on Monday to collect the other half of my winnings." As he made his way between the tables to the door, people were still patting him on the back as he went past.

It was past one in the morning as he stepped from the *veranda* of the cantina and made his way home. The wind was gusting and in the distance he could see streaks of lightning followed shortly by sounds of thunder. By the time he got home, a few large drops of rain had started to fall. It looked like the start of the long-awaited rains had finally come.

Victor finished what was left of the wine in the bottle and made his way out of the cantina. Nobody paid him any attention; they were all too busy talking about the game to care about a loser like Victor. And, after all, he'd had it coming to him for a long time. Victor staggered into the house around the back through the kitchen. The *paraffin* light was turned down low so he turned it up, took the pot of warm coffee from the stove, and poured some into an enamel mug.

The next morning Mrs. Aguiar found Victor sitting at the table passed out with his head resting on his arms on the table, snoring loudly. She emptied the ash from the stove, restarted the fire and made a fresh pot of coffee. She then went back to their bedroom and got dressed for church. She woke the children up and told them to wash and get ready for church. By the time she got back to the kitchen Victor was awake. He was sitting, playing with the sugar, picking up a spoonful and pouring it slowly back in the bowl.

Chapter 29

"Good morning, husband, would you like some coffee?" Victor never answered her. He continued to play with the sugar. It never bothered her that he did not answer; she was used to it. She poured him a mug of black coffee and put it in front of him. The girls came into the kitchen and greeted their father. He never responded or gave any indication that he recognized that they were even there. It was as if he were in a world of his own. It did not bother them either, as they were so used to their father being in a bad mood, especially when he'd had had too much to drink the night before.

"We are finished," he said to no one in particular, not looking up from the sugar that was slowly cascading from the spoon back into the bowl.

"Finished what, my husband?" she asked, not really paying any attention to what he was saying as she continued to prepare his breakfast before they went to church. Victor never went to church. The girls and their mother would have breakfast after church. "Finished, finished, don't you fucking understand, you stupid woman? We are finished, we have nothing left."

"What do you mean, Father?" asked Negome. "Have you lost money again at poker to Mr. Xavair and the commissioner?"

"Be quiet child," scolded her mother. "Can't you see your father is not well? He does not want to talk about it now. Go and get your things for church."

"No, Mother, I want to know. I'm not a child anymore and I control the finances of the store so I must know what our father has done. If he's gambled the money away again I must know how much, so we know how long it will take to pay the commissioner and Mr. Xavair back."

"It's all gone, the store, the house, everything, it's all gone, we have nothing left."

"Father, you can't be serious. You have lost to them many times before and they always let you pay them back. Surely they will let you pay them back again? We always paid the debt back with interest."

"No I'm afraid this time it's different, they will not let me pay them back, not even with all the interest in the world will they let me off this time. The commissioner will take the store and that Boxer Boy will come on Monday and take you."

'Take me, Father, take me where? What are you talking about? I don't understand—you are not making any sense." Negome was becoming very agitated with her father.

"You were part of my gambling the bet," said Victor, looking up from the sugar bowl at his oldest daughter.

"You mean you used me like money or property, to gamble with? What—do I mean so little to you that you could just use me in this way?"

"I had no option; there was nothing left for me to do. The commissioner told me that if I did not continue to play, he would tell everyone that I was cheating."

"Were you cheating, Father?"

"How dare you ask your father such a question? Have you no respect, child? Your father would never cheat, you should know that," said her mother.

"So you gave me to Mofola as part of your gambling debt, because the commissioner caught you cheating, is that what you are saying, Father?"

"Yes, that is correct, but it wasn't the way you're thinking."

"Father, it doesn't matter what I think, it's what the whole town thinks. First I'm a whore and now I'm a gambling debt."

They were late, the service had already started and everyone was standing singing the opening hymn. They went and sat at the back of the church, first kneeling to cross themselves, and then standing up to join in the last verse of the hymn.

Negome's eyes were red from crying. She had cried all the way to the church. She felt dirty, like a dirty dishcloth. How could her father do this to her after all she had done for him? She heard nothing of the sermon that Father Hogan was preaching. It was only when her mother nudged her with her elbow that she snapped out of her trance, and everyone was kneeling except her. She slid off the pew and knelt down on the wooden floor and prayed silently, "Blessed Mary, Mother of our Lord Jesus Christ, forgive the thoughts I have for my father." But they were only words. Still deep in her heart she despised him.

Father Hogan stood outside his church and greeted members of his congregation individually as they came out, chatting briefly to those he knew had been ill or had sickness in the family. Father Hogan knew most of his congregation, one could almost say intimately. Over the years he had visited them all at home on numerous occasions. The Aguiars were some of the first to leave. Although Victor never went to church, Father Hogan always made a point of asking Mrs. Aguiar how he was and how the business in the store was going.

She in turn would always give the same old answer that made Negome want to scream. Every time she said, "Thank you, Father. Victor is well and sends his greetings to you. Yes, the business in the store is going well. Good day, Father." Negome knew it by heart.

Negome was the last of the Aguiar family to be greeted by Father Hogan. He took both her hands in his and looked her in the eyes and he could see the terrible hurt there. "Be strong, my child," he said, "and may the Lord bless you in a special way." And with that he lifted her hands in his and kissed the back of each hand and squeezed them before letting them go again.

There were no secrets in Massangena that Father Hogan did not know of. He had heard about the plight of Victor in the cantina the night before from the woman who cleaned his small house. She brought him all the news and gossip of the small town on a daily basis.

They walked from the church entrance and out through the courtyard. Negome could feel the eyes of the people that left the church ahead of them staring at her. Members of the parish stood in small groups talking and spreading the latest gossip. It was the only chance that most of the community got to see each other when they came to church. Negome knew that they were talking about her family and when she looked at them they would look away and stop talking.

Her mother greeted various people as they made their way to the gate and out on to the muddy street. Negome despised her mother for her naivety and simple-mindedness; she came from a poor family in the northern district. Negome hated the fact that her mother could at times be so pigheaded and not see what her father was doing to the family. Every time he lost at poker her mother would simply say he was just having a bit of bad luck he would soon win it back again. Negome knew better; her father very seldom won at cards. He was just not very good at playing cards but he would never admit it and, over the years, he had become obsessed with the game.

Negome walked ahead of her mother and two sisters. When she arrived home she went straight into the bedroom and threw herself down on the bed, buried her head in the pillow, and cried. She felt so hopeless. Mrs. Aguiar and the two girls came home and went straight into the kitchen to make their breakfast. Victor was no longer sitting at the table; the cup of coffee, now cold, was still on the table where Mrs. Aguiar had put it.

The fire in the stove had all but gone out. Mrs. Aguiar took one of the fire tools hanging next to the stove and lifted off one of the steal cover plates. She poked the ashes and put the last two remaining logs from the wood box in the fire and closed it again. She then topped off the coffee pot and put it back on the hottest part of the stove. The two girls set the table for breakfast. They would always have a thick slice of their mother's homemade bread and jam and a cup of coffee when they got back from church.

"While the coffee is getting hot, please go and fetch some more wood from the shed," she said to the younger of the two girls. The youngest picked up the old wooden *paraffin* box used for storing wood and went out the back to the shed. The wooden slat door was closed and she tried to push it open but something was preventing it from opening. It felt like one of the bags of chicken meal had fallen against the inside of the door. She put the box down next to the door and pushed it with both hands, the door opened just enough for her to squeeze inside. It was rather dark in the shed, as there were no windows, and the only light came from the gap in the doorway, but whatever was holding it closed, had pushed it closed again as she squeezed inside.

Her eyes took some time to adjust from the bright sunlight to the gloom of the shed. She hated the shed; there were always rats and mice in there feeding on the chicken meal. She took a short step forward holding her hands out in front of her, scared that she may walk into something. Something brushed against her cheek. She put her hand up and touched what felt like a hand, it was cold and clammy. By this time her eyes were becoming adjusted to the gloomy light. She looked up to see a man hanging from his neck from a rope tied to one of the roof beams.

Negome had stopped crying. She had turned on her back and lay there as if in a trance staring at the ceiling, wondering just what they were going to do now. She was shocked out of her trance by an ear-splitting scream coming from outside the house. She jumped off of the bed and ran into the kitchen. Her mother and other sister were already running toward the shed where the screaming was coming from.

When Negome arrived at the shed her mother and sister were trying to push the door open. They all pushed together and the door suddenly opened revealing the body of Victor hanging from a rope tied to one of the beams just inside the door. As the door flew open the youngest sister came running out screaming and shaking. She collapsed into her mother's arms. She held her tight as the poor child shook and sobbed uncontrollably.

Negome, realizing that it was her father, became hysterical, shouting, "No, no, it can't be you, Pappie, please not you," as she held onto his dangling legs trying to pull him free. By this time all the shouting and screaming had alerted the neighbours and the people in the street. They came running into the yard through the back gate. They immediately saw what the commotion was all about and escorted the four hysterical women back into the house. Someone had run up the street to the police station and called the constable on duty to come and see what had happened. By the time he arrived at the shed there were quite a lot of people standing around the shed, all trying to get a look at the body hanging from the beam.

The constable pushed his way to the door and had a look for himself. He immediately recognized the fat little frame of Victor Aguiar and told one of the people standing there to go and call the commissioner from his house. When the commissioner arrived, he immediately took control of the situation and told all the people standing around to go home or go about their business. With the help of another constable they managed to lift the body up and then cut the rope from around his neck.

There was no official mortuary in Massangena so the body was stored in a   small   room at the back of the church. Bodies were often stored there while waiting for a coffin to arrive from Inhambane before being buried in the cemetery opposite the   church on the other side of the road.

Chapter 30

It had rained hard all through the early hours of Monday morning and at daybreak the rain stopped and the sky was slowly starting to clear. Mofola got up and went outside. The sun had just started to peep over the horizon; there were pools of water everywhere. Even the dogs were wet. The rain had blown in on them as they lay all curled up under the kitchen enclosure. They spotted Mofola and came running over to where he stood outside his room. He patted them and scolded them for shaking the rain off their backs all over him.

He walked over to the kitchen enclosure to see if he could find some wood in the wood box that had not gotten wet. By the time the fire was roaring, the rest of the *shamba* had started to come alive. Mofola was excited and could hardly wait for the family to get up so that he could tell them about his winnings from the night before.

The old man was the last of the family to get up. He was not well and Mofola could see that there was no spirit left in him. He shuffled his feet along as he made his way to the kitchen enclosure. "Good morning, Father," said Mofola. "The gods have been good to us; they have brought the rain."

"Yes, they have sent the rains," said the old man, "but it will be too late this year to save the grass. But if the rains continue, then it will help the grazing in the early spring. Maybe we will not have to feed the animals like we did this year, for the money is getting little and soon we will not have enough to feed ourselves and the animals."

"Father must not worry any longer about the money, for we will have enough to feed us all for many seasons without the rains and there will still be enough to send Father to the hospital in Inhambane."

"So tell me how is it that my youngest son, who has only worked two years on the mines, can have all this money and still have money to take his sick father to hospital? Did you rob a bank in South Africa or steal some gold to have all this money you speak of?"

"No, Father, I did not rob a bank or steal gold in South Africa. I won the money last night playing cards at the cantina." Mofola opened the bandana that was lying on the table, revealing the pile of bank notes.

"Here is enough money to pay for all that we need," he said, "and I still have other important news." The family had never seen so much money in one pile before, so they just looked at him in astonishment.

"What is this other important news you have?" asked his father.

"I'm going to get married to Mr. Victor's oldest daughter, you know, Negome," said Mofola excitedly.

"What is this all about a wife for my youngest? No one has spoken to me or even asked my permission, or is this no longer custom in these new times we are now living?"

"Of course it is still done, Father," said Mofola. "Please, everyone sit down and I will explain."

"Yes, please explain to a simple old man where all this money comes from."

Mofola explained to his family exactly what had happened from the time that he arrived back from South Africa. He told them how he tried to pay Mr. Victor the *ilobola* money for Negome and how Mr. Victor threw all his money on the floor of the store. He went on to tell them how he played cards with the commissioner, Mr. Costa, and Mr. Victor, and how he won money from them because they cheated and he saw how they cheated.

"The commissioner, Mr. Costa, and Mr. Victor would never cheat. I forbid you to say such things about these honourable men of the community," said the old man. "I will not sit here and listen to this nonsense anymore and he started to get up.

"No, no, Father, please let me finish. It is true what I'm telling you. You can ask the people in the community—they will tell you the same thing." The old man sat down again and Mofola continued with his story.

He went on to tell them about how the wine spilled on the cards and how the commissioner was so angry with Mr. Victor and how he told Mr. Victor to continue playing even when he was losing a lot of money. He told them that the commissioner and Mr. Costa had refused to lend him any more money, so Mr. Victor included his daughter as part of the bet. "That is how I won all this money," he said, pointing to the pile of money on the table, "as well as Negome for my bride."

The old man sat on the bench and said nothing, the rest of the family were as excited as Mofola, especially the two nephews. They were asking questions about how he saw that they were cheating and did Negome just climb up on the table as part of the bet. Everyone was now talking and asking questions except the old man, who sat quietly listening to all that was said. Slowly the old man got up, pushing himself up on his stick. He walked over to the small wooden table, lifted his stick, and brought it down on the table with a loud smack that brought an immediate stop to the talking and excitement.

"In this house we will have nothing to do with this," he said, pointing with his stick at the pile of money in the bandana on the table. This is the money of the devil. It is evil and will only bring shame and grief to our house."

"But, but," protested Mofola, "I won this money. It is for all of us and some we will use to take you to the hospital in Inhambane to make you well again."

"No, this money can never make me well. It is too evil." And with that he hooked the bandana with his stick and pushed it together with the money into the fire.

The heat of the fire lifted some of the notes into the air and everyone sat and watched as the notes slowly fluttered to the ground. No one moved; they were all too shocked by the old man's sudden reaction. They just stared at the money burning, shooting out little green flames as it slowly burned into a pile of grey ashes.

Chapter 31

Mofola had managed to save a few thousand *escudos* of his money that had not fallen into the fire. It would not be enough to start a new life with Negome. "Maybe the old man was right," he thought to himself. "It is the money of the devil." The money that he had brought from South Africa was to pay over to Mr. Victor for the hand of Negome. That money was now gone and he had Negome as his bride. There was really no difference; the extra money that he won was not his. That must be what his father meant when he said the money belonged to the devil. This was how Mofola reasoned with himself as he walked down the road toward town late that Monday morning to go and claim his bride.

It was past midday by the time he walked into town dressed in his best clothes and wearing his smart trilby hat. The town was fairly busy with trucks passing through, splashing up muddy water as their big wheels bounced through the many potholes in the road. Mofola was surprised that the store was closed. He knew that they closed between one and two, but it was only just past noon. He cupped his hands over the window and looked in, but there was no one inside.

Mofola asked one of the two people passing by if they knew why the store was closed.

"Did you not hear?" he said.

"No, hear what?" asked Mofola.

"Mr. Victor, he is dead. They find him Sunday morning. He be hanging from his neck in the woodshed."

"What?" said Mofola. "Who would do this to Mr. Victor?"

"No one do this to him; he do this thing to himself. When his wife and children, they are at the church, and when they come home the young girl she find him hanging by his neck."

Mofola was shocked. Why would Mr. Victor do such a thing? He must go and speak to Negome and see if she is alright. He walked around the back of the house. As he passed the old woodshed, he stopped and thought, that is where he and Negome used to meet and now they find Mr. Victor hanging from his neck in there. He walked on up to the house and knocked on the screen door. Mrs. Aguiar came to the door.

"Oh, it's you, and I suppose you have now come to take my daughter away as well?"

"No, no," lied Mofola. "I have just come to say how sorry I am to hear this sad news. Could you please tell her I'm here?"

"I don't know if she will even want to see you," her mother said and went back inside.

Mofola stood outside the back door and waited for quite a while before Negome came out. When he saw her he hardly recognized her. She looked terrible, and she had obviously been crying a lot.

"Yes! What do you want now?" she asked defiantly.

"I'm so sorry to hear about your father, I only just heard about it a few minutes ago from some men in the street. This is a terrible, terrible thing to happen."

Yes, she said, "it is a terrible thing you have done to us, you are so smart and yet you are so stupid, stupid. How could you do this to me? Were you not satisfied that you took all my father's money, his pride, and then you still were not satisfied, you took me from him as well? Why didn't you just put the rope around his neck while you were taking everything else from him?" she said, sobbing. "I thought you were different and cared about me, but you are just like all the other men— greedy, greedy, only ever thinking of yourself. I hate you and never want to see you again. If you think I will come with you, I would rather die before I do that." And with that she turned around and went back inside slamming the screen door behind her.

Mofola stood and stared at the closed screen door, not wanting to believe what he had just heard. His whole purpose in life had just been taken away from him again, it was as if someone had taken a knife and cut out his heart. He was devastated; never in his whole life had he felt so lost and without direction. He walked back home with a heavy heart.

At home he told his parents about Mr. Victor, and his father said, "Now you see, it is as I told you. If you play with the things of the devil, then one day the devil will come and fetch you. It was a good thing we sent the devil's money back to him. That daughter for Mr. Victor, she was not for you, she would have brought only trouble to our family. If it were that the gods wanted you to take this girl as your wife, then surely it would have been already." That was all the old man had to say about the whole affair.

On Wednesday they buried Victor in the cemetery opposite the mission church. Father Hogan conducted the service. There were not many people at the service, as Victor had not been very popular with the ordinary townsfolk. The commissioner, Costa, and his family were there to comfort the Aguiars. After the funeral there was a small wake at the cantina, which Costa paid for.

The commissioner walked back to the house with the Aguiar family after the wake and went inside with them. "Mrs. Aguiar, young ladies, please sit down. It is important that we talk about your late husband's affairs."

"I'll go and make some coffee."

"Please, Mrs. Aguiar, sit down, I think we've already had enough coffee. It is important that we speak now. There is no point in putting it off; the situation is not going to get any better and it is not going to go away."

"But I knew nothing of my late husband's affairs."

"Mother, sit down," said Negome. "The commissioner has something important to say and he wants us all to hear. Please, continue, Commissioner."

"Thank you, Negome. What I'm about to tell you does not bring me any pleasure," he said. "As you well know, Mrs. Aguiar, your husband has borrowed large sums of money from both Costa and me over the years."

"But he paid it all back," said Mrs. Aguiar.

"No, I'm afraid not. You see, he would pay back a little and then he would lose heavily again." The commissioner pulled out his little black book and showed it to the Aguiars. This is the amount that your husband owes me and Costa, and this amount does not include what he owes us from last Friday night's card game where he was cheating.

"I'm sorry to have to tell you this, but it is far better that you hear it now and we deal with the situation now rather than later. Costa and I have discussed the matter and we have reached the following conclusion. I will take over the store and the house to wipe out the debt owed to me and Costa and I will then pay Costa what is owed to him.

"Mrs. Aguiar, I have drawn up the necessary papers that will absolve you of your husband's debt." He placed a document in front of her on the table. "If you will just put your signature here and here," he said, handing her his open fountain pen. She took the pen from him and signed her name in the places he had indicated without even reading what was written. She trusted the commissioner implicitly.

"Now the next question is, what are we going to do with you ladies?" There was total silence. They just stared at the commissioner, waiting for him to come up with a suggestion. "Mrs. Aguiar, I know you have family up north and maybe you would like to take your family up there to live. I will also need someone to run the store for me and, if you like, you and your daughters can remain here and run the store for me. I will not be able to pay you much, but you will have a place to stay and enough money to feed yourselves. I will leave you to think about it for a few days and then you can tell me what you have decided."

"No, that will not be necessary. Commissioner, you have been very good to us over the years and very lenient with my late husband, and we will stay and run the store for you."

Negome had other plans for herself, and they did not include staying in Massangena and managing the store for the commissioner. For as long as she could remember she had worked in the store. She now wanted a change and she desperately needed to get out of Massangena. She had heard that they were always looking for woman to pick tea on the tea plantations in Rhodesia. It was hard work, she was told, but the money was good and accommodation and food were supplied.

Chapter 32

The bus from Inhambane going up to the Rhodesian border town of Espangabera came through Massangena twice a week. It stopped at the post office to off-load the little mail and any passengers, and to pick up any new passengers. Negome stood on the steps of the post office with some other people waiting for the bus to arrive, but as usual the bus was late. She wore a plain long brown dress; her hair was tied in a bun and covered with a scarf to try to keep it from being covered with dust that came in through the open windows of the bus. The few clothes she possessed were neatly packed in a small brown suitcase sitting on the steps at her feet.

She had said all her good-byes and had asked her mother and sisters not to come and see her off at the bus stop. They had all cried when she left the house to walk up to the bus stop at the post office, but she never shed a tear, the time for crying was over. In the past few weeks she had become very hard and bitter, and now she was stepping out into a new world. The prospects were quite frightening, as she had never in her whole eighteen years been out of Massangena.

The commissioner had helped her secure the travel documents she would need to enter Rhodesia and to work there. He had also given her enough money for the bus fare as well as a little to see her through for a few days. The commissioner had hoped that Negome would have stayed and continued to run the store, but she explained the reasons why she just had to get out of Massangena and he understood. Now, more so than ever, he wanted the rest of the Aguiar family to remain and run the store for him so he offered to help Negome.

He had also supplied her with a letter of introduction to a tea farmer he had gotten to know from the Chipinge district in Rhodesia, who would stop over in Massangena on his way to and from Inhambane. He told Negome to get to Chipinge and then ask the locals how to get to the Traverses' farm.

It was a long and dusty trip up to the border post at Espangabera and it took the rest of the afternoon to cover the hundred and sixty kilometres up the winding mountain road, including all the stops along the way unloading and loading passengers and their luggage. Negome spent the night in Espangabera at a cheap hotel. The next morning she crossed the border into Rhodesia and walked the few kilometres into the little town of Silinda.

Chapter 33

The Traverse family had been farming tea in the foothills of the Chimanimani Mountains for over twenty years. Reg had inherited the estate from his father who had died three years ago; his mother had died some years before, having suffered from recurring malaria fever. The whole of Reg's tea crop was exported to England via Beira or Inhambane. The market in the United Kingdom was very lucrative, having been established many years ago by his late father.

Because Reg's father had connections in England they had sent Reg to boarding school there and later to King George's Agriculture College in Kent. There he had met Elizabeth Farningham, whom he eventually married and took back to Africa, much to her parents' disapproval. Elizabeth or Beth as she was most commonly referred to was never a physically strong person, but what she lacked in physical strength she made up for in sheer guts and determination.

Reg had met Beth in his last year at college and they fell madly in love from their first date. They had married with neither of her parent's blessing shortly before Reg was due to go back to Rhodesia.

Africa can be a harsh place and Beth never really adapted to the hot and often dry conditions of the African bush, but she adored Reg and was determined to make a go of their relationship and also to prove a point to her ever-doubting parents.

They had been trying to have a family for a number of years. Twice Beth had fallen pregnant and within the first six to eight weeks had lost both the babies. The specialist in Salisbury had told her that she would have to take special care and slow down, if she ever wanted to produce a family. Two years after her last miscarriage Beth fell pregnant again. This time, both she and Reg were determined that she was going to keep the child. So during the first two months of her confinement she spent most of it resting in bed or out on the recliner couch on the *veranda* of the big farmhouse.

Reg was not happy that they were so far from a good hospital and at the last visit to their doctor Reg asked him if it would be safe for Beth to travel to her parents in the England. The doctor said that the crucial stage of the pregnancy was now past and that as long as she took it very slowly and rested well, there was no reason why she could not travel. However, he recommended that she not fly, as the high altitude and pressure could have a negative effect on her pregnancy. So it was decided after a few long distance telephone calls to her parents that she should go as soon as she could get a passage on a ship. At first Beth was not very happy with the decision. She did not want to leave Reg for such a long time, but finally agreed that for her and the unborn child's sake, it would be the right thing to do.

The three-week trip from Beira to Southampton via the Suez Canal as a passenger on a freighter was an absolute nightmare for Beth. She spent the major part of it lying in her bunk in the confined space of a tiny cabin with only a single porthole for ventilation. She was constantly sea or morning sick and could keep nothing down; as a result, by the time she arrived in Southampton she was so weak that they had to carry her off on a stretcher.

Janis and Pops were there to meet her; they were horrified when they saw her being carried down the gangway on a stretcher by two of the crew members. This was not their Beth that had left England nearly six years ago.

The next two weeks Beth spent flat on her back with her legs raised in the air at the Florence Nightingale General Hospital some ten miles from her parents' estate in Kent. She hated the hospital and missed Reg terribly. She missed her dogs and the wide-open space. Being cooped up in a small cabin for three weeks and now to be confined to a bed in a small hospital room was not her cup of tea. Janis and Pops came to see her every day. Janis would come laden with homemade bread and cream cakes, which she insisted Beth eat before they went home.

After two weeks Beth was allowed to go to her parents' home and convalesce there. Beth's mother fussed over her like a broody hen feeding her all the things she remembered Beth enjoyed as a child. In the beginning Beth enjoyed the attention, but after a while it started to get on her nerves and she longed to get out of the house to be on her own.

Another two weeks of rest and fussing by her mother saw Beth well on her way to recovery. The doctor confirmed at her last visit that the pregnancy was going well and, providing she did nothing foolish, she could now start walking. He said the fresh air and exercise would do her a world of good.

Beth could not understand why she had not heard from Reg. The only word she had received from him was when she was in the hospital and he had phoned to see if she had arrived safely. Her mother had taken the call and told her that Reg sent his regards and said everything was fine back on the farm. She could not believe Reg would have said so little, even to her mother, and that he sent regards and not his love, but perhaps he was phoning from the farm telephone. Reg would seldom use the farm telephone party line for business or private matters, as all the old biddies in the district would be listening in to his conversation.

Reg had promised to write once a week and it was now over six weeks and still there was no letter. Every day she would ask Pops when he went into town if there was any post for her. She knew the post from England to Rhodesia sometimes took over two weeks, even if it was by airmail. Surface mail, depending whether it went the long way round to Cape Town in South Africa first and then by train to Bulawayo, Salisbury, and then by bus to Chipinge, could take up to eight weeks. She had already written him four letters, always telling him how much she missed him and that she was getting stronger by the day and he need not worry.

Every day now she would take the two golden retrievers for long walks through the meadows and down the narrow winding lanes. The dogs were only too pleased to have someone to take them out for a run. It was now the end of August and the afternoons were still pleasant and warm. Beth had been reading for the better part of the morning. She had been promising the dogs that she would take them out after tea for a nice long walk through the fields and down to the river where they could go and play in the water.

As usual the dogs were in high spirits and raced off through the long grass, jumping and barking as they tried to catch the butterflies that fluttered from one yellow dandelion to another, sipping nectar. A rabbit, startled by the barking of the dogs popped up out of the long grass and took off across the meadow with the two barking dogs in hot pursuit. Beth ran after them shouting for them to come back, but they had other ideas, which did not include "come back."

The rabbit went through the hedge on the boundary of the property and into the thick scrub on the other side. The dogs ran along the hedge until they found a hole big enough for them to get through and they too went crashing through the undergrowth following the fresh scent of the rabbit. Beth was about five minutes behind them as she got to the hedge out of breath. There was no way she could get through the hole that the dogs had scrambled through, so she walked briskly alongside the hedge until she came to a stile that crossed over it.

She climbed up onto the top rung of the stile to see if she could see them, but they were nowhere to be seen. She could hear barking in the distance. Still calling for them to come back, she stepped down off the top rung of the stile, still looking out over the thick undergrowth, her hand up to her forehead shielding the setting sun from her eyes. As she stepped, her foot missed the next rung and she came crashing down her head hitting the wooden stile post as she fell, badly shaken, to the ground.

She lay there stunned for a few minutes then slowly she pulled herself up, holding onto the side of the stile. Her head was spinning and she felt nauseous. Suddenly she felt a sharp pain in her lower abdomen and she let out a scream as the pain intensified and she fell back down on the ground and lay there curled up in a ball. She could feel the warm wetness between her thighs and she knew that she had again lost the baby. That was the last thing she could remember before losing consciousness.

Chapter 34

When Negome arrived in Chipinge the next day, the little town was buzzing with people. She asked one of the locals what was going on, and he informed her that the tea picking season had started and the farmers were there recruiting labour.

Negome asked him where they were recruiting from, as she was looking for work. He informed her that she should go down the road to the petrol station. At the back of the petrol station there was a big open piece of ground that was where all the farmers parked their trucks and hired the pickers from, he said. Negome thanked him for the information and made her way down toward the petrol station.

Negome's good looks had always attracted attention. Even as a little girl, strangers would come into the store and would comment on her appearance. Although she was flattered, she was also often embarrassed by their remarks. Her long thick black hair that hung to her shoulders and those big brown eyes were very striking features. Negome was very self-conscious about her good looks and was always trying to hide them by wearing clothes that did not accentuate them. She found that if she wore her hair in a bun or she put on a scarf it would make her look a lot older than she actually was.

With her head tied in a scarf and her dark sallow Portuguese complexion she looked like a coloured girl. Negome could speak two languages fluently, namely Portuguese and *Shangane*, she also understood a few words of English that Father Hogan had taught her at the mission school.

Negome did not want to be obligated to anyone so she thought that if she could get work without asking for this Mr. Traverse, it would be far better for her. As she drew near the petrol station carrying her small brown suitcase she could hear the noise of the women shouting something over and over that she did not understand.

There must have been a hundred or so black women standing around the four trucks parked at the back. They were young, old, big, small, and some were only children, she doubted if they were older than ten years. Some of the older women looked as if they were at least a hundred years old.

Many of the farmers had already come and picked up the number of workers they required and had left again. It was the luck of the draw, sometimes you got workers that had picked tea before and other times you got inexperienced ones. As soon as a truck pulled up at the back of the petrol station, there would be a surge of women around it all shouting and waving their arms. "Take me, take me," they shouted in English to the person on the back of the truck who was making the selection. The person doing the selection would point to the worker he wanted and that one would be pulled up onto the back of the truck. This process continued until the farmer had the number of tea pickers he needed.

Reg had sent his black foreman Mapenge to town in the three-ton truck to go and get thirty pickers. Two other farm trucks pulled out with their load of tea pickers and Mapenge drove into the space that one of the other vehicles had occupied, blowing his horn as he inched his way through the mass of shouting women. Negome soon got the idea. Using her shoulders and her suitcase, she pushed and battered her way to the front and stood there waving her hand shouting, "Take me, take me."

"Yes, you with the orange scarf," said the black man on the back of the truck, pointing to Negome. She pushed her way to the side of the truck and handed her suitcase to one of the men on the back. Another put out his hand and pulled her up. Within ten minutes the back of the truck was full of jabbering women and Mapenge drove out from the recruiting area.

"So, did you get us a good bunch this year, Mapenge?" asked Reg, as Mapenge got out of the truck's cab. "I hope they are not a lot of whores and madalas like you got last time."

"No, Mr. Reg, these are all good strong women. See, this time we get there early and got good young ones."

"Yes, I can see that you picked all the young good-looking ones. I hope they can pick tea and are not only good for lying on their backs," said Reg with a touch of humour in his voice.

"Hau! Mr. Reg, how can the boss think like that of me? I'm a married man with children."

"Come on, Mapenge, I know you of old, by the time the picking season is over you will have slept with at least half of these and sired another dozen or so children."

The other two permanent labourers on the back of the truck laughed and one of them said, "Boss, Reg, he know Mapenge well, he like too much *ngyobe, ngyobe*."

"OK, Mapenge, we will soon see if they can pick tea. Get them off-loaded and settled down in their quarters. We start at five tomorrow morning," Reg said and then he walked back down to the house.

Negome had now been a week on the farm. She had never in her life been so tired. Her back ached from the constant bending and her hands were blistered from picking the tea tips. She wished it was Sunday because they did not work on Sundays, but it was only Friday and she still had two days to go before she could have a rest. They would start at five in the morning and work until eight. They would then have breakfast and then work until noon. From twelve to three was siesta time and the shift ended at six o'clock. She was not sure if she would make it through to Saturday six o'clock.

Chapter 35

It was four weeks to the day that Reg had driven Beth to Beira port to catch the boat to the England. The trip down to Beira took two days and the freighter would take a minimum of three weeks to Southampton depending on how many ports it called on up the coast. He estimated that the boat should have docked in Southampton by now. Tomorrow was Saturday and he would go into Chipinge and book a long distance call to Beth's parents to find out if she arrived safely.

He did not want to use the farm party line, as all the old bags sat on the line chatting all day and they would seldom get off the line for you. If they did, they would still listen in to what you had to say. That's why everyone in the district knew everybody else's business. Saturday morning Reg went straight to the post office and booked an overseas call. Betty, the exchange girl, said the delay would be about two hours. Reg went and did some shopping and had breakfast at the hotel. It was nice to have hot coffee and toast that wasn't burned to a cinder. He decided that when he got back he had to find another girl to work in the house. The one that Mapenge had selected for him was useless and she had to go. Beth did all her own housework and did not have a servant in the house. The only thing she did was to get Simon the gardener to do the windows once every two or three weeks.

At half past nine Reg was back at the post office sitting in the Ford pickup outside the telephone booth. He told Betty that he was sitting outside the booth and that she should ring twice when the call came through. In the meantime he sat and read the three-day-old newspaper he had picked up in the hotel lobby. The phone in the booth rang twice. Reg leaped out of the pickup cab and with two long strides he was inside the booth and had the receiver in his hand. "Hello, hello, Mr. Traverse, your call is going through. Please speak up, as the line is not very clear."

Reg pushed the receiver hard against his ear, he could hear voices in the distance and a lot of crackling and whistling noises, and then an unmistakable English voice came on the line. "Hello Mr. Traverse, did you make a person-to-person call to Mrs. Elizabeth Traverse?"

"Yes, that's right, can you put me through, please?"

"I'm sorry, Mr. Traverse, but the person you wish to speak to is not at that number, but I have a Mrs. Fatheringham on the line. Do you wish to speak to her?"

"Yes, yes, please put her on."

"Hold on, I'm putting you through now, please speak up."

"Hello, hello, is that you Reg? It's Janis here," came the not so distinct voice from the other side of the line. "Beth has gone into town with Pops. Yes, she's fine. We picked her up in Southampton two days ago. Yes, everything is fine. The pregnancy is going well, not to worry.

Yes, I'll tell her you phoned and give her your love. She will be disappointed that she missed your call. You too, Reg. Keep well. No, I won't forget to tell her. Bye, bye now," and the phone went dead.

Reg hung up the receiver and it rang again. He picked it up. It was Betty wanting to know if he was happy with the call and could she just put the charges onto his account. Reg said yes that would be OK and hung up again. He was disappointed that he had not been able to talk to Beth. He had been looking so forward to hearing her voice again, but at least he knew she was safe and that everything was fine.

At least she should have received two of his letters by now and gotten the news of what was going on at the farm. As promised, he had written every week and would write again tonight. What he could not understand was why he had not received any mail from Beth. She too had promised to write every week. Perhaps she was busy the first few weeks, getting checked up at the doctor and catching up on family and old friends. He got back in the pickup and drove the twenty odd miles back to the farm.

Chapter 36

The first thing Reg did when he got back to the farm was to find Mapenge and get him to find someone else to do the housework. He found him in the workshop. "Mapenge, where did you get that girl who is working in the house, is she one of the girls you owe favours to?"

"Does she work good, Mr. Reg?"

"No, Mapenge, she doesn't work good, she burns everything, the food, the clothes she irons, and I'm sure that given enough time she will learn to burn the water too."

"Hau! No, the water she can't burn that one, Mr. Reg."

"Well I'm not going to take that chance. You go and find me another one that knows something about housework."

"Maybe the boss can come down to the plantation and we look together. Then the boss can see which one he like."

Reg and Mapenge walked through the plantation. It was just before the noon break. So far Reg had seen and spoken to no one that he thought would be any better than the housemaid he already had. They had just gotten to the bottom of one of the groves and were looking down the hill on one of the other groves that was also being picked when the siren went, indicating that it was the lunchtime break.

Negome stood up and stretched her arms and back, she had her back toward Reg and Mapenge who were standing up on the hill some fifty yards away. She untied the scarf around her head and shook out her long flowing black hair, shaking her head from side to side to get some air through her hair that was wet from perspiration. Her action caught the attention of Reg. "Mapenge, what's that white girl doing in the tea plantation?"

"She one of the new pickers we get last week, but she no white girl, she coloured girl from Mozambique."

"Go and fetch her. I want to see this girl with the long hair."

Mapenge went down the hill and brought Negome back to where Reg was standing. She was quite nervous that she had done something wrong and was about to be dismissed or reprimanded. She did not know how long they had been watching her and what she could have done wrong. She stood in front of Reg in her old dark green dress that was now wet with perspiration. She knew from the other workers that Reg was the owner of the tea estate and the only other time she had seen him was the day they all arrived on the back of the truck. At that time she had no idea who he was.

"What's your name?" asked Reg in English.

Negome looked at him and shook her head.

"She only speak Portuguese or *Shangane*," said Mapenge. Reg readdressed her in *Shangane*, which he had learned as a child on the farm playing with the black children.

"My name is Negome," she replied.

"So where do you come from, Negome, and why are you here picking tea?"

"I come from Massangena in Mozambique, I came here to look for work," she said, still worried that she had done something wrong.

"From Massangena," said Reg, "I have been to Massangena many times on my way down to Inhambane. I know the commissioner there, what's his name?"

"Commissioner Carlos Chissano," said Negome.

"Yes, that's right, Chissano. So he is still there, how is he? I haven't seen him for a long time. I used to travel a lot to Inhambane via Massangena, but lately I have been going to Beira."

Negome told Reg that the commissioner was still there and he was well when she left Massangena two weeks ago. She mentioned that the commissioner had, in fact, given her a letter of introduction to a tea farmer by the name of Traverse, but she had managed to get a job on this farm so she did not need the letter.

"Is that so," said Reg. "Interesting, do you know who I am?"

"Yes sir, you are Mr. Reg," said Negome politely.

"Yes, that's right," said Reg with a smile, "but that's my first name. I'm Reg Traverse. So it would seem you ended up where you were supposed to be after all. Do you still have the letter from the commissioner?"

"Yes it is in the quarters," she said.

"Well, let's go and get the letter," said Reg, "I would like to see it." They walked back up the hill, Reg and Mapenge walking in front with Reg explaining to Mapenge something he wanted done. Negome followed a short distance behind.

Negome went and fetched the letter and handed it to Reg. The letter was still sealed and it had his name on the front written in a neat handwriting. Reg opened the letter and read it. He then looked at Mapenge and said in English, "I think we may have found the solution to my housemaid problems." Reg then spoke to Negome again. "The commissioner speaks very highly of you. It would seem that you efficiently ran your father's store until you decided to move out of Massangena. I think maybe your talents could be put to better use. How would you like to come and run my house for me until my wife gets back?"

Negome was relieved that she had not done anything wrong and to work at the house sounded a far better proposition than standing out in the hot sun all day picking tea. "It was very good of the commissioner to give me a good report, and, yes, I would be pleased to come and run the house for you, sir."

"OK let's give it a week and see how you do. I'll pay you the same as the tea pickers and if I'm happy with your work, then there could be an increase. The hours you work will be different; you will need to start at five thirty in the morning to have my coffee ready by quarter to six and then breakfast between nine and ten. In the evening you can go after the dinner things are washed and put away. I don't eat lunch, only some cold black tea with lemon, so if you are happy with those conditions then you can start tomorrow. Do you understand?"

"Yes, sir, I understand."

"OK then, Mapenge will show you around the house later this afternoon."

Reg then spoke to Mapenge in English so that Negome could not understand. "I want you to get your little girlfriend out of the house this afternoon. You can tell her what you want but she does not have a job in the house anymore. If you still want her to pick tea then that's OK with me and when that is done take Negome over to the house and show her the ropes."

Within a week Negome had reorganized the house, she had cleaned it properly from top to bottom, cooked dinner and breakfast for Reg every day and washed and ironed his clothes. Reg was so impressed he said to her in English the one morning when she brought him his breakfast, "God surely must have sent you."

The only word she understood was god, but she saw he was smiling so she just smiled back at him, flashing her lovely white teeth.

On Reg's insistence Negome moved from the tea pickers' compound to the old maid's quarters on the opposite side of the house. Ever since Reg's mother had passed away, the room had been used as a storeroom for some of his mother's furniture and things that he did not have the heart to throw away. He said she could use what she needed of the furniture and the rest could be put up in the big store shed next to the workshop.

She selected a few things such as a single bed and mattress, wardrobe and a small chest of drawers and chair; the rest she asked Mapenge to take up to the shed. She then washed and scrubbed the room from top to bottom and arranged the things she had selected back in the room. There were old curtains that she found in a cardboard box that she shortened to fit the window and a small rug for the floor. By the time she had finished, the room looked very nice. It was the first time in her life that she had a room to herself. Reg gave her an old Coleman *paraffin* pump lamp that gave out three times as much light as the hurricane lamp that Mapenge had given her.

After a month, Reg entrusted Negome with all the buying of the groceries for the house as well as the food stocks required for the farm labourers. She would go into town with Mapenge or one of the other drivers to get the necessary provisions for the week. Reg had now started to speak to her only in English and told her she had to speak to him in English. She was very shy to speak at first, but, as she got used to Reg, she started to speak and he would correct her when she got her tenses and words a little mixed up. Reg soon realized that this was a bright young woman. He would have to correct her only once and tell her something once and she would never make the same mistake twice. In fact, he had never been so organized in his life before, not even when his mother was alive.

Chapter 37

Ten weeks had now passed since Beth had left and Reg still had not received any correspondence from her, or been able to speak to her personally on the phone. He was still writing every week and had tried twice more to reach her on the telephone. Each time he phoned, Beth was out and he would end up speaking to Janis who would always assure him that Beth was fine.

No, she had no idea what was happening to the mail these days, and then she would make some stupid remark like, "Perhaps they were just dumping it all in the sea." It was most frustrating. Reg missed her terribly and even though he had lots of people around him all day he was still lonely, especially at night.

Reg spoke to Negome and told her that it was stupid for her to have to take her supper into her room to eat; after all, it was the same food and she should rather eat at the dining room table with him. It would be nice, as he was tired of always having to eat alone and it would also give her an opportunity to speak more and improve her English.

Every night Negome would sit at the dining room table with Reg and have her meal. As a result, her English improved in leaps and bounds. She could now carry on a conversation in English and Reg would have to correct her only every now and then. Reg enjoyed her company; she was so fresh and innocently naive about the world around her. She had a thirst for knowledge and he looked forward to the evening meals in her company.

Sometimes they would still be talking at ten o'clock and it would be close to eleven before she had finished cleaning up in the kitchen and could go to bed. She did not mind, as on those occasions Reg would come into the kitchen and say good night and tell her not to get up early, as he would make his own coffee in the morning.

Johan de Klerk, the farmer on Reg's western boundary, was turning fifty and his wife was having a small party for him. She had invited all the neighbours in the district including Reg. Annette was Johan's wife and she was Beth's best friend. She was more commonly referred to as Annie by her friends and family. Johan and Annie were originally from the Northern Transvaal province in South Africa. He was a still a staunch Afrikaner and they both spoke English with a strong *Afrikaans* accent.

Annie had phoned Reg a week ago and enquired as she often did about Beth, also complaining that she had not heard from her. She would joke with Reg, saying that Beth had found a new man and was therefore too busy to write. At the same time she had asked Reg to come to the party. Reg was at first reluctant to go.

"Annie, I'm not really a party person, as you know, and it would seem funny to be there without Beth," Reg told her.

"Come on, don't be such a stick-in-the-mud," she said. "It will do you good to talk to some white people again."

"It has not been that bad lately," said Reg, "as I do have the occasion to talk to my new housemaid in English."

Annie had heard all about this pretty young Portuguese half-breed that Reg had employed to do the housework and perform other duties around the house. She also wondered whether Reg had her performing any other more personal duties for him. She had written to Beth about this new maid and was anxious to hear what she had to say about the situation. She knew that Beth would not approve of another woman in the house. She had not seen the girl herself but the rumours in town were rife; she desperately wanted to meet this so-called maid.

"Oh! Have, you employed a white woman to do the housework?" she asked, knowing full well that the new maid was not white.

"Well, she isn't white. She is sort of half Portuguese and I have been trying to teach her to speak a bit of English," said Reg.

"Can she hold a decent conversation?" asked Annie. "I hear most of these half-breeds can be pretty stupid, as they tend to drink far too much."

"No, no, on the contrary, she's an exceptionally bright young girl," answered Reg, rather flustered with Annie's line of questions. "And to be honest, I can't ever remember her smelling of drink."

"How old is she, by the way?" asked Annie.

"I'm not sure," said Reg, "but I guess in her late teens or early twenties."

"Well then why don't you bring her along to the party," said Annie. "You then won't have to drive by yourself. Besides it would be nice for the kid to meet and speak to some young people her own age. She's about the same age as my Jane who will be home from university for the weekend to see her father on his birthday. She is also bringing one of her varsity friends to stay for the weekend. If I know my Jane, I'm sure there will be lots of young blokes at the party her sort of age. You can bet your life on it, half the young lads in the district are trying to get into her pants, so there will loads of blokes around for her to meet."

Reluctantly, Reg agreed to go to the party and bring Negome with him on Annie's insistence.

Chapter 38

The next day was the last Sunday of the month and Reg would provide transport for all his workers to go into town to attend the service at the Catholic Church. Negome would go along and they would all normally be back before midday.

Reg sat on the wide front *veranda* looking up at the Chimanimani Mountains as the hot midday sun danced off the shear rock faces making shimmering heat waves. He saw the dust cloud on the road long before he saw or heard the big diesel truck coming back from town loaded with people. He got up and walked around to the back of the yard and waited under the back *veranda* for the truck to arrive. Negome would take his post box key and clear the box for him on the Sundays she went to church.

Negome got out from the truck's cab with a pile of mail and a newspaper. She saw Reg standing on the back stoop and walked over to give it to him.

"So how was the sermon today, did you say a little prayer for me?" asked Reg with his head down sifting through the mail to see if there was a letter from Beth.

"Yes, Mr. Reg, I say a prayer for all the people including you."

"That's nice of you," said Reg, still focusing on the mail.

"Will that be all, Mr. Reg? I am very hot and would like to shower and change my clothes."

"Yes, you go and change and when you are finished come into the study. I want to talk to you about something."

Negome showered and put on a clean house dress and hung her Sunday dress up in the wardrobe. She walked over to the house and wondered what Mr. Reg wanted to talk to her about. The study door was open and Reg was working at his desk with his back toward the open door, he sensed more than heard Negome at the door and turned around in his late father's old rickety swivel cane chair.

"Ah! Negome, there you are, I was waiting for you. Are you feeling cooler now after your shower?"

"Yes, thank you, Mr. Reg. You said you wanted to speak to me?"

"Yes, that's right, come in and sit down," he said, pointing to an old leather chair near the window. Negome went and sat in the chair. "You know our neighbours on the northern boundary, the de Klerks, well, they are having a sort of birthday party next Saturday. It's Mr. de Klerk's fiftieth and his wife, Annie, has invited me to the party and is insisting that I should bring you along as well. She says that her daughter and a whole lot of other young people your age will be at the party. So what do you say?"

"That is very nice of Mrs. Annie to ask me to go to the party," said Negome, "but it will not seem right for me to go with you and everyone will be a stranger to me."

"That's nonsense, what's wrong with me taking one of my staff members to the party? Mrs. de Klerk has invited you, so what's wrong with that? Yes, you won't know anyone there but how are you going to meet anyone if you don't make the effort to go out and meet new people? This will give you the opportunity to speak English to other folk."

"But Mr. Reg, I have no dress to wear to this occasion and I will feel, how do you say, bad—no, ashamed—in my old clothes, especially with all the other young people dressed in their nice new clothes. I see them at church and I know that the other women look at me and laugh behind my back because of my old-fashioned clothes."

"Negome, this is not like church, people don't get all dressed up to go to a farm party. It's not really a party, it's a barbeque, where everyone stands around and talks and eats lots of food and drinks lots of beer. Most of the men will still be wearing short pants, I know I will."

"I understand, Mr. Reg, but for a woman it is different, I will feel uncomfortable in my old clothes. Look at this dress." She stood up and pulled the skirt open. "See how it has faded and it has been mended so many times before."

"I don't know, the dress looks fine to me," said Reg.

"Yes, Mr. Reg, that's because you are a man, women think differently."

"OK, I'll tell you what, my mother was quite a dresser in her time and she was about your size. Why don't you go into my parents' old bedroom and see what you can find to wear among my mother's dresses? I'm sure you will find something suitable. Then will you come with me?" asked Reg.

Negome could see it was pointless trying to argue with Mr. Reg, as he had made up his mind that she should go, so she reluctantly gave in and said, "All right, Mr. Reg, if I find something nice to wear then I will go."

"Good girl," said Reg, opening the drawer in the desk and taking out a bunch of keys. "Here are the keys to my mother's wardrobes. They are the two big brown ones, and one of these keys will fit. Go and see what you can find," he said, handing her the bunch of keys.

Negome had been in the room a few times before. Every so often Reg would unlock the room, open the windows and ask Negome to dust the furniture. Reg had left the room just as it was when his mother and father were still alive. He could not bring himself to clear it out and Beth said it was his duty and refused to do it for him. He promised that one day he would get around to doing it.

Negome found the keys that fit the wardrobe's locks. There were rows and rows of dresses on hangers, each with a white linen cover. She had never seen so many dresses before. She did not know where to start looking. Eventually she started lifting the covers and looking at the material, taking out some of the dresses made of lighter material and laying them on the double bed.

Mr. Reg was right, his mother had beautiful clothes and there were pictures of her on the dressing table when she was young. Negome could see that she was also a very beautiful woman. She removed the covers off several dresses and held them against her, twirling around to let them flare out, looking at herself in the long mirror fixed to the inside of the wardrobe door.

After much deliberation she chose one and put all the others back and locked the wardrobes and the bedroom door. Reg was still in the study when she went down the passage. She stopped outside the open door and knocked softly. Reg turned in the swivel chair. "Ah! Negome so did you find something you liked?" he asked.

"Yes, thank you, Mr. Reg. I think this one will be fine," she said, holding up the dress she had selected still in the cover. "Well that's it then, said Reg. "We go to the party on Saturday," paying no real attention to the dress she was holding up.

By the time Saturday had come she had tried the dress on at least half a dozen times. Was it too long, was it too low cut at the back, and so she deliberated every time she tried the dress on. She really did not want to go to the party, but she did not want to make Mr. Reg angry, as he had been so good to her. To tell him at this short notice she did not want to go would seem not to be right.

At three o'clock Reg was outside her room calling, "Negome, we should go, if you are ready."

She had been ready for over an hour sitting on the side of the bed, still not sure she was doing the right thing. She got up from the bed and opened the door.

"I'm ready, Mr. Reg," she said, standing in the doorway. The light coming from the window at the back of her highlighted her slim brown figure in the door frame, her long black hair cascading over her bare shoulders and down the front of the long white dress was a sight that Reg would remember for a long time. He stood there just staring at her.

"Mr. Reg, is something wrong, is the dress not good?" she asked with anxiety in her voice.

"No! No! The dress is fine," said Reg, realizing that he had been staring. "I'm just thinking that perhaps you should wear some different shoes that will go better with the dress. Come into the house. I'm sure we will find a suitable pair that will go with that dress in among my mother's things, she had at least twenty pairs of shoes if not more."

Chapter 39

It was a good thirty-minute drive to the de Klerks' farm. Negome sat in silence feeling very awkward and fidgeted with the pleats in her dress. She had bought some cheap perfume in town and this was the first time she had worn perfume. The scent was quite strong in the confined space of the pickup cab and she was wondering whether she may have put a little too much on. Reg had noticed it too and looked over at her and smiled and opened his side window to let in some fresh air. The wind blew Negome's hair into her face and she brushed it away.

"Sorry," said Reg, "I'll close the window again."

"No need to, Mr. Reg, it's fine, I have a ribbon." She took a white ribbon from her pocket and tied her hair at the back. Tying her hair back brought back to Reg the silhouette of her in the doorway with the light shining from the back window with her long black hair cascading down over the white dress. This was the first time that he realized how strikingly beautiful she was. He could not understand why he had not seen it before and now wondered if he was doing the right thing taking her to the party. Reg cursed Annie under his breath for insisting he bring her.

When they arrived at the farm there were cars and pickups parked all over the front yard. Annie saw them arrive and came out to greet them. "Hello, stranger, what's kept you away so long, or need I ask," she said and kissed him on the cheek, but all the time she was looking at Negome. "I assume this is your um"—and she paused a second or two not quite knowing what to call her, and said "new helper?"

"Yes," said Reg, "this is Negome and this is Annie. "Mrs. de Klerk," she corrected him."

"Sorry, I mean, Mrs. de Klerk."

"Come on inside and I will introduce you to my daughter Jane and her friend from varsity, they are home for the long weekend. It was so nice that she could be here for her father's birthday."

Jane had been told by her mother that Uncle Reg was bringing his coloured maid and that she should be nice to her, but she had not expected someone as strikingly beautiful as this. She was somewhat taken aback when Negome was introduced to her by her mother, who looked at her and raised her eyebrows.

"Come, Reg, let's leave the girls, they will be fine."

"Jane, you introduce, what's her name to the others, OK?" Annie hooked her arm into Reg's and proceeded to escort him from the *veranda* down to where they were having the barbeque at the bottom of the garden. When she got to where the men where congregated around the barbeque she unhooked her arm from his. "I'll leave you here in the good ol hands of the boys," she said, turning to go and speak to the wives who were sitting on fold-out chairs under the big acacia tree.

Johan was talking to a group of men. Reg went over to them and shook Johan's hand and said, "Happy birthday, you old fart, what is it sixty now?"

"Sixty, my fucking ass, you big shit, where have you been all this time? Now that Beth's away we don't see you anymore, or shouldn't I ask—hey, guys?" said Johan pumping Reg's hand in his huge banana-like fingers. Reg shook hands with all the guys standing around the fires, some with beers and others holding glasses of whatever poison they drank. It was not often that the people in the district got together and many months could go by without them ever meeting each other.

"So why so scarce lately?" asked Johan, grasping Reg's shoulder in a vicelike grip that hurt like hell. This was just one of Johan's sick ways of showing affection—he liked to see people cringe when he squeezed them. "With Beth overseas we don't see much of you anymore."

"You know what it's like in the picking season, you are so damned busy that you forget about the time and the days just seem to fly past," said Reg.

"Yes I can well imagine the time flying past if I had someone like that to do my housework," said one of the farmers, pointing to where Jane and Negome were standing on the back *veranda*, "I assume that's your new maid that everyone is talking about?"

"Hey! Reg, does she have a sister?" chaffed one of the farmers.

"Hey! maybe she'd come work for me part time," said one of the other guys.

"Come on guys, she's just a kid that needed a job. The commissioner down in Massangena asked me to give her a job, so what should I do, chase her away because she looks good?"

"Hey, Reg, man, don't take it so seriously, we're just pulling your piss a bit. Here, pour some of this down your throat," said Johan, handing Reg a cold beer. That was the end of that conversation and the guys went on to talk about more important things like fishing, hunting, and other farming-related matters.

The air was still and the smoke from the barbecue fires hung like low clouds over the garden, every now and then one would catch the whiff of the meat cooking and the old stomach juices would start to work, reminding you how hungry you were.

By the time the sun had dropped down behind the mountains a lot of meat and sausages had been cooked and a large number of beers had been consumed by the men. Reg was getting bored with the same old conversation about the problems in government, the low crop prices and the rising cost of living. He had already consumed too much beer and was feeling a little light headed; at least the youngsters were enjoying themselves. There seemed to be a constant stream of music, laughter, and clapping wafting down from the back veranda where they were playing records on the portable battery operated gramophone.

.Jane took Negome around to the back *veranda* where the rest of the young people were gathered, listening to the latest hit records that Jane had brought down from Salisbury. They were all doing the latest dance called the

Jive. Negome was fascinated. She had never heard this type of music before and had never seen people dance this way. It didn't take too long for her to become the centre of attraction—the guys all wanted to teach her the latest dance steps. This was getting up the nose of Jane and her friend Pamela; the guys were supposed to be paying them all the attention, not this little coloured bitch.

Jane called her friend over to the side, away from the other young folk and said, "We need to fix this little bitch before she spoils all our fun. Come, I've got an idea how we can sort her out." Jane took a large glass tumbler from the table where the bowl of fruit punch stood that Annie had made for the youngsters. Jane went inside and took a bottle of gin from the drinks cabinet and poured a hefty tot into the glass. She then went outside again and filled the glass with the fruit punch.

When the record came to an end and the dancing stopped she went over to where Negome was standing talking to some of the guys. "Negome, all the dancing must have made you thirsty, here's a glass of fruit punch."

"Oh, thank you," said Negome, accepting the glass, "I'm so thirsty—what is in it?"

"It's what my mom made this morning. It's got lots of fruit, as you can see, and lemonade."

"Yes, it tastes good," said Negome, taking a big drink from the glass.

By the time the two girls had fed Negome the third spiked drink she was flying. The alcohol had made her lose all her inhibitions. She had already untied the ribbon from her hair and was really getting into the swing of things. The guys were spinning her around and her long flowing dress would flare out revealing her shapely legs up to her thighs. Every time her dress went up the guys would cheer and whistle, while clapping to the beat of the music. Negome was enjoying herself; she could not remember ever having had so much fun before.

When the third drink finally kicked in, Negome could hardly stand. The room seemed to be spinning around faster than what she was and, as her partner spun her around, she fell on the red polished floor and lay there with her dress up around her waist.

Annie announced that the food was ready and everyone should come up to the house and help themselves to whatever they fancied. Reg started to drift up to the house with the rest of the guests. Annie came down to meet him and pulled him to one side. "It would seem that your little coloured housemaid has been making quite a spectacle of herself," said Annie.

"What do you mean?" asked Reg, somewhat surprised.

"She's passed out on the couch in the living room. It would seem that she has been into the drink. I told you these coloureds can't resist the booze."

"I think you had better get her home now, before she causes any trouble and embarrasses you in front of everyone."

"But where did she get the drink from?" asked Reg, as they walked together up to the house."

"I have no idea," said Annie. "She could have taken it out of the booze cabinet—it was open for anyone to use—or one of the guys could have given it to her, you know what the guys are like. Anyway while everyone is getting their food I think you should slip out the back with her."

Chapter 40

By the time Reg got up to the house, Negome was sitting up on the couch with her head in her lap. "What's the matter?" asked Reg.

"I don't know, Mr. Reg. I think I must be drunk."

"But what have you been drinking that would make you drunk?"

"I have only drunk the fruit punch that Jane gave me. It tasted so good and I was so thirsty. That's all I've had to drink. I don't understand why I'm feeling like this."

"OK," said Reg, "I think I get the picture."

"What picture?" Negome asked. "I don't understand."

"Don't worry, I think it's time we went home. Come on, let me help you up," said Reg. He took her elbow and guided her through the house out the back and into the Ford pickup truck.

They had not gone more than two miles when Negome said, "Please stop. I must be sick," but before Reg could pull up, Negome had vomited into her hands and onto her dress. Reg pulled over to the side of the road and ran around to the passenger side to try to help her out of the cab. Negome fell to her knees and brought up everything she had in her stomach. Reg helped her to stand up, she was in a mess her dress was soiled, she had vomit in her hair and all over her hands. Reg took out his handkerchief and tried to wipe away some of it but he was not very successful.

The rest of the journey home was uneventful, except that Negome was terribly embarrassed and could not stop telling Reg how sorry she was for all the trouble she had caused him. Reg said it was not her fault, that someone had played a mean trick on her and had spiked her drink. She did not understand what spiked meant and Reg had to explain to her what he thought had happened. Now it all became very clear to her that Jane and her friend were not as nice as she thought they were.

"Well the first thing we must do is get you cleaned up when we get you home, it's under the shower with you to get most of the mess out of your hair and off of Mom's dress."

Negome said nothing and sat quietly for the rest of the journey feeling very sorry for herself. She was even more upset that she had soiled the dress Reg had let her wear.

It was already dark when they arrived back at the farm and Reg told Negome to remain where she was; he was going to fetch a light. Negome, although she now felt much better, was long past protesting anymore. For the first time, she missed her mother and would have loved to have her there to comfort and reassure her.

Reg went into the house and lit one of the Coleman lamps and came and fetched Negome out of the pickup. He walked with her to the outside shower in the little enclosed courtyard that led into her room and turned the water on. "Let's get you under the shower and try to get most of this mess off you. The first few minutes or so the water was quite warm, as the water pipe that ran from the reservoir to the house and then to the servant's quarters was exposed to the sun for a good fifty yards and had as yet not cooled down completely.

Negome stood under the warm shower like a docile dog being bathed. Reg rinsed away the vomit that was on her dress and in her hair. By the time he had gotten her all cleaned up the water had turned quite cold and his shirt and shorts were wet through to the skin. Reg turned the water off. Negome stood in the shower cubicle dripping water and looking like a drowned rat with her long hair in knots and her lovely white dress clinging to her wet body. She was shivering now from the cold water and the nipples on her breasts pushed against her wet bra and dress like little brown puppy dogs' noses. Reg could not help but notice the beautiful curvatures of her body that were now emphasized by her wet clothes.

"Right, we need to get you out of these wet clothes and into something dry," said Reg, stretching out his hand to help her out of the shower. Negome stepped out of the shower cubicle, but because of her tangled wet hair in her eyes and the wet dress clinging to her legs she missed her footing and stumbled over the little step at the bottom of the shower. Had Reg not been there to catch her she would have fallen flat on her face on the wet cement floor.

They stood there holding onto each other, their wet bodies pressed against each other. Reg could feel her breasts pushing hard against his chest and he could feel himself becoming aroused. Negome felt the warmth and comfort of Reg's body with his arms around her. She had never been held by a man like this before and she could feel the manliness of Reg pressing against her inner upper thigh and she too was aroused.

Reg lifted his arms from around her and slid the straps of her dress from her shoulders. Negome lifted her arms from around Reg's neck and let them fall to her side. Reg pulled the straps down further over her arms, peeling the wet dress from her body. Negome stood before him only in her wet bra and panties. Reg put his arms around her and unclipped her bra; it slid off her arms and fell on top of her dress at her feet. He lifted her up and carried her into the room and laid her on the bed. Reg removed his wet clothes and lay down on the bed next to her.

Chapter 41

It was in the early hours of the morning when Reg slipped out of Negome's room with his damp clothes under his arm. It was pitch dark outside; the moon had already disappeared behind the mountains. Reg made his way to the house in his bare feet, hoping he did not step on a lazy puff adder that might be lying on the hard sun-baked earth trying to get what was left of the warmth. By the time he had covered the fifty paces to the house, his eyes had become accustomed to the dark, and he opened the back door, found the matches, and lit the lamp.

Reg looked at his wristwatch—it had just gone two o'clock. He went into the bathroom and ran a bath. The water was still warm in the boiler from the fire in the stove from that afternoon. Reg lay in the warm water thinking about what he and Negome had just done. At the time it seemed so right, but now that he was stone-cold sober he was having second thoughts. He cursed himself for being so damned weak in the moment of passion. He wondered how Negome would feel when she woke up in the morning.

By the time Reg had gotten into bed and managed to drop off to sleep, the alarm clock was ringing, signalling it was half past five and time to get up and face a new day. The dawn was just breaking, casting its weak light through the open curtains. He dragged himself out of bed and made his way to the bathroom. He felt like hell and wondered whether it was from the beer or the lack of sleep or a combination of both; he suspected the latter. He went into the kitchen and put a pot of water on the Primus stove to boil, he desperately needed a cup of coffee.

The sun was already peeping over the top of the mountain when Reg made his way down to the nursery to supervise the planting out of the seedling tea trees into small wooden boxes. They would remain there for the next year before being planted out into the plantation. It was tedious work and one had to be very careful not to damage the small seedlings when removing them from the seed trays. At nine o'clock the siren sounded that it was time for breakfast.

Reg walked back up to the house deep in thought and still feeling bad about what had happened last night between him and Negome. Now for the first time he did not really want to face her at breakfast. He felt guilty about what they had done, but he was also angry with himself for having let Annie talk him into taking Negome to the party. Because if she had not gone to the party then none of this would have happened and he would not be feeling as he did now.

Of course now he realized that Annie obviously only wanted to see for herself what she had heard in the town about his new maid. It was obvious from the comments and ragging he got from the chaps at the party that Negome was quite the talk of the town and now he had made what everyone was thinking about him and Negome factual. Well stuff them anyway, they could think what they liked; he knew that more than half of the guys that were there at the party would like to have done what he had done.

As he walked up the steps to the back screen door the smell of bacon frying came wafting down to meet him. Negome was standing at the stove with her back to the door as Reg walked into the kitchen. He greeted her. "Good morning."

Negome turned around. "Oh," she exclaimed, "you gave me a fright, Mr. Reg. I did not hear you come in, your breakfast is nearly ready. Please sit down and I will pour you a cup of coffee while you wait." Reg sat down at the small kitchen table. He always ate breakfast in the kitchen; he said it was too much of a fuss to eat breakfast in the dining room on a workday.

Negome put a large plate of bacon and eggs down in front of him and then cut him two slices of her home-made bread and put them on the side plate next to him. She then went about washing the cooking utensils in the sink. When Reg had finished eating she took his plate and inquired whether he had had enough to eat and could she pour him another cup of coffee.

"Yes, thank you. I have had plenty to eat but you can pour me some more coffee, please. Pour one for yourself and come and sit down, I want to talk to you about last night."

Negome did as he asked and sat down on the chair opposite him. "Negome, I want to apologize, say sorry for what happened last night between the two of us."

"Mr. Reg, there is no reason to be sorry. We were both a little drunk and it just happened. I was also wrong. I should have stopped you, but I let it happen because I wanted it to happen."

"Yes, that may be so," said Reg, "but I took advantage of your vulnerability and I didn't even stop to think that you may still be a virgin."

"Mr. Reg, please, it was going to happen one day anyway and I am glad it was a nice man like you, so please don't be sorry. It was very nice for me for the first time."

"Negome, it was very nice for me too, but I'm a married man and it should not have happened."

"Yes, Mr. Reg, I know you are a married man, but that does not stop you from having feelings. You have not been with your wife for a long time and maybe you needed someone and that someone just happened to be me. I have no regrets. This is our thing no one else needs to know about it. Please, Mr. Reg, you must not feel bad for me."

Reg could see it was pointless trying to reason with her. She had made up her mind about what she wanted to believe and that was that.

Chapter 42

It was quite awhile later that the dogs came running back, tired of barking and digging at the entrance to the hole that the rabbit had found refuge in. They found Beth lying unconscious at the foot of the stile. They licked her face and clawed her arm, but Beth did not respond. The dogs became very distressed, sensing that all was not well. They began to bark and whine and claw Beth even more vigorously. Suddenly, Sally, the older of the two dogs, ran back up along the side of the hedge to the hole they had scrambled through after the rabbit. She took off across the meadow barking as she ran. Red, the male dog, lay down next to Beth with his head on her leg, whimpering softly.

Janis heard the dog barking as it came up through the meadow and into the backyard. She was sitting reading in the drawing room, enjoying the last rays of the afternoon sun radiating through the bay windows and wondered what the dogs were so excited about. When Sally came running into the room still barking and ran up to her clawing her legs, obviously very distraught, Janis realized that there was something wrong. "Pops," she shouted, 'there's something wrong, I think something has happened to Beth."

Pops was in the study catching up on some work, and came hurrying out. "What do you mean something has happened to Beth? She has gone out for a walk with the dogs."

"No, something is not right. Sally has come home on her own and she is beside herself, look at her, she is normally not like this."

Sally ran out of the room and stood in the passage barking. She then came running in and jumped up at Pops, something she would under normal circumstances never do.

"Yes, I think you're right. Let me go and get my hat and stick and we will go and see what she is making all the fuss about."

Beth spent a whole week in hospital again, she had lost the child, and it was a little girl. She had also lost a lot of blood and the doctor said that had they not found her when they did she would not have survived.

Beth went into a deep depression. She did not want to see any of her friends or go out, and she remained in her room all day, sitting by the window looking out across the meadow where she had fallen. She would not come down for meals and even the food that Janis took up to her, she hardly touched. The doctor had seen her a number of times in the three weeks that she had been home from the hospital. He had prescribed some antidepressant tablets, but Beth refused to take them. Much as she hated to do it, Janis eventually sent Reg a telegram asking him to come over, hoping that he would be able to snap her out of the depression.

Chapter 43

Reg went back down to the nursery and Negome continued with the housework, but today it was different, there seemed to be a new enthusiasm in what she did. At eleven o'clock the phone rang two longs and two short rings, which was the ring code for the Traverses' farm. Negome's ear was attuned to the rings; the phone rang all day for other farms in the district, each one with their own ring code. She hardly heard them, but when it was their ring code she would react immediately. It was Betty, the exchange lady. She said there was a telegram for Reg at the post office and Negome should inform Reg immediately.

Negome stopped what she was doing and ran down to the nursery to go and find Reg. As soon as she had given him the message he took off at a run for the house, leaving Negome to follow behind. Reg got to the phone in the passage all out of breath; he did not realize how unfit he was. He picked up the handset and put it to his ear. For once there was no one on the line. He put it back on the cradle and cranked the handle three long rings and one short, which was the ring code for the exchange, and he picked up the handset again and waited for Betty to come on the line. After waiting for what seemed to have been an age, with no response he banged down the handset and vigorously cranked the handle again. "Christ, where the fuck is that bloody woman? She is never on the exchange board when you need her."

Just then Betty came on the line. "Exchange, can I help you?"

"Yes, its me, Traverse, I believe you have a telegram for me, Betty. Who is it from?"

"Hello, Mr. Traverse, It's from a Mrs. J. Fatheringham in Kent, England. I'll give it to your driver when he comes in to collect the mail if that's all right with you, just tell him to see me."

"The driver isn't going in today so, please, just read it out to me."

"You know, Mr. Traverse, I'm not allowed to do that. Anyway, you know if I did, it would be all over the district within a few minutes."

"Betty, I don't have time to drive into town today and I don't give a stuff about who knows what about me, the bloody public seem to know more about my affairs than I do anyway, so just read it to me."

"OK, OK, Mr. Traverse, if you say so. It simply says, 'reg comma pregnancy not going too well comma suggest you come over ASAP comma, not an emergency but she needs you full stop." That's it."

"OK, thanks, Betty, I'll need you to make some long-distance calls for me some time later on," he said, and put the handset down.

Reg went into the study to look up the numbers of a travel agent in Salisbury, he also got out his diary and then went back to the phone in the passage and got Betty back on the line and asked her to get the agent's number for him and to put a person-to-person call through to the Farninghams in England. Reg then went to the kitchen to find Negome. She was not there. He looked outside and saw her hanging up the washing on the line. He called to her. "Negome please come up to the study when you have finished hanging the washing. I need to talk to you."

Negome knew that whenever there was something serious Mr. Reg wanted to discuss with her, he would call her into the study. She was apprehensive every time he called her into the study. Today she was even more so, thinking that it must have something to do with what had transpired last night. She stood outside the study door, very nervous. Reg sat in the old swivel chair with his back to the door. Negome knocked softly, afraid she might disturb him. Reg turned around in the chair, "Negome, please come in, sit over there," he said, pointing to the big brown leather arm chair. Negome hated that chair, it seemed to swallow her up. She felt so insignificant and intimidated sitting in it.

"Negome, that message you gave me from Betty was from my mother-in-law in England," said Reg. "Apparently the pregnancy with Beth is not going too well and I must go to England as soon as I can arrange a flight out from Salisbury. Now I will be away for some weeks and while I'm away I would like you to sleep in the house. You can use the small spare room at the end of the passage.

"Mapenge will manage the farm; he knows what has to be done and has looked after things many times before when we had to go to Salisbury so many times with Beth during her first two pregnancies. I will also speak to Johan de Klerk and ask him to keep an eye on things while I'm away, so if you are unsure about anything or have a problem, you can phone him and he can be here within half an hour. The ring codes are written down for everyone and pinned to the notice board next to the telephone, I'm sure you have seen them before.

"I don't expect there to be any problems, but one never knows. Now, although we have been away for a few weeks before, the farm has never been left without one of us here for longer than two weeks, so there is a lot that has to be done that can't be done before I leave. I'm going to have to ask you to do many of those things, like buying the supplies for the farm workers, but you do that anyway, and draw the wages at the bank, pay the accounts, etc. Now I want to know, do you think you can handle all that? Because if you say no, I'll understand. It is a big responsibility, and then I will ask my retired uncle in Bulawayo if he can come down for a couple of weeks. I know I'm asking a lot of you but if I didn't have the confidence in you then I would not have asked you, so what do you think—or shall I give you some time to think about it?"

Negome sat in silence for a moment looking at her hands in her lap, and then she replied. "Mr. Reg, it is a big thing that you ask me and I am very, how do you say, happy? No not happy."

"You mean flattered," prompted Reg with a smile.

"Yes, that is the word, flattered, if Mr. Reg has the trust in me to do this then I will do my best to do a good job while you are away. I am also very sorry to hear that Mrs. Beth is having trouble with her pregnancy again. I know it is very important that you go as soon as you can, and I'm sure that Mapenge and I will manage while you are away."

Chapter 44

It was a week after Reg received the telegram before he could manage to get on a flight to London from Salisbury. He had tried unsuccessfully a number of times to get in touch with Beth's parents on the phone and had ended up sending them a telegram informing them of his flight details.

Mapenge had driven him to Salisbury in the Ford pickup; it was a long hot drive. Mapenge seemed to be taking his time and eventually, after telling him to drive faster, Reg told him to get in the passenger side and he drove himself, not that he was able to drive much faster but at least he was doing something. Mapenge was happy not to have to drive and was soon snoring with his head flopping forward each time he dropped off to sleep. Reg was not looking forward to the long flight to London.

Pops was there to meet him at the airport in the Austin Estate. Reg never got on with Beth's folks and they likewise never really accepted Reg as their son-in-law. They blamed him for all her troubles. They firmly believed that had he not taken her to that country of heathens and savages, then she would not be in the state she was in today. They drove most of the way in silence, Pops not really telling him what the problem actually was with Beth and Reg not pushing the issue. He had waited so long, another hour or so would not make any difference.

Beth had not been informed that Reg was coming, as they were never sure when he would be able to get a flight and did not want to get her all worked up. Janis took Reg up to Beth's bedroom. Beth had her back to the door sitting where she normally sat at the window staring out over the meadow at nothing in particular. "I've brought someone to see you, dear," said Janis. Beth continued to look out the window as if she had never heard her mother speak. She only turned around when she heard Reg's voice.

"Hello, darling, how are you?" It was the first time since the accident that her face lit up and she actually smiled.

"Reg! Oh, Reg! Is it really you?" she said, jumping up out of the chair and flinging herself into his out-stretched arms as he walked toward her. "Why did you take so long to come and fetch me?" she said with big crocodile tears rolling down her cheeks. "I thought you had forgotten about me and that's why you never wrote or phoned."

Janis stood in the doorway and when Reg turned and looked at her questioningly. She shrugged her shoulders, turned, and went back down the stairs. Like a flash it then suddenly all made sense, why he had not heard from her all this time. Her folks had obviously not been giv-ing her his letters and telephone messages and they had also not been posting her letters to him. He just held her in his arms. He knew that her folks were not particularly fond of him and that they did not approve of their marriage, but to do this to their only daughter was beyond his comprehension.

"I came as soon as I could. We were so busy at the farm and I had difficulty getting a flight out of Salisbury," he lied.

With Reg at her side, Beth's condition changed within a week, she started to eat properly and was soon able to go for long walks with Reg, hand in hand. Beth never questioned him about why he had not written and Reg never volunteered to tell her, but he guessed by now she had worked it out for herself.

Reg had not planned to be away from the farm for longer than three weeks at the most, but it was now six weeks in total that he had been away. He phoned the farm the day after he arrived in England and every week thereafter.

Although both Negome and Mapenge confirmed that all was well, he was not entirely convinced and had a feeling that something was not quite right. He could detect a distinct change in Negome's attitude over the past few weeks, but maybe he was imagining things. After all, he had never spoken to her on the phone before. It could well be that she was uneasy speaking to him on the phone so far away.

Reg had also booked a person-to-person call to Johan but Annie had taken the call; apparently Johan was not available. Annie was very cool on the phone and said very little, not even asking after Beth. She confirmed that

Johan had been around to his place to fix the pickup and everything seemed to be OK.

Reg was now even more worried and he cursed himself for not asking his uncle, Lyle Traverse in Bulawayo, to look after the place while he was away.

Every day Beth grew stronger, and what her folks had been dreading for so long soon came to fruition; a week later they were on a flight back to Africa.

Chapter 45

For the first three weeks on the farm all went well; there were no problems that Mapenge or Negome could not handle. They worked well together, each recognizing the other's skills and talents and therefore respecting one another. Mapenge never tried to come on to Negome. He knew that such a move would spell disaster for him should Reg find out about it, so he confined his romantic escapades to the tea pickers. Negome consulted Mapenge when she was not sure about something and he in turn asked her about things to do with the wages and other money matters that he did not understand. This way it all made for a good harmonious working relationship.

It was Friday and the end of the month. Wages had to be drawn and provisions bought. Mapenge and Negome went into town early; they wanted to get most of the shopping done before the bank opened at nine o'clock. Negome was in and out of the bank within half an hour. They then quickly finished the provision shopping and were on their way home by ten thirty. They had just come over the rise, having negotiated the worst stretch of corrugations in the road, when the engine suddenly cut out.

Mapenge got out, opened the bonnet, and looked inside. He pulled and wiggled some of the wires and checked the little glass fuel filter bowl to see if there was petrol in it. Everything was OK as far as Mapenge could see. He got back into the vehicle and tried to start it again and, although the engine turned over, it just would not start. Mapenge stopped trying to start it, as he was afraid he would run down the battery.

"I don't know what the problem is," he told Negome. "You sit here in the pickup and I will walk to the farm. It is not too far, maybe only two miles. I will go and get the big truck and we can then pull this thing to the farm and try to fix it there."

Less than an hour later Mapenge was back with the three-ton Bedford truck and the other driver. They hitched the pickup to the truck with a chain, towed it back to the farm, and left it standing outside the shed. Once they had off-loaded all the provisions into the store, Mapenge went down to the house and phoned the de Klerks' place. Annie answered the phone. "Hello, madam, it's Mapenge, can I please speak to the boss?"

"Hello, Mapenge, the boss is not here. He is down in the lands. He will be back at lunch time, can I give him a message?"

"Thank you, madam, please, will the madam ask him if he got time he can please come and look at the pickup, she is not starting."

"OK, Mapenge, I will tell him when he comes up for lunch."

When Johan went back to the house at one o'clock, Annie told him about the phone call from Mapenge. "*Ja,* that's typical of the bloody kaffirs. As soon as you leave them alone for a second, they fuck something up. I suppose I had better go and see what the problem is. I was going to go over there sometime anyway. As you know, Reg asked me to keep an eye on things while he was away."

At around three that afternoon Johan pulled up at the Traverses' place and sent one of the labourers that was working in the back garden to go and find Mapenge.

"So, Mapenge, what have you fucked up this time?"

"No, boss, I no fuck up nothing. The pickup, she just stops there by the hill before you come here to the farm, so we fetch the Bedford and we pull him here."

Johan got in behind the wheel of the pickup and turned the ignition on first to see if the petrol gauge was registering and that there was petrol in the tank. He then tried to start it, the self-starter turned the engine over but it would not fire.

He opened the bonnet and checked all the leads to the spark plugs. They all seemed to be making good contact with the plugs. He removed one of the leads and told Mapenge to put the gear into neutral and turn the ignition. As the self-starter turned the engine, Johan touched the spark plug lead to the engine block; no spark jumped from the lead to the block.

"OK, Mapenge you can stop, there is no spark going to the plugs, there must be something on the coil that's causing the problem." Johan pulled on the lead coming from the coil and it came out of the rubber grommet leading into the coil. "Ha! Here's the problem, Mapenge," he said, holding up the loose lead in his huge hand for Mapenge to see.

"That wire, she was already coming off when I come back from taking boss Reg to Salisbury," said Mapenge. "That road, she got too many potholes and bumps, the engine, she sometime misfire. Must be then that this thing, she start to make like that. Now there, up the road by the corrugations, this wire, she now really come loose."

Johan wiped the lead with a cloth and screwed it back into the coil terminal. "OK, Mapenge, try it again," called Johan to Mapenge, who was still sitting behind the wheel. Mapenge turned on the ignition and pushed the self-starter button, the engine turned over twice and then fired. He revved the engine a few times and then switched it off.

Mapenge got out of the pickup beaming, "I'm so pleased the boss can fix it so quickly and it not such a big problem for the boss."

"*Ja*, Mapenge, you see that's why I'm the boss—you need to have brains," said Johan, tapping his finger on his head, "to be able to fix things like this," and they laughed. "OK, so how is everything else here on the farm, any other problems you want me to look at while I'm here?"

"No, boss Johan, everything else, she is OK, there is no problem. Thank the boss that he come to fix the pickup so quickly."

"OK then, Mapenge, then I'm going back home seeing you got no more problems for this," Johan said, tapping his head again with his banana-size index finger.

Mapenge laughed and said, "Thanks, boss, but maybe some other time we can get a big problem for the boss to fix. Maybe the boss, he want to go down to the house to wash his hands before the boss drive home again."

"Yes, thanks, Mapenge, good idea. I'll go down and wash up before I go." With that he walked down to the house leaving Mapenge to park the pickup in the shed.

Negome was in the kitchen cleaning when she heard the screen door bang closed. She turned to see Johan standing in the doorway. "Hello, Mr. De Klerk. Did you manage to fix the pickup?" she asked,

"*Ja*, hello," replied Johan, somewhat taken aback by this good-looking coloured girl, "So you're Reg's piece of fluff?" he said as he walked toward the sink. "What you got to clean this grease off my hands?" Negome did not understand the first part of what Johan said but she understood the second part and grabbed the tin of Vim powder from the sink and poured a good measure into Johan's cupped hands.

"*Ja*, that's the stuff that should get it off."

Negome put the Vim tin back on the sink. Johan stood with his cupped hands over the sink. "Turn the water on so I can wet it, or do you expect the grease to just come off dry, hey?"

Negome did not understand the sarcasm but turned the cold water on for him.

"Don't be so fucking stupid, girl. Cold water isn't going to get this shit off, turn the fucking hot water on."

Negome turned off the cold tap and turned the hot one on. Johan wet the powder and rubbed the paste all over his hands, he then rinsed them under the running hot water tap, which by this time was steaming hot. The boiling hot water did not seem to bother him in the least.

Johan finished washing his hands and dried them on a towel that Negome handed him. As he gave her back the towel, he caught hold of her arm and pulled her toward him. "Seeing your boss isn't here to give you one I'm sure you won't mind giving me a little bit of pussy," he said as he grabbed her on her breast and started to squeeze it.

Negome, taken aback by his sudden actions, tried to pull away from him, but he held her in a vicelike grip. She then tried to slap him across the face with her free hand. "Let go of me," she shouted. For a big man Johan was very quick. He stepped back, and letting go of her breast he caught her hand as it skimmed past his nose.

"So the little bitch wants to play rough, does she?" And with that he spun her around so that her back was toward him. He held both her wrists in one hand behind her back.

"You are hurting my arms," protested Negome, "let me go."

"Well now, you should have thought of that before you started to get rough, shouldn't you?" Johan pushed her to the edge of the kitchen table and then pushed her down so that she was bent over it.

I saw you at my place the weekend of my birthday, showing the boys your legs up there on the *veranda*. A bit of a cock teaser, hey? He held her down with one hand while he loosened the belt around his fat stomach with his free hand and let his trousers fall to his feet. Johan never wore underpants—as far as he was concerned, underpants were like a necktie, a piece of unnecessary cloth that served no purpose in life other than to make you feel uncomfortable. He then lifted Negome's dress up over her head and pulled her panties down around her legs. She tried to lift herself up off the table, but he pushed her down again so that her head hit the table with a thump.

"Lie still, you little bitch, and feel what it's like to have a real man inside you." The sight of Negome's bare backside had Johan immediately aroused. "Nice piece of ass you got here, no wonder Reg tried to keep you a secret," he said as he caressed her between her legs with his free hand. Negome immediately tensed up. "Yes that's what I like nice and tight. With that he spat on his hand and rubbed the saliva on his penis to lubricate it and then thrust it into her.

Negome screamed as he penetrated her.

"Shut the fuck up, you silly bitch," he said slapping her twice about the head. "Do that again and I'll hurt you real good." It was all over in a few minutes. Having satisfied himself he pulled out of her, picked up the towel from the floor, and wiped himself. Then he pulled up his trousers and walked out of the kitchen. "You can now look forward to the next time," he said over his shoulder as he went out the door.

Johan got into his pickup and drove out the gate of the Traverse farm with a feeling of satisfaction. As he drove, he thought to himself, "That little coloured bitch, she actually tried to hit me. What the fuck did she think she was, white or something? That's the bloody trouble with the English; they just don't know how to treat their blacks. If you don't give them a good kick up the ass every day they get too fucking white. That stuck-up little cow had it coming to her. The next time she won't try to be so fucking clever."

Negome lay as she was, bent over on the table crying, her dress still over her head. She was not crying from pain but from being violated and humiliated in such a manner. After a while she got up from the table and went into the bathroom where she stood for a long time under a steaming hot shower.

Chapter 46

By the time he drove in through the gates of his own farm the whole incident was a thing of the past. It was nearly half past four, everyone would be knocking off in a short while and Johan wanted to go down to the lands to see if his workers had done what he had told them to do before he had gone up to have his lunch. "But I suppose I had better go and tell Annie that I'm back before I go," he reasoned with himself, "or she will no doubt shit herself if she finds out I have not told her I'm back."

Johan walked into the kitchen. "Hello is there anyone home," he called.

"I'm in here, in the living room," shouted Annie. Johan went up the passage to the living room at the front of the house and stood in the doorway. Annie was sitting on the sofa doing some needlework. "So did you fix whatever the problem was?" asked Annie, not even looking up from what she was doing.

"Hell, it was no big problem," said Johan. "The lead from the coil had worked itself loose. I had it sorted out in a few minutes"

"You would have thought that Mapenge could have fixed something as simple as that," remarked Annie.

"You must be joking," said Johan, "The fucking blacks can't fix things—they can only fuck them up."

"So if it wasn't such a big job, what took you so long?" asked Annie.

"Well, I thought while I was there I may as well go and see how things were going down at the nursery and that took some time," lied Johan.

"So what are you planning to do now?" she asked.

"I must quickly go down and see if those buggers have done what I asked them to do before lunch. They didn't know I was going to the Traverse farm so more than likely they have done very little while I was away," said Johan.

"Would you like a quick cup of coffee before you go?" asked Annie. "It's all made, perking on the stove all I have to do is pour it."

"*Ja*, that would be nice," said Johan. He only now realized that he had had nothing to drink since lunchtime and was quite thirsty. Annie put down her needlework and walked over to where Johan was standing in the door.

"There is also some fresh *vetkoek* that I made this morning, I suppose you won't say no to one of those either?" said Annie, as she squeezed past him in the doorway.

"You know me, doll, I'm always a sucker for your *vetkoek*," he said and gave her a hug.

Annie immediately pushed him away and stood back and looked at him. "You've been with that coloured bitch of Reg's, haven't you, de Klerk?"

"What do you mean?" protested Johan.

"Don't lie to me, de Klerk. You've been fucking that bitch. I can smell her cheap fucking perfume all over you, I would recognize that smell a mile off. She came here smelling like the cheap whore she is the day of your birthday."

"No ways," protested Johan, "I never touched her. The smell must have come off the towel she gave me to dry my hands when I went down to the house to wash them."

"Yes and then you fucked her, didn't you?" Annie was now incensed, she went back into the living room and took down her late father's Purdy double barrel shotgun from the gun rack. "You're some kind of sick bastard, de Klerk," shouted Annie over her shoulder as she broke open the gun to see if it was loaded. "I swear, doll, I never touched her. The smell must have come from that towel when I wiped the sweat off my face with it."

"Christ, de Klerk, do you think I was born yesterday?" she said as she turned around cradling the open shot gun on her arm. "You've been fucking the little *kaffir* tea pickers for years. Pa warned me about you a couple of times when he was still alive, but I was too blind to see it. I thought the old man was just trying to come between us because he never liked you. He saw through you right from the start. I only realized what Pa had always been trying to tell me was, in fact, true when that old maid of ours, Beatrice, came to see me. She told me that there are a number of little coloured children running around on the farm that have been sired by you, you are fucking pathetic, de Klerk.

"Now you know why I haven't allowed you near me for the past few years. You always thought there was something wrong with me. It's not me, it's you there's something wrong with, you're fucking sick and now I have had enough of your shit."

"Jesus Christ, Annie, what do you want me to do to convince you that I never touched the bitch? All I did was wash my hands."

"You want to know what you can do?" said Annie, snapping the gun closed, you can drop your pants and come over here so I can smell. I know you too well, de Klerk. You never wash after having sex.

"Annie, are you mad? I told you I didn't have sex with her, why won't you believe me?"

"Johan de Klerk, you have two options, you can drop your pants and come over here or you can fuck off and don't ever come back. I'm counting to three. If you are still there on the count of three I'm going to give you both barrels full in the nuts and you will never fuck a bloody thing ever again," she said, lifting the gun to her shoulder and cocking both hammers, click, click.

"Annie are you out of your fucking mind? Put that dammed gun down before you hurt someone."

"The only one that's going to get hurt is you de Klerk, ONE—TWO—THREE." Annie had no need to pull the triggers; there was no one to shoot at. The word two was not even out of Annie's mouth and Johan was making a fast getaway down the passage. He knew when to stand and argue with Annie and when not. This was obviously not the time to stand and argue, he knew her too well when she was in this frame of mind. She was more than likely to give him both barrels full in the nuts.

Annie uncocked the gun and put it back on the gun rack. She heard the pickup start up, and walked to the front door to watch as Johan drove out the gate. He would go straight down the road to their other neighbour's farm, Dave Cross, who stayed by himself. Dave had lost his wife some years ago. He was the only neighbor who would socialize with Johan; all the others disliked him intensely and only tolerated him because of her.

Chapter 47

Annie had met Johan at boarding school in Pietersburg, a small farming town in South Africa that was close to the border with Rhodesia. He was a day scholar and she a boarder who went home only for the long holidays. Annie was not particularly beautiful, but she was very bright, top of her class every year. She started to date Johan when she was in standard eight and Johan was in standard ten. Johan was the school's rugby hero, blond, good looking, and built like a Sherman tank. What he lacked in intellect he made up for in size and brute force. He came from a broken home with two stepsisters and a little brother. His mother had been divorced three times and his life, as far back as he could remember, was shear hell with the various stepfathers that had come and gone in his life from the age of three to sixteen.

Annie, on the other hand, came from a long line of farming stock. Her grandfather had been a wealthy cattle farmer in the northern province of South Africa who had two sons. When he died he left the farm to his older son and Annie's father received a sum of cash, which he used to buy a farm in Rhodesia. Annie could not remember her mother; she apparently died when Annie was only eighteen months old.

There was a lot of speculation about the way Annie's mother actually died but the consensus was that a leopard attacked her while she was out riding. Her horse had returned late in the afternoon of the day she went out, bleeding from deep claw marks on its side and back. A search party was quickly formed, but what was left of the body was only found two days later. A number of predators left spoor around the remains of the body, including a leopard. Annie's father took it very badly and blamed himself for letting her go on out-rides by herself. He never married again and, as a result, he worshipped the ground Annie walked on and always wanted the best for her.

The old man never took to Johan from the start. Annie would bring him home for the long holidays, her father said he was lazy and all he did was laze about reading comic books. On the other hand, Annie was besotted with him and did everything for him. They were married two years after she finished school.

The old man died of prostate cancer three years after Annie had given birth to Jane, her only child. When he died, he left the farm and everything he possessed to Annie, not even mentioning Johan in his will. He had been very critical of Johan and had informed her several times about his escapades with the tea pickers. Annie had always defended him against her father, believing that the old man was jealous and was trying to come between the two of them. It was only in the old man's later years that she slowly began to realize that what her father had been telling her all the years was, in fact, true.

Since her father had died, the production on the farm had declined. Johan always blamed the lazy black labourers, lack of rain, too much rain, or something else that was out of his control for the bad crops. There was always an excuse for everything that went wrong; it was never his fault or bad judgment.

The day her old retired maid, who had virtually brought her up, came to visit her and told her about Johan's goings on with some of the young tea pickers, was the day she had moved Johan out of their bedroom and into the spare bedroom. When Jane came back from boarding school and asked why her father was sleeping in the spare bedroom, Annie told her that her father's snoring kept her awake at night.

Chapter 48

The flight back to Salisbury was uneventful. They spent the night in a hotel in Salisbury waiting for Mapenge to come and fetch them. It was late in the afternoon when Mapenge eventually arrived at the hotel to pick them up. They left early the next morning before daylight and arrived back at the farm in the late afternoon, other than being hot and dusty, the trip was thankfully uneventful. Negome had been waiting all day for them to arrive. She saw them come in through the main gate and ran outside to meet them.

Reg had told Beth all about Negome and what a great help she had been in helping him with the buying of provisions and doing the general housework and cooking. He also told her what a disaster the other girl had been that Mapenge had sent them shortly before she left for England. He had told her that she was an Afro-Portuguese woman but had neglected to tell Beth how beautiful she was. Negome and the dogs came running up to meet them as they got out of the pickup. Beth had a completely different picture in her mind of what

Negome looked like and was quite taken aback by this lovely girl standing in front of her.

"Oh, Mr. Reg, Mrs. Reg, I'm so glad to see you," said Negome shaking Beth's hand vigorously. Reg came around from the driver's side and introduced Negome to Beth. "Negome this is my wife, Elizabeth."

"Pleased to meet you," said Beth, having recovered from the shock of seeing Negome for the first time.

"Me too. I'm pleased to meet you too, Mrs. Reg," she said, shaking Beth's hand again. Despite Reg not having told her how strikingly beautiful Negome was, Beth was immediately attracted to her.

Mapenge unloaded the luggage from the back of the pickup and helped Negome carry it inside. The dogs were all over Beth, jumping up and running around her, barking with excitement. Beth had run down to the house with the dogs running in front of her barking. She could not wait to get inside her home again and be among her own things. She went from room to room picking up little things here and there, familiarizing herself again with them. It was as if she had been away for years. The house was spotless and, from what she could remember, nothing was out of place. In their bedroom Negome had placed a glass vase filled with roses from the front garden.

Negome had moved out of the spare room and back to her own room when she got the phone call from Reg in Salisbury telling her that Mapenge should come and fetch them. Basically she had gotten over the incident with Johan but was worried about what was going to happen to her now that Mrs. Reg was back. Reg had made it quite clear to her in the beginning that this was not a permanent job. She did not particularly want to go and pick tea again, having now experienced what back-aching work it was.

She had taken the opportunity one day when she was in town buying provisions to ask the storekeeper if he perhaps needed someone to help him in the store. Old man Arthur Hamman was getting on in years and had gotten to know Negome quite well since she had been doing the buying for Reg. He knew that she was a bright girl and he could use someone with her experience. He told her to speak to him again if things did not work out for her on the farm. Negome did not particularly want to leave the farm; she liked it there and enjoyed what she was doing.

On the Saturday following their return from overseas, just after breakfast, Reg called Negome up to the study. Negome thought to herself, "This is the day that Mr. Reg tells me that I must go and pick tea again." Negome knocked softly on the open study door. Reg was seated in his rickety old swivel chair and Beth had flopped down in the big armchair with her feet tucked up under her.

"Come in, Negome," said Reg. "Elizabeth and I have been discussing your position here on the farm and have decided that it would be nice if you could stay on and help with some of the things around the house that Elizabeth might just not be strong enough as yet to handle on her own. Then there's the business of buying of the provisions and the paperwork that's associated with all that. I would also like you to continue with that, seeing that you did such a good job while I was away. So what do you say, Negome, would you like to do that?"

Negome was so pleased that she could have hugged them both, but she restrained herself and said she would be very pleased to do those things.

The following Monday afternoon Beth phoned Annie to let her know that she was home again and to pick her out for not writing to her while she was in England.

"You're upset with me," said Annie indignantly. "I wrote to you twice and when you never wrote back I stopped writing. I even told Reg jokingly that you had most probably run off with another bloke, so don't talk to me about not writing."

"Sorry, Annie, I 'm not quite sure what was going on while I was in England. I never received any letters from Reg either and he most probably never received any of mine and I wrote at least five letters to you. I thought no one cared about me anymore, including Reg. I thought I was going out of my mind. All the time my mother was telling me that maybe everyone over here was very busy and did not have time to answer my letters. It now appears that no one ever received any posts from me or me from anyone else.

"I know Mother wanted me to remain in England, but I never expected her to go to such lengths. Now I know why she always insisted that my father go and post my letters and collect the post from the post office. I wonder what she did with all the letters. Anyway, enough of that. When are you coming to see me, you old bag?" Annie explained that she was running the farm on her own for a while and could not get away, so it would be better if Beth could come over and visit her instead.

"Yes of course I'll come over to your place," said Beth, "but where's Johan?"

"It's a long story," said Annie, "not one for the phone. I'll tell you all about it when you come over."

"OK, Annie, then I'll give you a ring later on in the week and we can make a date. I just need to get my life together again, I'm not sure what I'm doing and what our maid Negome is still supposed to be doing."

"Oh, is she still there?" asked Annie with a little cynicism in her voice.

"Yes, we've decided to keep her on, she has done such a great job looking after Reg while I was away and—"

Beth never got to finish what she was going to say. Annie interrupted and said,

"Yes I'm sure she did, you give me a ring when you're ready," she said and then she put the phone down.

Beth stood for a while looking at the receiver in her hand, thinking, "That was strange of Annie to put down so abruptly." She shook her head and put the receiver back on the cradle and went back down to the kitchen to finish cooking dinner.

That night at dinner she told Reg about the conversation she had with Annie. Negome, of course, was no longer having her evening meal in the dining room.

"Maybe Annie has kicked Johan out at last," said Reg jokingly.

"No, be serious, Reg, I think there is something going on over there. I detected something in her voice— she wasn't the old Annie I used to speak to."

"Come on, dear, you're imagining things. I'm sure Annie is fine and Johan has gone off on one of his fishing trips with the boys or something."

"You know, Reg, now I know why I never received any letters from you. You did write, didn't you?"

"Yes, of course. As promised, I wrote you every week, but I gathered for some reason or other you never received any of them. Is that right?"

"Yes, that's right, and you never received any of mine, did you?"

"No, I didn't get any of yours either."

"Annie never got any of mine and I never got any of hers. Mom and Pops were not posting the letters or giving me any when they arrived."

"But how can you be so sure?" asked Reg.

"Because my mother always insisted that Pops post and collect all the letters at the post office."

On Friday Beth phoned Annie and made arrangements to go over there for morning coffee on Sunday at about ten. She promised to make Reg a nice dinner when she returned instead of the normal big Sunday lunch.

Chapter 49

When Beth got back to the farm just after one o'clock she was in a foul mood. She had been brooding about what Annie had told her all the way home and she now urgently needed to speak to Reg and went off to find him. She found him in the study catching up on some paperwork. She stormed into the study.

"How could you embarrass me like that?" she shouted at Reg. He spun around in his chair and looked at her standing just inside the door with her hands on her hips and her face all flushed.

"Embarrassed you about what?" he said calmly.

"Why didn't you tell me you'd taken Negome to Johan's birthday barbecue and the little slut got drunk and made a spectacle of herself in front of all Annie's guests? Do you know while you were away she had a fling with Johan and that's why he's not there?" she babbled, now almost in tears."

"Hey, slow down, slow down. Come and sit down and we can try to make some sense of all this."

Beth flopped into the big armchair. "I could have just crawled out of her house when she told me about

Negome and when I said I had no idea she was like that, she said, 'Oh, I'm sorry, I thought Reg would have told you about the little slut's incident here.' She said the whole town was talking about you and your little bit of black ass. Christ, Reg, how could you do this to me?" She was sobbing now, nearly choking on her words.

"Well I didn't tell you, because firstly I didn't want to upset you about something I didn't think was a big issue," said Reg.

"A big issue! Christ, Reg, did you really think Annie wouldn't say anything to me? How bloody naive can you fucking be?"

Reg knew Beth was very upset, as she never swore.

"She couldn't wait to tell me what a little slut you employed and although she didn't say it, I just know she wanted to ask me if you were sleeping with her while I was away. I felt so humiliated I could have shrivelled up right there and died."

"OK," said Reg, "now I don't know what Annie's told you, so now let me tell you what I know and you can then make your own judgment about what you think actually happened."

"OK, so you tell me your side of the story now. I'm all ears," Beth said cynically.

"About two weeks before Johan's birthday bash, Annie phoned me and invited me to come over for the party. I said I'd feel strange without you there and that I didn't mix well, being antisocial, and all that. Annie insisted I come over. She said I needed to talk to some white folks for a change. I told her that I had a new housemaid and that I had been talking English with her. Yes, Annie said she had heard in town that I had this new coloured maid and why don't I bring her to the party? She said Jane and a girlfriend were coming down from Varsity and it would be nice for the maid to meet someone her own age. She insisted I come and bring Negome with me.

"I thought about it for some time and also came to the conclusion that it would be nice for Negome to meet some new people, especially people her own age. I told Negome about it, but she was not keen to go, as she thought it would not be right. I insisted and told her that Annie thought it would be nice for her. She said she had nothing suitable to wear, so I let her scratch through my mom's old things—as you know, she had some nice dresses."

"Well, did she manage to find something among all that stuff in there?" asked Beth, wiping her nose with her hankie.

"Yes," said Reg. "she picked out a white dress that really looked nice on her."

"Yes that was another thing Annie wanted to know if it was one of my dresses that she had on," said Beth.

"So what did you tell her?" asked Reg.

"I said I didn't know, but it could have been and the thought of that made me even angrier."

"Beth, you know I would never let anyone touch your things, let alone wear one of your dresses."

"Yes, I know, but Annie had me in such a state I wasn't thinking straight," said Beth. "So you went to the party and Negome pinched some booze and got drunk."

"No, that's not how it happened," said Reg, and he told her about what Jane and her friend had done, spiking Negome's fruit juice because she was getting all the attention from the young guys that were there at the party. Reg told her everything, how she was sick in the pickup and how he had to clean her up—except for the part where he slept with her.

"Well, that certainly puts a different slant on the story compared to what Annie told me," said Beth.

"Darling, I hate to say this but I've told you many times Annie is bit of a troublemaker," said Reg. "She loves to exaggerate and put her own interpretation over as the facts."

"Yes, I know, love. I'm sorry I went off like that," said Beth and she got up out of the chair and came and gave him a hug.

"But what do you make of the story that Johan had a fling with Negome while you were away?" asked Beth. "She has definitely kicked him out."

"Well, maybe we should ask Negome, let's see what she has to say. I'll go and see if she is in her room," said Reg, lifting himself out of his chair. Reg saw Negome sitting outside on the grass reading. "Negome," he called from just outside the back door, "could you please come up to the study for a few minutes? Beth and I would like to speak to you about something." Reg went back up to the study and sat down in his chair again.

"Did you find her?" asked Beth. "Yes she was outside sitting on the back lawn reading."

Negome came into the study. Reg pulled up a chair and told her to sit down.

"Negome we need to ask you about something that apparently happened here while Mr. Reg was in England," said Beth. "Now we don't want you to be scared to tell us, and we will not be angry with you. All we want to hear is what happened to you and Mr. de Klerk when he came here that day to fix the pickup truck."

Negome put her head down in her hands and said, "I'm very ashamed to say what that terrible man, he did to me." And she started to cry.

"Reg, I think maybe you should go out and let me handle this, said Beth.

"OK, if you think that would make Negome feel easier I'll go and make some tea."

Beth got up from her chair and went and stood next to Negome. She put her arm around her and said, "You just tell me in your own way what happened that day, start from the beginning."

Negome told Beth in a fair amount of detail about the whole incident, starting from when she and Mapenge went to town and the pickup truck broke down. Beth was appalled when she heard the whole story and how Johan had raped her on their kitchen table. Beth and Negome went into the kitchen and Beth made them a mug of tea each. Reg had drunk his tea and gone up to the workshop. They sat and talked for hours Negome told Beth about her past and Beth told her about all her troubles.

Reg came into the kitchen and said, "Are you two going to sit here talking all afternoon and forget that your old husband, who you promised a nice big dinner instead of lunch, is practically dying of hunger?"

"I'm so sorry, Mr. Reg, that I have taken so much time to talk to Mrs. Reg," said Negome, getting up from the kitchen table.

"No, I'm only joking," said Reg, "please sit down, Negome. I was just wondering what you two were gassing about for so long."

"It's girl talk," said Beth, "and you don't want to know."

"OK , I get the message. I'm going back to the study to finish off what I started on earlier," said Reg, "seeing as you girls have now occupied the kitchen."

It was not long after Reg had left the kitchen that Beth came into the study and plunked herself down in big armchair. "That bastard, de Klerk, raped her right here in our kitchen," said Beth, "and now she thinks she may be pregnant."

"Pregnant?" said Reg, his attention suddenly fully on what Beth was saying. "by whom?"

"By Johan, stupid, who else? She was a virgin before he raped her."

"Oh! How was I supposed to know?" said Reg. "I just thought it may have been someone else."

"Look, Reg, just because she's half Portuguese and half black, it doesn't necessarily mean that she sleeps around; you men all think alike."

"You know that's not what I meant," said Reg.

"No, I don't. Just what did you mean?"

"Nothing. Just leave it. I'm sorry. I forgot how sensitive you are about these things."

"No, I won't leave it. Do you know something I don't know?" asked Beth getting a bit ratty.

"No, I don't know anything, I just thought that she may have been seeing some one. Hell, I've been away for over two months. I don't know what she's been up to while I was away."

"I'm sorry, love. I'm just so dammed upset about this whole thing with Negome. As if the poor girl has not had to endure enough in her past, she has to now get raped right here in our home by our neighbour. That bastard, de Klerk, I could spit I'm so mad and now I'm getting all ratty with you as if it were your entire fault she's pregnant," said Beth.

"That's all right, love; I'm just as upset," said Reg. "I can't believe Johan would do something like that. I know there was always talk in the town bar that Johan liked the young tea pickers, but I though it was only bar talk."

"Apparently not," said Beth. "He has been screwing around for years. Annie tells me that there are a whole lot of coloured kids running around their farm that are as a direct result of Johan's sexual escapades."

"So, if she knew about his goings on for so long, how come she kicked him out only now and how did she find out about Negome?" asked Reg.

"She said it was a dead giveaway. When he came back from having raped Negome, he apparently gave her a hug and she could smell her cheap perfume on him. Annie said she would have recognized the smell of her perfume a mile away. She said that Negome was wearing it when you went to their place on Johan's birthday."

"Yes, that's right, I remember now, I had to open the pickup window it was so overpowering," said Reg.

"Well, when she confronted him with it, he apparently denied it and she got the shotgun and chased him off the property. She said that was the last straw, or as Annie so nicely put it, his last fuck on my place."

"Look, I don't want to know all the details, but is she sure she's pregnant?" asked Reg.

"Well, she says she hasn't had a period for months now and she says she is normally like clockwork, but I will take her into town tomorrow to see Dr. Lewis, said Beth.

"And if she is pregnant what is she going to do?" asked Reg.

"I don't know but she has made it quite clear she doesn't want the child and could we please help her to arrange for an abortion."

"Abortion, that's a pretty strong action to be taking, isn't it?" asked Reg.

"Well, do you have any other suggestions?" asked Beth, getting all defensive again.

"No, not really, it's just that an abortion is just so damn final, that's all," said Reg.

Chapter 50

On Monday morning Beth took Negome into town to see Dr. Lewis. Dr Lewis was well into his seventies and had been the Traverse doctor long before Beth had come on the scene. The Traverse and the Lewis families were old house friends when Reg's mother and father were still alive. Beth waited outside in the waiting room while the doctor examined Negome.

Dr. Lewis stuck his head out of the door and asked Beth to come into the consulting room. Negome was sitting opposite the doctor at his desk. "Come in, Beth, pull up a chair." Beth pulled up a chair next to Negome and sat down. "Well, it would appear that our young lady here is pregnant, I would say just over three months. She tells me that she does not want to have the child and could I arrange for her to have an abortion.

"Of course I've explained to her that the law of the land does not allow for abortions to take place unless there are extenuating circumstances. But if she were to lay charges of rape against the perpetrator, the law would perhaps look more favourably on her case and maybe allow her to have a legal abortion."

"But she must also realize that a case of rape would have to be thoroughly investigated, which could take months and months. Then it would have to wait to go to court and that too could take months. By that time the child could already be a few months old."

"I would seriously suggest that she skip the abortion route and rather go for maintenance, but she would still have to prove in a court of law that the person who she claims raped her was indeed the father of the child. Negome, would you please go and wait in the waiting room? I would like to quickly have a private talk with Mrs. Traverse." Negome got up and went and sat in the waiting room.

"Beth, I would strongly suggest that you take Negome home and talk to her and try to get her to see that in this country with her being a person of colour and the perpetrator being apparently white, the odds, I'm afraid to say, of her getting a conviction against the white man are next to nothing. I would suggest she have the child and try to do her best to support it the best she can."

Beth thanked Dr. Lewis for his frankness and went out into the waiting room where Negome was sitting. Neither of them said much on the way home. Each sat with her own thoughts.

It was lunchtime when they arrived back at the farm. Beth could see that the whole ordeal had drained Negome so she told her to go and relax for the rest of the day. Reg came up from the lands for his customary glass of cold tea at lunchtime. Beth told him what Dr. Lewis had said and suggested. Reg said that he was not surprised; he had expected Dr. Lewis to say something along those lines, as the law was quite clear on abortion.

For the rest of the afternoon Beth went about her work around the house with her mind firmly fixed on something else. At dinner that night, Beth wanted desperately to ask Reg something but she was scared that he would respond negatively to her suggestion. Finally over coffee she had plucked up enough nerve to speak to him. "Darling, I want to ask you something, but I want you to really think about it before you give me your answer," said Beth."

"Now, what is it you've got up your sleeve?" asked Reg curiously.

"I don't quite know how to put it, so I'm just going to say it straight out," said Beth nervously. "I would like us to adopt the child that Negome is going to have. I can't have any children and this could be the only chance that we have of ever having a child we can call our own. Please, love, just think about it. I have given it a lot of thought and that's what I would like us to do."

"Wow! that's quite something," said Reg rather taken aback. "I don't know what to say, I mean you know that it is Johan's kid, how's that going to affect us?"

"I know its Johan's child, but only we will know that and what difference does it make in the end? It will still be our child and we will love it like our own," said Beth.

"Have you mentioned this to Negome yet?" asked Reg.

"No, I've not discussed it with her yet, as I first wanted to get your consent. I didn't want to get her hopes up and then we tell her we don't want to take the child. That sort of thing can really upset her even more than she is at the moment."

"I know we are desperate to have a child we can call our own, but are we prepared for something like this? What will the folks in town think of us adopting a child from one of our workers? You can bet your life on it that Annie will be broadcasting it all over town before you can say jackrabbit," said Reg.

"I know and I've given that some thought too. We could send Negome to Auntie Maureen and Uncle Lyle in Bulawayo. Then Annie will think we have fired her because of what she told me happened while I was away. Negome can continue to work for them and when it gets close to the time for her to have the child I can go up and be there with her. Nobody will know where the child came from," said Beth getting all excited. "We can say we adopted it from an orphanage."

"It would seem that you have worked out a fair bit of detail already in your mind," said Reg.

"Oh, there's plenty more. I've got it all figured out. Just you say yes and leave all the details to little old me. Come on, love, what have we got to lose, hey?" said Beth, now almost pleading with Reg to say yes.

"Well, I suppose it's OK, said Reg, "but you had better—"he didn't get to finish the sentence as Beth had jumped up from the table and was smothering him with kisses.

"I knew you would agree," she said, still with her arms around his neck and continuing to kiss him.

"OK, OK, that's enough, enough!" shouted Reg. "You're going to throttle me if you don't stop that."

"No, love, I would only have throttled you if you had said no," she said jokingly as she let go of him and went and sat down again.

Beth wanted to go and tell Negome what they had decided, but Reg said no,

Beth should wait until the morning; things like this need to be discussed in the daylight, he said. Beth hardly slept that night. She could not wait for the dawn to break and it was time to get up. She desperately wanted to tell Negome about what she and Reg had decided.

The morning came at last. Reg got up as soon as the alarm clock went off at half past five. Beth normally turned over and went back to sleep again until Negome brought her a tray of tea at seven. This morning she sat up in bed watching Reg dress in the light of the flickering candle. Reg never bothered to put on the Coleman lamp in the early morning; the candle was all he needed to see to get dressed. "You're awake early," said Reg as he stooped over her to kiss her good-bye.

"Yes, I couldn't sleep. I kept thinking about the child we are soon going to have."

"Now, I don't want you setting you heart on something that isn't a certainty," said Reg, as he made his way to the door.

"Don't worry, love, I won't. Please ask Negome to bring my tea early today, as soon as you have gone to work."

Reg went down the passage to the kitchen. He could see the light under the door leading from the passage to the kitchen and knew that Negome was already there making the fire. The kettle was already on the primus stove to make coffee.

Negome came into the bedroom and greeted Beth good morning. She placed the tea tray next to Beth on the side table. She was about to leave when Beth said, "Don't go, Negome, I want to speak to you. Sit on the stool over there," she said, pointing a small footstool. "Mr. Reg and I have been discussing your predicament and we wish to adopt your unborn child, of course, with your consent.

"We will send you to our family in Bulawayo and you can have the baby in a good hospital. I will come and be there with you when you have the baby," explained Beth excitedly. Negome sat and stared at the floor in front of her not saying anything. "Isn't that exiting?" asked Beth.

Negome slowly lifted her head. "This really is a big thing you ask of me. I am not sure that I can carry the child of that man inside me any longer. Would you and Mr. Reg be happy to look after this child" she asked, pointing to her stomach, "knowing that it was from an act of violation that the child is now growing inside me? This child can one day grow up to be like his father and we do not need more people like that in this world."

"I can understand how you feel," said Beth, "but what will you do if a legal abortion is not possible? You will be stuck with a child that you hate. As you know, I can't have any more children and this may be our only chance to have a child that we can call our own. You would be helping us and we would be helping you. Yes, we know it is a child that was conceived under terrible circumstances and that there is the chance that the child may have some of its father's character, but equally the child must have some of your wonderful character and, who knows, maybe your character will be the dominant one."

"I am very confused," said Negome, "I must think about it, I did not plan this thing for myself and now this thing grows inside me and as it grows so am I reminded every second of the violation. I want to rid my body of this curse so that I can get on with my life the way it was."

"Please don't do anything before you speak to me, if you are sure what you want to do, then we will try to find a doctor, maybe in Mozambique that can help you," said Beth, with disappointment in her voice. She had expected Negome to be overjoyed with the news. Instead she was obviously not happy to even carry the child for the full term.

Negome thanked Beth for her understanding and help and went back down to the kitchen to prepare breakfast. She was very grateful in her mind for the help and support that the Traverses were giving her, but she did not want to put this burden now on their backs. They had been so good to her and already they had done enough, she must sort this thing out for herself. She would talk to Mapenge; he would surely know someone who could help her.

Reg came up from the plantation to eat breakfast with Beth. Negome served them, and when they were done eating, she cleared the table and then went outside. That's when Beth told Reg what Negome had said. Reg could see that Beth was obviously very disappointed; she had not expected Negome to have reacted so negatively to her proposal.

"I told you, love, not to get your heart set on this thing. Negome has her reasons and, let's face it, if it wasn't meant to be, then it wasn't meant to be."

"Oh, that's such a typical male philosophical answer, so where does that leave us now in terms of having a child?" said Beth getting a bit ratty with Reg.

"Look, I can understand that you are disappointed," said Reg, "but let's give Negome a chance to think about what we proposed. After all, this is a very big decision for her and whatever she decides, the outcome of that decision will no doubt have an effect on her for the rest of her life."

"Yes, I know you're right. I just wanted her to be as excited as I was, that's all," said Beth.

"OK, love, I'm out of here. You just be patient and think positively. Things have a way of turning out for the good in the end."

Negome washed the breakfast things and packed the dishes away. By twelve o'clock she had completed all her chores and walked down to the commune kitchen next to the staff quarters to go and find Mapenge. She had never told him what happened to her with Johan de Klerk, the only ones she had spoken to about it, were Reg and Beth. Negome found Mapenge in the canteen; he was sitting with a group of other workers eating his lunch. She went and sat at another table with a group of women she knew and waited for him to finish his lunch.

When he had finished, she went over and asked him if she could speak to him in private. Negome told him she was pregnant, but she would not disclose who the father was.

"Why you not tell me you want to have a child? I would make you a very nice child," said Mapenge.

"I did not want to have a child, explained Negome, "it just happened and now I must get this child that is growing inside me out, can you help me?"

"Yes, I think I can help you, there is a *sangoma* who stays not too far from here. She is very good with these things, but next time you want to make a child, you come to me, I not make you pregnant if you don't want."

"Mapenge, I have told you many times I don't want to sleep with you, I like you as a friend and we are a team together."

"But you sleep with this other guy, is he also not a friend?" asked Mapenge.

"Look, Mapenge, this person who did this to me is no friend, so please don't ask any more questions, just tell me how I can go and see this *sangoma*."

"Just you tell me, this guy, did he force you? You tell me who he is and I will kill him if he force you. OK, you tell Mapenge?"

"Thank you, Mapenge, I am very thankful you want to help me like that, but, please, just you tell me how to get to the *sangoma*."

Chapter 51

On Friday at lunchtime Mapenge came down to the house and told Negome that he had arranged for her to see the *sangoma* on Saturday afternoon. She must take five pound sterling and an empty cold drink bottle with her. He would send his youngest son to take her there and they should leave by midday, as it was about five miles to walk through the bush to the *sangoma*'s *shamba*.

Normally on Saturday Negome finished work at twelve o'clock and then she was off for the rest of the weekend. Most Saturdays the Traverses went into town and once they had left, there was very little for her to do in the house. She would knock off after she had cleared and washed the breakfast things.

Shortly before twelve o'clock Mapenge's son David came down to fetch Negome to take her to the *sangoma*. It was hot walking in the midday sun and they had a fair amount of climbing to do. David set a fast pace, walking a long way in front of Negome so that any conversation with the young boy was impossible. When Negome would lag too far behind, he would wait until she caught up and then he would set off again. When they could see the *shamba* some distance away, David stopped and pointed it out to her. He said he would wait under the tree for her to return and that was the sum total of his conversation.

The *shamba* was made up of four huts; one was a lot bigger than the others. A high reed fence encircled the *shamba* with a small entrance passage. A young woman met Negome at the entrance and told her to wait until she was fetched. Negome went and sat on a rock under a tree near the *shamba* entrance, out of the hot sun, and waited. She was grateful she could rest and catch her breath before she saw the *sangoma*, as she was wet with perspiration, David had set a fast pace and toward the end she had struggled to keep up with him.

It was not too long before the young woman came and fetched her, leading her along the reed passage into an opening between the huts. In front of the larger of the huts three women sat on grass mats on the ground. The one in the middle was obviously the chief *sangoma* as she looked to be very old, although it was hard to see, as she was lavishly made-up with white clay paint, coloured beads, and draped in bright cloth. "I see you, my child," said the old lady, beckoning to Negome to come and sit opposite her on the grass mat.

"I see you too, Oh Wise One," replied Negome respectfully as she sat down in front of her on the grass mat.

Negome knew about the sangomas. Her mother visited one up in the mountains near Massangena and her mother would always speak respectfully of her. The old lady took an old tobacco bag that was lying next to her and emptied the contents onto the mat in front of her.

The bag held an assortment of small odd-shaped bones, a dried-up monkey's hand, smooth-coloured stones, a silver coin that Negome did not recognize, a Coca-Cola bottle top and a thimble.

The old lady pushed the objects around with a stick that was decorated with coloured beads and had a large wisp of hair from a Zebra's tail tied to the end. Every so often she would swat at the flies with the hair wisp. Every time she changed the position of the objects, she would chant while rocking backward and forward. All the time the other two women would also chant and rock back and forth.

The old lady suddenly stopped her chanting and the moving of the contents of the bag that lay scattered in front of Negome. "I see, said the old lady pointing with her beaded stick to the coin, 'that you are like this coin; you are not from these parts. Your mother is very sad and your sisters are missing you." She went on pointing to various objects as she spoke. "Your body has been violated by an u*mlungu*," she went on, pointing to a flat white stone that was touching the thimble. "You are also with child," pointing to the hand of the monkey. "Your father tells me that he is sorry for all the pain he has caused you and that he does not wish you to send this child that is within you to him. He says that he is not prepared for it, but he will do his best to look after it, if you must send it to him.

"So child, why do you not want this child that is growing so strong in your womb?" asked the old lady.

"I'm afraid that this child may grow up to be like the man who sired it, said Negome.

"And is that so bad?" asked the old lady.

"Yes, I think so," answered Negome. "Well then, let us see what we can do. Did you bring me something?" she asked. Negome produced the bottle and the five pound note, the woman on the left of the old lady took the bottle and put the five pound note on the mat in the middle of all the other objects.

The woman who took the bottle went into the big hut and after a while she came back with the bottle half full of a brown liquid with a screwed up piece of newspaper for a stopper. She gave the bottle to the old lady who took it and, while tapping it with her stick, said, "This is the *muti* for the child within you. If you really have decided that you do not want this child, you must first fill the rest of this bottle with your body fluid that comes from your womb first thing in the morning. You must then go down to the river and drink it all at once. You will need a friend who can help you; you will feel a great pain just before the child comes away from the womb. When the pain comes, you must walk into the river and let it flow away."

Negome thanked the *sangoma* and took the bottle and got up from the mat where she had been sitting. "I greet you well," said Negome.

"Go well, my child, take care, remember what your father has said." And with that the old lady got up, helped by her two assistants, and walked bent almost double into the large hut.

Negome found David where she had left him and without saying anything, he got up and started to walk back along the winding path followed closely by Negome. The return journey was much easier, as it was mainly downhill, and they arrived back while the sun was still high on the western horizon. When the farm was in sight, David ran off and that was the last Negome saw of him.

All the way back, Negome was thinking about what the old *sangoma* had told her. She was now even more confused than before. The part where the old lady told her about what her late father had said was most disturbing. Then there was the thing Mrs. Beth had told her about adopting the child, all these things weighed heavily on her mind. Negome decided before she did anything, she would talk to the priest, Father Murphy, on Sunday.

On Sunday after the church service, Negome went and stood in the line waiting for her turn to go into the confessional booth. The line was not long and soon it was her turn to go and make her confession. "Father, I have sinned," confessed Negome.

"What is the nature of your sins?" asked Father Murphy.

"Father, I am not married and I have had sex with two men, one with my consent and the other time without and now I find myself pregnant from the one that violated my body."

"I see," said Father Murphy, "and are you planning to marry either of these men?"

"No, Father, that is not possible, as both of these men are already married."

"How do you know that you are pregnant?"

"The doctor has confirmed that I am at least three months pregnant," said Negome, getting all choked up and starting to cry.

Father Murphy had heard confessions of this nature many times before. Rape and sex outside of the marriage and incest were common among the black community. "How long after the first incident did the second one occur?" asked Father Murphy.

"Only about three weeks," replied Negome, still sniffling, "and I do not want to have this child of the man that violated me. He is bad and his child will also be bad."

"Have you had any other sexual relationships before these two?" asked Father Murphy.

"No, Father, this was the only time,"

"I see," said Father Murphy. "So then the first man took your virginity?"

"Yes, Father, that is so," said Negome still sobbing.

"Was the first relationship an act of love or an act of lust?" asked Father Murphy.

"It was not lust, Father, it was gentle and loving."

"You know, child, God works in mysterious ways. It could well be that the child you are carrying is, in fact, the child of the first man. Our God is a God of love and he would not have chosen the man that violated you to make you pregnant."

It had never occurred to Negome that Reg could be the father of the child growing inside her "I don't understand, Father," said Negome. "Why would God then send a second man to violate me like that?"

"As I said, God works in mysterious ways and he has a plan for each and every one of us, do you believe this?"

"Yes, Father, I believe that, but his reason is still not clear to me," said Negome now feeling a bit better. "God's reasons are not always that obvious, child, but if you pray, God will surely reveal to you his reason. Now go and sin no more."

On the way home, Negome said she would rather ride in the back of the truck with all the other people. She stood right at the back of the big Bedford truck with the cool wind blowing through her long hair. Negome thought about what the old priest had said. "God works in mysterious ways," she kept repeating to herself over and over in her mind.

Dark clouds were looming up from the west with lightning streaking across the sky in front of them. It started to rain, and everyone was trying to huddle up behind the cab to try to avoid getting wet. Negome stood where she was. She didn't mind the rain—it was cool on her face. There was another big flash of lightning that streaked across the now black sky followed by a loud clap of rolling thunder.

"That's it, that's it," shouted Negome to no one in particular. The others crouched behind the cab didn't even hear her above the driving rain and thunder. "That had to be it," she said to herself, it was as if the flash of lightning had suddenly made her realize the whole purpose of her ordeal. "Of course, God works in mysterious ways and has a plan for each one of us. Mrs. Beth can't have a child, so God sent me to bear the child for them. God knew that Mrs. Beth would not have accepted the fact that Mr. Reg had made love to me, so God sent that man de Klerk to violate me and he would then get the blame for the child I was carrying. Oh gracious God, she said out loud, lifting her hands to the heavens, how wonderful you are."

Chapter 52

As soon as the truck stopped, Negome was the first to climb down from the back. She removed her shoes, lifted up her wet dress that was clinging to her legs, and ran through the pouring rain down to the main house. She opened the screen door and called to Beth, she did not want to go into the kitchen and drip all over the floor. Beth was in the living room when she heard Negome call and immediately thought there was something wrong. She knew that Negome would normally have come in and knocked on the living room door.

"Goodness, child," said Beth, "look at you, you're sopping wet. Come in and let's dry you off before you get sick."

"No, no, Mrs. Beth, I'm fine, I just come to tell you I want you and Mr. Reg to adopt this child that grows inside me." Beth took hold of Negome's wet hand and pulled her into the kitchen. "You just stand there while I fetch a towel to dry you off." Beth walked up the passage to the bathroom with the sound of the protesting Negome still coming from the kitchen. Negome stood in the middle of the kitchen waiting for Beth to return.

Her dripping wet clothes had formed a pool of water on the red polished cement floor around her bear feet.

"Who's that you're talking to?" asked Reg as she went past the study where he was working. "It's Negome," said Beth sticking her head in the door. "She has just come back from church and she is sopping wet. I'm getting a towel to dry her off."

"They must have gotten caught in the storm," said Reg, calling after Beth as she continued up the passage to the bathroom. He thought it a bit strange for Negome to come and bother Beth just because she got a little wet, but perhaps she had a reason. He continued with his paperwork.

Beth came back with a large bath towel and a blanket. "Here, let's dry you and get you out of those wet clothes," said Beth as she dried the still protesting Negome. Beth made her strip down to her bra and panties right there where she stood and then wrapped the blanket around her. Beth picked up her wet things and put them in the sink. "Come sit here at the table and let's talk about this big decision of yours."

Beth poured them each a mug of hot coffee and they sat at the kitchen table across from each other. "The decision as what to do has been very heavy on my mind," said Negome. "Ever since I knew that I was going to have a child, I could find no reason why God would do this thing to me, and today the priest told me that God works in mysterious ways. On the way home, I suddenly knew why I was having this child," she said.

"And what was that conclusion?" asked Beth, now intrigued to hear why Negome had changed her mind.

"You see, Mrs. Beth," said Negome, "God could see that you could not have a child and he knew that I was grateful to you and Mr. Reg for what you have done for me so he sent this man de Klerk to make me pregnant so that I could have this child and give it to you for all your kindness to me. This is God's and my gift to you and Mr. Reg."

Beth was so moved by what Negome had just said that tears came rolling down her cheeks. She got up and went around and held Negome in her arms. "Thank you, thank you," was all she could muster. Beth went and sat down and gathered her composure. Maybe there is a God up there after all, she thought to herself.

Beth told Reg the exciting news. They discussed the plan Beth had put together before Negome had agreed to let them adopt the child in more detail. On Monday Reg and Beth drove into town to phone Auntie Maureen and Uncle Lyle in Bulawayo. After hearing the condensed version of the Negome ordeal, they agreed to accommodate Negome and find her a job while she was there waiting to have her baby. Being a retired advocate, Uncle Lyle had many contacts; he would also arrange to have the adoption papers drawn up for them to sign when they brought Negome up to stay with them.

Lyle Traverse had been an attorney and advocate for over forty years before he retired at seventy. Having seen and heard many things in his life, he had learned when to ask and when not to ask questions. Lyle and Maureen were a little taken aback when his nephew informed them that they were going to adopt an unborn child of a half-caste Portuguese girl who worked for them.

They said nothing and would reserve their judgment until after they had seen the girl and heard the full story.

Reg and Beth made arrangements to take Negome up to Bulawayo the following Friday morning and to return on Tuesday the following week. Beth had told Negome to tell her friends that she was going back to Mozambique and that Mr. Reg was going to Inhambane and was giving her a ride as far as her home town.

"So my little friend is going back to her mother to go and have the child," said Mapenge. "That is good, but before you go, I want to know who do this to you so I can cut his balls out."

Negome laughed and said, "Mapenge, you are not angry that the person did this to me, you are angry because it was not you who's baby I carry."

"No! You see, my friend, I am two times angry because of this thing. I tell you long time before I make for you a beautiful baby but you no want and this other guy he do this to you, now I think I nearly get three times angry."

Reg and Beth had decided that it would be better if Reg took Negome up to Bulawayo alone, as the workers on the farm all believed that she was going home and Reg was giving her a ride on his way to Inhambane.

They left the farm in the early hours of Friday morning. As usual it was a long hot drive up to Bulawayo and Negome and Reg had plenty of time for small talk. "This is truly a wonderful thing that you are doing for us," said Reg after travelling for some time, "especially for Beth. This has brought her a new lease on life. This last week she has not stopped talking about the baby. She is planning to change the spare room into a nursery and I must get Mapenge to go search through the junk in the shed and find my old crib. She wants me to clean it up and repaint it. Well, I'm sure you know all about these things, as she talks to you all the time about them. But how do you feel about all this, are you not sad that it's not you planning the birth of your first child? How do you feel knowing that you will never see your first child grow up in front of you?"

"Yes, Mr. Reg, my heart is very sorrowful on the one side, but on the other side it is very joyful, for God has chosen me to be the carrier of your child."

Beth had told Reg what Negome had said that Sunday when she got back from Church that Negome now believed God had sent Johan to rape her so that she could have this child and give it to them. This was her and God's gift to them for all the good they had done for her. "Yes, Beth has told me," said Reg, "and we are very grateful, it is just such a shame that this child has to be the result of such a terrible incident."

"Oh! No, no, please don't say that, Mr. Reg, this child that I carry inside me is not the child of that man de Klerk."

"It's not?" said Reg, somewhat astounded after all the fuss she had created over the fact that Johan had raped her and made her pregnant. "Then whose child is it?"

"It is our child, Mr. Reg."

"How do you mean our child?"

"That night after the party when we made love, Mr. Reg, that was the night that the seed of this child was planted inside me."

"But how can you be so sure it is not the child of Mr. de Klerk? A few weeks ago you wanted to abort the child because you felt the child might grow up to be someone like de Klerk."

"I know but I was confused then. I did not see God's bigger plan for all of us. All I could see was my own misery. You see, God has spoken to me and now I'm as sure as I'm sitting here that you, Mr. Reg, are the father of this child."

"But you can never be so sure," protested Reg. "It could be either of us."

"Mr. Reg, trust me, my eyes have been opened and if you don't trust me then trust God, for it was His Will," said Negome, getting a bit upset that Reg did not want to believe that it was his child. She was sure that he was going be very happy to hear that it was his child.

"Maybe you don't want that this is our child," said Negome with a little sob in her voice as she touched her stomach.

"No! No! That's not what I meant," said Reg, realizing that he had upset her. "Oh course I'm delighted that the baby is mine and not from de Klerk, but Beth will never accept that we slept together to make this child."

"Yes, Mr. Reg, you are quite right. Mrs. Beth would never accept that we slept together, that is why Mr. de Klerk had to come and violate my body so that she would believe that it was his child. This is now a great secret between you, me, and God. No one else need ever know that this is actually your child that I grow for you and Mrs. Beth inside me. You see, Mr. Reg, God, He works in mysterious ways."

"Yes," said Reg, "I'm beginning to see that."

Very little else was said for the rest of the trip, with both deep in their thoughts.

By the time they had driven through the centre of town and out to the small holding on the outskirts of town it was four thirty in the afternoon. They were tired, dusty. and thirsty by the time they arrived at his Uncle Lyle's house.

Lyle and Maureen had been waiting for them to arrive. They heard the pickup come up the driveway and went out to meet them. They were not quite sure what to expect. Reg had not said much about the young girl whose child they were going to adopt, only that she was an Afro-Portuguese girl. Where should they accommodate her, in the house or out back in the servant's quarters, where will she eat, with them or with the rest of the servants?" These were some of the questions that went through their minds.

Reg parked the truck on the side of the house, got out and walked back to where his aunt and uncle were standing at the front of the house. He gave Maureen a big hug and kiss on the cheek and vigorously shook Lyle's hand.

"Good to see you, my boy, looks like Beth's been feeding you too well," he said patting the little paunch that Reg was developing.

"That's the problem, Uncle Lyle," said Reg laughing, "between Beth and Negome's cooking I'm fighting a losing battle. Come, let me introduce you to Negome."

Negome stayed in the cab but when she saw them coming down the driveway in the side mirror she got out and waited for them by the side of the truck. Maureen could see that this was no ordinary black farm girl who picked tea for a living. This girl was special. She was struck by her simple beauty. Despite the fact that she had been travelling all that time she looked lovely, her thick black hair cascading down over the shoulder of her long cream dress, the dark chocolate eyes in that sallow skin. A light breeze caught a wisp of Negome's hair and blew it across her face. She lightly brushed it aside and tucked it behind her ear.

"Yes," said Maureen to herself, "I can see why Reg and Beth have agreed to adopt the child of this lovely girl."

Reg had some business to do in town on Saturday morning and it gave him and his uncle an excuse to get out of the house, as all they had heard was the jabbering of the two woman. Lyle and Maureen had three daughters, all married. Two were living in South Africa and the third, the youngest, was living in Salisbury. They had six grandchildren and Maureen had been at all the births of her grandchildren. As far as Maureen was concerned, having babies and being involved with the births of babies was all part of a day's work. Negome could not have chosen a better person to be looking after her interests than Maureen; she was like an old broody hen.

Maureen had quickly fixed up the room of her youngest daughter for Negome. The room was still pretty much the same as it was a year ago when her daughter got married and left home. She emptied the wardrobe so Negome would have some place to hang her things. Negome was embarrassed.

"Please, Mrs. Maureen, I can sleep out back with the other servant girls. You make too much trouble for me."

"Nonsense, child, you will stay here in Joan's old room where I can keep an eye on you. Anyway, Reg tells me that you are a good cook so I have decided that as long as you are here you can earn your keep by preparing the meals for us. I'm tired of cooking just for the two of us. Lyle insists that we have a full cooked meal at dinner, so, my dear, you have just got yourself a job."

On Monday they all drove into town to go and sign the adoption papers at the magistrate's court that Lyle had got drawn up by one of his ex partners. Reg was anxious to get back to the farm. He did not like leaving Beth too long on the farm by herself because of the political unrest that was taking place. There was nothing else left for him to do in Bulawayo, so he decided that he would leave after lunch. He gave Maureen and Negome a squeeze good-bye and as he did he whispered in Negome's ear.

"Now remember if there are any parties, stay away from the fruit punch."

"Oh, don't you worry, Mr. Reg, I never will touch that stuff again."

"Beth will write to you. As you know, if we phone, the whole world will know our business. Two weeks before you are to give birth, Beth will come up and be with you. Auntie Maureen will keep in touch with Beth on the phone if there are any emergencies. I'm sure they will work out some code or something to fool the old biddies who listen in on the party lines." Reg got in the pickup and waved good-bye as he reversed down the driveway.

It was nearly midnight by the time Reg got home, he was dead tired, and twice he had nearly fallen asleep at the wheel. He had to stop and get out and walk around to wake up. He didn't bother to put the truck in the shed and parked it outside the back door. Beth had woken up when she heard the pickup come through the gate. She lit the candle, slipped on her night robe, and went through to the kitchen to meet him.

Chapter 53

Mofola knew that he could no longer stay in Massangena. The whole town knew what had happened between him and Victor at the poker table and now Victor was dead. He had no intention of getting into any trouble with the commissioner again. Not that he had anything directly to do with Mr. Victor's death, but he knew how the police worked and if they wanted to blame him, they would find a reason to do so.

The next day Mofola told his mother and father that he was going to leave again, as now there was nothing for him in Massangena. Mofola had packed the few things he needed into his suitcase early that morning and, having greeted his father, he and his mother walked to the gate together.

"But where will you go, my son?" asked his mother. "You have only been here for such a short time and now you want to leave again. Why don't you stay? Your father is not well and we need a strong man here at home."

"No, Mother, this place is not for me, it is as if the gods are telling me that I should leave this place. All that it has brought me is sorrow and pain. I will go and find work in Inhambane and when I have enough money I will return to the mines in South Africa." Mofola hugged his mother. "I will write to you when I have work," he said as he looked back over his shoulder and made his way down the track to the road leading to Massangena.

Mofola had given his mother most of the money that had not burned but he had kept enough to buy a bus ticket to Inhambane and enough to see him through for a few weeks. At midday the bus stopped outside the post office. A few people got off and more got on. For the first hour or so, Mofola had to stand, as all the seats were occupied but at the next bus stop a lot of people got off and he managed to get a seat. It was late the following afternoon when the bus finally pulled into Inhambane Station bus stop. Mofola waited for his suitcase to be unloaded from the top of the bus and then set off for his old friend Roberto's house.

The family greeted Mofola like he had been away for another two years. It felt like years, with all that he'd been through, although it was only six weeks ago that he sat outside Roberto's house waiting for him to come home. How things can change in such a short time. Just six weeks ago he was a wealthy man going home to fetch his bride, and now he was a poor man without even a dream to hold onto.

As usual, Roberto was not at home. He had been contracted out by his company to transport cement from the cement factory at Dongo thirty kilometres from Beira to the Cahora Bassa dam. The dam was sited on the Zambezi River up in the Tete Province, a trip of over five hundred kilometres. This was the job Roberto was telling him about the last time they met. Roberto's wife, Magrete, told Mofola that Roberto came home for only a few days at the end of every second or third month and that he would just sleep for three days solid. He would wake up, eat a little, and then go back to sleep again. She said the job was very tiring, he was working fifteen to eighteen hours a day, and there was hardly time to eat or sleep. The money was good, but she was afraid that the work would kill him or he would die in an accident.

Magrete told Mofola that Roberto was due to come home at the end of the week and he was welcome to stay as long as he liked. Mofola was hoping that Roberto would be able to get him a job on the dam site or put him in touch with the recruiting people up there. He had heard that this was going to be the biggest dam in Africa. He had no idea how big that was, but he was sure they could use someone up there with his mining experience.

It was past midnight on Friday when Roberto arrived home, the children were all asleep in bed and Magrete and Mofola were still sitting in the kitchen talking, when he walked in. They greeted each other like long-lost brothers with much hugging and backslapping.

Roberto stood back and looked at Mofola. "You know, my friend, when I saw you the last time when you walked out of the cantina that night. I thought that you might do something stupid and land up in jail again or get yourself killed, but look—here you are, again alive and well."

Roberto greeted his wife and she took the few things he had brought with him and went and put them in the bedroom. Mofola and Roberto sat opposite each other at the small kitchen table and Magrete put the kettle on the Primus stove to boil for coffee. Despite the fact that Roberto was cheerful and happy to be home, Mofola could see that he had lost a lot of weight, his eyes were sunken in his head, and he had dark rings around them. He looked grey and tired.

Magrete went to bed and left the two men to talk, but it was not long after she had gone to bed when Mofola insisted that Roberto join her, as he could see that Roberto was practically falling asleep at the table. "You go and sleep, my friend; we have plenty of time to talk before you return to Cahora Bassa."

Roberto finally woke up at two in the afternoon the next day, hungry and thirsty.

"Well, my friend," said Mofola, looking at Roberto as he came outside where he and the boys were kicking a football around, "I must say that you look much better now than you did last night. I mean, you are still ugly," he teased, "but at least now you are rested and ugly."

"If you think I'm ugly, when last did you look in the mirror?"

Magrete came to the door and looked out. "Hey, do you lot want to stand there and argue who's the ugliest or do you want some of the chicken I just cooked?"

Over lunch Mofola told Roberto about what had happened since the last time they had been together in the cantina up in Massangena. Roberto was quite shocked to hear that Victor had taken his own life and said Mofola had done the right thing by leaving, as they would have blamed him for it just like they framed him before.

"They are looking for good people up at the dam site and you, with your mining experience, you can get a good job that pays well," said Roberto. "If you like, you can come back with me on Monday."

Monday morning before it was light Roberto and Mofola left the house after saying their good-byes to the family. They walked the few kilometres to the depot of the company United Transport, which had the contract to transport supplies up to the dam site near the small town of Songo. The truck was all loaded, ready to leave, when they got there. By the time Roberto had completed all the paperwork and filled the big truck with diesel the sun was already peeping up over the ocean.

It was late Tuesday afternoon when they pulled into the town of Songo. The town was about five kilometres from the actual dam site. The little town had grown over a hundredfold in the past two years. There were now places to shop, a communal church, recreation facilities, and many more amenities for the construction workers, administration people, and their families, who now accounted for the larger part of the population of the small town.

They parked the truck at the back of United Transport's offices where it would be unloaded. Roberto went to check in and see if his supervisor could put a word in for Mofola at Zamco's recruiting office. Zamco was the company that the Portuguese had founded to handle all the administration, supervision, and general management of the construction of the Cahora Bassa dam.

Roberto came back after ten minutes and said that he would need to check again tomorrow morning with his supervisor to see if he had managed to do anything for Mofola. Meantime, they would go back to the compound where Roberto was staying.

The next day Roberto would start his shift again. Soon after he had spoken to his supervisor he would leave to go and pick up a load of cement from the factory at Dondo, a round trip of eleven hundred kilometres. At an average speed of forty-five kilometres per hour it would take the better part of twenty-four hours. This did not include the two hours at either end for the loading and off-loading of the fifty-kilogram bags of cement and a chance to catch up on some much-needed sleep. It was gruelling work, six days a week and in those six days he would do a minimum of four trips, often pushing it to five and then sleeping for eighteen hours on the Sunday. The money was good and Roberto said he would continue for as long as he could. The rail link from Dongo to Moatize could not cope with all the cement needed at the dam site, so they had a convoy of trucks carrying cement running continuously from Dondo to Songo.

Next morning before sunrise Mofola and Roberto were outside United Transport's offices. They did not have long to wait, as business in Songo started early as the noon temperature reached thirty-five degrees centigrade and higher on most days. Roberto's supervisor had a letter for Mofola that he was to hand to the security guard at the entrance to Zamco's recruiting offices. When they arrived at the offices, the line was already around the block. Mofola handed the envelope to the security guard at the gate and was told to wait there while he took it inside to the person whose name was written on the front of the envelope.

At that stage Roberto bid Mofola farewell and made his way back to the transport truck depot at the back of the United Transport's offices where his truck and co-driver were waiting for him.

Chapter 54

It was already midday by the time Mofola was called from the gate by another security guard. He was escorted into one of the many prefabricated offices inside the two-metre-high fenced yard. Crammed inside the small office was a single desk and many filing cabinets all around the walls. Behind the desk that was piled high with papers and files, sat a short fat Portuguese man with small round reading glasses perched on the tip of his oversized nose. He addressed Mofola in his home language, *Shangane*. "This letter tells me you have worked on the gold mines in South Africa. What job did you do there?" he asked without looking up from the letter that was lying open in front of him on the desk.

"I was working as the boss boy for the white miner," replied Mofola. "Do you have an SA Reference Book and any papers from the mine you worked on?"

"Yes, I have them here," said Mofola, opening a large brown envelope that he had brought with him. He placed the papers and his SA Reference Book in the outstretched hand of the man behind the desk. The man systematically went through the pile of papers and paged through Mofola's Reference Book.

"These seem in order," he said, handing the papers back to Mofola. "We will start you at the basic wage of six hundred *escudos* a month and if you prove yourself to your supervisor then we can give you an increase. You will work as a driller in one of the tunnels being built near the dam site. Go down to door seven and hand them this paper and they will give you your kit and tell you where to go from there."

Mofola found door number seven quite easily, as there was a queue leading to it that extended halfway up the long *veranda*. By the time Mofola had collected all his gear, gotten all the instructions and been medically checked, it was already late afternoon. He was now standing with a group of about twenty other labourers waiting outside the East Gate for the company's bus to pick them up and take them to their quarters.

While they were waiting, everyone was looking up at the big notice board that was suspended above the double gates they had just come through. It showed an aerial photograph of the area that the dam water would cover once it was completely full. Mofola could not make out any details other than hills and mountains, as the scale was too small. A red line had been drawn around the outer circumference where the high-water mark would be once the dam was full. He could see that many of the hills and some of the mountains would either be covered with water or they would form islands in the lake.

He was amazed at the size and area this man-made lake would eventually cover. On the right-hand side of the photograph was a write-up and a drawing of the dam wall as it would look when completed. The write-up said the lake would extend more than 250 kilometres (156 miles) upstream and would be the third-largest man-made lake in the world. The dam wall was going to be 160 metres (525 feet) high and 305 metres (1,000 feet) wide. The drawing showed an arrow pointing to a small object at the base of the wall that looked like a match-box; the caption said it was a full-scale picture of a bus. They all stood there talking excitedly about the magnitude of this project; they could not believe that such a huge wall could be built and that they were actually going to be part of it.

The living quarters were not unlike the ones on the gold mines in South Africa. There were many South Africans working on this site and their years of experience on the gold mines had shown that this model worked well. They had therefore adopted a similar model for this site. Mofola was put in a dormitory with eleven other labourers.

The next morning they were taken by bus down the steep and winding road into the Zambezi River gorge. They would be working in the chamber that was being cut into the solid granite side wall. This chamber would eventually house the huge electrical generators. Mofola had seen big chambers before in the South African mines, but this chamber was huge. He was told that you could fit two of St Paul's Cathedrals in this chamber. He had no idea how big St Paul's Cathedral was, but he knew it must be a big building. Mofola asked why this chamber had to be so big and was told that it was going to house five of the biggest generators ever made. Each generator would be able to supply enough electricity for a city of over one hundred thousand people.

This was a lot different from the small stopes in the gold mines that were barely a metre high in places. Here the ceiling or hanging-wall was sixty metres high, and one had to stand on hydraulic-lifted scaffolding to drill. The principle was basically the same and that was to drill and blast as clean a cut as possible and to penetrate as far as possible with every blast. After two weeks Mofola got the hang of it and started to get a feeling for the type of rock that they were cutting into. He was sure they could improve their daily metreage by drilling a different pattern and using a different blasting sequence.

That day, after they had finished their shift, he explained his idea to the white South African foreman who was in charge of the section where they were working. At first he was reluctant to listen to what Mofola had to say but, after speaking to him, he realized that Mofola knew what he was talking about and decided that they would try Mofola's idea on the next shift. He figured they had little to lose if it did not work, as they were weeks behind schedule anyway, so another day or so would make little difference.

The company offered generous bonuses for clean cuts and for being on schedule, but not one of the five teams of ten miners had yet been able to achieve a bonus. The granite rock was full of fissures and became very unstable. A piece of the south wall had collapsed, killing six miners and injuring many more. It was very difficult to get a clean cut from the blast, as the rock tended to break along the fissures and that was not always the direction that they wanted to follow. In the section that Mofola was working, they had managed to get back on schedule within three weeks, using his drilling and blasting techniques. With the new technique the cut was much cleaner and they were able progress an extra metre with every blast.

Word soon got around that team three was doing well and the head supervisor wanted to know what they were doing differently. When he learned that it was a new drilling and blasting technique developed by Mofola, he immediately promoted Mofola to drilling and blasting supervisor. Within two months the chamber was on schedule for the first time. Now it was the cementation team that lagged behind; before they were constantly waiting on the mining teams progress before they could line the chamber with a thick skin of concrete to strengthen and prevent any collapse of the hanging-wall and long-walls.

Mofola had been working at the dam site now for just over eight months. There was never much of a chance to take time off, as they worked twelve hours a day and six days a week. Mofola did not mind; work never frightened him. Besides, he had made more money in the past eight months than he had made in the two years working on the South African gold mines. He had seen very little of Roberto as a result of all the time he spent working.

Early one Sunday evening, Mofola was sitting outside his dormitory when Roberto came around the corner and said, "Hey, Mr. Big Shot supervisor, have you forgotten your old friends now you're such a big shot?"

"Roberto, my old friend, I never get to see you anymore, you are always on the road when I enquire about you."

The two friends sat talking way into the night. Roberto said, "It's getting late, my friend, we both have to be up early tomorrow and I need to get some more sleep before I start the week again. Hey! I'm going home at Christmas for a few days—why don't you join me?"

"That sounds good," said Mofola. I'll speak to my boss and see if I can take some days off."

Chapter 55

Roberto had arranged to take a truck back to the Beira depot and then pick up another truck with a load that had to go down to Inhambane. They left Songo early Saturday morning and, as the truck was empty, they made good time, arriving in Beira in the early afternoon. The truck they were to take to Inhambane was already loaded and ready to go, but they decided to sleep the night at the company's hostel and leave early Sunday morning for Inhambane.

Mofola and Roberto had each taken a six-day leave of absence; they weren't due back at work until the Tuesday after Christmas. Roberto had not been home for over two months so his family was excited to see him. They also made a big fuss over seeing Mofola again. It was nice not having anything in particular to do. The boys were home from school on holiday so they would all go into town in the morning and do a bit of shopping for Christmas. Mofola bought a few things they could not get in Songo and some gifts for the boys. In the afternoon they would go down to the beach with the boys and fish or just swim and lay around.

Wednesday night Roberto said he had to go to a meeting and Mofola should come along as his guest. Mofola wanted to know what sort of meeting it was.

"Don't worry," said Roberto, "its just a little political meeting, someone is giving a talk, and you'll find it interesting."

"I don't know," replied Mofola. "I'm not very interested in politics."

"Come on, I want you to meet some of the people—they could help you one day."

Reluctantly Mofola went along to the meeting. It turned out that it was a secret meeting of one of the banned political parties called RENAMO, which stood for Mozambique National Resistance. This political party, like the other banned party, FRELIMO (Front of the Liberation of Mozambique), were two of the main political groups that were against the present Portuguese colonial government.

Mofola knew that FRELIMO had initiated an armed struggle against the Portuguese colonial rule last year. He had heard that they were a Marxist group supported by Russia, and that they were particularly active in the rural areas of the Northern Province. Everyone working on the dam had been warned that there was always a threat of a FRELIMO attack on the dam site and, as a result, the government had stationed troops in Songo as a security measure. The government-controlled newspaper had been full of propaganda against the two parties and the people had been warned that anyone caught collaborating with any of these banned political groups would be shot.

"So what did you think?" asked Roberto, as they walked home after the meeting.

"My father always said you work with whoever's in power and with their system, be it good or bad. It's the system and it does not matter how bad it is, it's still better than no system," Mofola said. "I have had my share of getting involved with the local government and I don't want to get mixed up in anything political or anything that's against the law."

"Yes I can understand how you feel, but if there's going to be a change we need to make sure that the right change comes about. If FRELIMO is successful we will again have a one-party state, only this time it will be a Marxist rule and we will be worse off than we are now. RENAMO is for a multiparty democratic type of government where we all have a say in how the country is governed. Don't you want that for your future and the future of your children?"

"You see, Roberto, that is where we are different, I believe in what I can see and feel, not in a lot of talk that mostly comes to nothing. When I was a young boy I used to hide in the long grass at night and listen to the elders talk and pass the pumbe around. I remember what they spoke of and how they will change things. I'm a grown man now and still the things they promise are not done. If the system changes then I will work with the new system. I believe that if a man works hard he will benefit, but if he sits back and always complains about this system or that system he will always be a poor man."

Roberto could see it was a futile exercise to discuss politics with Mofola, so he changed the subject.

The rest of the week went by very quickly; Saturday was Christmas day, the boys were very excited about getting gifts from their parents as well as from Mofola. Roberto's wife had cooked their favourite fried chicken and fried potatoes. The next day, Sunday, they had to leave again and catch the bus going to Beira, as there were no trucks going up from the Inhambane depot. Monday morning they were on their way back to Songo with a fully laden truck. Mofola was well rested and was eager to get back to work and see what progress his team had made while he was away. He was glad to see that they had made good progress and it was clear that they had now mastered the techniques that he had taught them.

The Thursday, two weeks after he got back, a messenger came down from the site office and told him that he was to report to the site manager's office the next morning and not to go down to the main chamber. Mofola wondered what the problem was and why the big boss wanted to see him. The only thing he could think of was that perhaps they were not happy that he had been away for such a long time.

Early the next morning, long before the offices opened, Mofola was waiting outside the site manager's office. He did not have long to wait. The site manager arrived and called him into the office.

"Sit down, Mofola. I suppose you are wondering why I sent for you. Well, don't worry. I have heard only good things about you. It would seem that your drilling techniques and blasting skills have allowed us to get back on schedule down in the main chamber. I have therefore decided to pull you off the main chamber, as I think the teams down there have now gotten the hang of it. I want you now to concentrate on the south diversion tunnel.

"Come and look over here," he said, getting up from behind his desk and beckoning Mofola over to one of the big tables where drawings where piled high. He pulled a drawing out from under a pile and spread it out in front of them, placing bolts and nuts on the corners to stop it from rolling up again. It was an overall view of the dam site.

"You see, here is the south wall of the gorge below the dam wall. We need to dig a tunnel from here that is fifty-five metres from the base of the wall. It will extend four hundred and fifty metres to here," he said, pointing with his pencil to a point up stream of the dam wall. "The tunnel has to be thirty metres high and twenty metres wide and it must first penetrate at an angle of thirty-five degrees into the side wall over here. When it reaches a point that is parallel with the middle of the dam wall it will turn seventeen degrees and cut back toward the side wall and eventually emerge here where I pointed before. At this point we will build a coffer dam to direct the water into this tunnel. This will be the main diversion for the river. We will also build a much smaller tunnel on the north side; this tunnel will take care of the flood waters.

"So, Mofola, what do you think, how long will it take?"

"It is a big tunnel, sir, and it will be more than half a kilometre long," he said, following the tunnel line on the map with his finger.

"Yes, I know, but we need to finish it just after the second flood season, which will be toward the end of March 1968, depending on when the rainy season starts and ends. That's about two years and two months from now. Once the tunnel is complete, we will start with the excavation of the base and side wall foundations for the dam wall. From next week, I want you to start with the training of three new teams. I want them to work eight-hour shifts until the tunnel is complete, do you think you can get it done in time?"

"It is a big job, sir, but we will do our best. Maybe the gods will be good to us, sir, and let us finish in time."

"Well, you had better pray hard to those gods of yours because there will be a big bonus of forty thousand *escudos* if you finish on time."

The manager went and sat back behind his desk, picked up the telephone, and spoke to someone. "Send Grobler in to see me," he said, and put the phone down. "So, Mofola, from next week Monday you will report to the new project manager for all the tunnelling.

Forty thousand *escudos*, thought Mofola to himself, was more than he could earn in four months; that was a good bonus. Just then the office door opened and a big white man walked into the office.

"You wanted to see me, sir," he said.

"Yes, Jannie, this is Mofola. He will be working with you on the tunnelling. He has also worked on the mines in South Africa, so you two should work well together. He is to be credited with getting the main chamber back on schedule."

Chapter 56

Negome's pregnancy went well with no complications. She was able to help Maureen around the house and do a lot of the household shopping. Lyle loved her cooking, it was spicy and different. Since she had taken over the cooking he had put on a few pounds, mainly around the midriff. Maureen fussed around Negome making sure she went to the hospital for her regular checkups and rested when she thought she should. The doctor predicted that the baby would arrive mid to late January. Maureen had communicated the dates to Reg and Beth, and they planned to come up just after New Year's or sooner if necessary.

Ever since Ian Smith, the prime minister of Rhodesia, declared independence from British rule, travelling had become a risky business. The two main opposition political parties namely ZANU (Zimbabwe African National Union) and ZAPU (Zimbabwe African People's Union), both Marxist liberation movements, had been staging protests and demonstrations in the main cities. They were vehemently against this Unilateral Declaration of Independence, commonly referred to as the UDI.

Things on the farm were much the same; politics seldom filtered down to the remote areas. There had been some talk in town about the UDI. As can be imagined, it was quite widely reported in the press and on the radio. Reg and Beth travelled up to Bulawayo on the first weekend after New Year's, leaving the management of the farm in the capable hands of Mapenge. They arrived in Bulawayo not having encountered any incidents of stone throwing, as reported on the radio the day before.

The following Wednesday, January 12, 1966, at 2.45 p.m., Negome gave birth to a beautiful six-pound fourteen-ounce baby girl. Beth had sat through the whole birth, wiping Negome's brow squeezing her hand, and generally giving her support. The baby had a mop of jet-black hair and a little nose that curled up at the front. Once Negome was out of the delivery room and in a private ward, Reg went to see how she was. The baby had been taken to the nursery and the rest of the family—Beth, Maureen, and Lyle—were there "ooing" and "aaing" over her.

Reg kissed her on the forehead and squeezed her hand, "I believe you did a great job," he said.

"Did you see her, Mr. Reg? She is beautiful. She has your eyes and nose."

Reg smiled and said, "No I haven't seen her yet. I first wanted to make sure that you were all right."

"Go and see her, Mr. Reg, you will see she is your child without a doubt."

Reg made his way down the long hospital corridor to the nursery, his mind racing back to the night he took Negome's virginity, wondering if it was his child or that of Johan de Klerk and would he ever know. Reg walked into the nursery to what sounded to him like a hundred babies all crying and screaming at the same time. Beth saw him come in and went up to meet him.

"Come and look, Reg, she is just too adorable," she said, pulling him by the arm to one of the many cribs in the nursery. She was asleep with only her head showing, the rest of her was tightly bundled up in a little white blanket. He could see her little up-turned nose but not her eyes, as they were closed. He had heard that a baby's eyes change colour after six weeks anyway, so how could Negome know that they were his eyes?

They had decided to name the baby Neita, which means lovely flower. They wanted a name beginning with "N" to remind them of Negome. Neita would remain in the nursery for the next few days or until she had reached an acceptable weight. They had all decided that it would be better for Negome if she did not see Neita again.

Reg did not want to leave the farm for too long a period, especially with the political upheaval on the go and decided that he would return Friday morning early and come back and fetch Beth and Neita when they were ready to come home. Reg had spoken with his shipping agent in Beira and he had agreed to fix Negome up with a job and find her suitable accommodation as soon as she arrived there. On his last business trip to Beira, Reg had opened a savings account at the local bank in Negome's name and had deposited £3,000 into the account.

Lyle had purchased a train ticket for the two-day journey to Beira. Negome would catch the train from

Bulawayo down to Salisbury and from there down to Beira. Negome wanted to leave as soon as the doctor said she could travel; she knew the longer she remained in Bulawayo with the Traverse family, the more difficult it was going to be to leave her baby behind. Lyle had also arranged all the necessary travel documents through his old contacts. On Tuesday morning just six days after giving birth, Negome waved good-bye to Maureen and Beth as the train to Salisbury pulled slowly out of the station with much huffing and puffing and smoke billowing from its smokestack.

Twice a day once in the morning and once in the afternoon Beth would go to the hospital to see Neita. The little one had lost four ounces the first few days but had put the weight back on. The doctor had told her that she could fetch Neita on Thursday afternoon. He was sure that by then it should be fine to take her home. Maureen was a great help to Beth with the baby, having had three children of her own. Beth would be forever grateful for all that Maureen and Lyle had done for her, Reg, and Negome. But now she wanted to take her baby and go to her own home. The second weekend in February Reg arrived to take his new family home.

There was much excitement back at the farm when the farm workers heard that Beth had a new baby. Beth had a great time showing off her baby every time she took Neita out for a walk around the farm in her pram. Father Murphy had agreed to christen Neita at the following Sunday morning service. Father Murphy, knowing of Negome's pregnancy and having heard that she had gone back home to have the child, put two and two together and came up with the conclusion that Beth and Reg's adopted child could well be Negome's, but he kept this to himself.

Its funny when you don't see people regularly, time seems to have little meaning; the townsfolk knew Beth had gone to the England to have a child and simply believed that this was the baby. Everyone at the morning church service was commenting on how she had Reg's blue eyes and cute little nose. Annie had heard from her maid that Beth had been away and had come back with a baby girl. They had not spoken much since the Negome incident and Annie telling Beth that everyone suspected Negome was Reg's piece of fluff.

Chapter 57

Internationally Ian Smith's UDI went down like a lead zeppelin and, as a result, the United Nations declared economic sanctions against the regime. Early in January of 1966, Reg received a letter from his agent in London, explaining very apologetically, that unfortunately they could no longer trade with Rhodesia because of the United Nations ruling.

It seemed that the whole region was having problems. In Mozambique the Front for the Liberation of Mozambique (FRELIMO) had started an uprising against the Lisbon-controlled colonial government. Lisbon was also under international pressure to grant independence to its colonies. As much as Mozambique economically needed the trade with Rhodesia, it dared not break the sanction rule imposed by the United Nations. It would only draw more attention to its own dilemma and, therefore, reluctantly Mozambique had to close its borders with Rhodesia. South Africa. On the other hand, being Rhodesia's only ally, it didn't give a damn and continued to trade with Rhodesia and allowed them to ship via their sea and airports.

Reg, like many other farmers and manufactures of exportable goods, had to quickly find alternative routes to their export markets. He would need to travel to England as soon as possible and hopefully come to some mutually agreed compromise with his British agent, such as shipping via a middleman in South Africa. Fortunately Reg had never given up his British passport and was thus able to fly to the England via South Africa.

The British agent also had lucrative markets in England and Europe for Reg's tea and they too did not want to lose these sales and were more than happy to reach to a compromise. They agreed to accept Reg's teas if shipped via South Africa and providing all markings referring to Rhodesia were removed and the shipping was done through a third party in South Africa. Payment would be the same, a percentage would be paid into Reg's English banking account and the balance would be transferred to the South African third party, so that every thing looked legitimate.

The South African agents, knowing the political predicament that Rhodesia was in, charged the Rhodesian exporter a hefty fee for their services. In Reg's case, all this amounted to was the sticking of a few labels on the fifty-pound boxes of tea and making out some new papers. For this service they charged him twenty percent of the final declared sale price.

By the middle of the year the uprising had escalated into a full-scale war, which soon became known as the Rhodesian Bush War by the supporters of the UDI. The unrest had now shifted into the farming communities and farms closest to the major cities became easy targets. Farmers had taken to double-ring fencing their homesteads with dogs running loose between the two fences. An emergency radio communication system had been set up that linked the nearest military post and the entire farming community onto a common frequency. Each farm was issued a code name. Telecommunication was no longer an option, as most of the lines had been cut and repairing them was a total waste of time and money; no sooner had they been repaired, than they were cut again. In the rural areas, radio became the only means of communication.

The majority of farm workers were not politically motivated, and were not involved in the armed struggle, they were only interested in having a good job, earn a reasonable wage and being able to have a small piece of land on the farmer's property where they could build a home and grow a few crops. However, as the armed struggle continued, the farm workers were being intimidated into performing various misdemeanours on the farms. Those loyal to the white farmers had their wives and children raped and murdered and their homes burned to the ground.

Some of the labourers moved closer to the main homestead while others simply disappeared into the thick bush and set up small shacks where they lived off what they could hunt or steal. Farming became increasingly difficult with the constant labour disruptions and rationing of gasoline, diesel fuel and other commodities. Transport of goods had to be accompanied by an armed military escort. No one travelled at night unless in a convoy and then only when emergency situations made it necessary.

Every white male over the age of eighteen was called up for active duty in the military for a period of three months on and three months off. By the time little Neita turned two years old, Reg had already been called up twice. By the end of November of the following year he had been more on active military duty fighting in the Bush War than he had been farming. Every time he was away, he worried about the farm and the vulnerability of Beth and Neita. They had also erected a high double security fence around the farmhouse, but even this gave him little comfort when he was away.

Tea production on Reg's farm had dropped to a third of what it was before the war started. Mapenge had moved his family into the room that Negome had used and many of the others workers were camped out around the sheds and the nursery. As the war progressed, the insurgents were becoming increasingly desperate to make a point and, as a result, became more and more brazen. Reg knew it was only a matter of time before the attacks on the farms would filter down to the far eastern borders where they were situated.

It was around one thirty in the morning when Reg was awakened by the two-way radio blaring next to his bed, "Bingo, bingo, bingo, being attacked, need assistance, bingo, bingo, urgent help needed."

Reg grabbed for the radio and pressed the send button. "This is Bulldog. I read you, bingo, we are on our way." As he pulled on a pair of shorts and a T shirt, more and more callers were responding to the request for help.

Beth woke up and asked, "What's going on?"

"It's Annie's call sign "bingo," she's being attacked."

Beth, now full awake, sat up, "Oh! God, Reg, she's all alone out there."

Another voice came over the radio "Jackal, Jackal, we will all meet on the prearranged main road rendezvous" "Jackal" was the call sign for the small military outpost in town.

By the time they got to the top of the crest looking down on the farm a mile away they could see the glow from the flames. As they drove through the farm gates they could see that the shed was burning profusely. Everyone was extremely nervous knowing how vulnerable they were in the light from the flames, and the dancing shadows cast by the flames made them even more jumpy.

They walked toward the main house, their automatic weapons at the ready. It was quiet except for the crackling of the fire. The whole place was deserted, and the labourers had obviously run off or had been warned to clear out or face the consequences. As they drew nearer, they saw the tractor was standing half way up the three front steps to the house. The attackers had used the tractor to ram their way through the security fence and the steel security gate on the front door of the house.

There were two bodies lying in a pool of blood on the front *veranda* underneath the window. Next to one of the bodies there was a hacksaw with its broken blade lying in two pieces next to it. All the windows in the front of the house were shattered. The front of the house had obviously been raked with bullets fired from AK47 semiautomatic rifles, as there were spent AK47 shell casings lying all over the front garden and lawn.

Reg and one of the other farmers went inside, shining their flashlights back and forth as they made their way up the main passage. At the entrance to the living room Reg's flashlight beam fell on a pair of legs on the floor protruding through the doorway. They stepped over the body. It had a big gaping hole where a chest should have been. Shining their flashlights around the room they discovered another body lying in a pool of blood on the polished wooden floor with half of his head blown away. Annie lay sprawled across the big couch that was facing the door, there was a gunshot wound through her stomach and another in the side of her head; she was still clutching a double-barrel shotgun in her left hand, and lying at her feet was a smashed two-way radio.

They searched the rest of the house for any other insurgents that may be lurking inside but found none. From the look of things, Annie had put up a brave and desperate fight, despite the fact that she was wounded. It was fairly obvious to see what had happened. The insurgents had used the tractor to ram the fence and then shot the place up. Thinking they had killed all who were inside, they then tried to cut the steel burglar bars with a hacksaw taken from the shed.

Annie must have been hit in the stomach with the initial hail of bullets. There was a trail of blood leading from the bedroom. She must have crawled to the front window and shot the two insurgents who were trying to cut the burglar bars. On the carpet next to the window there were five spent thirty-eight special revolver shell casings. It looked like she then crawled all the way to the living room, grabbed the shotgun, and went and sat on the couch waiting for them. She must have smashed the radio that was lying at her feet, not wanting it to get into the insurgents' hands.

The insurgents, not being able to get through the window, drove the tractor up the short flight of steps and rammed the door until it gave way. Annie blasted the first two as they came through the living room door with the shotgun. Before the rest could get to her she used the last round in her revolver to take her own life. The revolver was gone but the spent shell was lying on the couch next to her body. They then ransacked the house looking for more weapons and money, leaving the shotgun, as it wasn't a weapon of their choice. Before taking off into the bush, they set fire to the shed.

The shed fire was too intense to get even close enough for the garden hose to be of any effect. The best they could do was to make sure it did not spread to the other outbuildings. Reg got on the radio to Beth and told her he was OK but that Annie had not made it and that he would be home after sunrise.

As soon as it was daylight the dogs would be brought in and the military would go through the motions of following the insurgents, knowing full well that the chance of capturing any of them was slim. It was the same pattern they had encountered in other attacks, a quick hit-and-run by a small band of between six and ten insurgents. They would then split up and all go off in different directions to lick their wounds and then regroup again in a week or two at some prearranged rendezvous. They wore no uniforms so when they were not armed they looked just like any other person and this made following and capturing any of them very difficult.

Reg got back home just after eight that morning having left the authorities to do what they had to do. Mapenge saw Reg drive in through the gate and went to speak to him. "How is the madam that side?" he asked.

"Not good, Mapenge, the madam, she is dead," said Reg starting to walk down to the house.

"That is too bad, boss Reg, she was a good person. And will the boss Johan now be coming back?"

"I don't know, Mapenge," said Reg over his shoulder as he carried on walking, "we will have to wait and see what happens."

Reg told Beth what had happened and that it looked like Annie had taken her own life not wanting to give the insurgents the pleasure of torturing and molesting her before finally killing her. Both Reg and Beth agreed that would have been Annie's style. Beth was sorry that she had not had more contact with Annie, but things had never been the same between them since the Negome incident.

"I wonder what will happen to the farm now?" asked Reg

"I remember Annie telling me that she had left the farm to her daughter," said Beth. "You know how she felt about Johan. I remember the last time we spoke her saying, 'that fucking bastard Johan de Klerk won't get a bean if I happen to die before him.'"

"I heard that Johan had gone back to South Africa anyway," said Reg, "he apparently was working as a mechanic at a garage in Pietersburg. I believe that Jane had gone to live with him after she finished her studies at varsity." 'that's such a shame," said Beth.

"I know that Jane worshipped the ground her father walked on and would hear no wrong about him. Hell, that must have really upset Annie."

That night Reg and Beth decided that it was just too risky staying on the farm and that Beth and Neita should go and live with Beth's parents in England until the war was over and some semblance of normality returned to the region. It was a big decision. Beth was torn between wanting to be with Reg and the safety of Neita. Also her relationship with her parents had never really gotten back to what it had been prior to her accident and losing the baby. Reluctantly she agreed that in the interest of the safety of Neita she would go.

They heard that there was a small military convoy leaving Salisbury in two days for the South African border post at Messina, the convoy would travel down on the main road to Masvingo and then onto Messina. As the main road to Masvingo was only twenty odd miles from the farm gate, Reg decided that this was an ideal opportunity to travel with the convoy to South Africa. Rather than go into town and have all the hassle of trying to reach Beth's folks on the military radio-telephone, they decided to pack up Beth and little Neita, travel down to South Africa, and make all their travel arrangements from there.

The trip down to the South African border post was thankfully uneventful and they spent the first night in a small hotel in Pietersburg. From there they managed to contact Beth's folks in the England. The next day they motored down to Pretoria and booked into a hotel. From there they were able to book Beth and Neita on a plane leaving Jan Smuts International airport for London Heathrow airport that Sunday morning. Reg stayed with them for the next two nights. Early Sunday morning he took them to the airport just outside of Pretoria and saw them safely off.

Chapter 58

Neither Mofola nor Jannie gave any indication in the office that they knew each other, but as soon as they got outside Jannie slapped Mofola on the back and shook his hand vigorously like he was an old lost friend he hadn't seen in years. This was totally out of character for Jannie being a staunch Afrikaner from South Africa, but he was genuinely pleased to see Mofola. "What the fuck are you doing here?" he inquired.

"I have been here for nearly nine months," said Mofola, "working down in the main chamber."

"How long the boss been here?" asked Mofola.

"Well the company flew me in with their plane last week," said Jannie. 'they recruited me up in Jo'burg about a month ago. I saw in the *Sunday Times* newspaper that they were looking for someone to run the tunnelling division here and the money was good. So I applied and they gave me the job and now I'm here. Man, I'm glad to see you," he said, slapping Mofola on the back again. "At least I have someone I know and can work with here.

"They have even given me a small office in that pre-fab building over there," said Jannie, pointing to one of the many prefabricated asbestos buildings that had sprung up on the Songo plateau just above the gorge on the south bank. These were the site offices for the many companies who had contracts on the Cahora Bassa project. All the main offices were situated in town. Most of the plant needed for the construction work like the stone crushing and concrete mixing plant, the cement silos, diesel generators, compressors and all that were situated on the south bank above the dam site.

"Come, we go and drink some coffee in my office, this hot sun is killing me," said Jannie. The office was sparsely furnished, a chest high trestle type table that also had piles of drawings on it seemed to take up most of the office space. There was a small desk stuck in the one corner with a chair behind it and one in front. Jannie went and sat behind the desk and beckoned Mofola to sit on the other chair in the front. Jannie picked up the phone and dialled a number, there was a short delay then a voice answered, "Yes, this is Jannie Grobler in office 34B, can you bring us two mugs of coffee, please? Yes, milk and two sugars will be fine," he said, and put the phone back on the cradle again.

"So tell me," asked Jannie, "what have you been up to, you told me when you left the mine you were going home to get married, did you bring your wife here to Songo?"

"No, my boss, it did not work like I plan," said Mofola, and he went on to tell Jannie what had happened between him and Negome. The two sat and chatted like old friends who had not seen each other for some time. They spoke about the people they had worked with on the mine, about the funny incidents and the not so funny ones like when Vissie blew himself up.

Mofola felt a bit awkward, Jannie had never treated him like this before and he did not quite know how to handle it. Jannie was also a bit uncomfortable, not quite sure how to conduct himself not having been in a country before that did not officially practice segregation. They went on to discuss the tunnelling project and how soon they could recruit and train three teams.

The South African company, Mining & Shafting Pty Ltd., were the successful tenderers to win the contract for all the drilling and blasting of the various chambers and diversion tunnels. They were a highly reputable and successful company who specialized in this type of work. Like Jannie, all the white miners and engineers on the site had been recruited and brought in from South Africa or from Europe. They were given contracts that ranged between two and four years depending on the type of work that that particular employee was employed for.

Most companies with contracts on the Cahora Bassa project had a policy to first try to recruit married men, as they were more stable having their families there with them. Despite this policy there were over five hundred bachelors on the site.

Jannie had been given a two-year contract with the option to extend for a further year if they needed him longer and he was prepared to stay on. Jannie would fly back to Johannesburg in South Africa at the end of the month and fly back again the following day with his wife Sonja. They would stay in the furnished guest quarters until their furniture arrived and they could then move into one of the company's prefab houses.

This was Jannie's second wife, his first wife having died of ovarian cancer four years before he married Sonja. Sonja was twelve years Jannie's junior and was the eldest daughter of his former neighbour in South Africa. Sonja had been Jannie's first wife's best friend right up to the time of her death. In the last months of her illness Sonja had been by her side constantly caring for her and doing her best to make her remaining days as comfortable as possible.

Sonja was an exceptionally attractive woman and many said she looked like Doris Day, the film star. Jannie had seen Sonja grow from a young teenager into a mature woman. The two families had always been very close. Due to a hysterectomy in her early years, Jannie's wife could never have children and Sonja became like her adopted daughter. No one would have said that Sonja and Jannie would make a couple, but Sonja had seen through Jannie's exterior roughness and aggressive attitude a long time ago. This was mainly a front as deep down he had a loving and caring nature that came out strongly during his first wife's illness. Sonja was also no fool, she knew Jannie was short tempered and she had seen this materialize when someone rubbed him up the wrong way.

The marriage did not go down well with Sonja's parents. They said that Jannie was too old for her and she should marry someone her own age. This was also one of the reasons Jannie took the job on Cahora Bassa as they needed to get away from Sonja's side of the family who were always interfering and telling her what and what not to do.

Jannie worshipped the ground that Sonja walked on and bought her everything her heart could desire. This was also one of the reasons why Jannie was so obsessed with earning good money. She always wore the latest fashion and was the talk of many of the other woman on the mine property. In her school days, Sonja was captain of the girl's athletic team and she played a mean game of tennis.

Early Monday morning at six AM sharp Mofola reported to Jannie's office. "Before we start putting a team together I would like to see the site and the conditions down there," said Jannie, so why don't you and I jump in the *bakkie* and go down to the riverbed and you can show me around." Management had provided Jannie with a three quarter-ton pickup truck to get around and to transport some of the more fragile material down to the site such as explosives that were stored at a magazine two kilometres away on the outskirts of the town.

They donned their hard hats and jumped into the truck and drove down the winding treacherous road that was cut out of the sidewall to riverbed some four hundred meters below. They stopped three quarters of the way down, as Mofola wanted to show Jannie the main generator chamber where he had been working. They drove a short way into the cavern and parked the truck out of the way of the big tipper trucks that were constantly coming and going.

In all Jannie's mining career he had never seen such a large manmade cavern. They walked to the work face.

There were people and machinery all over the place and the noise from the machinery was deafening, one could barely make oneself heard over all the noise. The only way Jannie could describe it, was organized chaos.

They walked around trying to stay out of the way of all the activity, Jannie was trying to take it all in, he could not get used to the sixty metre height of the cavern and how they blasted such a huge face. They walked back to where the truck stood away from all the hustle and bustle and noise. "How do they blast such a large section?" Jannie wanted to know.

"They go in stages," said Mofola, "working from the top down to the floor. The hydraulic scaffolding takes them up and down."

"I see what you mean about these fissures," said Jannie, pointing to the fissures in the side wall that had not been covered in concrete. "They run just like we had in "C" section *stope* at Roodepoort Frontier Mining. So you used that same drilling pattern we used on that section," said Jannie.

"Yes, boss, only here I make the holes closer. First I try ten inches but then the rock it break too rough, so I make the holes six inches and we get this finish," said Mofola, running his hand over the side wall.

"Good man," said Jannie, "I see you did learn something from me."

"I learn plenty from the boss," said Mofola, "all I know about this work I learn from the boss."

They continued down the road to the riverbed, parked the truck and walked over to the side wall where the outline of the tunnel exit had been painted by the surveyors in yellow road paint on the side of the rock face of the cliff wall. "This is going to be a big tunnel," said Mofola."

"Yes, it will be big, because it has to take all that water there," said Jannie, turning around and pointing to the river flowing in the background, "I hope it will be big enough—that's a lot of water that is flowing there."

They stood watching the brown turbulent waters of the mighty Zambezi River flowing past them some fifty metre away.

"Let's go upstream and see where the tunnel is supposed to start," said Jannie.

They got back in the truck and drove slowly up the rough road that had been bulldozed out of the dry part of the riverbed and stopped at a point about five hundred metres upstream, where there was a similar outline of the entrance painted on the cliff wall. Here the gorge was a lot narrower and the water edge was only ten or so metres from the sidewall.

There was a construction crew there busy with the foundations for the half-moon wall that was to protect the entrance to the tunnel from the flood waters once they broke through, hopefully in about eighteen months time. This wall would be removed once the construction of the sliding gate was complete. Once the cofferdam protecting the main dam foundations was complete, the river would be diverted through the tunnel until the main dam wall was built.

About halfway up where the entrance was marked on the rock face, running left to right, was a white painted line and written above the line, three letters. "What do those letters 'HWM" say?" asked Mofola, pointing to the big letters.

"That's the high-water mark during the flood season," said Jannie.

"Hau! I hope the surveyors can do a good job. If it's flood season I don't want to break through anyplace other than here where this wall is," said Mofola, pointing to where the construction crew were throwing the foundations for the protection wall.

Once the construction of the elaborate winches and roller-sliding gate was complete and in place, the sliding gate would then be lowered to the closed position to protect the slides from any debris that may lodge itself in-between them when the half-moon protection wall was imploded. The gate would then be hoisted to the open position allowing the water from the cofferdam to flow through the diversion tunnel. The gate would remain open until the main dam wall was complete. It would then be closed for the last time allowing the dam to fill up. A three- metre-thick concrete plug would then be constructed behind the gate to strengthen the gate and seal it forever.

Two months had passed and although the tunnelling was progressing well, it was slower than what they had expected. The rock formation down this low in the riverbed was different to that of the main generator chamber situated a hundred metres higher up. They had to experiment for the first two weeks to find the optimum drilling and blasting technique. They were basically using the same method of drilling from the top down and could fit two blasts in per eight hour shift one top half and one bottom half.

Jannie was concerned that they may overshoot the allotted time given to complete the tunnel and mentioned this to Mofola one day when they were both in the office together.

"We need to drill the complete thirty-by-twenty-metre wall and make one blast, not two as we are doing now. Then the front-end loaders and dumper trucks can come in once and we can then move back in and start the next round of drilling, this way we could save two to three hours per blast."

"That would be a good plan, boss," said Mofola, "but we need two teams drilling top and bottom at the same time and we can't have two teams working the face together."

"Yes, I know, but look here," said Jannie, pulling a piece of paper out of the drawer with some sketches on it. "This is the hydraulic scaffolding we are using; the floor here is made up of thick planks spaced with a one inch gap between them to allow the debris and water from the drills to fall through to the floor below. Now what if we make this floor a solid metal floor," said Jannie, "and we slope it slightly from front to back, here," he said, pointing with his pencil to the edge of the steel floor, "we weld a twelve-inch-wide and six-inch-deep trough that carries the slush and water, to this flexible down pipe which drains onto the floor. This way we can have another team drilling under the scaffolding. So, Mofola, what do you think, can it work?"

"I think maybe this is a good plan. The boss must ask the manager if he can get the engineers to fix this for us quick, quick over the weekend," said Mofola.

Within a week they had all the teams drilling together, using Jannie's modified scaffolding. Not only were they gaining three to four hours a blast, the cut was much cleaner because it was only one blast. This meant less work for the people who were lining the tunnel with concrete, saving even more time.

Chapter 59

It had taken six weeks for Jannie and Sonja's furniture to arrive. Mofola had helped them to move out of the married quarters into the house that had been allocated to them. It was the last house right at the bottom of the street. Their nearest neighbour was at least a hundred metres away. Jannie was happy with the location, being a private type of person he did not want to see his neighbours sitting on their front porch.

Sonja knew Mofola, as he had come to cut their grass and work in their garden in South Africa after the Vissie incident. It just seemed practical for Mofola to just continue to do it here at Songo. He did not mind, it was extra money for him and the garden was quite small compared to the garden in South Africa. He would come every second week on a Sunday morning and cut the little bit of lawn and dig out any weeds and generally keep the garden looking neat and tidy.

Sonja had developed quite a little social life in the village and had very little time to do any gardening work, so she was grateful that Mofola was willing to do it. She played tennis twice a week. Wednesday was ladies day and Saturday was mixed doubles. There were needlework classes, cooking classes, book clubs and then there were, what Jannie called "old hen's parties." Some of the ladies would meet at one or other's home, once a week on Friday morning and have tea and cake and generally gossip about anything that went on in the village.

Jannie, on the other hand, was not a socialite, but he would occasionally walk down to the recreation club on a Saturday afternoon after work and sit outside with a cold beer and watch Sonja play tennis and read the week old newspaper from South Africa. Sonja would then shower and change in the ladies locker room and they would then generally end up having an evening meal at the club restaurant before going to watch the outdoor movie.

Jannie would normally try to avoid sitting near any of the tennis players so he would not have to socialize. Everyone knew Jannie and they left him very much to himself, but occasionally one or two of the guys would come and sit and talk to him. On one such occasion two of the male players were having a beer with Jannie while Sonja and her partner were showing a lot of form on the tennis court.

"You had better watch that little Frenchman, André," one of them said. "Sonja and he are a formidable team;, they will more than likely walk away with this year's doubles championship trophy."

That evening at the club restaurant Jannie mentioned what he had heard. "Congratulations, I believe that you and that Frenchman André are going to win the doubles championship this year," said Jannie casually.

"Well, you know what they say, it's not over till the fat lady sings," said Sonja, "and we still have two matches to play next week. If we win those, then we will win the championship. We will have to wait and see what happens."

"The guys tell me it's a forgone conclusion; you two are a formidable and unbeatable team."

"Well yes, we are a good tennis team, André is a strong player, he played on the professional circuit in France some years ago before he went back into engineering, and he has taught me some of the finer things about the game."

Besides rugby, Jannie had very little interest in any sport other than fishing, he much preferred to make an arrangement with Mofola to go and fish. Often on the Sundays that Mofola did not work, the two of them would take the *bakkie* and drive down to the river with the fishing rods and spend the day fishing for Tiger-fish and Barbell. What with tennis on Saturday and Jannie fishing every second Sunday, Sonja and Jannie saw very little of each other.

The lifestyle in the Songo township was not unlike the lifestyle in some of the small mining towns in the more remote parts of South Africa where all your needs were provided for by the mine. The only difference here in Songo was the high security because of the FRELIMO uprising. The township and office area above the gorge were fenced in with an eight foot high double fence with military police guarding all the entrances and exits and patrolling the perimeter twenty-four hours a day, seven days a week.

The security was tight and military personnel could be seen around every corner and bush. The Portuguese Government believed that the dam site was a prime target for the liberation movement to sabotage. Although the Cahora Bassa had huge international interest and any attack on it would attract a huge international press, FRELIMO left it unscathed, except for the odd rocket attack on the cement convoys coming up from Tete. It would seem that FRELIMO was dead against destroying or disrupting the building of any future assets.

This may have been the case but the government could not take any chances and every worker was given an identification badge with their photograph on the front. These ID cards as they were known were also colour coded. Only certain colours had clearance to go into certain areas. Both Jannie and Mofola had yellow status that allowed them into most areas unsupervised.

Chapter 60

When Mofola started work on the Cahora Bassa site he wrote to his mother, informing her that he had a good job and was no longer planning to go back to the mines in South Africa as he could earn good money here on the dam project. He would write to her every month and enclose a postal order for three hundred *escudos*. He had been working with Jannie for over eight months now and the tunnelling was ahead of schedule. All in all he had been working on the site for just over sixteen months and in all this time he had received only two short letters from his mother written by one of the sisters at the catholic mission. In the last one he received just two months ago she mentioned that his father was now bed ridden, but that Yussaf his brother had returned from the mines in South Africa and they were coping fine.

Mofola was not surprised to find a telegram was waiting for him at the office when he came up from his shift. Even before he opened it Mofola had a feeling it was bad news about his father. He opened it and read the short message; he read it again, the date said it had been sent three days ago. He stood there looking at the telegram not seeing the words. His mind flashed back to that last day his father had rejected all the money he had won and tossed it into the fire, and wondered if things would have been any different had he taken the money and gone to hospital.

"Bad news?" asked Jannie.

"Yes, it's my father," said Mofola. "He has died and they will bury him tomorrow."

"I'm very sorry," said Jannie. "I know you said your father had been sick with phthisis, it gets us all sooner or later. You had better take some leave of absence and go to the funeral."

"Thank you, boss, but it is too late to go home for the funeral. It will take two or maybe three days to get to my home. I will go at the end of the month to see how my mother is," said Mofola.

Two weeks later on a Friday morning Mofola managed to get a ride with one of the empty trucks going down to Beira, he got off at the cross roads at Inchope and from there caught a bus to Gogoi where he spent the night. The next morning he caught another bus to Espangabera on the border of Rhodesia and from there onto Massangena arriving there late Sunday afternoon.

Mofola noticed that a number of tents, shacks and small mud huts had sprung up all around the various towns and villages he had passed through and Massangena was no exception. Except for the shacks and huts nothing else seemed to have changed in the town as far as he could see, he did, however, notice that there was quite a presence of military personnel and their vehicles in the town and on the outskirts. He got off the bus at the Post Office and walked down the dusty street past the police station. It brought back unpleasant memories of his jail term there. It now seemed such a long time ago.

For a Sunday afternoon there was quite a bit of activity in town and he put this down to the influx of small-time farmers in the outlying areas having given up their farms and moved into or closer to the towns, for fear that FRELIMO would attack them in the remote areas. One thing that Mofola had learned when he attended that political meeting with Roberto is that this was a tactic employed by FRELIMO to put pressure on the Portuguese Government to step down. With the influx of hundreds of people into the towns and villages, the government was forced to provide shelter, food and water for these folk. This placed a huge financial strain on the Lisbon controlled government. FRELIMO was very shrewd and did not attack any of the families that were connected to the royal family. They knew full well that if they one day succeeded with their struggle they would need the support of the tribal chiefs to run the country.

The cantina was full of people on the inside and outside sitting on the knee-high wall that extended around the perimeter of the *veranda*. Mofola looked over at the store and, being a Sunday, it was closed. As he walked past he wondered if Negome was still working there or was she now married, having been promised to Costa Xavier's son by her late father.

It was Mofola's intention to slip into town, see his family for a few days and slip out again without attracting any attention. As much as he would have liked to see Negome again, the pain he felt at their last confrontation when she told him she would rather die than go anywhere with him, was still fresh in his memory.

He walked on up the road past the mission school and looked over at the cemetery across the road from the church and wondered if his father had been buried there or in the burial plot up on the hill behind the *shamba* where his grandparents and one of his sisters that had died at birth were buried. The dogs started to bark and came running up to him as he walked through the gate.

His sister-in-law Maria and his mother were sitting in the cooking shack and heard the dogs barking, Maria got up and looked around the side to see who was coming through the gate. Recognizing him, she shouted, "Its Mofola," and went up to meet him.

"When we heard the dogs barking we thought it was Yussaf coming back from town," said Maria embracing Mofola. "Every time I see you, you become more handsome," she said, putting her arm around him and walking with him back to the cooking shack.

"And you have become even more beautiful," said Mofola with a big grin on his face.

Mofola's mother came out from the cooking shack, "I see you, my son," she said, coming up to him and holding him in her arms.

"I see you too, Mama, I'm so sorry I could not get here for *Baba's* funeral, I came as soon as I could," said Mofola.

"I know, my son, your father will also understand, he suffered much in his last days but he never complained, it is better now that he has peace and is with his father and Mother in the land of the spirits," she said, pointing up in the direction of the burial plot behind the huts.

They sat in the cooking shack talking, the sun had already started to dip behind the distant mountain range and a light evening breeze swirled the smoke from the smouldering fire around the enclosure. "Where are the boys?" asked Mofola.

'"They are down at the cattle paddock milking the cows," replied Maria. "They will be so excited to see you."

"You said Yussaf was in town?" asked Mofola.

"Yes, he spends a lot of his time there," said Maria,

Mofola sensed some tension in her voice and left it at that.

"Before its dark I would like to see my father's grave," said Mofola and got up to go.

"Wait," said Maria, jumping up. "I will come with you."

"Thank you Maria, but I would like to be alone," said Mofola and walked up to the graveyard situated on a small hill overlooking the *shamba*. Mofola opened the gate and went through it and into the stone walled graveyard.

Three of the graves had gravestones, the fourth had none and the ground was still fresh and lay heaped up over the length of the grave. Mofola stood at the grave facing the setting sun. "I see you, my father, it's with a sad heart I stand here at the foot of your grave not having seen you before you left on your final journey. But then I take comfort knowing I will forever see your face high in the clouds and I will feel your presence as the evening breeze brushes my cheek and I hear the sound of your voice in the rustling of the leaves. Never again will I have to walk alone, rest well, *Baba*."

Dusk had now turned to darkness. Mofola made his way back down to the *shamba*. He could see the glow of the fire now burning bright in the cooking shack. Mama was preparing the evening meal. There were two pots on the metal frame standing to the side of the fire with some burning coals under them. The boys heard Mofola calling the dogs that had followed him up to the grave-yard and they came running out from the cooking shack shouting his name.

They sat and ate with the boys bombarding Mofola with question after question. Maria eventually sent them to bed so that she and Mama could have some time to talk to Mofola without all the questions and interruptions. Mofola had learned that Temba's wife and daughter had gone back to her parents' *shamba* after the funeral and would be away for some weeks. Mofola's mother stood up and said she was tired and was going to bed.

"Tonight I will sleep better," she said, "having seen you my youngest." She took one of the *paraffin* lamps and made her way to her hut.

A few minutes later she came back again carrying the lamp in one hand and a short *assegai* in the other. "Your father said you should have this," she said, handing the *assegai* to Mofola. "He said I should tell you to take care as everyone who creeps into your house at night is not necessarily a thief. He said you would understand."

Mofola took the *assegai* from his mother and smiled to himself, "Yes, *Baba*, even in death you have the last word."

"Your father's illness has put many more grey hairs on your mother's head these past months," said Maria, after the old lady had retired to bed.

"Yes, I see that," said Mofola.

"She misses the old man terribly."

"So what is it with my brother that he has to spend so much time in town?" asked Mofola.

"Since Yussaf came back from the mines he has not been able to stay here at the *shamba* with the old man being so ill. He said he could not listen to the old man coughing and struggling to breathe. He spent a lot of time at the cantina drinking so that when he came home he did not hear it, and now he just drinks to forget."

"Did Negome marry Costa's son?" asked Mofola.

"Did you not hear?" said Maria. "Negome left some days after you left, she went to work in Rhodesia. The commissioner, he took the store from Mrs. Aguiar. We heard that Mr. Victor owed him a lot of money, so he took over the store as payment. Now Mrs. Aguiar and her two other daughters run the store for the commissioner."

"Where in Rhodesia did Negome go?" asked Mofola.

"No one seems to know—her mother has not seen or heard from her since she left."

Mofola went and slept with the boys in their hut; he was dead tired and fell asleep immediately only to be woken up a short time later with Maria shouting at Yussaf. It was about his drinking and spending their money on drink.

"This is not your money, shouted Yussaf, "you did not earn this money, it is the money that I have earned working on the mines. I will spend it as I please, it is not for a man's woman to tell him what he can and cannot do."

Mofola had got up early, when the boys got up and went with them down to the cattle paddock to milk the cows. He carried the milk up to the *shamba* and the boys herded the cattle out into the fields. Mofola sat with his mother and Maria in the cooking enclosure talking, the sun was already high in the sky when Yussaf came out from their hut in a pair of shorts and staggered across to the cooking shack where he heard the talking.

Yussaf stood at the side of the enclosure and greeted his mother. "I see you, Mama,"

"I see you, my son," she replied, not looking up from the pot she was stirring next to the fire.

Mofola sat with his back to the wall where Yussaf was standing. He greeted Yussaf. "I see you, my brother."

Surprised, Yussaf stuck his head around the corner to see his younger brother sitting there.

"Mofola, it is you, my brother," said Yussaf coming around the corner to greet him.

"Why did you not tell me last night my brother was here?" enquired Yussaf, glaring at his wife.

"Because you were too drunk to stand and I did not want your brother to see what a drunken fool you were."

"You mind your tongue, woman, or one day I will cut it out." Yussaf scooped some water into a basin and stood it on a small table outside of the enclosure.

Mofola watched his brother splash water over his face and arms.

"Let me go and get dressed and then we can talk," he said over his shoulder to Mofola as he walked back to their hut. Maria took the basin of water and sprinkled it around the floor of the enclosure to dampen the dust; she wiped it with a cloth and put it back on the shelf where it had come from.

For the better part of the day, the two brothers spoke about their respective jobs and the people that Mofola knew back in South Africa.

"This is no place for me, my brother," said Yussaf. "I will never be a farmer and I don't want to be a farmer, I will go back to the mines, this is not the life for me."

"Why don't you come back with me to the dam? They are always looking for people with experience, and soon they will be putting in the big generators and they will need people who can work with the electric," said Mofola. "And the money, she is very good."

"Thank you, my brother, but I will go back to the mines in South Africa," said Yussaf.

Mofola knew that it was not the farm life that Yussaf hated; Yussaf had another wife and two children back in South Africa and that was the reason he wanted to go back there to the mines, but he said nothing. There was no point in having a confrontation with his brother. It was his life and he could not tell him how to live it. Yussaf wanted Mofola to go with him into town that afternoon but Mofola told him that he would be leaving early the next morning and would rather spend the last hours with their mother.

Chapter 61

Mofola arrived back in Songo late on Thursday afternoon. It had taken him nearly three days to get back. As he was not able to hitch a ride, he had to catch a number of buses and they stopped at every little village. He went to the office, but Jannie was not there so he left him a message that he was back and that he would start work the next day.

Friday morning Mofola reported to Jannie at the office to see if there were any changes he should be aware of before he went down to the tunnel to supervise the first shift. Jannie and Mofola would alternate morning and afternoon shifts on a weekly basis. The morning shift would start at 6:00 a.m. and go through to 2:00 p.m. in the afternoon. The clean-up teams would move in working a four-hour shift to 6:00 p.m., when the second drilling and blasting team would move in and work until 2:00 a.m. early that morning followed again by the clean-up crew who would then work through to 6:00 a.m. They had it down to a fine art and it all worked like a well-oiled machine with very few hiccups.

The south tunnel was now nearing completion two months ahead of schedule. It was just as well the rainy season had started early up in central Africa and the Zambezi River was in full flood. The survey team had been down at the face every day now for the past week taking measurements. The water had risen up to a metre from the top of the protection wall around where the entrance to the tunnel would hopefully blast through.

All work in the tunnel had been stopped for the past two days and everything had been removed from the tunnel; only essential machinery and equipment needed for the final breakthrough remained at the work face. The surveyors estimated that there was no more than eighteen feet to go before they broke through. Jannie and Mofola were at the work face discussing the next crucial step with members of Mining & Shafting management. It was decided to drill a pilot hole that should go right through using a twenty-foot extra-long drill-rod with a special diamond tip. The surveyors made a big X with a fat yellow crayon marking the spot where they wanted them to drill the hole.

Mofola went back to the entrance of the tunnel and instructed his drilling team to come up to the work face. He showed them where to drill and they moved their pneumatic equipment into place and started to drill the pilot hole. Jannie estimated that it would take them about six hours before they broke through. Once they break through it was decided that someone would descend on a rope to see where the drill actually broke through on the outside wall. This was the only way they could access the area as the road was now several metres under water.

Five hours into the drilling time Jannie went down to see how they were progressing. Mofola had stayed at the face to supervise the drilling. Jannie indicated to Mofola to move back to where the noise of the compressor and drilling was less intense. "How's it going?" shouted Jannie.

"We changed over from the twelve-foot to the twenty-foot rod about two hours ago. We are now at the seventeen-foot mark," replied Mofola. "We'll know in an hour or so if our surveyors were on the mark."

"You call me when they break through," shouted Jannie.

"OK, boss," shouted Mofola, and he went back to the work face.

Jannie went and waited at the entrance, which hopefully soon would become the tunnel exit. The project manager had also come down from his office and asked how things were progressing. Jannie informed him of the status and that Mofola would call them as soon as they break through.

An hour and a half had elapsed since Jannie had been up at the face and he was becoming anxious as to what was happening and was just about to walk up to the work face again when he saw Mofola coming toward him.

"What's happening?" he enquired.

"We are now at nineteen feet," said Mofola. "I stopped the drilling—what the boss want me to do?"

"Nineteen feet," said Jannie.

"*Ja*, boss. I stop the machine, she is now just this far from the face," said Mofola, indicating about a foot with his hands.

They all walked back up to the work face, the compressor had been shut down, but all the floodlights were still on lighting up the work face and the surrounding area like it was a theatre stage production.

"So what do you think, Jannie?" asked the manager.

"I don't know how tight that drill-rod is; it's a long way into the face. I would hate for it to stick and we have to abandon this hole and start a new one again. What do you think, Mofola, how tight is that drill-rod?"

"She not so tight, boss, maybe we can go another six inches and see what happen."

"OK, let's do that," said Jannie.

The compressor started up and they started drilling again, it couldn't have been more than five minutes when the noise of the drilling machine suddenly changed pitch and surged forward with the front of the chuck hitting the rock face. They backed the drilling machine up until the drill bit cleared the hole and then shut down the compressor.

"I think we are there," shouted Mofola to Jannie and the manager who were standing back from all the activity at the work face.

"Switch the lights out and let's see if we can see any light at the end of this little tunnel, said Jannie, walking over to the work face. Jannie stood at the pilot hole and signalled for the lights to be switched off. He looked into the hole and let out a loud "Yahoo! We have light at the end."

They immediately lowered one of the surveyors down the outside wall to see where the hole had broken through. The surveyor confirmed that the pilot hole had come through at a point six inches to the left of the centre line and that it was now OK for them to proceed with the drilling and blasting using the same line they were on until they broke through. Jannie said that he would get the full team back for the afternoon shift.

"Come on, you two," said the project manager, referring to Jannie and Mofola, "let's go up top and have some coffee. I think we need a dash of something in it after all that my nerves are shot."

"Thanks," said Jannie. "It will take some time for the riggers to get the scaffolding back in place before we can start drilling again."

Two days later using a lighter charge they broke through into the daylight. Everyone was standing on a ledge of the cliff about fifty metres diagonally above where the tunnel would break through. They first saw the puff of dust and then heard the explosion as the side of the wall burst open. A loud applause went up from the group standing there and smaller pop, pop could be heard as the Champagne bottles were opened.

Chapter 62

It was now up to the engineering teams to erect the complicated roller slides and fit the huge steel gate that would eventually shut off the water from the Zambezi River that would soon be diverted through the tunnel. There job now complete Jannie and Mofola temporarily moved their teams into the main chamber to help out there as they would not be able to move over to the north wall to start the shorter and smaller north tunnel until the river subsided.

Once the river was flowing through the south tunnel they would be able to get to the north wall. At this stage the only access to the north wall was via a swing bridge spanning the gorge, anyone with any fear of heights was not encouraged to use this means of crossing. At this stage there was also no road cut out of the north wall so there was no way to get any heavy equipment to that side of the riverbed.

With the pressure now off to complete the south tunnel Mofola and Jannie went back onto a normal eight-hour shift. They had each received a generous bonus well above what was originally promised for finishing on time.

For Mofola every day, week, and month now seemed very much like the previous, they flowed from one into the next with monotonous regularity. He had not see nor heard from Roberto for at least two months and was wondering if he was OK, as there were frequent reports of FRELIMO attacks on the truck convoys coming up from Tete.

Despite the fact that there was a rampant war being fought in the rest of Mozambique, at the dam site and in Songo life went on from day to day with very few attacks launched on the town or site . Like any small town community there would always be the odd bar brawl, the odd affair and the rumour mongering and gossiping among the woman. The fact that there were more single men on the site than there were married couples would inevitably lead to some confrontation. The married men constantly had to deal with the single men making passes at their women, while the women enjoyed the extra attention.

A rocket attack on the township was the talking point for the best part of the week. There were no casualties or damage to property the rockets had fallen and exploded on an open piece of land within the fenced area. The main point of conversation was why the insurgents had directed the rockets into an open piece of land when they could just as easily have aimed at one of the many buildings, or for that, at the explosives magazine situated on the outskirts of the town. This would have made a spectacular show. Speculation was that they wanted it to be known that for the time being they choose not to attack the town but they could do so if they so chose.

It was a particularly hot and humid Sunday, even at that early hour of the day, especially down in the gorge where Mofola and Jannie were fishing. They had parked the *bakkie* and taken their fishing gear and shade tent and walked a few hundred metres downstream where the river was much wider and the flow was less intense. They had erected the shade tent, baited up, and cast their lines into the river and were sitting under the canopy out of the sun waiting for that big one to take the bait and make a run.

"Today is the day I'm going to get that big bugger that has been eluding me for the past few months," said Jannie. "I feel it in my water."

"Talking of water, what did I do with the bottle of ice water I took out of the refrigerator; did you put it in the bag?"

"No, boss, I not see any water, where did the boss have it?" asked Mofola.

"I remembered to put it in the fridge last night; I must have forgotten to take it out again this morning. Shit, man, we won't survive down here without water. I had better go back and fetch it," said Jannie.

The drive up or down into the gorge even on a Sunday without all the trucks going up and down the winding road took the better part of thirty minutes. Jannie left the *bakkie* in the road with the engine running and quickly ran around the back of the house to the kitchen door. He did not want to make a noise, as he knew that Sonja liked to sleep in on the days he went fishing. His intention was to grab the water bottle and slip out without disturbing her. As he opened the fridge door he thought he heard voices coming from the bedroom—maybe it was just the noise from the air conditioner in the bedroom. What the hell, he thought to himself, that doesn't sound like the air conditioner. It sounds like Sonja's and someone else's voices.

Jannie closed the fridge door and walked softly up the passage to their bedroom, the door was half ajar and he could see that there was someone else in the bed with her. Sonja was moaning with pleasure. "Oh yes! Oh yes!" she cried, "don't stop, please, oh yes."

Jannie burst into the room. "What the fuck's going on here," he shouted, taking the whole scene in at a glance.

Sonja was lying naked on the bed with the naked French tennis player on top of her. Jannie grabbed the Frenchman with both hands around the back of his neck and dragged him kicking off his wife. He held him up against the wall with his legs dangling off the floor and hit his head against the wall. "You fucking little French prick, you want to teach my wife more than just the finer points of tennis, it would seem. Now let me teach you some of my not so finer points," he shouted, all the time banging the Frenchman's forehead against the wall until his head went through the asbestos panel wall and his feet stopped kicking. Jannie let him go and he dropped to the floor like a bag of meal. "I'll teach you to fuck my wife, you little French piece of shit," he shouted. Climbing in with his boots, he kicked him again and again.

All the time Sonja was screaming hysterically for him to stop as she hammered him on his back. Jannie was in a blind rage and oblivious to all that was going on around him other than what he was doing to the Frenchman. Sonja stopped screaming and hitting him and sat on the floor curled up in a little ball, sobbing Eventually Jannie stopped kicking the Frenchman and collapsed exhausted to his knees on the floor in front of Sonja.

"Why, why?" he shouted at her, banging his fists on the floor, "I gave you every fucking thing you desired."

The Frenchman was obviously dead. He had died of strangulation long before Jannie dropped him to the floor. Jannie went outside and drove the *bakkie* into the driveway. He went and picked up the body and put it in the spare room with the Frenchman's clothes and closed the door. Sonja sat on the bed with a sheet wrapped around her, still sobbing.

"What are you going to do with him?" she asked, in between sobs.

"I don't fucking know yet. Maybe I'll have him stuffed. You can hang him on the wall as your tennis trophy," said Jannie sarcastically, "I'm going to go and fetch Mofola down at the river."

"You can't leave me here alone with him in there," she said, pointing in the direction of the spare room.

"Why, do think he's going to come and fuck you again?" said Jannie. "No such luck, my dear, that was his last fuck. I'll be back later," he said and stomped out of the house still fuming.

Jannie drove back down to the river and by the time he had walked back down to the fishing spot he had calmed down and the reality of what he had done started to sink in.

"I think the boss he maybe forgot about me," said Mofola. The boss was right, look at this fish, he is the biggest one we ever catch. Did the "boss find the cold water?" rambled Mofola excitedly.

"Mofola, we have to go. I need to get back to the house, the madam, she is not well"

"OK, boss, I'm sorry the madam, she not well, we can pack up quickly. They packed up and carried the stuff back to the *bakkie* and drove back up to the house.

Mofola helped unload the fishing gear and carried it up to the house. "Can I put the fishing rods in the spare room, boss?" asked Mofola as he went into the kitchen.

"No, no just leave them there on the kitchen table," said Jannie. "The madam, she is not going to be happy if we put these on the table, boss."

"Mofola, just do as I say, and go back to your quarters. I will see you at work tomorrow."

Mofola detected that something was not right with his boss. He put the rods on the table and went back out of the door. "I see the boss in the morning," he said, closing the screen door behind him.

Jannie went into the bedroom and found Sonja dressed and packing a small suitcase on the bed. "What the hell do you think you are doing?" he asked.

"I'm catching the company plane back to South Africa tomorrow afternoon. I can't stay here with you knowing what you have done," said Sonja.

"What I have fucking done! Christ, you little slut. If you hadn't been fucking that French prick this would never have happened. Yes, maybe it's better you go, because the way I'm feeling at the moment, I could kick the shit out of you too."

Early the next morning Jannie arranged with management for Sonja to get on the afternoon plane to South Africa, making some excuse that she had to see a specialist, woman problems, so they managed to squeeze her on. At one thirty they drove in silence to the small airport just outside of town. Jannie dropped her off and did not bother to say good-bye or wait to see her onto the plane.

From the airport Jannie drove straight down to the main chamber where his teams were now working, he parked the *bakkie* and went in search of Mofola. "When you finish your shift this afternoon, Mofola, I want you to come up to the house, I need you to help me with something. Is that OK?" asked Jannie.

"No problem, boss. I come straight away or I can come after I go to the change room?"

"No you change first then you come," said Jannie. "We need to clean that big fish and cut it up. It takes up too much space in the fridge. "OK, I will be there by the boss's house about half past six.

Early that evening, Mofola knocked on the back screen door, expecting Sonja to come to the door, but Jannie called from inside. "Is that you, Mofola? Come on in, I will be there shortly." Mofola stood just inside the kitchen screen door waiting for Jannie. A short while later Jannie came out of the spare room and walked into the kitchen.

"Sit, sit," said Jannie, indicating that Mofola should sit at the kitchen table. "We need to talk. Do you want a beer?"

"No thank you, boss. I must work tomorrow."

"No, I think you need a beer," said Jannie, walking over to the fridge and taking out two bottles of Lion Lager beer brought in from South Africa by the company store. He went to the kitchen cabinet drawer, got an opener, and opened the beers and handed one to Mofola. Jannie sat down opposite him.

"Cheers and good riddance to bad rubbish," he said, clinking his bottle against Mofola's beer bottle.

Mofola was not sure what to say or do. He was again in an uncomfortable situation. He had never before sat drinking with Jannie and it did not feel right to him.

"Tell me," said Jannie, taking a big slug from the beer bottle, "do you have a wife yet? No, now I remember, you came back to get married but things did not work out for you, that's right, hey?"

"Yes, boss, someday maybe I get married, but first I must find a good woman," said Mofola.

"Yes," said Jannie, "good women are difficult to find. Let me ask you a question," said Jannie, having another swig of his beer. "If one day you get married and one day you come home unexpectedly and you find another man in your bed with your wife, what would you do?"

"That one is not a difficult question," said Mofola. I kill him right there in the bed and then I kill that woman after him. No problem. We black people, we don't accept that."

"You are very serious about that," said Jannie.

"That is a serious problem, boss. It also need a serious ending."

Jannie got up from the table, beer in hand and said to Mofola, "Come, I want to show you something."

Mofola got up and followed Jannie into the passage and to the closed door of the spare room. Jannie pushed the door open to reveal the Frenchman now fully dressed lying on his back on the spare bed.

"Why that boss sleeping here?" whispered Mofola.

"Do you know this man?" asked Jannie.

"Yes, I sometimes see this boss down by the main chamber. He works with the people who put in the electric generator," whispered Mofola.

"You don't have to whisper," said Jannie, "he will not wake up."

"Why he not wake up?" asked Mofola. "He sleep very deep?"

"No, Mofola, he is dead, that's why he will not wake up. You see, on Sunday, when I came to fetch the water, I found him sleeping with my wife, so I killed him," said Jannie, taking another swig from his beer bottle.

"Hau! I can see this was a serious problem. Did the boss kill the madam too?"

"No, Mofola, but I can tell you honestly I really wanted to kill her as well. She has left me and gone back to South Africa to her parents, she flew out this afternoon." Jannie went on to tell Mofola about what happened on Sunday when he came up from the river to get the bottle of cold water.

"Yes," said Mofola, "I wonder why when the boss come back to the fishing and we have caught this big fish, but the boss I see is not happy to see the big fish and so we go home. Now what we do with this one?" asked Mofola, pointing to the Frenchman on the bed.

"Yes, I'm afraid that will be another problem," answered Jannie. "I thought maybe we can throw him in the river while it is still flooding. The body will quickly wash downstream and soon the crocs will find him and that will be the last anyone will see of him, what do think?"

"I think maybe that is a good plan but how we get him down to the river without the military police seeing us?" asked Mofola.

"I was also thinking about that," said Jannie. "I thought we could carry him onto the swing bridge and throw him from there but the guards are watching both sides. We can't go out of the property because they search every vehicle and if we go down to the river where we fish they will also see us. They are all over the damn place."

"So the boss maybe has another plan?" asked Mofola.

"I think maybe yes," said Jannie. "You know all those sandbags that are stored in the shed at the back of my office, the ones they use for stopping the water when they build the walls? Well, we fill the *bakkie* with those bags and come back here. Then, when it's dark, we take some of the sandbags out and put him at the bottom and cover him with sandbags.

"We then drive down to the river and into the tunnel. Nobody is working there at night and there is no guard posted at the new entrance, as nobody can get in from that side except if you climb down with a rope. We can take the long extension ladder and then carry the body up onto the protection wall and throw it into the river, it will be dark as all the tunnel lights are switched off. What do think?" asked Jannie.

"I think maybe this plan can work, but what can we tell the guards down by the tunnel when we want to drive in?" asked Mofola.

"We tell them management heard that there is more water coming down the river and we need to check on the height of the flood water to make sure the wall is OK and if the waters are rising up too high, we must pack these sandbags on top of the wall. The guards, they know us well, so I don't think there will be a problem."

"I think the boss has a good plan. We need to go now and get those sandbags and the ladder loaded," said Mofola, "before it get too late."

The security guards stopped them at the bottom of the road under the floodlights. Jannie told them their little story and the guards waved them on. They drove the heavily laden *bakkie* through the dark tunnel and out the other end. Jannie parked the *bakkie* with the engine still running and the lights shining on the protection wall in front of them. Mofola untied the ladder from the *bakkie*'s carry rack and extended it to reach the top of the wall. They then rolled the sandbags off the body and lifted it out.

Mofola helped Jannie heft the body onto his shoulder and held the ladder as Jannie slowly ascended the ladder like a fireman doing a rescue; only here there was no rescue taking place. Jannie reached the top of the ladder and simply tipped the body into the fast flowing river a few metres below the top of the wall. They rolled the sandbags back and rearranged them a bit to compensate for the missing body, tied the ladder back onto the carrier and drove back out.

As they passed the guards Jannie slowed down and said, "It looks OK. The water is not too high so we don't need to pack the bags on top of the wall. Thank you."

The guards said OK and waved them on. Much relieved having accomplished their mission, they took a slow drive back up the winding road to go and off load all the sandbags and store the ladder in the tool depot shed.

By the time they had finished off-loading both Jannie and Mofola were bushed. "I'll drive you down to your quarters," said Jannie, "and thank you for your help."

"No problem, boss, we do a good team job again tonight."

They drove in silence to the compound situated about two kilometres from the town centre. Jannie dropped Mofola off and then he drove back home again.

The Frenchman was not really missed until Friday. His work colleagues in the office just assumed he was down in the main chamber and those in the main chamber assumed he was in the office. Friday afternoon a memo came around sent out from Zamco management to all the offices. It basically was notifying everyone that André Du Plezee was missing and asking if anyone had seen him since last Saturday.

An official investigation was conducted by the military police on site and after two weeks of intense questioning and investigation he was simply listed as missing assumed dead. Apparently it was André's custom to rise early on most Sundays and go for a walk and then he would end up having breakfast at the club. This was a ritual that he followed with regularity and his colleagues and the staff at the club verified this. As one can imagine for the next few weeks the rumours were rife as to what had happened to the cocky little Frenchman.

Because André and Sonja had been associated together at the tennis club and she had recently returned to South Africa, she and Jannie were automatically placed under investigation. They were listed as possible suspects linked to his disappearance. The police questioned Jannie and searched his house. Jannie had covered the hole in the wall with a picture. The police found nothing in his house that could incriminate him. The SA Police were contacted and they apparently went around to Sonja's parents' home and questioned her there. She basically told them that the last time she had seen him was Saturday afternoon at the club.

Jannie had reached his own conclusion that Sonja and the little Frenchman had been having an affair for quite some time. What he deducted was that Sonja would tell André at tennis on Saturday that Jannie was going fishing the next morning. André would then get up early as usual and go for his Sunday morning walk. On the days that Jannie went fishing he would slip into Jannie and Sonja's house for some pre-breakfast exercise. And because their house was at the bottom of the street no one ever saw him enter or leave.

Chapter 63

Jannie remained at Songo to complete his two-year contract. He was not asked to renew his contract for a further year, as the management of Mining & Shafting Pty Ltd. were of the opinion that they could now dispense with his expertise, as the teams had now started on the smaller north tunnel and they were progressing well with very little supervision needed from Jannie. They concluded that he had served his purpose well and was now an unnecessary expense.

Mofola continued to work at the dam site and was basically now the supervisor for all the drilling teams on the north tunnel project. Now that Jannie had left, Mofola had his Sundays to himself again. One Sunday afternoon, a few weeks after Jannie had returned to South Africa, Roberto came around to the compound to visit Mofola.

"Hey! At last I find busy Mr. Big Supervisor. Do you know how many times I have been coming around here to see you on Sunday?" asked Roberto, shaking Mofola's hand in the traditional African style.

"I'm sorry, my friend, these past months we always seem to be missing each other," said Mofola.

"You mean years, my friend," joked Roberto.

"So tell me then what has kept my friend so busy these last months?" asked Roberto.

"Come, let's go and sit over there," said Mofola, pointing to one of the benches under a big baobab tree. "Maybe you have some time, we can talk?"

"It's not me that has no time, it's the big shot supervisor," teased Roberto.

The two friends sat and spoke until it started to get dark and the floodlights came on. Mofola told him all the news about himself, but leaving out the part where Jannie killed the Frenchman.

"It seems you have been quite busy, my friend," said Roberto. "Are you ready for another short holiday in Inhambane?"

"Yes, that would be good, I really need to get away from this place for a while, but you promise me no political meetings, OK?"

"No problem, my friend, I won't take you to any political meetings. Anyway it's far too dangerous to attend any gatherings at the moment."

"So when are you planning to go down to see your family again?" asked Mofola.

"I'm planning to go the week after we get paid. That is in ten days, if that's OK with you. We can leave here on Friday morning for Beira and I have to back here in ten days."

"That will be good," said Mofola. "I will speak to the project manager and see if it's OK to take some time off."

"Fine then, I'll be back here late Thursday night and if you have managed to get off we will leave early the next morning."

As before, Roberto had arranged with his manager for him take an empty truck back to the Beira depot and then pick up another truck with a load that had to go down to Inhambane. Mofola had no problem getting time off as everything was running well on the north tunnel. They left Songo early Friday morning and, as the truck was empty, they made good time arriving in Beira in the early afternoon. The truck they were to take to Inhambane was already loaded and ready to go. Roberto said that he was not tired and that they could leave straightaway and drive through the night.

Roberto asked Mofola if he could collect the consignment papers from the office while he filled the truck up with dieseline. The co-driver normally got all the paperwork sorted out, but as this was not one of the company's regular scheduled trips Roberto would have no co-driver.

Mofola went into the office and told the woman at the counter he was there to collect the papers for the consignment that the driver Roberto Gumane was taking down to Inhambane. She picked up the phone and spoke into it and then said to Mofola, "You can wait over there, pointing to a small waiting room on the side, and someone will be with you shortly."

Mofola went and sat with two other men in the waiting room and started to look at some of the magazines that were lying on the table.

Five minutes later, a woman came in and asked, "Who needs the papers for the consignment going to Inhambane?"

"Yes, that's me," said Mofola, standing up and putting the magazine back down on the table. He then looked up at the person standing in the doorway. To his surprise, he saw that the person standing there was Negome.

They both recognized each other, and at the same time, each said the other's name, exclaiming. "What are you doing here?"

They then both started to talk at the same time again and stopped and started to laugh. The other two men sitting there were looking at them, so Negome said, "Let's go outside." They went outside and Negome said, "I'm so pleased to see you," and gave Mofola a big hug.

Mofola was taken aback, not quite sure if he should reciprocate, remembering their last confrontation, so he just placed his hands on her hips not really returning affection.

Roberto had bumped into Negome some time ago at the office. He recognized her from the few times he had gone into the store to buy something when he was driving the Rhodesia route via Massangena. That's why he'd been trying to contact Mofola for months. Negome did not recognize him from those times and he said nothing to her that would associate himself with Mofola as he knew the history between the two of them. He then put this little trip and plan together knowing full well Negome would issue the consignment papers he would need. He stood and watched them from around the side of the truck and smiled as he saw them embrace.

Is that the best you can do to greet an old friend?" she asked, stepping back with her hands on the side of her hips.

"I'm sorry," said Mofola, "seeing you again after all these years, I did not know how I should react."

"Well, you can start by at least giving me a proper hug," she said.

Mofola stepped over to her and took her in his arms. They just stood locked in each other's arms neither wanting to let go. Negome broke the silence and said, "I'm sorry for what I said at our last meeting. At the time I was in shock. I just wanted to hit out at everyone around me. Especially the ones I loved, you, my mother and my two sisters. I know better now, it was not your fault. My father took his own life. Because of his stupidity and greed, he brought the tragedy on himself."

Negome broke their hold and placed her hands with outstretched arms on his shoulders and looked straight at him. "Can you ever forgive me?"

Mofola looked at her with tears in his eyes. Hearing those words, it was as if someone had lifted a huge burden from his heart. "How can a mere herder of cattle and goats not forgive one as lovely as you?"

THE END

Ilobola Glossary

1) Afrikaans	This is a language that arose from the Dutch settlers in South Africa in the seventeenth century
2) Afrikaaner	The nationality given to the white folk who spoke Afrikaans
3) Assegai	Spear
4) Baas	Boss, master
5) Baba	Respectful word for an older man
6) Bakkie	Pickup truck
7) Bliksem	Assault, hit
8) Boer	Afrikaaner farmer
9) Bob	One shilling (sterling)
10) Braai	Grill or barbeque
11) Calabash	Type of gourd, when dried can be used as a vessel.
12) Cheesa-stick	Igniter stick used to ignite explosives
13) Egoli	Gold
14) Escudos	Portuguese currency; In the sixties 80 escudos = one pound sterling

15) Eshafti   Mine Shaft

16) Fanagalo   Lingua franca, language spoken in the mines.

17) Golovan   Tramming Car

18) Highveld   Up on the high plateau, highland

19) Houtkop   Wood head, disparaging name

20) Ilobola   Dowry given to parents for their daughter's hand in marriage.

21) Impi   An African warrior from the Zulu tribe

22) Induna   Chief/elder of the tribe

23) Ja   Means Yes

24) Kaffir   Derogatory term for a black person; from Kafiristan in Asia

25) Klap   Slap, normally with the flat hand on the side of the head

26) Kudu   Large antelope

27) Lasher   A person who shovels ore into a tram car or ore-pass

28) Litie   Young boy

29) Lowveld   Low lying area, could be hot and dry

30) Madala   Old person

31) Maize   Field corn, not sweet

32) Muti   Medicine, mainly homeopathic

33) Nee   Means No

34) Ngyobe   To have intercourse

35) Paraffin   Kerosene oil

36) Piccanin   Young black boy; also a miner's assistant

37) Pombe   Sour beer made from millet, a type of grain.

38) Rondavel	Round huts with mud plastered walls and a grass thatched roof.
39) Samies	Sandwiches
40) Samp	Field corn, dried, and the kernels crushed coarsely
41) Sangoma	Traditional healer, witch doctor
42) Shamba	Cluster of huts together
43) Shangane	An African native tribe from the southern part of Mozambique
44) Skokkejaan	A potent self brewed alcoholic drink, like moonshine
45) She/He	In the African culture the tenses are often reversed in speech
46) Stope	Narrow tunnel sometimes only a few feet high
47) Swazi	An African native tribe from the kingdom of Swaziland
48) Takkies	Sneakers, tennis shoes
49) Trek	To travel
50) Umlungu	White person
51) Veld	Grassland or open fields
52) Veranda	Porch
53) Vetkoek	Type of doughnut
54) Voertsek	A harsh word to tell one to go away
55) Zulu	An African native tribe from the Natal province of South Africa

Made in the USA